# FAREWELL, EVERYTHING

●○

VÉVA PERALA

Translated by
H.B. CAVALIER

nowhere press

*Translated and adapted by H.B. Cavalier*

First Edition

First printing, November 2019
Revised during a deadly pandemic, August 2020

ISBN 978-1-73408-660-7

Nowhere Press
PO Box 314
Corvallis, OR 97339

nowherepress.com
farewelleverything.com

*Book design by Ian Cavalier*
*Cover illustration by H.B. Cavalier*

Twenty percent of the net profits from sales of this book will be donated to the following 501(c)(3) nonprofit organizations: the Sierra Club Foundation, Prevent Child Abuse America, and RAINN.

*For R.H.D.*

*I miss you.*

# CONTENTS

# DENIAL

ANGER

BARGAINING

DEPRESSION

ACCEPTANCE

# ONE

Osha didn't have much when he got to Valena. His things had waxed and (mostly) waned as he drifted south. He'd lost clothing, photographs, a whole bottle of pills. But since leaving the nomads and going it alone, everything had settled. Sensibly. Memorizably.

1 coat

2 scarves

3 hats

4 pairs of pants

5 notebooks

6 shirts

7 pairs of underwear

8 mismatched socks

9 weeks' worth of medication (if taken as directed), and

10 crisp, freshly minted Pan-Archipelago Union bank bills

He didn't count his ink pens or guitar, sleeping bag or tattered shoes – that'd be like counting fingers and toes. What mattered was that, for the first time in more than two years, he knew exactly what he had and exactly where it was. It was neat. It was orderly.

It was a particularly bad time to be robbed.

For nine halcyon nights, he'd slept in a driftwood hut, right where Valena's boisterous bayfront gave way to the calm of the North Woods. It was a forgotten place, one that barely existed at high tide, yet hardly a deer trail stood between it and the crowds Osha sang for. Nobody was even buried there: no small feat in Valena, where headstones rose like mountain ranges, half a dozen bodies under the average house. Courtyards and parks, even cafés served the dead – choking the streets with incense, littering the alleys with flower petals. But Osha was alone on his little beach. The hills of town rolled around him like electrified waves, but they never reached him there. Nothing did. Safe in his cove, he knew only serenity.

So it was quite the shock to be woken one night by a boot in the gut and dragged from his sleeping bag by his hair.

Blinded by instinct he fought, loosing a thorny vine of curses and a slew of misplaced kicks. But steel on his shin soon stopped that – and everything else along with it. No timid wind. No chirping insects. The whole black bay held its salty breath. Osha's heart alone thumped on, an ancient drum in a fossilized world.

In the still, he could make out two digmen: sharp arrow hats over moon-white grass, angular uniforms over lazy ferns. Osha had never known why digmen were called "digmen." He'd never seen them dig anything. Holy men dug the graves in the Union, and prisoners dug the rail lines. But the nickname fit better than their official title. Even with the language barrier, Osha could plainly tell that "Officers of Peace" didn't suit them any. Dangling from one of their hands was a baton on a chain – exactly the width of the bruise that would soon appear on Osha's leg. Slowly it swung, the pendulum of a clock: time remembering itself.

A blinding light flared up. Osha's eyes slammed shut.

"Vagrancy is forbidden, you know." A man's voice, smooth and cold as marble.

Osha failed to steady his own. "I'm not a vagrant, sir."

One of the digmen snickered.

The other one didn't. "What are ya, then? A nomad?"

More snickering. "Not with that pasty face."

Shakily, Osha rose to his feet. "I—"

They went for his ribs this time, icy baton knocking him backward and bent. It took a minute to unfold, and by then they were much closer. Osha had yet to visit a place where he felt tall, and he certainly wasn't tall here. Not that size mattered against men with guns.

Especially when they reeked of beer.

He took an extra step back.

"Come on, go easy on him," the one with the light chided. "He probably can't understand. You're not from around here, are ya kid?"

Osha was still fighting for breath. What's more, he wasn't sure he should answer.

The man cocked his head. "How much ya got on ya?"

Osha narrowed his eyes. "What?"

The baton swung out again, slamming into his side.

"We're the ones asking the questions! Answer!"

But he didn't answer. He turned and ran.

It seemed rational enough, tearing through the wet wild, empty-handed in a foreign country. His bare socks, soaked heavy with mud, didn't protest any. Neither did his racing pulse. Pain fanned through his ribs with his gasps, but it was a useful sensation. Motivating.

He stopped when he reached the boardwalk, doubled over and panting. Escape beckoned under the streetlamps, crisp and vivid: gleaming stones across the boulevard, cavernous alleys, stairways to safety. If he could only catch his breath.

It was usually bustling here, so close to the market, but there were no crowds to lose himself in now. The place was abandoned.

Almost.

One lone woman, blue-gray and brown against the yellow leaves, emerged from an alley and paused. A witness, at least – for whatever that was worth. Haloed in frizz beneath the hazy light, she was looking right at him. And just as the digmen came crashing out of the brush, she raised a single gloved hand. "Osha, darling! *There* you are!"

He'd never seen her before in his life.

The digmen slowed their approach, scrutinizing the woman as she splashed across the cobblestones. A twisting tornado scarf. A storm cloud of gauzy fabric atop tiny velvet slippers. Head pinned with feathers. Cheeks blushed in perfect circles. Voice like a ringing bell: "I've been looking all over for you!"

The digmen turned to Osha now. Like *he* could explain this.

"I'm so terribly sorry, officers," the woman gushed. "Was he troubling you? He's new to town, you know, and does lose his way."

The digmen looked incredulous. "You expect us to believe this hobo's *yours?*"

"Why, of course!" Her eyes went wide. "He's my cousin. Can't you see the resemblance?"

The men erupted now, spewing lava laughter. "Listen, sister," one of them jeered, "whatever stunt you're tryin' to pull, I'm not buying it. This guy's got a full campsite back there and not a sign of papers—"

"That's because they're at my house," the woman cut him off. "His name is Osha Oloreben, he's nineteen years old, and he's here on a temp visa for health purposes." A small purse appeared, fished from the misty seas of her skirt. And the catch of the day: a shimmery, silver-finned calling card. "My address. I can verify everything in the morning." Curtly, she stuffed it into one of their fists. "Now, if you would be so kind, we really should get home. This cold can't possibly help my cousin's condition."

The digmen scowled.

Osha feigned a grin. "It won't happen again."

The warmth of the woman's glove enveloped Osha's fingers. She squeezed. "Shall we?"

# TWO

Their departure was swift. Osha craned his neck back toward his beach, but it was only getting farther away. "My things—"

"Tomorrow." The woman hooked her elbow on his, pulling him close. "It's not safe."

In silence, they made their way past the market, past shuttered storefronts and vacant booths, into the knot of downtown. By day, those streets were flooded with music, buskers and bands trading songs for the melodic jingle of spare change. Drums flayed near the docks, cellos moaning at the temple gates, poets roosting on benches like metaphor-plagued hens. A whole spiraling galaxy of street stars – with Osha among them, a happy satellite. No one ever stopped him, no matter how much noise he made. No stiff-lipped landladies, no business owners, not even digmen – none of the people who chased off the nomads when they played. It almost made him doubt the Union's infamous austerity. *Almost*.

At any rate, scrawny northerners were held to entirely differently standards than full, riotous nomad bands. Going solo had its downsides, but money and common courtesy were not among them. It was certainly more work – athletics as much as art – but stomping and strumming on his own, he could earn in a day what the Sobini band made in a week, easy.

Maybe too easy. A little more exercise would've done him good.

Osha was walking so fast now, trying to keep up with this woman, that he hadn't the breath to ask what they were even doing. Not that she didn't seem safe. To the contrary, she radiated a kind of calm that made fleeing the law with a stranger feel perfectly ordinary.

They neared the streetcar station, trolleys sleeping in their shadowy brick cocoons. A fat, round clock hung over the yard, held in place by eight arched legs like a great steel spider. Osha still wasn't used to clocks. The nomads didn't care for them, and they certainly weren't popular up in Oclia. What use was time when the sun barely skimmed the horizon? To number the hours hardly seemed fair in the Arctic. Clinging to something so arbitrary only caused problems.

"Damn! Half-past midnight," the woman tsked. "Just missed the last ride."

See? Problems.

She shrugged. "Guess we gotta ankle."

So on they went, without pause. Past the fish grotto. Past kitschy sailors' pubs and antique shops. Past shipping crates and street murals and pungent, brackish dumpsters. Under yellow balloon lights, they crossed the broad, flat bridge that skimmed the neck of the bay, and left downtown behind.

"Where are we going?" Osha finally managed.

"To my house, silly. Where else at this hour?"

"How much farther?"

"Not far. I live right up there, in Perala House." She pointed at the wall of hills, the looming giant that lay before them. On its lazy contours hung a string of ancestral homes, flickering jewels trimmed with naked tree-branch lace. "I'm Nadya, by the way. Nadya Perala. Maybe you've heard of me?"

Osha shook his head.

"Good." She seemed relieved.

"But you've heard of me?"

"No. Why would you think that?"

"What you said back there—"

"Was I right?"

He nodded. "Aside from having papers."

"Oh, what fun!" She beamed, hands clasped at her chest. "It's so exciting when that happens."

Osha couldn't press the issue. The climb was dizzying. Flight after dark flight of stairs cut through unkempt yards, squeezing between fences warped and heavy with vines. The conical glow of streetlamps lit each lane they crossed, but the stairwells were dark. Cavernous. Steep. Osha was left winded, nose bleeding.

Nadya eyed him warily.

"Happens all the time," he wheezed.

"Well, hurry then. We'll clean you up at home."

Osha's legs were shaking by the time they arrived. A mere cottage beside its extravagant neighbors, Perala House bloomed in the shadows of two ancient evergreens like a daisy on a brick-laid stem. Osha tripped on the uneven path, on jutting roots and loose stones, stubbing his numb, near-naked toes twice before reaching the porch.

Nadya shushed him. "My brother's asleep."

Osha envied him.

Nadya ushered him inside, switched on a lamp, and collapsed onto a sofa – melting like wax in the heat of her home. She looked no worse for wear from their trek, though. Far from it. In the light, her features were clear: brown cheeks, smooth nose, a smattering of freckles under almond eyes. Quite lovely to look at lying there. Languidly, she stretched out an arm, gesturing toward the far side of the room. "The bathroom's over there. You look like you might be sick."

She wasn't wrong.

Peering into that bathroom's mirror, Osha hardly recognized himself. His own face was never a mystery to him – growing up, he'd seen it whenever he looked at his sister. Sleepy doe eyes, a sensitive openness, a vague touch of idiocy. And since leaving home, those features had kept her clear in his mind. But shadows were creeping in now, painting angles that made him something less approachable. His penance, perhaps, for abandoning Faia to their mother, to poverty, to the Oclian wastes.

Even after cleaning off the blood, the mirror was unforgiving. The bluish stains around his eyes just wouldn't wash away. True, he was tired, but not *that* tired.

He pulled up his sweater to inspect the damage he'd sustained. No skin broken, but his side had gone calico with bruises – new ones mean and purple on top of the old. He didn't have to check his leg to know it was the same. He was a veritable rainbow of accidents.

He was turning into a ghoul.

Creeping about in a stranger's house, no less.

What was he *doing*?

He pinched himself (bruising be damned), hoping to end this strange dream, to wake somewhere in his cozy, coherent past – with the nomads, with Neta or Nitic or Julis – but Nadya called for him before any wishes were granted. Uselessly, he raked his fingers through his hair. It had seemed so wild back home, in that sea of smooth raven-black. Centuries earlier, as the ocean washed up waves of refugees trading their blistered homeland for Oclia's soggy valleys, Osha's ancestors had slipped in quietly – and illegally – from another direction entirely, bringing with them a hair style, religion, and uniquely precarious luck that set them apart from their neighbors to that very day. In the province of Rimolee, however, next to manes like Nadya's, Osha's tangled waves seemed lifeless and flat.

Still messy, though.

Like his luck.

He emerged sheepishly, keeping his distance, reluctant to step into the light in which Nadya basked. She'd removed her seafoamy little cardigan. It lay on the arm of the sofa, that river of a scarf unfurled beside it, cascading down to the floorboards. A gentle warmth washed over Osha as he edged closer, like all those soft fabrics were wrapping around him. A sense of security. The notion that everything would be just fine, mind you, don't worry your little head. He'd felt it before. He'd followed it all the way here. It rolled off Nadya like mist from the bay. Cottony. Sedating. A little disorienting.

"I have to apologize for my house," she said. "It's been tidier in the past."

"Are you kidding? I should be the one apologizing."

"Whatever for?"

Osha fumbled for words, but found none more appropriate than: "For my face."

"Oh, fiddlesticks. All you need is a good night's sleep. Even the friendliest chat with a digman can take years off your life. I know *I'm* exhausted. In fact, I can't move an inch. I'll just have to sleep—" she yawned, languorously "—right here." She rolled onto her side, reaching out once more for the lamp chain, batting at it ineffectively before finally getting a grip. "There's a bed under the stairs. Make yourself at home."

Then she switched off the light, leaving Osha alone in the dark.

# THREE

The room was little more than broom closet. No windows, empty walls. The bed was flyspeck; had Osha been any taller, he wouldn't have fit. The mattress was flat and creaky, the sheets thin, and the nightstand was wobbly and lopsided.

It was the nicest place he'd slept in years.

He was slow to rise in the morning, less than eager to part with the good life now that he'd been reminded of its flavor. But he was hungry, and perhaps there was more to taste.

So he made his way back to the front room.

In the glare of day, Osha could plainly see the mess Nadya had referred to. Bookcases stood like sailors, keeping watch over a rough sea of wooden crates, paperboard boxes and dusty antiques, wet with frothy clutter spray. Plants were crammed into any available spot, stringy herbs trickling into pools of umbrella leaves. Magazines and scrap paper dipped dangerously close to the open hearth – as did scrolls. Scrolls like the nomads kept stowed away in old trunks: ancient maps, recipes, forgotten laws dating back all the way to the floods. But Nadya's likely didn't detail land division or pigeon roasting. Hers were sheathed in gold and embellished with religious symbols.

A menagerie of esoteric knickknacks were scattered throughout the wreckage: crystals of all colors, decks of cards, rusty keys on steel hoops. Bones. Quite possibly human bones. Some had been painted, eloquently adorned with whimsical patterns.

Didn't stop them from being bones, though.

Crowds of sepia faces hung above the deluge, insulated by glass plates bearing flowery names and long-ago dates. Dark faces, like Nadya's – the likes of which barely existed up north.

The furniture seemed an afterthought, a mismatched collection drooping over a dull, drab rug. Nadya was no longer on her sofa – a sleepy swath of light lay in her place, having let itself in through the broad front window. Osha tiptoed toward it, around animal skulls and open boxes, over bowls of ash and herbs, between candlesticks and leafless branches, and looked outside. Far below spread downtown, weather-beaten and quivering, shrinking before the bay's scolding finger like a guilty child. Osha had seen truly grand metropolises in his travels, stone blossoms smothering the earth under heavy petals – but Valena was not one of them. It splayed haphazardly, crumbling and sloppy, locked in a losing battle with the wilderness.

Much like Perala House itself.

Osha turned back to the mess. He was hardly squeamish, but life had taught him some hard lessons about germs. How could a woman so glamorous, so coiffed and graceful, live like this? Spoiled food. Moldy flowers. Crab shells.

A record player. One single offering for the living amid so many for the dead. At last, a sacred fetish he understood.

It'd been ages since he'd enjoyed such luxury. He itched to turn it on, to let the music wash over him, to close his eyes and fall into it. But then he saw the records themselves, scattered at the player's paw-like feet, some not even in their jackets. Some visibly scratched.

Sacrilege.

The whine of a teakettle rose up, weaving its way round a heavy door, past the vines and mushrooms chiseled into its frame. And then, abruptly, it stopped.

In its wake: a chorus of muffled voices.

Cracking the door just a little, Osha could hear much more clearly.

"You know I can't do that," Nadya was saying. She stood at the counter of a tiny kitchen, kettle in hand, recognizable only by her voice. Her lavish dress had been traded for the simple robe of a priestess, loose and shapeless on her thin frame, colors muted, muslin wrinkled. Her hair, mahogany in the morning light, was twisted up and tied with a ribbon. The visible crescent of her cheek was free of makeup, freckled, bronze and fresh. Only her earrings suggested any penchant for luxury – strings of tiny scarlet gems raining all the way to her shoulders. "What if it's discovered?"

Another woman answered her, nasal and impatient: "Oh, come on, by who?" She sat at the dining table, next to a man. Like Nadya, these two were at least a decade older than Osha – though they'd aged well, to say the least. Each possessed the kind of delicate, curated beauty that Osha's mere presence might sully. And they did nothing to hide their opulent tastes. "You think your temple pals are gonna care? Or your brother? Like he's got any friends to tell. Never even comes downstairs."

Nadya made her way over to them, one steaming teacup in each hand. "My father's a Union man, you know, and—"

"Big deal! He's an *engineer* – hardly an authority figure. You'd think he was the goddamn capital ambassador, the way you worry. Besides, how often does he even visit? Sagoma's not exactly next door."

"Is there no one else you can ask?"

"Just say yes, already! It arrives tomorrow!"

"No." Nadya returned to the counter for her own mug. Osha could feel that warmth again, that invisible cloak she wore, bubbling around her as she moved. The whole world vibrated with her vocal chords. "Surely someone else can help with this problem of yours."

The other woman scoffed. "Like it's not your problem, too!" She looked familiar: sunburst of golden curls, excessively made-up face, round blue eyes like bugs with those lashes. Slumped in her chair, arms crossed, her pencil-thin brows knitted with a stage-worthy pout.

"I want no part of this, Iza."

"Perhaps I can persuade you," the man tried. From head to toe, he was the color of damp sand – slick hair, sharp features, and double-breasted coat all blending together. Tall and weedy, he dipped his narrow fingers into a pocket and withdrew an envelope. "Confidential from Polon Larami."

"You can't be serious!" Nadya nearly dropped her teacup. "Show me."

He taunted her with it, waving it wickedly until she managed to snatch it up. Then came the quiet crinkle of paper, followed by a long pause. When Nadya spoke again, her voice was choked with emotion. "But I thought—"

"We took care of that." There was humor in the man's tone. "He's in Erobia now."

"Erobia?" Nadya looked up from the letter, mouth agape. "I wouldn't think that's a safe place for him."

The man's reply was curt. "Some things are best hidden in plain sight."

Nadya folded the letter back up. "But not all, Holic." She bit her lip.

"I'm sorry to put you in this position, Nadya, but it's a miracle to even have this equipment." The man spoke slowly, purring like a cat.

Meanwhile, the woman at his side squirmed. "Just stop being such a pill, Nadya! There's nowhere else to put it!"

But Nadya was firm: "You can't run a radio station from my house."

Osha's heart skipped a beat. "Radio station?"

All eyes turned to the door.

Osha hadn't meant to say that aloud. He ducked back behind the wall.

"Good morning, Osha." Nadya singsong voice followed him. "Won't you join us for tea?"

He stepped in timidly, offering a wave. "Good morning."

The blond didn't mince words. "Who's this bum?"

"Iza, this is Osha Oloreben." Nadya nodded from one to the other. "Holic, Osha."

The man extended a hand formally, jaw set. "Holic Tiademis."

"Are you kidding?" Osha slapped the man's fingers. "Holic Tiademis!"

Holic drew back like he'd been hurt.

"The actor, right?" Osha searched the faces around him for understanding. "Your name's on posters all over town."

"Ah." Holic wasn't moved by his enthusiasm. "I see."

"Holic and Iza are with the Barsamina Company," Nadya explained.

Osha gaped at the woman now, drinking up her doll-like face. "You're Iza *Barsamina*?"

She raised a brow. "What's it to you?"

Nadya moved behind Osha, taking him by the shoulders and steering him to a chair. "Ignore her. She'll warm up."

Reluctantly, Iza extended a hand. Palm up: no kisses welcome. "My apologies, um. . . ."

"Osha."

"Osha," she deadpanned. "What kind of name is that?"

"Oclian."

"Guess that explains the accent."

Osha grinned. "Hopefully it's not too thick for radio."

Iza's ever-expressive face dropped skepticism in favor of outright shock. "Nadya, you have got to stop taking in strays! This one's got the nerve of a rubber ball."

Now it was Osha's turn to raise a brow. "A rubber ball?"

"A rubber ball! A crook. A nomad. Always bouncing away from the trouble they cause."

Osha scowled. "Are you calling nomads crooks?"

"Settle down, you two." Nadya placed some tea before Osha, meeting his glare with a smile. "Osha's a good kid. I found him after the show last night, getting chewed on by a pair of digmen. Mind you, he's done nothing wrong – he just doesn't have anywhere else to go."

Osha raised his cup to Nadya before taking a sip. An absolutely scalding sip. As soon as the tea passed his lips, he spat it right back out.

Iza crossed her arms again. "Charming."

Holic slid a napkin toward him, silent.

Nadya ignored all of them. "He's staying with me and Loren until he finds a place of his own."

Osha dropped the napkin. "I am?"

"Well, of course, silly. What do you think you're doing here?" Nadya drifted back to the counter, a ghost in her long dress. "Besides, we met for a reason. The spirits gave me your name and—"

"The spirits!" Iza threw up her hands. "I should have known."

Nadya fanned the words away with her hand. "Would you like anything to eat, Osha?"

"Yes, please."

Holic slunk close to him now, snake-ish. "Oclian, you say?" He hissed. "An independent! Our esteemed Union hasn't yet got its hands on your territory."

Osha snorted. "They wouldn't want it."

"And what brings you so far from home?"

"The weather."

Holic smirked. "Snow and ice aren't your cup of tea?"

Osha's actual cup of tea was still piping, billowing hot and humid in his face as he leaned over it. "Not a fan of the wind, either."

"And you're looking for a place here? In Valena?" Holic's voice was low, almost frustratingly soft – especially compared to Iza's. Words like the tendrils of steam that swirled between them: "One might say we're house hunting, as well."

Nadya shot him a wary look, struggling with the thin, knotted string of a cloth sack. "Holic, please."

But his words slithered on: "You seem interested in radio."

"You leave him out of this."

"Oh, come on, Nadya." Holic straightened himself, facing their busy hostess. "The boy knows what we're up to. May as well hear his thoughts."

"Well, isn't that considerate!" Iza heaved a sigh, rising to her feet. "Seeing as you're so interested in *my* thoughts, I'll be out having a smoke while I collect them."

With a wry smile, Holic watched her huff off toward the door, skirt and curls and chest all bouncing. Then he turned back to Osha. "I take it you've gathered we need a place for our station."

Osha glanced at Nadya, but she kept her head down, rightly focused on wielding an impressive knife. "Why can't it be here?" he asked.

"Well, look around." Holic unwound his spindly arms, spreading them wide. "A radio station demands a bit of space and, despite its reputation as a boarding house, *space* is something that Perala House sorely lacks. But perhaps—" He paused.

Osha blew on his tea, waiting for him to go on.

"Perhaps," Holic repeated, eyeing his fingernails. "Let's say . . ."

Osha's foot began to tap.

". . . once you establish a residence . . ."

Fingers, drumming on the table.

". . . if it's at all possible . . ."

Temples, throbbing.

". . . you might be interested in—"

Osha burst. "Look, I'll do anything if you let me play on the radio! Anything! I'll store the damn thing in a tent if I have to!"

Nadya paused her chopping, glancing over her shoulder, eyes wide.

Holic's eyes, for their part, narrowed to slits.

Osha shifted in his seat. "If that's what you're asking, that is."

The man tilted his head. "Play?"

"Music. I'm a musician." He tried the tea again. Still too hot. "You wouldn't have heard of me, though. I've never been on the radio. Not solo, at least. Played backup for Nitic and Ivra Sobini – but who am I next to them? Gotta start somewhere, though, am I right?"

Holic's head tilted all the more. "The Sobini band?"

"Learned from the best!"

"So you want to play *nomad* music?"

"Well, no. I've got my own songs."

Nadya stepped between them, setting a silver tray in the center of the table. "Breakfast is served!" A cosmic creation: grapes, cheese, chopped apples and almonds shining like rays around a blazing, oat-roll sun. Nadya looked proud of her artistry.

Osha swallowed his disappointment. He missed eggs. He missed meat. He didn't miss the blubbery stews he'd endured at home, and he appreciated the produce in these parts – but the religious proscription of meat-eating in the province of Rimolee was something he could do without. Temple folk – like Nadya, evidently – didn't even eat fish. In an archipelago! It was lunacy.

But he was in no position to complain. Nor did he really feel like it, with Nadya pouring her ethereal syrup over everything. Things felt so strange with her nearby. In a good way. With a smile, he took a roll. "Looks delicious. Thank you."

"Now, I wouldn't get my hopes up too high, *Osha*." Holic said his name like it tasted bad. "We can't broadcast very widely. And to be completely honest, our programming plans haven't moved beyond radio theater. We haven't even considered musical entertainment."

"Consider it." Osha's words were emphatic, if muffled. He swallowed his mouthful and cleared his throat. "Just tell me when."

Holic's thin lips curled up. "Tomorrow?"

"I'll have a place by sunset."

"Osha," Nadya pressed gently, "don't you think it's a little premature for a promise like that?"

"Not at all!" He batted away her doubt. "Luck's on my side. I'm here, aren't I? Rather than in jail. Or worse."

She looked like she might laugh. Or cry. Or ask him to leave.

He probably should have left luck out of this.

"It's decided, then." Holic pushed back his chair and stood. "For now, we'll make room in this mess if we must – but move things in with you just as soon as you find a roof. A mutual favor. Positively fizzing."

"Fizzing," Osha repeated, more to feel the word in his mouth than anything. It was a new one; he made sure to add at least one a day.

Holic clapped his hands together, satisfied. "Now if you would excuse me. I'll be joining Miss Barsamina on the patio. Care to join, old boy?"

"Don't mind if I—"

"Osha doesn't smoke," Nadya cut him off.

"Actually, sometimes—"

Nadya shook her head.

"Well, in that case—" Holic gave a little bow "—enjoy your meal." And he left.

Osha took a crestfallen bite.

"You shouldn't smoke, Osha. Not in your condition."

He glared at her. "What condition?" That wasn't a word he liked, in any language. It cut clean through whatever fuzzy magic she'd woven, leaving a cold, gaping hole.

Nadya lifted a clump of grapes from the tray and laid them on a napkin in front of her. "Didn't you stop traveling for your health?"

He shrugged. "I just needed a break."

Nadya's face was a ball of grape-chewing concern. "But the spirits—"

"I'm fine," Osha snapped. "The spirits don't know what they're talking about." Conversations like this never ended well. He hadn't come so far from home just to be fussed over like he'd never left.

Nadya sighed. "Well, you should still rest a while. There's no need to rush – especially on account of some harebrained scheme of Holic's." She rose yet again, robe sweeping the dust from the floorboards as she returned to the counter. "It's supposed to rain later, so you'll probably want to get your things soon. But do come back quickly."

*His things.* Osha's heart sank. He was finally able to take a sip of his tea, but there was no joy in it. "You think my stuff is still there? You don't think the digmen made off with it?"

"I didn't think you had anything valuable."

"Come on now." Osha tossed a handful of almonds into his mouth. "I'm not a beggar."

Nadya glanced back at him.

"I'm a vagabond."

"Well, then. For all your vagabonding—" She drew close again, presenting him with a small blue booklet. "Here are your papers. You'll need them every time you go out." Her expression darkened as she passed them to him. "*Every time*, Osha. You're not up north anymore. This is occupied territory. You're in the Union now."

Osha was holding a visa. An official, leather-bound, Pan-Archipelago Union-issued visa. Every detail, flawless. Triple-looped ribbon, golden and glossy on the cover. Inside: his name, home province, even his birthday printed dark and clear. And an address! It had been so long since he'd had a real address. Perhaps now he could write home, send money, let his sister know he was still alive. How distraught Faia had been by thoughts of his death.

Then again, after two years, it might be best to keep playing dead.

At any rate, "You don't know what this means to me."

"Sure I do. That's why I did it."

"But how?"

"The spirits."

"No, no. The visa itself."

Nadya turned away once more, giving a small shrug. "I have my ways."

# FOUR

Nadya wasn't the first to mistake Osha for penniless. In the business of busking, his recent earnings seemed more pity than praise, especially when he was feeling sick. It was a bit of a blow, given the effort he put into performing, but by and large he was grateful. It generally worked in his favor, after all. Especially when digmen assumed little of him as well – as they clearly had on the beach, deeming his prized possessions garbage and abandoning them all in a jumbled heap.

Mostly all, that is.

At least half of his things were crushed by what remained of his hut. Mud-caked notebooks, bent by the logs, were only damaged more by Osha's recovery attempts. Half-written songs tore. Unsent letters slipped from his frozen fingers, dropping into tide pools. His favorite hat (which hadn't been cheap), was filled to the broad brim with water, a featherless felt bucket. His bag, too, was smashed within the ruins – *some* of his clothes still inside.

His shoes were gone.

His guitar was gone.

His pills were gone.

Up along the narrow sandbank he spied a shirt, soaked and clinging to a rock. Just beyond that, a sock, similarly taken, tossed and returned by the bay's lazy tides.

With Nadya's blessing, Osha had borrowed a pair of her brother's shoes. They were surprisingly comfortable – much warmer than ones with holes in the soles. He was reluctant to remove them, but did, tying them to his bag as he followed the soggy laundry trail away from town, toward the maternal hush and shush of the ocean. His toes blanched in the icy water as he skirted the overgrown banks, but he was rewarded for his efforts. Stirred in with sea stars, anemones and glowing, gelatinous nudibranchs were sweaters, scarves, pants and pens. A strange but satisfying soup.

A haze rolled in as he crept along, carrying with it a sound that gave him pause. Otherworldly, it seemed. A low, ghastly wail, drowned out only by the rhythmic groans of the foghorn. Osha scanned the horizon. It seemed to come from Shipwreck Beach – those twisted ribs just across the bay, tortured metal claws ever-popular with picnickers, historians and grave-robbers. "Ghosts," he muttered to himself. "All this death worship's keeping the dead awake."

Not that he believed that. There were plenty of superstitions in the northern taiga: gods and demons from the other side of the world, as well as native beasts sleeping in the surrounding mountains. Wooden shrines festooned with bells marked the rural intersections near his childhood home, and the cities of southern Oclia boasted prayer houses grand enough to rival any of the temples in Rimolee. But Osha was young when he left that area – too young to be converted or possessed or spirited away. Instead, he came of age amid black ice and endless night in the industrial wastes of Lanestabra, at the tiptop of the world, where no one had time for that sort of thing. Osha's family could barely muster the energy for one lonely god.

Shaking the wailing from his ears, something on the water caught his eye. Small and shiny. Familiar. A jar.

His pills.

He cursed. They were not close. He would definitely have to swim for them. True, he'd looked forward to swimming when he ran away – but maybe a little farther south. Sagoma, perhaps. The hidden surfing coves of the capital looked quite nice. But Rimolee? Watching the bottle bob in the howling gray, he considered his options. This water was awfully cold, but his medicine did have a way of warming him up. In fact, Osha had yet to suffer something it couldn't help. Food poisoning, nosebleeds, hangovers. Those pills were prescribed for one purpose only – a disease he'd never even had – yet they'd carried him through the past few years like a life raft.

It'd be nice to have them.

Osha slipped off his shirt first, then his pants, hanging both from a tree branch. And there he stood, skinny and shivering, bruises paved with goosebumps, eyes fixed on the bottle. It wasn't getting any closer. He took a full, deep breath. "Come on, Oloreben, this is nothing." Behind his mother's back, he'd swum round ice floes, trekked through blizzards, been buried to his neck in snow by school bullies. "You're from the *Arctic.*"

He plunged in, the shore giving way rapidly, frigid water sucking him down. Collapsing his lungs.

From the dry comfort of a nearby perch, a murder of crows exploded with laughter. "Come say that to my face!" Osha shouted in Oclian – first language of frostbite and hypothermia. The birds understood. They rose up, a squawking black cloud sailing south, back toward town. "Cowards!"

The clamor drifted off, leaving Osha alone with the hollow cries of the fog and his own ragged breathing. And a rather unsavory task. It was a short swim to the bottle, but he swore the whole the way. Upon reaching it, he immediately turned back for the beach.

That's when he saw the house. Peeling and rickety, it stared back at him with windows wide and curious. Hardly inconspicuous, yet he hadn't noticed it earlier at all. It sat in a clearing right on the water, just around a rocky bend from where he'd left his things. It even had its own dock, worn and splintered, jutting out into the bay. And tied to its side: a wooden rowboat. Had Osha walked only a few more steps, he would have seen it.

A boat. He could have taken a boat.

He wheezed his way ashore and stumbled into the weight of the air. As quick as he could, fumbling with buttons and folds, he found the driest thing in his bag and mopped himself off. Still damp, he dressed. It was best to hurry. With any luck, he could warm up in that house.

Or if not luck, pity might serve him well.

He paused only to pop the cork from the pill jar – or liquor bottle, as it were. The jars the doctors used were much smaller, and far too easy to lose in the hedonic whirl of nomad life. He'd thought it wise to consolidate, and that had obviously been a good move. His pills were fine. They'd survived their misadventure unscathed, if a little cold.

Tucking the jar into his bag, he pressed on toward the house.

In less than a minute, he arrived. It was jarring, in fact. Like it had moved even closer. The shaggy lawn seemed warped somehow, pulsing, as though recovering from the shift. The tiny stones of a half-moon beach clacked in mass with the bay's push and pull, like a crowd of tiny hands clapping. Welcoming him.

He took a moment to look around. A sleek new train bridge slithered through the sky, a distant rainbow over the dunes of Shipwreck Beach. And beyond that, the arc of Valena's famously long jetty, warning lights just barely visible from where he stood. Even with the mountains missing, swallowed by the darkening clouds, it was a lovely view.

Osha followed a muddy path from the dock, cutting through wet grass up to a sunken front porch. There, the trail became a road, winding toward obscurity and obliteration among the soaring cedars. This house didn't belong in a city like Valena. Valena had only existed for two-hundred years – this place was easily twice its age. It could have fallen from the mountains, from some ghost town built by landless refugees back when the sea was still rising. It sported the same sharp angles as those old farmhouses, even as it wilted from neglect. Moss and seedling trees sprouted like unkempt hair from its roof, yet somehow it seemed sturdy. Comfortable. Inviting.

At least from where Osha stood, teeth chattering.

He knocked on the door. No reply. So he tried the knob: unlocked. "Hello?" He called into the darkness. "I don't mean to intrude."

The room flared up in response, a blinding blaze. Osha stumbled back onto the porch, nearly falling down the stairs. But his racing heart soon stilled. It was just the lights turning on. Nothing more.

"Who's there?"

No one answered.

He stepped inside.

Aside from a thin layer of dust, the place was immaculate. Nothing like the outside at all. The main room was vaulted to accommodate the towering windows, a wall of eyes on the choppy water. The adjoining rooms featured sliding doors inlaid with stained glass flowers, framed in a dark, cherry wood that matched the ceiling beams. And the walls – they'd been painted with something that wasn't even paint, a color that wasn't a color. Something warm and watchful and calm that reminded him, somehow, of Nadya.

Only one piece of artwork was hung, right above the rounded mouth of a stone fireplace: two flat discs, one dark and one light, both studded with jewels. The craftsmanship was extraordinary, curves as soft and smooth as young skin. Supple. Alive. Beaming into the room with a dim but unmistakable glow. Surely it was a trick of the light, but it almost seemed to move – one circle slowly overtaking the other, slipping over the shimmering, metallic hoop that surrounded it.

An eclipse.

Osha smiled. He'd seen an eclipse before, as a child. In fact, it had been a pivotal moment in his life, one he remembered often: the sun swallowed up by some faceless creature, darkness falling over day like a bedsheet. A darkness that never lifted, in his case. His mother moved him and his sister to the ends of the earth the very next day, leaving lush hillsides, a drunken father, and Osha's feeble happiness far behind.

There were flickers of light, of course. It wasn't *all* gloom – especially after joining the nomads. The roar of bonfires, the low burn of lanterns. The warm glow of Julis Balestro. Julis, who'd also seen the eclipse. His whole band had gone on a whim, traveling hundreds of miles for the event, ultimately placing him and Osha in the exact same park at the exact same time – totally unknown to one another. A baffling coincidence under an equally baffling sky. It was this rare memory that brought them together years later, and as their friendship deepened they attempted to re-create it – passing paper cutouts over Julis's lamp, eyes on the shadows above his bed.

A poor substitute for the real thing.

Or the replica Osha turned his back on now.

Lights sparked on eagerly as he moved off into the house, fireworks in every room. He appreciated it, though he didn't know who to thank – as far as he could tell, no one was there to flip the switches. One door opened to a bathroom with candles already lit. Another led to a staircase, plummeting into a stone cellar where strings of spherical lanterns spread like fruiting vines across the ceiling. A narrow table filled most of the space, flanked by benches long enough to seat a dozen strangers (or more, were they close friends). At one end of the room, a set of shelves offered up a sizable, albeit dusty, selection of vintage wines. At the other, another open hearth – fire crackling away within.

A second flight of stairs curled up from the ground floor, onto a landing – a balcony of sorts, overlooking the main room. Two bedrooms sprung from its sides, and another bathroom as well, angular and odd below the peaked ceilings. The windows slanted like tired old men, leaning heavily upon their frames. Propped ajar, they let in the insistent complaints of the foghorn, along with a thin wisp of fresh, green air.

Just one of many lovely smells. The house was full of them.

Both bedrooms were stamped with the sweet aroma of nut oil, and up from the kitchen drifted the bold spices of holiday cooking. The scent of woodsmoke and beeswax permeated everything, and yet there was not a sign of human life.

Osha found precious little furniture. Beyond the cellar table, there was only a bed, clean and neatly made in one of upstairs rooms. He sat there, head in his hands, trying to digest the past twelve hours of his life: the digmen, that woman, this house. But it was all a bit too rich – indigestion set in, his belly began to ache, and he lay down. Tenderly, the bed wrapped its downy arms around him, and he closed his eyes.

 Only a few minutes had passed, he was sure of it – yet when Osha sat up again, the room was different. Brighter, perhaps. And at his feet, neatly folded, was a set of clean, dry clothes. He wasted no time unfolding them. They were exactly his size, every piece.

No reason not to try them on.

A full-length mirror stood now, in the corner, beside crisp, gossamer drapes just beginning to take shape around the windows. He studied his reflection: gaunt though he was, he didn't look half bad in proper dress. The sweater's thick weave filled him out some. The pants were fitted and sharp. And the boots he found beside the bed were downright classy – fastened with large, moon-like buttons, smooth as silk. The clothing wasn't flashy; it boasted the same cloudy tones he was used to. Yet never in his life had Osha worn such finery.

He made his way back downstairs, savoring the fleecy fabric against his skin, following the heady aroma wafting from the kitchen. And there, greeting him cordially from the stove top, was a sumptuous tray of fresh-baked pastries. Square cakes, to be exact; easily his favorite food. He'd first had them in Erobia – less than a mile south of the Oclian border, where the world became a banquet. Gone was the pickled herring, gone the unleavened bread, replaced by flavors so varied and delightful that, by the time he reached Rimolee, Osha could barely button his pants. All that weight was gone now, though. A lingering stomach bug had seen to that, leaving him as bony as he'd ever been.

And ever so hungry.

Square cakes came either sweet or savory, and spread before him now was a wide variety of both. Salmon with dill cream and capers, honeyed cinnamon chicken, chili apple, mixed berry, eggs and cheese, all folded delicately within sourdough frames. No two were alike.

The first he tried was fig. *Cardamom* fig. How Julis loved cardamom. Called it "starry" and "sensuous" – and used it to excess. Made half their meals taste like medicine.

But this was no time to think of Julis. With such a bounty before him now, why dwell on what he'd lost? Besides, cardamom tasted lovely like *this*. He ate with abandon, washing it all down with cold, clear water from the sink tap.

After such decadence, Osha could hardly touch his filthy things. Carefully, so as not to soil his new sweater, he fished his visa and pills from his bag and slipped them into the borrowed shoes. Otherwise empty-handed, he headed for the door.

And then stopped.

There, propped in the entryway, was his guitar – pleading like a pet dog to not be left behind. Osha knelt uncertainly, running his fingers over the water-warped surface. Its scratches, its dents. All the things that marked it as his own. "Don't worry, little guy. I wasn't gonna forget you." He squinted. Something had changed. "I just didn't know you were here." He lifted it and strapped it on, its weight natural and comforting. Only then did he notice the new strap. Midnight blue velvet. "Looks like we both got dudded up, didn't we?" Running his thumb over the strings, he strummed gently, just once – and frowned. It sounded different. It sounded better. Damn near perfect, in fact. "What do ya know? You even got your sixth string back."

Osha opened the door to leave, but found himself stalling yet again. The eclipse was tugging, pulling his gaze back, begging for attention. He couldn't help turning around, stepping toward it like a sleepwalker. So well-made, so vibrant. Certainly not carved from wood. Not glass, not clay. Too warm to be metal. Too *vital*. Perhaps it was – what was that stuff called? – plastic. That magical substance of old. Never decomposed. Never died. It just lingered forever, buried beside basements and bones, a man-made layer of the earth's crust. He'd dug for it as a child, but with little success. No ancient cities lay beneath Oclia's tundra. It hadn't been very habitable before the Great Thaw. Inconceivably, it had been even *colder*.

Honestly, Osha wasn't sure if he'd ever seen genuine plastic. But he was certain, beyond a shadow of a doubt, that he'd never seen anything like this eclipse sculpture. "I'll be back," he assured it.

The fog had lifted outside, taking the wailing with it, but still the sky pressed low with the threat of rain. Osha wasn't keen on getting wet again, so the bicycle on the front porch was a welcome sight. Surely, riding through the forest had to be easier – and quicker – than slogging back down the shoreline. Especially now, with the tide coming in.

He'd guessed right: the gravel path merged smoothly with the ribbony roads tying back the mossy hair of the North Woods. And though he'd never been on them, he knew just where to go. Guided by the same mindless faith that drove his fingers through songs, he found the North Gate checkpoint in less than five minutes, just as the streetcar showed up. He kept his head down, avoiding the eyes of nearby digmen, but couldn't suppress his smile. Hoisting his bike up the trolley steps, it seemed that his luck, after years – generations, even – was finally turning around.

# FIVE

The streetcar stopped mere blocks from Perala House, but by the time Osha reached the door he was drenched. Rain overflowed the gutters, torrents in front of the windows. Through those liquid curtains, he could make out Nadya's silhouette, swaying and pacing in the firelight. Waiting for his return.

So he didn't bother knocking. He just threw open the door. "I found a house!"

But it wasn't Nadya standing there. Or Iza, or Holic, or anyone he'd ever met. It was a stranger gawking at him. A slack-jawed statue. Wiry glasses reflecting the fire, flames for eyes. Had he turned his head, his enormous mane would have entirely hidden his face – but he didn't turn.

He kept right on staring.

Nadya emerged from the kitchen then, but rather than introduce them, she froze. "Oh, Osha, look at you!"

"I know! Fizzing, am I right?" Proudly, he smoothed his sweater, but as he looked down to admire himself, he saw a fat, red drop fall to the floor. Licking his lips, he tasted blood.

"Let me get you something." Nadya slipped back into the kitchen, leaving the two strangers alone again.

Osha tipped his head back and pinched his nose. "Osha."

"Loren."

"Pleased to meet you."

So this was Nadya's brother, stiffly removing his spectacles, wiping the lenses with the hem of a loose brown sweater. The resemblance was striking. Loren was clearly the younger of the two, but beyond that they could pass for twins: same lithe build, same long neck, same full lips. But the similarities were only skin deep. Loren was hardly charming him. In fact, he outright glared, arms crossed.

By the time Nadya reappeared, washcloth in hand, Osha's throat was full of blood. "Sit down," she said. "Let me clean you up." Osha did as instructed, smiling at Loren as Nadya pressed the damp rag to his face.

Loren headed straight for the stairs. "It's been great, Nadya, but I gotta go."

"Oh Loren, must you?" Nadya's shoulders sank. "Won't you meet Osha?"

Loren nodded. "I met him."

"It's alright." Osha took the rag from Nadya. "I've got it."

Empty-handed, she rose, hurrying after her brother. "Loren, don't be this way. Talk to me."

"There's nothing more to say, Nadya!" He was angry. "This is your mess, not mine."

"Look," Osha interjected, "if this is about me—"

Both frizzy heads snapped toward him, all eyes flashing. "It's not!"

Osha slouched into the sofa, shrinking behind his bloody cloth.

"Loren, I know you don't like this." Nadya was begging. "But I don't have a choice."

"You're not innocent here, Nadya. You've had plenty of chances to get out of this. Don't come asking for help now—"

"I'm not asking for help."

"Good," Loren spat back, "because I can't offer any."

"Maybe I can," Osha cut in once more. This had to stop. The one time he'd argued with his own sister, it hadn't ended well. Faia couldn't talk, of course, so misunderstandings were few – but when their quiet peace did fall, the battle was more gruesome than any he'd ever fought. And he'd fought a lot.

"Yes, Osha?" Nadya looked deflated.

"I found a house."

She mustered a feeble smile.

"Well, isn't that *berries*," Loren huffed. "Glad *that's* been cleared up." Again, he moved toward the staircase. "Good luck with the rest." And with that, he stomped up the steps and disappeared.

Nadya sighed. "I'm sorry about that, Osha."

"Could've been worse." Osha dabbed at his nose. It had slowed somewhat. "He seems nice."

"He is." Sagging and sullen, Nadya returned to his side. "It's me. I've gotten myself into quite a pickle." Even now, that soothing pulse throbbed around her, impervious to any troubling produce she might have. It seeped under Osha's skin, tingling, numbing. Such a familiar feeling. Like fingers through his hair. Light sheets on a summer night. Julis's whisper in the dark. But more. Much more. If Nadya moved any closer, he might dissolve.

"I did find a house," he said again.

"Did you." Eyes locked on the fire, voice flat and dry as a cracker.

"It's really something. Private beach access. The works."

"Sounds lovely."

"There's more than enough space for a radio station."

She faced him then, eyes glistening, waves bubbling. World melting. "Would you talk to him?"

"To who?"

"To Loren!"

"What am I supposed to say to him?"

"I don't know." Nadya turned back to the fire. "Tell him I'm sorry."

In the dancing shadows, she chewed her lip. Osha watched her collarbones rise and fall above the low neckline of her robe, his spine going liquid with her sighs. He wanted to comfort her, but more than that, he wanted to touch her – to feel her bare skin, to check if she was even solid. Hesitantly, his hand inched toward hers.

But she stood. "And give him his shoes."

Then she walked away, past the stairs and into her room.

# ﬩

Loren didn't answer when Osha knocked on his door. So he knocked again. "Hello? Anyone?"

There was nowhere else he could have gone. The stairwell led to nothing else, not even a hallway. Osha was left balancing on the top step, a hair's breadth from the door, hoping that if it did open, it wasn't into his face. He was pretty tired of nosebleeds.

More knocking. "I can hear you," he lied.

"Who is it?" The voice was quiet, muffled.

"It's Osha."

"Who?"

"We just met."

The door opened – away from Osha, thankfully. Just a crack, enough to reveal one gleaming, rectangular lens. "What do you want?"

Osha held up the shoes. "I borrowed these."

The door swung wide now, welcoming him into a cocoon of heat. Walls constrictive, ceiling low, the room would've been uncomfortable for someone of any stature. Fortunately, neither of them fit that description. Windows bookended the space, aiming for the illusion of length, but only making it feel narrower. The furnishings were sparse: a mattress on the floor, a ticking electric heater. Not even a shelf for the jagged stacks of books shoved against the wall.

Yet Osha could barely move a foot.

Ceramic pots paved the floor, hosting all colors, shapes and sizes of the most elegant, alien-looking flowers he'd ever seen.

"Sorry there's nowhere to sit," Loren mumbled.

"Not a problem." Osha smiled at the blossoms, somewhat enjoying the surprise ambush. Staked and tied, they reached out longingly. Dense pink clusters pressed against lanky stalks of magenta-striped and plum-speckled spiders. Ruffled, sunny faces kissed tiny, airborne doves. And lower down, amid thick, rounded leaves, were more still – every bit as stunning, if a little secretive. Osha knelt to get a closer look.

"Careful!" Loren snapped. "They're rare. Most orchids come from quite far away."

"Orchids," Osha repeated. That was a new word. And on a tag between the roots of a creamy specimen, yet another: *Luna*. Glancing about, he saw more, all scrawled sideways on headstone-like labels. "How sweet. You named them."

Loren bristled. "Just for keeping track. They're not easy to grow." He gestured toward the wall. Taped above his books were scraps of paper – dozens of them – curling like scales in the humid air. Transplant records, care instructions, meticulous notes. "They're expensive and finicky and so hard to keep alive, most people don't bother."

Osha smirked, stroking the stringy black whiskers of an especially impressive one. "Sounds like you and I have a bit in common, little guy."

Loren drew a breath through his teeth, blowing out slow. "You need a lot of patience to get them to bloom. I'm the temple's only orchidist."

"You're what?"

"What does it look like?"

It looked like he wanted to kick Osha out, that's what it looked like. But of course, that had nothing to do with flowers. "It looks like you and Nadya have a lot of plants."

"They're mine. *All* of them. *I* take care of them. Nadya couldn't keep a weed alive. She's lucky I let her use them."

This guy was a peach and a half. Osha couldn't remember the last time he'd had such a friendly conversation – barring the digmen, of course. He stood, clearing his throat. "And what does she use them for?"

"Medicine, of course. What do you think?"

"Medicine?"

"Do you know *nothing* about her?"

Osha shrugged. "She doesn't know anything about me."

Impatience invaded Loren's whole body, reducing him to a twitching, squirming rodent. "What are you even doing here?"

"I wanted to thank you for these." Osha offered up the shoes, dangling them by loose laces over the flower pots. Loren yanked them away. "And Nadya says she's sorry."

Loren sighed audibly, scowling at nothing. "What else did she say?"

"Not a word." Osha stepped cautiously between the orchids, toward one of the windows. The chilly afternoon seeped through the thin glass like ink into water. The rain had stopped, but the sky was still falling – tumbling down now as a heavy, sloppy sleet. "What's going on between you two, anyway?"

"That's none of your business."

"Fair enough."

"It's Nadya's family."

"*Nadya's* family?" Osha snorted. "Isn't she your sister?"

"Half."

"Ah." Osha fixed his gaze on the view. Beyond peaked roofs and twiggy branches, he could see the twinkling lights of downtown. A sliver of the matte gray bay. A single blinking boat. Quite different than the view he'd had from his own attic room in Lanestabra – when he, too, lived with his sister. What a lonely life that had been. Osha had always envied large families, noisy ones like the Sobinis. The more chaotic the better. The nomads had made him feel loved and ignored in perfect proportion. It was in these small, cold, too-close families that trouble brewed.

"It's her father's side. The whole damn family. They're just. . . ." Loren's eyes shifted, face softening a bit as he searched for the right words. "They're not good for her."

"Come now, she seems like a good judge of character."

"You sure about that?" Loren raised a brow, sizing Osha up. "You hardly seem like a good judge of character yourself."

"Well, I *am* talking to you."

"What do you even know about my sister?"

Osha shook his head, palms up. "She talks to ghosts?"

"Oh, brother." Loren rolled his eyes.

"She's a far sight better than the digmen she saved me from."

"Saved you?" Loren nearly laughed. Quite the sight, him smiling. Osha hadn't thought him capable. "Kid, she's not the saving type. Helpful, maybe, if you're—"

"Stop," Osha raised a hand. "You can be as mad at Nadya as you want, but I don't need some attic rat too lazy to move from his mom's house telling me who to hang out with."

Loren stared at him for a moment. A long moment. Unblinking. Inanimate. Only after Osha was sufficiently uncomfortable did he even breathe. At last, he licked his lips, shifting his weight. "I take care of this house," he stated coolly. "*Someone* has to."

"And your mother?"

"Do you see her anywhere?" This man was made of stone. "She's dead."

"Oh." Osha looked down. "I'm sorry."

"I don't want your pity."

Osha looked back out the window. The topic of dead moms had always been a tricky one. Having spent years trying to escape his own, it was difficult to imagine *missing* her. Years ago, at a wake, he'd asked a bereaved child if she'd actually loved her deceased mother. It hadn't gone over well. These days, he opted for silence.

"Your papers."

Osha glanced over his shoulder. "What?"

"This was in my shoe." Loren was visibly nettled, visa in hand.

"Oh! I forgot all about that! Thank you."

"And this?" Next came the pill jar. "What is this?"

"Sorry about that." Osha shook his head. "It's been quite the day."

"Is that so." Loren handed over the medicine and turned away. He had no trouble with the maze of orchids. He moved through the room like a dancer. Ducking into his closet, he traded his shoes for a small tin box – *cigarettes* – and with unfettered ease made his way back to Osha. "You mind?" He didn't wait for an answer before opening the window.

"You smoke?" Osha found that surprising.

"On days like this I do."

"Doesn't your sister mind?"

The match cracked, an explosion of sparks. "She doesn't know."

"What do you mean she doesn't know? She's *psychic*, Loren."

"Psychic?" He smiled again. "There's a thought." The lenses of his glasses flashed orange as he took a long drag. "The last thing Nadya needs is more voices in her head. She's got enough bad influences as it is." He exhaled slowly, the smoke not so different from Osha's own foggy breath in the icy air.

But different enough.

"Come on, now." Osha drummed his fingers on the windowsill. "You're not gonna offer me one?"

Loren obliged with a frown, grudgingly opening his tin for another cigarette. And with the flick of a match, Osha filled his lungs with rich, thick smoke. His first glorious cigarette since leaving the nomads. "This is incredible! What is this?"

"Mostly sage and mugwort."

Osha took another drag. Earth and heaven in equal measure. "I guess I'm used to mullein."

"There's that, too. And lavender. I made them myself."

"They're delicious, Loren." This, on top of square cakes. On top of clean, warm clothing. The shiny new bicycle. The roof over his head. *This.* "This is the best day of my life!"

Loren laughed outright. "How many of those pills did you take today?"

"Ah, if only they worked like that." Osha blew rings, dizzy with pleasure. "Laugh all you want, but yesterday I lived a completely different life. But look at me now! Rubbing elbows with actors, going on the radio."

"The radio?"

"Well, I haven't gone on air yet. But it's happening. Once I show Holic and Iza—"

Loren's face fell like a rock. "What are you doing with those people?"

Osha startled at the cold in his voice. "We're starting a radio station."

"You know what that station is for?"

"They've got some daytime drama, but—"

"A drama!" Loren scoffed, smoke swirling as he shook his head. "It's a drama, alright. Trust me, kid, you don't want to be part of that."

"Don't 'kid' me." Osha squinted at him. "What do you have on me, anyway, a month?"

"I'm twenty-six."

"I could pass for twenty-six."

Loren fully guffawed now, and loudly.

"Forget it," Osha grumbled. "Just because you're older doesn't mean you know what's good for me. I wasted the best years of my life being nagged and—"

"Best years!" Loren nearly dropped his cigarette.

Osha raised his voice over Loren's cackling: "I may be young, but I'm not the one holed up at my family house. I've been around. I know what goes on in this world."

Loren continued to laugh. "Do you?"

"And I've managed just fine on my own."

"Are you sure?" Loren leaned over the windowsill, tapping ashes from his cigarette. "Correct me if I'm wrong, but aren't you homeless?"

"Not anymore! I've got the kind of house people only dream of." Osha spread his arms toward the darkening bay, the evening blue forest. "Waterfront property, wine cellar – whatever you want, it's got it."

"And where is this dream home of yours?"

"Right over there, in the woods."

"The North Woods?" Loren's brow knitted. "Say what you will about those pills, but you're on *something* if you're seeing houses in the North Woods."

Osha let his hands drop. "What are you on about?"

"That's sacred land. It's illegal to build there." Loren shrugged, like there was nothing more to it. "I've been to countless ceremonies out there, and never seen so much as a tool shed."

Osha was incredulous. "There's a house. It's as real as I am. With food and clothes and anything you'd ever need."

"And you just decided it was all yours."

"No one else was claiming it."

"How nomad-esque." Loren took another drag, studying him. "You and I live in different worlds, kid."

Osha tossed his cigarette out the window, its shrinking glow extinguished by a fat drop of slush as it vanished in the shrubbery. "There's a house in those woods, old boy. You'll see."

# SEVEN

Night welcomed him warmly. Hotly, in fact, with a steaming shower. It had been ages since his last one, so it took time to wash away the past. Under the fingernails, especially, history could be tenacious. He shaved away the few hairs his face could produce, anointed himself with whatever oils hid behind the mirror and – smelling a bit like a nomad medicine cart – slipped into the downy clouds of his bed. Happy. Loren may not have liked him much, but nighttime most certainly did.

Morning, however, did not.

Morning hated his roiling, boiling guts.

And Nadya was no help. In the blinding daylight, she echoed her brother's claims with a certainty that made Osha's head throb. "You must be confused," she said. "Those groves are consecrated. Surely this house is somewhere else."

"Just let me take you there." He rubbed his temples, his eyes, his whole face. He didn't have the energy for an argument. The living room swayed. His stomach churned. And worst of all was the glistening horror outside – something Osha thought he'd escaped, but no. Snow. Not even Nadya's magic could take the edge off that.

"Holic and Iza are already on their way." She glanced nervously toward the door.

"That's fine." This was beyond exasperating. "I'll take them there, too."

"But—"

"It'll be fine, Nadya. Just give me a minute and I'll be ready to go."

Osha made his tipping, tilting way to the bathroom, locked the door behind him, and threw up. Half a cup of tea, unmistakably tinged with blood. "Not again."

He sat against the wall, hands shaking. Aching. Thinking of his sister. It was beauty, usually, that brought her to mind. He'd wish she could try a new dish, or laugh at a streetside comedian. There were festivals she'd love, concerts, glistening cities like Sabelso and Anatine. But times like this also reminded him of her. Her worry for him – how it would drive her sobbing, shrieking, hair-pulling insane. He was only two sneezes from death to Faia, always. A skinned knee: emergency. Flu season: fatality. It was good that he'd left. She was better off not seeing him like this.

Osha closed his eyes and refrained from missing her.

There was a knock at the front door. Nadya's footsteps moved toward it.

"Iza, dear, come in! Make yourself comfortable."

"Lovely morning, isn't it?"

"It is!"

"Such an early snow!"

"Care for some tea?"

Osha buried his face in his arms, innards aflame. Nadya's voice was a slight comfort, at least.

"Where's Holic?"

"In the car, with the equipment. Wrapping it in blankets! Simply petrified it'll catch cold."

Iza's laughter, however, was enough to make him sick again.

He hooked his fingers on the brim of the sink and pulled himself up. His reflection rose with him, pallid and glossy-eyed in the mirror. A few splashes of water made him more presentable. He dampened his waves, smoothing them back and out of his eyes. It wouldn't stay like that for long, he knew, but the effect was helpful.

"Any trouble passing the gates?" Nadya's soft song continued.

"Oh, I wasn't there. I was giving my hands a milk bath. They get so dry in this weather!" Iza's heels clacked across the hardwood as she spoke. "Gabris worked it out somehow, as usual. Helps to look so stodgy."

"And he'll get back to Anatine alright?"

"Of course he will. It's not like he has *resistance radical* stamped on his visa or anything. He's a *librarian* for goodness' sake – and it shows."

Osha slid the bathroom door open a crack. The two women were sitting now, side-by-side before the fire, backs to him. If he wanted to, he could slip out unseen and duck under the stairs for his pills.

And want to, he did – believe it or not.

For nearly half his life, he'd avoided those pills. No idle task, either: he was expected to take them three times a day. Gritty and enormous, they were painful to swallow whole and downright vile if crushed – and invariably saddled him with some of the very symptoms they were meant to treat. Nausea. Sweating. A covetous view of nonexistence. He once flushed an entire shipment down the toilet, right in front of his stricken mother. Of course, that stunt earned him nothing but the torture of weekly injections. He'd be taking his medicine one way or another.

But things had changed. Without his anxious mom and the endless parade of doctors, medicating was voluntary. A pleasure, even. And without barbarous school bullies breathing down his back, he could indulge unafraid. Without everything that had him skipping school, avoiding home, falling in with dockworkers and nomads, taking a pill was no more complicated than, well, taking a pill. He had a new life now, full of exotic places, exuberant parties, and people who weren't afraid to touch him. And medicine was only medicine.

Awfully hard to swallow, though. He couldn't do it without water. He needed something to drink. Pill in mouth, he made his way to the front room, lips tightly sealed.

"Well, hello there," Iza stood as he approached, a dizzying blur of busy, conflicting patterns. "And who might you be?" She held out a hand for him. Palm down.

He couldn't resist. In spite of everything, he leaned in and kissed it.

"Oh, Iza!" Nadya laughed aloud. "Surely you recognize Osha!"

"My!" Iza's eyes widened, but she didn't pull her hand back too fast.

"You certainly clean up well."

Osha lifted his teacup from the table and took a sip. It wasn't enough, though. The pill was still in his mouth.

"So, Osha," Iza pressed, oblivious to his plight, "what's this I hear about a house?"

The flavor was leaching onto his tongue now, frothing and bitter. He held up a finger, lifting the teacup once more. This time he managed to swallow it, but not without a struggle.

Nadya frowned. "Are you feeling alright, Osha?"

"Fine," he croaked. "Just swell."

"Are you sure? When you were in the bathroom I thought I heard—"

"Itch in my throat. Couldn't be better."

"Alright, you two, enough chit-chat." Iza took her seat, crossing her legs, resting her chin on a sturdy fist. "We've got business to attend to."

Osha sat as well, the room pulling away from him like a vacuum. He closed his eyes for a moment, reopening them with a smile. "I did find a house," he began. "An abandoned house—"

"Abandoned?" Iza raised a brow. "Does it have electricity?"

"It positively sizzles."

"Because I'm not interested in squatting."

"We wouldn't be."

"But someone has to own this place."

"I doubt it. It's in the North Woods." Osha smirked at Nadya. "And from what I gather, the North Woods are public property."

Iza frowned. "Says you. There's nothing out there but stone circles and bone piles. No one even goes but witches. Isn't that right, Nadya? You would know."

The pill hit Osha's stomach like a bomb, an explosion in a stormy sea. He breathed in. He breathed out. Soon, the spinning room would still. The feverish aches would dissipate. Even the bruises would fade. Just as long as he didn't vomit again.

Iza leaned forward, laying a hand on Osha's arm. "Look, bunny, I'm sure you've found something, but it's either not a house, or it's not in the North Woods."

Osha swallowed. "Why would I lie?"

She leaned back, toying with her hair as she looked him up and down. "I don't know one thing about you, northerner. Who's to say you're not gonna give us an earth bath?" She pursed her little cupid's-bow lips. "And to die now? Looking like I do? At least let me do my nails."

# EIGHT

The snow was melting fast in the streets, beaten to an ugly slush by morning traffic. Good thing, too – city cars were ill-equipped for winter weather, and altering them in any way was strictly forbidden. Careening downhill from Perala House, slipping and skidding all the while, Osha found himself actually missing Oclia. Or at least Oclian snow tires. Valena's vehicles were the same as any in the Union: matte brown, boxy little things, rarely updated and heavily regulated. Any resident could rent one, but the how, where and why of driving was yoked to a bureaucratic noose. Screenings, paperwork and checkpoints smothered even the shortest drive in anxiety, if not futility.

In an empire hell-bent on unity, the choking of travel struck Osha as a little off. Not that he knew much about politics.

What he did know went something like this: before the seas rose up, drowning highways and histories, all the provinces were one. One piece of land, under one single banner – from the Nameless Province all the way up to Oclia (by most accounts). That fabled nation of old stretched east as well, far beyond the mountains, into a no-man's land not even nomads wanted to visit. But Sagoma, Pan-Archipelago capital in both culture and command, wanted to rebuild it. Driven by madness or arrogance or pity for their less developed neighbors, Sagoma smeared its nationalistic mythos over the islands like fingerpaint – heavily armed artists commanding a whole militia of colors. They knew what was best, after all, for they alone had salvaged the past from the floods and fires of yore. They alone remembered, when no one else could.

Some had even made a point to forget.

Like Rimolee.

Most places let the old ways rot, burying them deep lest someone try to revive them. Civilization itself had nearly died with them, after all – curiosity was too great a gamble. City names were changed, remodeled, disguised. Some originals still existed, though Osha wasn't very good at identifying them. He knew the "San" and "Santa" towns around Sagoma were originals, but beyond that? Rumors abounded, of course, conflicting, convoluted titles attached to every old town he passed through. Antediluvian neighborhoods, with their sprawling wooden structures and weather-blasted, bird-legged signs, harbored heartbreaking trauma, ghastly legends, and particularly cheap boarding houses – with a rather garish aesthetic, in Osha's opinion.

But he didn't want to *destroy* them.

The temple of Rimolee, however, had a different take.

The temple had sprung from a network of rural safe havens, communal farms tended by pacifists while urban areas wallowed in chaos. From all over the world, they'd gathered medicinal plants – many hallucinogenic – and in glasshouses they bred them, selling them to the troubled populace as a pathway to peace. And it worked. Those little communes bloomed into cities, their economy sprouting a new religion, and a gentle hush fell over a once violent land. In light of the greed that had fueled such turmoil, temple folk favored asceticism, vegetarianism, and other things that made Osha cringe. But who was he to judge? The Rimolean theocracy had ruled in total peace for over two-hundred years before the Unionists marched in. Shunning hedonism wasn't *all* bad.

Indulgence wasn't all they blamed, though. *Everything* that came before was at fault. The priesthood had heaped history up in great piles and set it aflame. Countless technological advances went up in ashes. Political pacts: ashes. Social constructs: ashes. Troves of literature, art, music, innocent music: all of it, ashes. Honoring the past in full was sacrilege. The dim mysteries at the root of life got due respect, as did the pious pilgrims of the past few centuries – but for all their morbidity, the temple was awfully picky about the dead they chose to worship.

Iza Barsamina was clearly not a devotee. As Nadya drove and Holic guarded his precious cargo, Iza sipped spiked tea from a thermos and mourned all they'd lost: "Look, you guys, I know you don't believe me. But how else do you explain those theaters? They certainly weren't for plays. My cousin visited one once, down by Sagoma. Says there's huge spools of tiny pictures – whole strings of 'em, wound up like thread, kept in tins like cigarettes. It isn't magic, it's science, and someday soon—"

"You've got to stop reading those silly magazines," Holic cut her off.

"Says the guy who believes in air trains."

"*Planes*, Iza. They were called *planes*. And there are fields filled with them right here in Rimolee. You don't have to go to the damned Nameless Province to see them."

Osha had seen those planes. Mountains of decay between the trees like deflated, dead whales. He'd seen an old theater, too, where once people shot pictures like bullets into a wall that had long since collapsed (perhaps from the onslaught). He'd clambered over crumbling buildings, uncovered rusted cars the size of small houses, explored exclusion zones said to off-gas ancient, alien chemicals. Down abandoned back roads, alleyways, and underground with the nomads, he'd seen it all. And he wanted to say so, but not like this. Not in a jerking, skidding car. Not with Valena's white cloak burning his eyes. His medicine had never failed him, though – and Nadya's presence was an immeasurable help. Already, his shaking hands had stilled. Soon, the knots in his stomach would untie, and he'd be free to join the conversation.

For now, though, the incessant chatter was unbearable.

"Eat flies, Holic!" Iza screeched. "How can you say that a hunk of metal can fly but pictures can't move?"

"Simple mathematics, my dear. Aerodynamics. Precisely what these city cars lack."

"Well, you're right there. Not at all like the old cars. Why can't we model these after those? We know how – some fella in Anatine built one himself."

"Our cars are mass-produced, Iza. The Union has no time for details."

"You don't know a thing, Holic. The old cars were mass-produced, too. Every person alive had one – even children! They had everything before the floods. My stars, were they sitting pretty."

"Obviously not that pretty," Nadya chimed in.

Iza crossed her arms and pouted.

"You're being maudlin, my dear." Holic smirked, one brow raised – likely the most expressive face he could make. "Don't let nostalgia lie to you. Nostalgia is nothing but fear. We all fear the future as we can't know it, but history is safe. We all know its story."

"There's a claim! We can't remember the half! – least of all you. And isn't *that* terrifying?"

"What's done is done. There's nothing to worry over in the past."

"Like hell there isn't! It'll sneak back up on you, you know that. Like that fella from the wine bar who—"

"What's done is done." Holic was firm. "I'll say no more on that account."

"We know all we need to know about history, Iza," Nadya said, "and it's plenty terrifying. We know exactly what not to do."

Iza scowled magnificently. "Your people are the reason we're living like this today – stuck in these shoddy cars, worshiping the dead."

Holic's eyebrow was back up, sharp and ready to attack. "Sounds to me that *you're* the one worshiping the dead, dear."

"You know, you might be right. I'm sure not the one burning up the wisdom of the venerable ancestors here—"

"The temple didn't cause the floods." Nadya wasn't humored. "It's only Union PR that makes the past seem so glamorous. At the height of your so-called golden age, people were miserable. Materialism was God, and the gifted seen as crazy! Plant medicines were outlawed, the laws of nature undermined – powerful healers were killing themselves in grief. Can you imagine?"

Iza snorted. "Like I'd expect a witch to understand!"

"All those nice things you dream of just drove people mad with greed, Iza." Nadya looked genuinely disturbed. "Ravaging the land, poisoning the water. Killing off whole species and inventing new ones to replace them!"

"Oh, not that again. How many times have I told you: the passenger pigeon is not an invention. It was *rescued* from extinction. Brought back from the dead! People *saved* it."

"You're both wrong," Holic interjected. "There's nothing unnatural about that bird but its habitat. The flocks were forced over the mountains by the Eastern Wars."

"That's what they *want* you to believe," Iza scoffed. "Our boy Osha will settle this."

Osha blinked.

"There's loads of passenger pigeons in Erobia, right?" she pressed. "Surely you've seen them in your travels."

He had. And as far as he was concerned, the world would be better off without them. Black sky rivers. Feral clouds. Deafening, discordant dung storms. He cleared his throat. "Well, they certainly don't *seem* natural."

"What about the woolly mammoth?" Nadya spoke up now.

Now mammoths, he loved. Their eerie, disembodied trumpets echoing through Oclia day and night, their rare and terrifying appearance. Majestic, earthy gods. Dream singers. They were sacred in the taiga, revered for everything from keeping the ground fertile to keeping the world turning. In the ice, though, they were hunted. Poverty and shortages notwithstanding, Osha always felt bad about eating them. He drew himself up. "What about them?"

"They're man-made, aren't they?"

"Impossible." He shook his head. "Nothing's more Oclian than woollies."

"But I heard—"

"Can it, priestess," Iza waved a hand. "Chatty as you are with spirits, you'd think you'd be more on board with necromancy. You temple folk burned some of your best spells with those old books."

"With good reason. Those were dangerous technologies—"

"That could raise the dead!"

"While nearly destroying life as we know it! Have you forgotten the fires? The floods? Those violent diseases – especially up north! What was that epidemic called, Osha? From the melted ice? Or was it tundra?"

He shrugged, reluctant to talk about illness while feeling so ill.

"Unspeakable diseases," Nadya insisted.

"Treated with the best medicines in history!"

"They locked people in sanitariums to die, Iza!"

"It's true." Osha could attest to that. Oclia's plagues had littered the landscape with hospitals, now abandoned, crumbling and haunted. Only a few were still used – no longer for human experiments, in theory. "It was awful."

Iza ignored him. "You keep telling yourself that. But on some level, priestess, even you know the truth. The ancient civilizations were simply more advanced than us. A golden age was lost, and the powers that be just don't want you to know. The arts and academics flourished, and *everyone* was wealthy."

"You sound like a Union sympathizer, Iza," Holic chided. "Why not just move to Sagoma? See your moving picture theaters. Study the old ways. Join the campaign to better our lives!" He took on a familiar tone, a rolling, impassioned timbre that often flooded Union airwaves, sometimes cutting songs off midway: "Connect us all through the ancient technologies! Unite the islands as they were meant to be!"

"Who is that guy, anyway?" Osha asked.

"The ambassador?" Holic looked bemused.

"Whoever it is you're mimicking."

"Oh, Osha!" Iza's eyes were wide with disbelief. "You *must* know the ambassador. He's grown so popular, he's practically second-in-command."

"Ambassador?" Osha shook his head. "What kind of ambassador spends so much time on the radio? I thought—"

"Nevermind what you thought." Iza plucked his words from the air and tossed them aside. "He used to be more of an emissary, but the poor man's run out of countries to visit now that everything's the same place. So he just hops around the occupied territories, giving his pretty little speeches, boosting morale—"

"Boosting morale? Is that what you call it?" To Osha, interrupting a good radio program was much more likely to *crush* morale.

"It's good to hear you haven't fallen under his spell," Holic said coolly. "He has a way with words that most find quite compelling."

"And his face certainly helps," Iza added with a smirk. "If there's anything good about him, it's his genes. Though if you ask me, the hair's gotta be fake. Definite bottle blond."

Portraits of officials were everywhere in the Union: train stations, post offices, even pubs. Waiting for ferries or tea or a warm meal, Osha would study their regalia, their mustaches, their hats and high brows – but never gave much thought to who was who. He wasn't proud of his ignorance. He wasn't proud to have no idea who this man was. But politics had always bored him, and life was only so long.

"That's not all that's fake about him," Holic hissed. "His concern for Sabelso, his sorrow for that tragedy—"

"Oh, brother," Iza butted in. "He *caused* that. The things he says! Pretending to bring us all together while inciting violence and distrust. Buries it under pomp and poetry, of course, but anyone in their right mind can tell what he means."

Holic nodded along. "Hypocrisy."

Osha knew Sabelso well. Knew its vibrant, lively streets. Its stunning architecture. Lush gardens, sandy beaches. Block parties where he and Julis had danced until dawn. But he knew nothing of violence and tragedy there. He wanted to ask, but couldn't get a word in.

"Outright lies!" Iza cried. "Like claiming to be Rimolean! The nerve! And everyone knows that's just to cover his tracks. Anything to keep us from knowing who he is."

Holic snorted in disgust. "Won't even say his name!"

"With such a public role, he's got a right to his privacy." Nadya defended the man. "Think of the veils and masks of the priests—"

"Applesauce!" Iza bit back. "Witches dress for self-negation. Blending in with the divine and all that rot. Our ambassador is *hiding* from the masses, not seeking oneness."

"Dodging stalkers," Holic mused.

"And murders!" Iza concurred, lit with a dark glee. "Someone could shoot him. Stab him. Kidnap him for ransom."

Nadya shushed her. "Don't talk like that. He's a human being."

Iza crossed her arms. "*Now* who's the Unionist?"

The car grew quiet. Blissfully calm. Osha's head, at last, was beginning to clear.

But Iza would have none of it. "Anyway—" she shattered the silence like glass "—so maybe the old technologies weren't perfect. So what? All I'm saying is we're not living up to our potential. We're being lied to. Union, independent, resistance – *all* of us. And you don't have to dig deep to learn the truth. It doesn't take a genius to know where the old ways *really* came from." Nadya and Holic heaved heavy sighs, but Iza was undeterred. "That's right: spacemen."

# NINE

The towering gates at Valena's north exit were shut and locked, stopping up the road like a dam. In the snow at their base, digmen paced and smoked, scribbling in damp, wrinkled notepads. Bored and cold and poised to interrogate any looking to leave.

"We don't have to cross here, do we?" Iza asked.

"No," Osha assured her. But nothing looked as it had the day before. The paths that spider-legged off into the forest were lost in the white drifts. Still, he could feel the house out there, casting him a line. All he had to do was let it lure him in. "Take that road right there."

"That's a road?"

"Trust me."

Iza looked despondent. "I was right. He *is* gonna kill us."

"Shh! I need some quiet." Osha was groping blind. "Take a left after that stump." Thinking was no help at all. Fortunately, his brain wasn't yet up to that task. "Another left there." The house hummed, musical, ringing in his bones like the aftermath of a heavy gong. He could only listen. "Turn right there."

"Where?"

"Back there. You just passed it."

"Strange. I didn't even see that."

Osha's irritable gut was dealt a blow as they jerked to a halt and began the squirrelly process of backing up.

Nadya was shaking her head. "I don't think I've ever been on these roads."

"Neither have I," Iza agreed. "They'll never find our bodies."

Between the trees, the jagged mountains could be seen, reliable as a compass arrow. Osha found their presence soothing, the way they just sat there. Still and dark. Like the inside of his eyelids.

"Osha." Iza tugged his sleeve.

He'd closed his eyes. "Sorry."

"No, it's, um . . ." she tapped the side of her nose silently, brows knitted.

Osha felt his nostrils. Wet. Blood on his hand. He sighed. "Does anyone have a handkerchief?" The others shuffled through their things, coming up with nothing but apologies. So – with the Barsamina Company's biggest stars looking on – Osha tilted his head back and pinched. If he didn't feel so awful already, his pride might have been wounded – but most of his woundedness had been used up for the day.

Anyway, they were almost there. The house was just coming into view. They parked and climbed out of the car, not one word spoken. Complete, unbroken silence.

Osha gathered snow below the porch, cleaning his face and hands. Bit by bit, the ground grew gory, like the scene of some wounded animal crawling off to die. Clinging lightheaded to the railing of the stairs, he wondered how big that carcass would be.

Holic patted him on the back as he passed, sauntering up the steps like he owned the place. "We've all been there, kid."

Nadya and Iza were much slower to approach. So slow, in fact, that they didn't move an inch. The snow had glued them in place.

"It's straight out of a ghost town," they were whispering.

"It must be four-hundred years old."

"At least."

"Why haven't I seen this from the water?"

"I haven't seen it from anywhere."

On and on they went, about sailing and ceremonies, beachcombing and treasure hunts that surely brought them to this very spot. But never in their lives had they seen this house. They blinked and blinked and stupidly blinked, giving it ample opportunity to disappear should it wish. Yet it remained.

Osha had no patience for their confusion. "Come on, it's freezing!"

Iza raised her eyebrows. "I'm surprised to hear that from you. You should be used to much worse."

He turned from them as they drew near, his nose continuing its red cascade over the railing. It had slowed some, but wasn't giving much thought to stopping. The sudden weight of Nadya's hand on his shoulder came as a shock. Pulsing. "Aren't you coming with us?" Her voice, too, slipped under his skin, a gush of static. For a moment, Osha could only stare.

"Sure," he finally mustered. Wiping at his nose, he smiled. "There's some old sheets upstairs."

While the outside of the house hadn't changed – dripping, mossy rock that it was – the inside was lighter. And not just from the snow. The air itself seemed to weigh less. All the spectral smells were stronger, more alive – and intermingled now with the faint aroma of music. Osha wasn't certain, of course. He couldn't recall having smelled music before, and the flavor of blood was surely tainting things. But it seemed rather distinct.

Nadya and Iza had frozen yet again, in the entryway, leaving Osha to push between them in his crimson rush to the staircase. In his wake, they whispered – and their voices carried. All throughout the house he could hear them. Clear up into the loft, right on his heels, their words followed.

"Are those moving?"

"What?"

"Those discs. Like the sun and the moon – right up there."

"Well, that is a little strange."

"Something doesn't feel right, Iza."

"Don't get all superstitious on me now. This place couldn't be more perfect."

"What about that foghorn? Don't you think it's a little loud?"

"Unwind a little, will ya? What could go wrong?"

"Anything, with strangers involved like this."

"Oh, psh. Osha seems alright. A bit loose at the seams, but he's young – maybe it's just a phase."

"I do hope he's alright. I've yet to see him at his best."

"Assuming he *has* a best."

"You're too kind," Osha shot down, leaning over the loft's low wall.

"Well, would you look at that." Iza beamed up at him. "A stage!"

He offered a broad, bloody grin – "It's a natural amphitheater!" – and turned his back.

A lamp switched on as he entered his room, atop a tall wooden dresser – and beside that, a full change of clothes. On a rack near the door hung a long black coat. The bed had been smoothed, pillow fluffed, an extra blanket folded at the base. And on top of it, his hat! His favorite hat, feather and all, as crisp and clean as it had ever been. As Osha lifted it, a bundle of handkerchiefs tumbled out, crumpled clouds falling to the bed. Deep maroon (so as not to be bothered by bloodstains), each was embroidered in black with O.E.L.O. His initials. He lifted one to his nose. It smelled of lavender.

Sinking into the bed, he waited out the bloodbath, listening to the muffled movements of the others. They were in the kitchen, directly below. He could make out nearly everything they said:

"What do you have there?"

"Strawberries!"

"Where on earth did you get *strawberries* this time of year?"

"Right there, on the counter. There's more in the basket."

It wasn't long before Osha felt better. Better than he had in years, in fact. When he stood again, his legs were strong. Energized. Hopeful. The pill was in full effect, his nose was dry, and good God, did he love strawberries.

But not as much as he loved pianos.

And there one sat, right in the loft, natural as a bee on a blossom. A beautiful black upright. The only instrument he'd been formally trained on, Osha hadn't played one since leaving home. He'd made do, as he tended to, leaning on nomad ingenuity. The Sobinis pieced together all sorts of abominations – handmade melodicas, surgically altered accordions. But a real piano? That ranked higher than indoor plumbing as a reason to settle down.

Slowly, he approached the bench. Very slowly, he lifted the fallboard. Very, very slowly, he placed his hands over the smooth ivory. And there he held them, reverently, drawing in a deep breath.

There it was: the smell of music.

"I'm going to play you now," Osha whispered to the keys. "Just so you know. I wouldn't want to startle you."

Then in he dove.

The sound was staggering. Full and rich, the vibration almost too much for his skinny bones. But he played anyway, as he always did – just as the music wanted. Obediently, his voice joined in, tripping over each note, stumbling from one syllable to the next. Doing the song's bidding.

He'd made good money with this up north, easily covering the cost of the medicines he didn't need. All over Lanestabra, he played – at weddings, at funerals, at all the archaic religious functions his grandmother dragged him to. But even when he had to sit up straight, don a weird little hat and sing in a language that had been dead for millennia, he felt just as he did now. Open, relaxed. High as a kite. If he stopped to think at all, he'd wreck it completely, so he didn't. After years of practice, he could play disassociation like any other instrument. Were it not for tips (both instructive and monetary), he wouldn't have a clue if he was any good. He leaned on witness accounts like a sleepwalker, baffled come morning by misplaced books and mysterious bruises.

And that's what he sang about now: sleepwalking. He'd outgrown the habit, but it had stained him, and its ink leaked into every song he wrote. The one he sang now was particularly rancorous, recounting that long ago night – mere weeks after leaving the taiga – when he'd wandered, unconscious, away from his aunt's house and into that contaminated marsh. His family fished him from the broken ice. The doctor stitched up his wounded thigh. But there was no recovering from the toxic water that had seeped in, a poison poised to dissolve him from the inside out in maddening cycles of torment that would leave him begging for merciful death.

Or so he was told.

Ultimately, the only torment Osha suffered was the stigma – that inevitable, animal response to the unknown. He was more than happy, at first, to deflect some bullying away from his sister, but it quickly wore him down. Until the day he left Lanestabra, Osha was little more than the disease he was said to carry: a prehistoric plague, hatched from frozen tundra during the Great Thaw. A parasitic swarm teeming in the tidal marshes of countless northern bays. He was to be fussed over or feared (depending on who you asked), and above all granted precious little freedom.

Before running away, music had been his sole sanctioned pleasure – and a convenient dumping ground for the algae blooms of angst that flourished in that stifling environment. In the first years after his diagnosis, he bore the tension like a shield; if he dropped his guard, the enemy within would surely wake, teeth bared. But with music he could unwind. He could let go. He could *vent*. From the nomads, he learned to hide his bitterness in drinking songs, to let his sorrows be swept away by violent waves of melody. His stories became whatever his audience wanted to hear, his past passing for a bad dream or a bad relationship, a bad government or a bad crop of potatoes. Pretty much anything bad, really. This tendency toward vague, mass catharsis made songs like the one Osha played now a hit. Especially at pubs.

He'd written this one for the piano, and he hadn't forgotten how to play it on one. He rode the whole song without missing a note.

When he finished, the room below exploded with applause.

Osha's hair had fallen, a black curtain over his eyes. He brushed it back as he smiled at his audience. With a bow, it tumbled down again.

Iza bounded up the stairs toward him, curls bouncing as she grasped his shoulders, words fluttering from her mouth like moths: "Why didn't you say you could do *that*? What *was* that?"

"Just something I wrote." Osha smoothed his hair again, firmly.

"Just something," Iza repeated, incredulous. "What do you call it?"

"'Farewell, Everything.'"

"A touch dark, but still. You got any others?"

"A few."

Nadya appeared in the loft now, too, eyes wide. "You said you play on street corners for peanuts!"

"Just guitar." His hair fell back over his eyes. "And yes, downtown, right by—"

"Madness!" Iza shrieked. She cupped Osha's face in her hands and squeezed. "A talented fella like you could be famous!"

"Well, put me on the radio then!"

"Holic, darling!" Iza called down. "Be a dear and bring in the equipment. Set it right here, in this very spot!" She beamed at Osha. "And then, bunny, you can put whatever you just did straight on the airwaves."

# TEN

Jumbled mass of wood and wires though it was, setting up the radio station took little time, and even less work – almost as though the house itself did it. That was unlikely, though, for the house was awfully busy with other things: draping the windows in thin, light curtains, sweeping off the roof, beating back the covetous fingers of the North Woods. The kitchen filled up, shelves loaded with pots and pans, a teakettle, jars of rice and flour, dried fruit and nuts. Food sprung up in the cupboards, the refrigerator, even the oven. Hot meals, almost every evening. On top of all that, how could the house have any time for the station?

Thanks to the aural demands of Iza's program, the floor of the loft grew crowded as well, all but carpeted with instruments: a violin, a trumpet, several drums. Chimes. A small harp. Glass jars of all sizes. A thin sheet of tin. Most were borrowed from Barsamina Theater, but under Osha's roof they behaved just as the piano did: perpetually ready, quietly tuning themselves when no one was around.

People were almost always around, though. They came through in droves. Yet for all the traffic, it proved exceedingly difficult to introduce anyone new to the territory. By the end of the first week, Osha was drawing up detailed maps replete with natural architecture, fleeting views, rail lines – absolutely anything that might point the way. To no avail.

The protests were all the same: "There's no road there."

"It's narrow. It's gravel. It was probably too dark last night to see." Osha's exasperation grew each time his directions fell short. It soon became clear that guides were needed. At times, literal handholding was necessary, as though escorting a blindfolded initiate to a secret clubhouse.

Most guests were actors in the midday drama – something Osha rarely stuck around for. He didn't mean to be rude, but he'd already lost hours, days, weeks of his life to such things. Dull romances, transparent mysteries. Growing up, every female relative he had would crowd into his mother's small, dark row house to swoon over stilted platitudes hissed by invisible heartthrobs. He'd done his time.

The actors were friendly enough, if a bit private. They all wanted to hear Osha play. To learn about his travels. To know what he thought of the Pan-Archipelago Union. But no one offered much about themselves, and none were half as gracious as Nadya.

Nadya, who was never among them. Nadya, who apparently didn't like the house. It made her uncomfortable, Iza informed him. The gifts, she said, the pastries, the sweetness of the water – it somehow rubbed her the wrong way. Something superstitious, something about death and ghosts. Osha didn't believe a word of it, though. Who in their right mind would take issue with free food? He knew the real reason behind her avoidance. He'd encountered it before. It had much more to do with him than any old building. There was no shortage of reasons to avoid *him*, and each was well-grounded and logical. It didn't take a psychic to see them. Anyone could.

Including Iza.

Not that it stopped *her* from coming over – Iza all but moved in. Her crowded family house cramped her style, or so she claimed. But she didn't seem too comfortable with Osha, either. He embarrassed her. Privately, she was kind, generous with compliments, and more than willing to discuss music – even placing personal requests for his radio program. Publicly, though, she treated him like a pesky little brother, someone to push away, something to hide. His music was too morbid, his nose too bloody. She'd cross-examine him on his plans, tracking his whereabouts almost as doggedly as his mother had, trying to patch together a social life that didn't involve him.

But it was a small price to pay to play on the radio.

For both of their sakes, Osha tried to keep a routine: each night, the airwaves were his. Lit by the liquid glow of the eclipse, he could play whatever he wanted, however he wanted, as long as he wanted. The only problem was his own fuzzy head. He couldn't remember all the lyrics he'd lost on the beach, stomped out by digmen, torn by shaky hands – and there'd be no turning to Julis now. No borrowing from him like a backup brain. In the dreamy swirl of Julis's reality, where flavors had feelings and sound came in color, Osha usually found what he was looking for. But even without those rainbowed recollections, he remembered the melodies. To fill the gaps, he'd improvise, adopting material from Iza and her friends. With their help, he rewrote one song after another:

> *"It's the clothes I don't put on*
> *"The half-heard lyrics of a song*
> *"Words never really understood*
> *"With . . . that? . . . I've? . . . um . . ."*

"That always carry on too long," Iza suggested.

> *"Another dinner served up cold*
> *"Salted by the sands of time*
> *"Seasoned with the dust of death*
> *"Served up with . . . a . . . slice of lime?* Damn."

"All history intertwined."

"But that hardly makes sense."

"Oh, like it ever does!" Iza was insistent. "Your songs are so vague, you can make 'em whatever you want. Just sing it tonight, bunny – you can change it later if you need to."

The prompts worked. Never as well as one would expect, given the enthusiasm of the drama crowd, but still. He used them, and his ever-tired mind was grateful for the help. On top of late nights and long days, the banal task of inventing new lyrics – or even translating old ones – proved too much for him. Just having a conversation was taxing enough.

Sleep was deep, but never seemed adequate. He'd wake refreshed and ready, but almost as soon as he left the house, the heaviness would descend. The aches. The pains. The shakes. He wasn't going to stay home, though. He had some truly bad art to escape. Any show that cast Holic (of all people!) as the love interest could hardly be called entertainment. The script was so choppy and false that Osha would end up feeling sick either way. So every morning, just as the actors trickled in, he'd strap on his guitar and ride his bike into town.

There, the music never stopped for any cockamamie dramas.

He'd claimed a bustling spot, sandwiched between food carts and a café, three blocks from the market and mere feet from the streetcar line. Prime real estate, and he knew it. So it shouldn't have surprised him, one chilly morning, to find his corner infringed upon. The musician wasn't in his territory, per se, but the music certainly was. It paced up and down the street, under the great grave arches of Valena's founders, between the fat, greasy taffy puller and the sallow, scowling pastry vendor. It walked right up to Osha and stood there, making it impossible to play a single note.

A slender figure was behind it all, ratty-haired and bearded, haloed by the light of the café. A positively ancient man, teetering on spindly legs, knotted fingers quivering pitch-perfect on the strings of his violin.

A melody far more beautiful than anything Osha could produce. His heart sank. To ask the man to move, to fill that void with his own obnoxious bellowing, would've been criminal.

Osha slipped past him without comment, into the café, where he could wonder what to do next without freezing. May as well rest a while. He whittled away an hour huddled in a corner, cupping a steaming mug, thawing. He pretended to read the news, to care about the fliers zealous Unionists had slipped between the pages, announcements that the ambassador would soon be visiting Valena in person. But he didn't give a damn. He was watching the violinist, swaying in time with his tune. Oozy music, muted and warped through the windows, it burst forth bold and clear each time someone opened the door.

That old man wasn't going anywhere.

At last, Osha rose, lifting his guitar with a whisper: "A day off will do us some good, buddy. And if this happens again, there's always the park." Lugging himself back into the cold, he passed close to the violinist. Tattered jacket. Musty, saltwater smell. A gray hat lay at his feet, expectantly. Empty.

That wasn't right.

Osha stared into the felt-lined void for a moment, baffled, before plunging his hands into his pockets for a couple of folded bills. Bending down, he dropped a heavy coin on top so that the money wouldn't blow away.

The old man muttered something.

Osha stood. "What's that?"

He stopped playing to repeat himself, slowly, with a nod. "You're looking up." His voice was deep and resonant, if a little gruff.

Absently, Osha touched his coat, his scarf – all fine new things. "Thank you?"

"I've seen you here before," the man explained. "And I didn't mean to impose. Been coming here for ages, myself, but I'm old news. More than happy to bow out for new talent."

Osha was struck dumb.

"I can pack my things."

"No, no, don't," Osha stammered. "Play as long as you want. I can just cross the street." He gestured at the hat on the ground. "It's not like this side's that lucrative today."

A strange look crossed the violinist's face. It would have been hard to read on anyone, but the magnificent wrinkles he'd amassed obscured nuance all the more.

"You're pretty good," Osha told him. "It's a real shame you're not making more."

"Ah, I've made enough money for one life." The man smiled at him. Whatever emotion crept under his skin deepened. His brows lowered. His eyes gleamed. "You're staying out at the Waiter House, aren't you?"

Something wasn't quite right about the old man's voice. Maybe it was just the noise of the street – echoing engines, bicycle bells, the rattling streetcar – but his words seemed to come from very far away. Osha leaned forward, cupping an ear. "Excuse me? The Water House?"

The man chuckled softly. "Well, it does have quite the bay view."

"I'm sorry, I . . . this isn't my first language."

"You don't say." He winked. Raising his voice (as though fluency was a matter of volume), he tried again: "Waiter House, I said. Your place – it's called the Waiter House."

Osha shook his head. "How do you know where I'm staying?"

"Well, where else would you be staying?" That vague look on his face collapsed then, with a sigh. "Spent some time out there myself, a long time ago. Didn't know what else to do, after the wife died. Took to drinkin' heavy, but that house took good care of me. Looks like it's taking good care of you, too."

Osha just stared.

"Ah, yes," the old man nodded to himself. "If you have to be there, it's good to be there. No one's gonna bother you, that's for sure. Not unless you invite 'em, of course."

"Why—" Osha was suddenly unsure how to use words at all, in any language. "Why is it called Waiter House?"

The man's wild white brows rose, his forehead folding upon itself beneath its cap of wiry hair. "Well, it waits on you, doesn't it? Not much more to it than that. It waits on you while you wait."

Osha blinked. "What am I waiting for?"

The violinist laughed outright now, throwing his head back. "Ah, boy, what's anybody waiting for?" He let his eyes linger on the sky, pausing thoughtfully. "You just let that house take care of you," he said. "Enjoy it while you can."

And with that, he lifted the violin to his shoulder and closed his eyes.

# ELEVEN

It was just before the solstice when Iza asked Osha to leave. "I'm not talking about forever. Just for the holiday." She uncrossed and recrossed her ankles, feet propped on the sofa's armrest, stocking tights as red as the blood from Osha's nose. "I don't wanna tighten the screws on you like this, but I got friends coming down from Anatine, and we could really use the space."

"You can't kick me out of my own house," Osha said to his handkerchief. "It's the middle of winter out there."

"Technically," Iza raised a finger, "it's just the beginning of winter. And anyway, who said this was your house?"

"I'm the one who found it."

"I hate to break this to you, bunny, but your nomad pals weren't the best role models. Life's not actually a game of finders keepers."

Osha sighed, eyes on the flames of the fireplace. His nose wasn't letting up. It had been going like this all afternoon, leaving him woozy and weak. Four pills in three days, and still this. And it was worse when he left home. Much worse. "Where am I supposed to go?"

"Why don't you stay with our little witch for a spell?"

"Nadya?" Osha felt his face grow hot. Yet another terrible sensation.

"It's been a while, and what with the torch you carry for her, I'm sure you'd love to catch up."

Osha glared at her. "I barely know her!"

She raised a brow. "In my experience, mystery fuels the hottest fires." Syrupy smile, voice dripping. "Look, I know you're some kind of prude, Osha, but cut yourself some slack. Everyone has feelings like this. Welcome to manhood."

"Catch hornets, Iza." He was happy to hide behind his handkerchief then, cheeks burning. The last thing he wanted to do was mar Nadya's ethereal beauty with his filthy hands. In fact, he didn't want to lay hands on *anyone*, filthy or otherwise. True, he'd been attracted to certain nomads: Nitic for his talent, Neta for her wit. Julis, for being Julis. And true, he'd stumbled into Julis's arms on occasion – but alcohol was requisite, and their embraces never led to much. Clumsy kisses, timid touch. Nothing more. Those sorts of feelings had simply passed him by. And it was a good thing, too. Otherwise, the string of rejections he wore round his neck would be far more uncomfortable. Even Julis distanced himself eventually. Friends blamed Osha, said his own ambivalence had pushed him away, but Osha knew when he wasn't wanted. And since these nosebleeds started, he didn't feel wanted anywhere.

Besides, whatever feelings he had around Nadya were of another breed entirely. No fabled butterflies fluttered in his churning stomach. Just nausea from swallowing blood.

Which, of course, Nadya's soothing presence might alleviate.

"You don't think she'd mind?"

"Are we talking about the same Nadya here? You could rob her at gunpoint and she'd call it sharing." Iza pulled one of her tight little locks out straight and released it. It sprung back in her face. "In case you forgot, she took you in off the street without even knowing your name."

"She knew my name."

Iza sat up, lips pursed. "Mumbo jumbo," she muttered. "One of these days that girl's faith is gonna get her in some real trouble. Who's to say those ghosts she talks to are even trustworthy? Can't imagine there's many rules in the afterlife. What's the incentive to tell the truth?"

"You really believe she talks to spirits?"

"Of course not. I'm not sure what she does, but whatever it is, it's all in her pretty little head. That girl's drunk enough dream soup to drown the whole province."

"Dream soup?"

"Vine tea! Priest in a brothel, Osha, do you even know where you are? Those temple goons may as well have vine tea for blood."

Osha readjusted his handkerchief.

"Speaking of which—" Iza smirked "—you could use some yourself. Might help that leaky schnoz of yours. They claim it can heal anything – after you upchuck for hours and see death, that is." She wrinkled her nose. "Mostly on account of the flavor."

Osha cringed. He'd been doing that just fine on his own. With each passing week, he lost another day's work to sore, sweaty sickness. Soon, it seemed, he wouldn't have any days left at all.

"Might inspire some new material, to boot," Iza continued. "Those witches sing new songs every time they drink that crap. Creepy ones, too. Just your style. Wish I could say it'd make you less morbid, but I can't lie."

Osha held his handkerchief up for examination: not a single spot was clean anymore, but circumstance forced it back to his face. "*I'm* morbid?" He sponged off his wet mouth. "Look at yourself. This whole town is a cemetery!"

"Honoring the ancestors and obsessing over your own demise are not the same thing, bunny. I get that death's part of life and all, but you only die *one time*. It doesn't have to be in *every song*. You gotta give us something new! Take all those half-written songs and make 'em into something lively. If you want my opinion—"

"I don't."

"Nadya's just the right person to help you with this. I've been to her ceremonies – she's a natural poet, believe me. She's got the gift. Runs in her family, ya know." Iza leaned forward, fingers curling claw-like below her chin. "What a perfect way to use your time away."

"Time away?" Osha straightened, frowning. "Hold on, I never agreed to leave."

"Now why on earth would you pass up this golden opportunity?" She rose and moved between him and the fire, a dark silhouette, hands on hips, hair glistening beneath the eclipse. "You could spend the holiday with the woman you love, getting help with your songs, a vine tea ceremony, a cure for whatever ails you – and instead, you're choosing to spend it with some lazy old rocks drinking catlaps and griping about bad dates?"

Osha felt dizzy. "What?"

"*What* indeed! I'd be asking myself the same thing! If you knew what's good for you, you'd get yourself up to Perala House posthaste! Opportunities like this don't come up every day. Only a fool would say no."

# TWELVE

The solstice was celebrated everywhere. In Erobia, it was a time of remembrance, a time to visit old friends, a time to spruce up old shrines. In Oclia: a bare spark in the limitless dark of winter. One lonely item on a mighty short list of reasons to forego suicide.

And in Rimolee, it was a traffic jam.

Valena positively bubbled with festivities. Bustling crowds. Billowing smoke. Through the steamy, rain-flecked windows of a packed streetcar, Osha could see shoppers and merrymakers and openly heavy drinkers. He even glimpsed the old violinist, undulating with his dipping bow, his music lost to the cacophony. The whole priesthood was out, ghosts in the throng, veiled beyond recognition and exquisitely embroidered, ringing their bells, burning their herbs, waving their multicolored flags. Houses and storefronts wore their finest as well, arming themselves against the bleak skies with a phalanx of luminous bulbs. The people, the cobblestones, the boardwalks – everything glowed.

Outside of Nadya's street, that is.

All that greeted Osha there was a checkpoint. Not yet complete, thank God, but well underway – chains and boards and warning signs worked diligently by three somber women in gray. Leaving gaiety and safety behind, Osha stepped down the streetcar steps and moved toward them. Heart clenched, lungs crushed. Since that night on the beach, he broke a sweat at the mere sight of a uniform, and now he was surrounded.

So he smiled. "Happy holidays."

The officers grumbled, heads down.

Not one to overstay his welcome, he pushed on. Fast.

There was no escape, though. Digmen were planted on practically every corner: the least attractive streetside trees Osha could imagine. Eyes on his boots, he pushed past their well-armed branches, steely foliage and suffocating shadows. Possibly the longest two blocks he'd ever walked, and he'd walked a lot. His whole life in Lanestabra was one long walk – stumbling home from blood draws, high on test medications, unsure if he'd survive determining why he wasn't dead. But this was worse. He knew what he was up against with doctors. The Pan-Archipelago Union, though – they threw curveballs.

Only when Nadya's house came into view did he relax. And even then, it was Nadya causing it – ever leaking that sedative ooze of hers. By the time Osha saw her, she'd already glued him in place, molasses all around him. Molasses in which he could finally breathe easy.

Nadya was in a celebratory mood – by temple standards, at least. Clad in her shapeless robes, lost below a beaded shawl, she knelt in the wet grass of her front yard with a platter of dried plants. Unnoticed, Osha watched her pile the leaves onto a couple of stones, mumble a brief prayer, and light them on fire. A saccharine aroma. Swallowed up by the hungry smoke, she began to sing. A song for the dead. Of course, those were headstones she bent over – what else would they be? – though so old and worn they passed for mere rocks. From where Osha stood, he could make out no names or dates, and he doubted that Nadya could either, even with her lips pressed directly upon them.

She sang in the loping language of the holy people – the same language as the digmen, in fact, the language of Sagoma, though such an ancient version that most couldn't understand it. Time had done to it just what it had to those gravestones. Osha could glean a little, could feel out the message, but could never chant like that himself. Even if he knew all the words, his mouth was too trained by the sharp, metallic lilt of Oclian, lips whittled to wires far too thin for such full-bodied music. The vining, floral sounds that grew in warmer climates always tied his tongue in knots.

But they were pretty.

Nadya's fingers danced to her song, drawing esoteric little signs in the cold air. A stray curl slipped from under the hem of her veil, falling over closed eyes, but her hands were too busy to brush it back. In the hush of that sacred, fizzy space, Osha could hear the rustling of her dress, the clink and clunk of the prayer beads round her neck, even the bell-like jingle of her silvery earrings.

She'd thoroughly drugged him, and she didn't even know he was there.

For a moment, Osha forgot why he'd come. He forgot the guitar in his hand, the bag on his back, the muddy notebooks inside of it. He thought of nothing but hope. Hope that Iza had been wrong. Hope that he was only confused, drunk on Nadya's inscrutable warmth. For in spite of his checkered health history, he'd yet to catch a bona fide case of love sickness. He could only hope his luck hadn't run out.

And just like that, it did.

Not quite how he feared it would, but still.

A vise closed on his arm, a hand so large and strong that Osha braced for his bones to snap. It shook him, knocking his hat to the ground.

"Guards!" Thunder, right in his ear. "We have an intruder!"

As though from thin air, the digmen appeared. Four of them. Four sets of smoldering eyes. Four loaded guns.

"Nadya!" She was already coming, but the world was closing in much faster. "Help!" She'd saved him once before, after all.

And her capacity for rescue was truly astonishing.

"Uncle, stop!" she chided. "Let him go!"

"This lecher? Watching my niece from the bushes?"

"He's my friend!"

Osha's arm was released, but he was hardly free to go. A wall of starched gray coats stood between him and salvation.

Nadya pushed between them. "I'm sorry, Osha! I'll straighten this out."

Osha couldn't thank her. His chest was caving in.

"Osha, you say?" The man behind him spoke again. "The Osha we discussed earlier?"

"Yes, Uncle. Osha Oloreben."

"Well, why didn't you say so?" He laughed. The laugh of a grizzly bear. "Apologies, everyone! False alarm!"

The digmen retreated, vanishing into the ether from which they'd emerged. Osha didn't drop his guard, though. Memories of midnight baton swings were alive and well in his throbbing ribs. He wanted to reach out, to pull the fuzzy quilt of Nadya's company closer, but someone else got to her first. Stepping around Osha, head hung low, the man bowed before Nadya's disapproving frown. A humble giant.

"I'm afraid paranoia's gotten the better of me. I've hardly been here an hour and I'm already setting off sirens!"

"It's alright." Ever-cordial Nadya. "But perhaps we should get inside now. The weather's taking a turn anyway."

They linked arms, Nadya and this beast, like old friends – like it made any sense at all – and began to walk away.

Osha didn't move.

"Aren't you coming, Osha?"

He swallowed.

Nadya pulled away from the man, soft-smiling and soothing. "It's only my uncle Nico. He doesn't mean any harm."

Osha looked the man up and down. Tall and powerfully built: a wall with yellow curls. All boat shoes and cable-knits, he looked like a captain. Possibly of a pirate ship. "Are you sure?"

The titan stepped forward now, extending a hand. "Do forgive me." His blue eyes crinkled at the corners. "I can't help but feel protective of my favorite niece." He beamed at Nadya before turning his grin back to Osha. "And I recognized that look on your face immediately. I was young once, too, you know."

Osha blinked.

The man burst out laughing.

"Come on, Osha." Nadya bent and lifted his hat. Straightening its feather, she placed it gently in his trembling hand. Waves of persuasion rolled off of her, washing fear away. "I'll make you some tea."

Drunk though he was from her touch, Osha didn't take his eyes off her uncle as he led them toward the house. The man rambled on, excusing himself, laughing at violence like it was harmless. Such a familiar voice, though Osha couldn't guess why. An eloquent cadence. A fine baritone.

Loren was waiting on the porch – and from the look on his face had been there a while. As they drew near, he locked eyes with the giant. "Remember what I said."

"I know, I'm sorry." The man waved him aside. "Honest mistake, my boy."

Loren turned to Osha now, barely repressing a smile. "You alright?"

Osha scowled. "Fizzing."

Loren followed them through the door, into the warm smell of baking bread, but not into the kitchen. He lingered in the entryway while

Osha unloaded his things, unable to shed his smirk. All but *laughing* at him. Still, Osha wanted him to stay. "You're not going to join us?" It wasn't a question. It was a plea. Loren had told him about Nadya's family. Loren had tried to warn him. Loren, perhaps, would protect him.

But Loren just shook his head – "You're on your own, kid." – and disappeared up the stairs.

Treachery.

Osha slunk into the kitchen and took a seat. Across the table, Uncle Nico watched with undisguised delight. Teeth white and glistening. Jaw strong and chiseled. A well-shaved, pluck-browed wild cat. Too clean-cut for the pirating life, now that Osha thought about it. A crime boss, perhaps. *Executive* marauder.

Nadya set a tea tray between them and began to fill their cups.

"I must say," the lion purred, "it's a real pleasure to come face-to-face with the notorious Osha Oloreben. I do so respect your work."

Notorious? "My work?"

"That's enough, now," Nadya cut in. "You're embarrassing him."

"Oh come now, after all you and Loren told me about him, how can I not confess my admiration?"

Admiration? "You told him about me?"

Nadya looked stern. "Remember what we said, Uncle."

The man nodded obediently. Satisfied, Nadya floated off – into the front room, humming and muttering, fingers along the walls. She tapped each framed photo as she passed it, but didn't stop to look at them. She was clearly focused on things that Osha couldn't see. He could feel them, though. Cool steam rising from the boxes stacked around them. Shadowy eyes boring into his back.

And crystal blue ones staring straight at his face.

Osha lifted his cup more to hide than to drink.

Nico shook his head. "Ghostly rubbish," he tsked. "The things she learned from her mother!" Drawing himself up straight, he raised his voice: "But enough of that! Why don't you tell me of your travels?"

"Travels?"

"Not to offend," Nico smirked, "but your accent isn't keeping any secrets. And what's more, I can see it in your eyes. I've ventured fairly far myself, you know. We've both been bitten by that bug, my friend."

*Friend?* "No bugs here, sir," Osha clarified. "Though I am from the north." He pointed up like it meant something.

"Indeed, it shows. And I must say, I'm glad you've left your bugs at home. I hear they can be quite ferocious." He winked. "Oclia or Erobia?"

"Oclia."

And just like that, the man was speaking perfect Oclian: "Land of bugs, indeed! Did some proverbial plague chase you out?"

"In a sense."

"Ah, I could see no other reason to leave. It's a regret that I've never visited your country. But your neighbor, Erobia – that's a fine land. Among the finest I've seen. Majestic and fresh. A right fountain of youth. Pity the conflict there. Those people were so robust before sanctions. Chilling, what disobedience does to the health."

Osha didn't know what to say.

Nico chuckled, chair creaking, a great beast leaning back. "Oh, but listen to me! Rambling on so hopelessly at this time. It'll pass, of course – it will all pass. These skirmishes only serve to refine our purpose. A 'baptism by fire,' as they'd say in the old days. Ours is a great nation, is it not? And I do *so* look forward to the day when Oclia claims its place on our map, as well."

Osha managed a terse smile. "I'd like to see Oclia join the modern world, too."

"Ah, but you're too harsh. I'd hate for it to lose that rugged, natural beauty. Since boyhood, I've especially admired the taiga of your Central Mountains."

Osha perked up at that. "I was born there!"

"Were you, now?"

"I moved to the North Coast when I was twelve, after my parents split. But I'd go back whenever I could, to see my dad." Nevermind that no dad-seeing ever took place – that his dad had simply vanished in a barroom, drowned in a bottle. Even a week on the couch of distant relatives beat life in Lanestabra. Any echo of childhood was more melodious than the deafening roar of rage.

"All that way? And to think—" Nico nodded toward his niece

"—people here won't even leave their mothers' homes!"

Osha shrugged. "I don't mind traveling."

"Ah, so you don't!" The giant laughed again, in his giant way. "That, too, shows." Smoothing his shirt, he straightened. "Well, consider us kindred souls. I left home around your age, as well. Made it all the way to the capital! Hitched rides and train-hopped with my best friend – extraordinary artist, that one. Paid his way with paintings, but me? Had to settle for poetry! Recited on street corners for food! Really honed my voice, so to speak, but what a way to live! You need a good friend for a life like that, and I had one. The kind you can be free with. The kind you can trust – a rare commodity this day and age."

Rare indeed. In all his travels, Osha had only found one.

"If you ever find a friend like that, don't you dare let him go."

Osha looked down. His hands were shaking.

"Sadly, I lost my own quite young. Artists tend to have some streak of madness." Nico's gaze grew distant, a foreign sadness invading his features. "It can be a dangerous act to balance – not unlike politics, in its way. A partisan split of the mind. Damn fool went crazy and killed himself." He snapped out of his reverie, hands clapping together. That was that. "Spent too much time cooped up in studios, if you ask me. Not enough good, clean air. And what a loss! He never did see my success in Sagoma. Never lent his vision to our cause." He cleared his throat. "But enough rambling on. I'm sure to bore you to tears."

"That's enough, you two!" Nadya called from the other room. "How am I supposed to know you're not making fun of me?"

"How could I make fun of my favorite niece?" Nico reverted to Rimolean so smoothly, Osha was left wondering if they'd been speaking Oclian at all. "Besides, wouldn't your ancestors give me away?"

"They translate feelings, Uncle. Not foreign languages."

"Well, I for one like a little clarity in my beliefs," Nico muttered. "But to each their own."

Nadya appeared at the door, hands on her hips. "I know you think poorly of mystics, Uncle," she said. "I know the capital is full of charlatans and parlor tricks – but that's only because the soul's been taken out of it. I'm not looking to make any money from this." Her voice remained sweet, but her eyes were flashing. "You're in Rimolee now. You can leave your skepticism at home."

Nico sneered. "And here I thought it'd make a nice gift. A thanks for your hospitality."

Nadya shook her head – "You're too kind!" – and turned her back on them. Back to her chants. Back to her ghostly dance.

Nico gave Osha a wry look, then extended a hand. "Do forgive me, son. I haven't even introduced myself," he said. "Nico Dov, of Sagoma."

"Osha Oloreben—" Osha paused uncertainly "—of the islands?"

"That's the spirit." Nico's handshake was charged with vigor. "The Union could use more youth like you." Releasing his grip, he turned, reaching toward a coat hung over the back of his chair. Osha hadn't seen it until then, obscured as it was by his broad form. But he saw it now: gray folds, gleaming glass emerging from deep pockets. Seamlessly, Nico twisted the cap from his bottle and poured. *Glug glug glug* into his teacup.

*Glug glug glug glug glug* into Osha's. Suspicious.

"Now, how about a round in Sagoman, shall we?"

Osha cringed. "I'm afraid I can't."

"You can't?" Nico scowled. "Osha Oloreben, of all people! Cannot speak our national language!"

"I understand it alright – just can't speak that well." Osha shifted uncomfortably. "Yet."

The beast took a dainty sip and sighed. "Well, I suggest you learn quickly. Within the year, that'll land you in prison."

That was news. "Prison!" Osha made a silent vow to keep up with current events. Not to mention language acquisition.

"Cohesion is the key to strength, my boy, and our Union must maintain it at all costs. Words are slippery enough without poor translations muddling things. Throw in nonsense like Oclian religious slang – animal spirits that aren't animals, years with names and personalities! No, no. Too much diversity makes a culture crack."

"I suppose I understand." Osha wasn't lying. His family had never believed what most Oclians did. Like aliens in their own country, they had their own holidays, their own God, even their own patois – and Osha had felt this difference keenly.

"Ah, but you only *suppose*. If you spoke Sagoman, though, you'd think properly. You'd *know*."

Nadya blew back into the room then, a glossy-eyed breeze, sleeves spread like wings. "Oh, I just love this time of year! The veil's so thin, the spirits are simply buzzing! Can't you feel it?"

"It's why I'm here." Nico patted her arm, palm large enough to crush her. His bottle had vanished. "Well, that and business. But the trip couldn't have been better timed."

"Are you an officer?" Osha asked.

Niece and uncle exchanged glances. "Why do you ask?"

"Multilingual, on business from the capital. . . ." Osha opted not to mention what had happened outside. "You seem like a military man."

Nico eyed his drink, swirling dark waters. "Something like that."

"My uncle is a Union employee," Nadya conceded quietly.

"You say it like something to be ashamed of," the man chided, sitting up straight in his chair. "Your own father is among Sagoma's leading engineers. You of all people know the good we do for backwater places like this. Think of that Shipwreck Beach of yours, just down the way. How many boats have washed up there since that train bridge was built? None! And we have the Union to thank for that." Nadya opened her mouth, but Nico kept right on talking: "Besides, think of the spirits! We *are* paying homage to them, after all, are we not? Studying their lives, honoring their achievements. What do they have to say about it? Or *feel* about it, as it were."

Nadya's voice was flat. "Why don't you ask them?"

Nico turned back to Osha with a grin. "They've never been particularly forthright with me." Lifting his cup, he took a long drink.

Not poison, then. Osha tried a sip as well. Fire.

Nadya looked thoughtfully from one of her guests to the other. "Sobriety helps."

Nico laughed aloud. "You can't hide a thing from Perala women!"

Nadya ignored him, looking instead at Osha. "So, Osha," she pressed, "to what do we owe the pleasure?" Those foamy waters still swirled about her, frothy, anodyne waves – but her words were jagged little things, popping the bubbles. "Have you come to pay your respects?"

"My respects?"

"To the ancestors."

"To be honest, I don't really speak with them much."

Nico chuckled, lifting his cup again.

"You can make it up to them, then." A smile fluttered down upon her, spreading wide, colorful wings. "You can help prepare the offerings."

# THIRTEEN

Temple doctrine viewed both solstices as potent spiritual portals. Something about perfect balance, shifting windows, open doors. Compelling, but arcane. Osha didn't fully understand. Not that he listened to Nadya's explanations very carefully.

He was drunk.

Alongside a serving of religious pomp, Nadya plied her guests with food. Braided loaves of bread, fresh from the oven. A bowl of oranges. A plate of cheese. Taffy, twisted in shining wrappers. All of it meant something divine, but none of it was enough to counter the effects of Nico's flask. Again and again, Nadya refilled their teacups, and again and again her uncle contaminated them as soon as she turned her back.

Ideal work conditions, if Osha did say so.

And work they did.

Smack in the center of their food, Nadya placed a massive steel pot – easily the size of the whale vats boiling in Oclia's seaside markets, where blubber was sold by the jarful. This pot, however, was filled with waxy green leaves, and a pile of twisted branches, thick and long as Osha's arm. Knives were passed around, and so began the business of whittling wood. It was a familiar chore; Osha had helped old nomad women mulch sticks and leaves for their own frothy potions. But there was no laughing and smoking and spitting through toothless gaps now. Nadya chanted balderdash from her scrolls as she pared down the wood, working her wrist at a pace that Osha was awed by. Sloppily, he scraped away, awkward and slow as Nadya crooned her soothing lullabies, his head caught in a tingling mesh. The more she sang, the less Osha could do.

"What exactly are we making?" he asked sleepily.

"Why, this is a Rimolean delicacy! Have you not heard of vine tea?" Nico wrinkled up his nose. "Delectable."

"You've never even tried it, Uncle—"

"But I've smelled it!"

"—and the flavor is hardly important."

"Then what is?" Osha asked. "What's so important about it?"

Nadya looked vaguely hurt.

"I'm just trying to understand."

Nadya stopped her whittling. "These plants—" she gazed upon them, reverent, frustrated "—they're guides, bridging the gap between this world and the next. They call down the spirits. They show us death."

"Death?" Osha snorted. "Why would you want that?"

She smiled. "Osha, life can lie. Our bodies tell us we're separate, but in reality our souls are shared with others, our health and happiness intertwined with everything around us. It's death that brings us back together, death that shows us how the universe lives within us, and us within it. Our joys are the world's joys. Our pains are the world's pains."

"Darling, the world is always in pain," Nico cut in, mouth full of bread. "Might I remind you: we are at war. And yet I feel fine."

"But that's exactly why we do this. So that we don't become lazy or permissive. So that we become conscious of what we're actually always feeling." Nadya resumed her work. "All the ancestors want is for us to learn from their mistakes. Not *repeat* them."

"Sounds like resistance credo to me. Sometimes I wonder where your allegiance lies, my dear niece. With your temple or with our Union?"

"The two aren't mutually exclusive."

"Your mother felt otherwise."

"I'm not my mother."

"At any rate—" Nico took another bite "—you can't drug away something as timeless as violence."

"This isn't a drug. And war isn't timeless, nor is it universal. One only needs to seek the truth and—"

"Truth is relative."

"Is it?"

"Well I'm not drinking it," Osha announced loudly. "War or no war, I'm too young to die."

"Oh, but Osha!" Nadya turned her eyes on him. "You more than anyone could benefit from it. In your condition—"

Now it was Osha who stopped, slamming his knife on the table with a clang – lucky he didn't cut his hand.

Nadya saw her misstep.

Nico missed it, though. He raised a brow. "What condition is this?"

"*No* condition!" Osha took a drink. "She's got some weird idea—"

"She has a lot of ideas, doesn't she?"

Nadya sighed.

"Listen." Nico set his whittling aside, as well. "Let's say you and I step outside, Osha. Conversations like this never lead to good places, and condition or no, the fresh air will do us some good."

"Please." Nadya went soft again, the air around her mush. "It's the solstice. Let's have no troubles between us."

"No troubles at all, Nadya," Nico insisted. "I'm simply feeling like a round with the racket. You know mine is a sporting life – cooped up too long like this, I hardly know who I am! And a strapping youth like Osha here is more than a worthy opponent. Surely a natural at the net!"

Osha shook his head. "The net?"

"And all those little headstones littering the lawn? Why, they'd make perfect goal lines!"

"Uncle!"

"Your death worship may be a bit macabre, but it has its uses!"

"Come on, man." Osha had nearly emptied his cup. His third cup. "It's cold out there, and I'm no athlete."

"Lies! Your posture, your complexion – you're the very picture of fitness."

Osha examined his hands briefly. Bony. Stark white. "You sure about that? My mom wouldn't even let me snowshoe."

"You've got better genes than most, my boy." Nico's expression darkened. Something had changed. Some shift Osha couldn't quite place. "No contamination in that bloodline." Something in his voice. His tone. "Not like this Perala muck." Of course. He was speaking Oclian again.

"What?"

"Everything wrong with my niece comes from her mother."

Osha narrowed his eyes at him. "What's wrong with her?"

He gestured around the room. "This morbidity. This filth. That boy, Loren." He scoffed. "Brown women know nothing of fidelity. They're built to roam, as they say. It baffles me that the Peralas have a family house at all. Nomad stock, the lot of 'em."

Osha glanced at Nadya – sad, alone, deaf to them. "What are you getting at?"

Nico laughed. "Believe me!" Back to Rimolean. "All you need is a little exercise!" He tore another chunk of bread before continuing, words muffled. "A good hearty round in the outdoors!"

Nadya said nothing.

Osha emptied his cup.

"I suppose you're more the creative type, though. A musician, I hear, is that right?"

Osha nodded, happy to change the subject. Thrilled, in fact. "Oh, Nadya, that reminds me! I've got a favor to ask you." He blushed, then, remembering his predicament. "Well, two favors, actually."

Nadya watched him expectantly, but kept shaving her vine, rhythm unbroken. Osha would have chopped off a finger.

"Iza told me that you're something of a songstress," Osha said.

"Oh, I don't know about that."

"That night we met, I lost a few songs. Parts of them, anyway. Iza thought you could help me with them."

Nadya stiffened, eyes darting to her uncle. "How?"

"She thought you could rewrite the lyrics."

"Did she?" She seemed anxious.

"I can't remember what I wrote," Osha confessed. His memory had certainly served him better in the past. Or at least he thought it had – maybe he'd forgotten. "And songwriting's not really my strong point."

"If music isn't your strong point, Osha, I don't know what is."

Osha wasn't sure if that was a compliment.

"What's the second favor?"

He lowered his gaze. "I need a place to stay a while."

Nadya relaxed at that. Chuckled, even. "Did Iza kick you out?"

He glanced back up, but said nothing.

"She did!" Nadya's jaw dropped. "How dare she!"

Nico's mouth was full yet again. "Who's Iza?"

Osha drew himself up, feeling sheepish. "She's—"

"No one," Nadya snapped. "Just an acquaintance."

There was a knock at the door. Nadya rose and moved toward it, dropping her knife on a stack of boxes along the way. In the clutter of Perala House, it was as good as lost.

Holic had come to visit, and with him a man Osha had never seen. He was tall – taller than Holic, but not quite Nico-sized – with dark waves pressed and shining on a regal forehead. His aquiline nose propped up a pair of wiry, circular spectacles, and through them he caught Osha's eye immediately – as did Holic.

Neither looked happy to see him.

"Hello, Holic," Nadya greeted them cordially. "And Gabris, it's been far too long."

Nico rose to his feet, lifting his drink with him. "Friends from the temple, my dear? Come to join the festivities?"

"My uncle Nico." Nadya gestured toward him. "Of *Sagoma*," she added with emphasis.

Holic and Gabris sized him up, then descended on Nadya like a storm cloud, voices so hushed Osha couldn't hear a word.

Nadya alone didn't lower her tone. "Not now."

More muttering, directly into her ears.

"No." She shook her head. "Leave him out of this one."

Gabris pulled an envelope from his coat, shaking it at Nadya before allowing her to take it.

Nico moved toward them, listing to and fro. "What's all this about, exactly?" he asked, the smile in his voice thinning with each word. "All this whispering's hardly polite, you know."

Nadya looked toward the kitchen, letter pressed to her chest. Defeated. Osha may have missed the conversation, but he had no doubt it upset her. "They're just some friends of Iza's," he said to Nico, hoping to peel back a layer of distress. "Probably here to work out my housing situation."

Nico continued his drunken waltz into the entryway, and Osha followed mindlessly. The tension was thick, though he had no idea why – and even less so why he was getting in the middle of it. But he didn't like seeing Nadya uncomfortable, especially given how comfortable she kept him – a comfort that only grew as he waded closer.

Quite the sensation, especially mixed with booze.

He pushed past Nico. Past Nadya. Right up to Holic, smacking him on the shoulder. "How goes it, old boy? Any news from my house?"

Holic's face softened as much as it could (which wasn't much), and he shook his head. "Allow me to apologize on Iza's behalf. She's hardly flexible with the plans she makes. But I must say, I'm happy to see that you've found yourself a warm bed here."

"Oh, Osha." Nadya's suffering deepened, waves of sympathy in her churning waters. "You weren't hoping to stay here, were you?"

"Only for a couple days."

"I'm sorry, but my uncle is already staying in the spare bed."

The spare bed! Osha shot Nico a look. He couldn't possibly fit!

"The temple, though!" Nadya brightened. "The temple has a hostel. Not the most comfortable, I'm afraid, but it's free, and there's always space. Loren can take you there." She called to him: "Loren! Loren, will you come down here?"

Osha could feel something stirring as he stood there, under the layers of liquor and confusion and Nadya's soothing, silent berceuse. Something aching, deep inside of him. He didn't want to leave now. "Shouldn't I at least finish with the offerings?"

"Oh, no, don't worry yourself with that. You've done plenty already. A tremendous help."

The room darkened. She was kicking him out, just as Iza had. So it went. Osha never did have much luck with friends, aside from the nomads. And even then.

He tried to tamp down thoughts of Julis, but it wasn't easy. The man eyeing him now – the only one he'd yet to meet – looked frustratingly similar. Older, of course. Perhaps a shade lighter. Definitely cleaner. But not even the glasses could lessen the impact. "You must be the Osha I've heard so much about." Like Holic, he'd enhanced his features with makeup: a touch of eye shadow here, a hint of lipstick there. Probably another actor. But the kindness in his eyes seemed authentic. "Gabris Hintica." He extended a hand. "I was hoping I'd see you here."

"You were?"

"I'd like to put in a request, for your show tonight."

"Gabi, please." Nadya looked distraught. Panicked, almost. Yet that mollifying aura of hers had never been so heavy. Almost suffocating.

Osha felt woozy. "I have a show tonight?"

"Don't you know?" Gabris's high brows rose even higher. "You're slated at Barsamina Theater! Biggest solstice bash in town. Much bigger – and dare I say, more pleasant – than whatever Nadya's cooking up in that pot over there."

Osha was speechless.

So Nico spoke for him: "Barsamina Theater. Is that so?"

"Loren!" Nadya called again. "Do hurry!"

This time, Loren opened his door. "What is it?" His feet thumped down the stairs, drumming along to his complaints. "What's so important that I can't have half an hour—" He stopped at the sight of them. "Oh."

"Osha's in need of a room at the temple tonight," Nadya explained.

"I don't need to go right *now*—"

"Please, Loren." Nadya was insistent. "Would you be so kind?"

Loren's eyes darted from face to face, finally settling on Osha. No more pleased with his presence than the others.

"And be quick," she added. "It's supposed to snow this afternoon. I'd hate for you to get stuck."

Osha was starting to feel sick. Nadya's magical airs cranked up in response, but the effect was merely disconcerting. Perhaps he *did* want to leave. This had hardly been a pleasant afternoon, after all. First accosted, then rejected.

And now praised.

"I must admit, I'm a tremendous fan," Gabris rattled on. A dizzying paradox. Osha felt nauseous. "I've been positively dying for a live performance. If you would do me the honor—"

"Osha has to go, Gabris," Nadya interjected. "Perhaps you can talk about this later – if he shows at the party."

"*If* I show?" Osha felt a pang in his gut. To play at such a venue, for such a glamorous audience, on such a vital occasion— "What in God's name could stop me from playing at *Barsamina Theater*?"

"If you felt ill or—"

"Will you stop with that!"

Loren stepped close, taking Osha by the arm: "We should go."

"I do hope to see you tonight, old boy," Gabris said as Loren pulled them toward the door. "Many people are expecting you. *Many* people."

Nico made a noise. A chortling laugh. A disgusted scoff. Maybe just a cough.

Loren tugged at his elbow, but Osha wouldn't budge.

"No pressure, of course." Gabris beamed. "But do know there's a full backing band for you, prepped and ready."

Osha broke from Loren's grasp and clambered toward the coatrack. Head spinning, scarf twisted, he grabbed his guitar. Grinning over his shoulder, Osha found Nadya chewing her lip. Nico towered behind her, silent and stern.

So what if they didn't want him? A full band did.

"Come on, Osha," Loren prodded. "Let's go."

"We'd so love to see you there, old boy."

Loren opened the door, a gush of icy air flooding in. Osha turned to face the room one last time. A smile for everyone, whether they wanted it or not. Nadya, with her bubbling narcotic waves. Holic, thin and crisp as paper. Nico nodded curtly.

Gabris grinned expectantly. "So?"

"I wouldn't miss it on my life."

# FOURTEEN

Only after they left did Osha realize what he'd forgotten: his bag, his hat, his notebooks. But Loren was in a hurry. His things would have to stay behind, with the cocoon of Nadya's presence – and the pills that could take the edge off her absence. Osha felt it as soon as they reached the street: an invasive ache, dull and heavy in every limb and digit. Rejection stung alright, but what he felt now went beyond bruised emotions.

He hurt.

"Slow down, Loren. You're making me sick."

"That would be the booze, kid."

"How do you know I've been drinking?"

Loren laughed. A terrible laugh, vibrating in his bones. The veins of his temples, his neck, his arms and legs – his whole body throbbed. Heat in his belly. Crackle in his lungs. And how his hands shook.

Maybe he had been poisoned, after all.

Loren kept the conversation light. "So I take it your house is real."

"You should come visit sometime."

"I can't say I'm big on your scene, Osha."

"I've noticed."

"You really should stay away from those people."

"Your *sister* is one of those people, Loren."

"I'm well-aware. And if you knew what was good for you—"

"I do!"

"Do you? Look at you."

Osha swallowed. His stomach was certainly siding with Loren on this one. "You gonna tell me to skip the party, too?"

"You'd go either way." Loren shrugged. "I'll just have to go, too. Somebody's gotta keep you out of trouble."

They reached their stop just in time for the streetcar to leave without them. Not that it mattered – they were barricaded in, checkpoint finished and open for business. The women Osha had seen setting up were now joined by men: five digmen in all, leaning lazily on the beams and chains of the blockade. Eyes narrowing as he and Loren approached.

That sobered Osha right up. Leaning toward Loren, he whispered: "Keeping me out of trouble, huh?"

"I got this."

One of the men – bareheaded and bald, cigar clenched in his teeth – parted from his colleagues to greet them.

"Good afternoon, officer." Loren's tone was suddenly as saccharine as his sister's. "And a happy solstice to you."

The man skipped the formalities. "Where are you going?" Rimolean words, but distorted by an accent even more onerous than Osha's.

"The temple, sir."

The digman stepped closer, smoke shooting from his nostrils like a bull exerting dominance. "And you?"

Osha glanced at Loren, but the officer was looking at *him*. "Um, the same, sir."

"'The same' what?" Short and heavy though he was, he was far from unintimidating. The triple-looped ribbon was stitched to his lapel, his boots, even the side of his hat. This guy was a true patriot.

"I'm also going to the temple."

"Sir," he snapped.

"I'm also going to the temple, *sir*."

"With that?" He kicked about Osha's legs. "With a guitar?"

"It's the solstice, sir," Loren reminded him. "So, you see—"

The officer held up a hand. "I'm not talking to you." Edging closer to Osha, the man drew hard on his cigar. A blinding, blue puff, directly into his eyes. "Erobian?"

Osha blinked. "Sir?"

Stiff, starchy gloves grabbed his shoulders. "Answer, northerner!" Thumbs digging into his collarbones, shaking him. "Are you Erobian?"

Osha coughed. "No, sir." Eyes burning.

"'No, sir,' what?"

"I'm not Erobian, sir," he panted. "I'm Oclian."

The digman thrust him back. Tapping the ashes from his cigar, he watched as Osha gingerly rubbed his shoulders. "Purpose of visit?"

"My health," Osha answered. If they had anything about him on record, he sure didn't want to contradict it.

One furry brow rose to a point. "And your complaint?"

At a loss, Osha unbuttoned his coat. Tugging down the neck of his sweater, he revealed the digman's own handprints. He had no doubt there were bruises there already – and mean ones at that. It was a little embarrassing, but worth a shot. "A bleeding issue."

The officer glared down his nose, saying nothing. But something new stirred in his expression. Guilt? Pity? One could hope. After a long appraisal, he drew back and held out a hand, palm open flat. "Papers."

Osha gave them over, grateful they were in his coat pocket, eager to be done with this. But the digman's smoggy face contorted all the more as he thumbed through them. After a moment of supreme tension, he burst into laughter. "You expect me to believe the *ambassador himself* notarized this?"

Osha's mouth dropped opened, but what was he supposed to *say*?

"It's authentic." Loren spoke instead, voice drained of sweetness. He handed over his own ID, straight-faced and cold.

The digman's resolve wavered visibly as he compared the two booklets. Drawing in a breath, he fluffed himself up, but it was a lost cause. Somehow, some way, he had been defused. "Fine," he muttered, handing back their papers. "You're free to go."

Osha was reeling.

It began to snow.

Osha looked over his shoulder as they slipped around the barricade. Over his shoulder as they approached the streetcar stop. Over his shoulder as they waited at the tracks, leaning close to Loren with a whisper: "What the hell just happened? The ambassador?"

Loren shrugged. "It's not important."

"It sure seemed important back there."

"Don't worry about it. Everything worked out, didn't it?"

"The *ambassador*, though?"

Loren sighed, eyes on the floating flakes, the fine dust of white collecting in the street. "Nadya has her ways."

"So I've gathered."

A still quiet fell along with the snow. The adrenaline was wearing off, nausea replacing it. Osha looked over his shoulder.

"So, what's this bleeding issue you have?"

Osha smirked. "Just a case of convenient bruises." He touched them absently. "Guess I was lucky to be attacked by your uncle this morning."

"*Nadya's*," Loren shot back. "He's *Nadya's* uncle." Furrowing his brow, he eyed Osha's neck. "But I didn't see him touch you there."

"How much did you really see?"

"I saw enough," Loren grinned. "'*Help me, Nadya!*'" he taunted. "'*Come save me!*'"

Osha groaned – from embarrassment, from discomfort, from stress. It had been quite the day.

"Just stick with me, kid." Loren gave him a pat on the back – a bit too hard. "Like I said, I'll keep you out of trouble. And I'll do a much better job than my sister."

# FIFTEEN

From the streetcar, Osha could see the thin line of the jetty, tripping the ocean's waves into an explosion of inlets and bays. He'd never traveled that route, never seen the views granted by the high ridge circling town. It almost made the trip pleasant.

But he was shivering and sore – and so distracted that he couldn't ask Loren the questions knocking about his head, bouncing from one side to the other as the trolley took its tight turns. The edges of his vision snapped and sparked, shadows flapping with bat wings, exhausting him. By the time the temple appeared – domes and spires natural in the hilly landscape – Osha felt he'd aged decades.

And Loren noticed. "How much did you *drink?*"

"I don't know."

"Well, we're almost there." He rose, reaching over Osha's head to pull the bell cord. "You can always call it an early night."

"Are you kidding?" Osha did his best to pull himself together. "Do you have any idea how long I've waited for something like this? To play for that kind of crowd? To be in those lights? To really be *heard?* I've practiced my whole life for this!"

Loren dropped a hand onto his shoulder. "That's not a very long time, kid."

"I'm going up on that stage tonight if it kills me."

"Well, hopefully it doesn't come to that."

A high wall surrounded the temple, separating the casual bustle of Valena from its sacred mysteries. Osha had only seen the buildings from afar – a great beast in the mist, stabbing the sky with its shining horns. The gates were always open, but he never crossed that threshold. Never really felt welcome.

That didn't stop him now, though. Following Loren off the streetcar, he walked right in.

Osha stopped to bow at the entrance, hands clasped, head down before the slender statues flanking the path: two weeping women.

Loren raised a brow. "What are you doing now?"

"This isn't—?" He straightened uncertainly. Oclian temples – even simple tree shrines – required a certain show of reverence. Osha had never followed Oclia's prevailing creed, but he didn't take chances either. The ever-angry God of his own religion had taught him that much. "It's just what we do up north."

"I see." Loren smirked.

Clearly, Rimolean obeisance took a different form.

They moved on.

A magnificent park unfolded before them. Gnarled, ancient trees on grassy knolls tattooed with elaborate stone designs – circles, triangles, fractals. Peppered throughout were not just tombs, but expansive mausoleums, draped in woven leaves, buried beneath so many flower petals they looked like they'd been struck by a pink and violet blizzard.

And soon to be buried by a *real* blizzard.

Here and there, the veiled holy ones bent, busily re-etching names and dates into headstones, meticulously resisting the finality of death. No one acknowledged the two of them at all. Osha felt self-conscious nonetheless. Uninvited. Underdressed. Loren, on the other hand, strode confidently between the phantasmal figures, like corduroy was orthodox.

"Are you a temple man, Loren?" Osha eyed the patterned fabric dragging behind a cloaked priest. It was easy to picture Loren's slender, stoic form drifting like a ghost among these people, neck heavy with beads. The same otherworldly flame burned behind his eyes that Osha saw in nearly everyone they passed.

"I went to school here." Loren answered. "I work in the greenhouses. But I didn't seek priesthood like Nadya, if that's what you're asking."

Osha studied the semi-cloaked faces. "Why does everyone here look like that?" He gestured loosely in front of his eyes, unsure how to describe what he saw.

"Why are they covered? It's symbolic. We're all the same, so—"

"That's not what I'm talking about."

Loren glanced at him, a strange smile playing on his lips. "Are you asking about their eyes?"

Osha nodded, swallowing, queasy from conversation.

"I'm surprised you noticed that," Loren mused. "I didn't think you were that observant."

"You don't have to flatter me."

Loren laughed. "These people have seen other realms, Osha. Working with the plants, offering themselves as channels, guiding us back to our natural place in the cosmos. Trying not to burn the whole world down again." He shook his head. "And didn't Oclia get the worst of it? That old plague of yours – wasn't that from the Great Thaw?"

Osha nodded, innards lurching with the movement. "Melted tundra."

"And what do they do now?"

He licked his lips. "It's not such an epidemic anymore, so—"

"No, what do they do to heal? To ground themselves. To keep themselves from being a bunch of nostalgic, idiot Unionists?"

"They don't take vine tea, I know that."

"Well *you* could certainly use it."

"Not if it makes me an ass like you."

Loren laughed again. "That wasn't an insult! I'm talking about your health."

"There's nothing wrong with my health," Osha grumbled.

Loren shot him a look. "Then what are your pills for?"

"None of your business."

"Suit yourself." His features softened again, gaze turning back to the graves and greenery. "But you should know the plants. We've been breeding them for centuries. They're from all over the world. Only a few are entheogenic, but they've all got uses."

"What's that mean – *entheogenic*?"

"It means they awaken the divine within, opening you up to the energy that connects all things across time and space."

"So they get you high."

Loren sighed.

Their path constricted as they walked, buildings angling closer until, ultimately, they were squeezed through a threshold no more than three feet wide. And on the other side, an entirely new world opened up: a grand courtyard, the likes of which Osha had never seen. Above their heads, icicle-like lanterns dangled from metallic hoops, warm and yellow against the bleak sky. And at their feet, the fine tip of a giant, tessellated star. Just one in a flickering galaxy of marble constellations embedded with gemstones all around them.

The sight took Osha's breath away, but Loren seemed unimpressed.

They passed fountains bubbling into triangular pools, mosaics of fishes and water lilies. Traipsing across the gold-embossed center of it all, their feet fell on an elaborate compass, a crackling firework of arrows, each direction an explosion of foreign symbology. Beautiful nonsense.

Nauseating.

They stalled for a moment, halted by a class of children funneling through another narrow passage. The students moved like a heavy cloud in their robes, each clutching a small book as they followed their teachers onto the celestial patio. Loren greeted one of the adults like an old friend, though how he recognized the man behind the veil was beyond Osha.

Just past the children lay yet another surprise – one even more spectacular. A titanic glass house, sharp and crystalline, wedged snugly between its stone and brick neighbors like an icy mountain. Greenery pressed against its walls, leaf-hands pawing the windows. Vines were visible, twisted helixes thick as thighs, draping like curtains. A veritable jungle had been encased here, and in its grandiose prison it thrived.

"This way." Loren held the door, then closed it swiftly behind them.

"This is incredible, Loren."

"Isn't it." He removed his glasses, fogged over completely from the humidity. "Ms. Belcov manages the hostel, but she's on vacation. We'll have to get the key from her daughter." He didn't look very happy about that. "She works here with me, so. Just wait." And with that he disappeared, swallowed alive by the hot, sticky wilds.

Osha drank it all in. Like when he first saw the lush slopes of Erobia, or Rimolee's sopping rainforests, he could barely believe his eyes. He reached out to touch a rubbery-looking cluster of red – perhaps a flower, though he couldn't be sure. Yes, it was solid. Real. He could never quite accept that the world produced life like this. Lanestabra's flat, icy wastes simply took up too much of his mind.

He wiped his hair back from his forehead. He was starting to sweat.

"You're sure lucky to catch me here!" A female voice wove out of the wetness, loud and getting louder. Loren's responses were muffled, but the woman was clear as the roof over their heads. "The fishmonger's putting on a bash across the way, and it's a riot! I only left to get my coat."

Out of the jungle she sauntered, swaying and sultry, scantily clad – especially by temple standards – arm in arm with Loren's stiff form. A teenaged waif built entirely from hair grease and rouge. Smiling and slurring: "Sorry if the rooms aren't up to snuff, Lori. Ma didn't think anybody'd need 'em, so—" Meeting Osha's gaze, she stopped in her tracks. "Oh my God. Is this him?"

Osha raised a shaky hand, but Loren answered for him: "This is Osha, yes. He'll need at least two nights and—"

"Oh no, dearie, you gotta get that fella over to healing quarters. I ain't takin' that in."

Osha frowned.

"Rika, he's fine. He's had a few too many drinks—" Loren forced a grin "—but who hasn't?"

The girl ducked behind his shoulder. "Look at him, though! Even his nose is bleedin'!"

Osha reached toward his face, but felt nothing. Fingers dry and clean.

"You're getting carried away, Rika," Loren chided. Gently, he guided her closer to Osha. "Come on, focus."

"I guess you're right." She shivered somewhat. "I mighta overdone the giggle juice, I suppose." Stepping toward Osha, she sized him up with knitted brows. "Still, though. This guy's got *somethin'* under his skin. Don't know *what* I'm looking at!" She rubbed her eyes, slinking back to Loren's side. "Might have to borrow those cheaters off ya, Lori, 'cause according to my peepers this one's a goner."

Osha was only half-sure what this girl was saying, but was fully certain he hated it.

"Excuse her, Osha." Loren tried to pull away, but the girl clung tight. "Rika's only recently trained as a healer. Her skills aren't quite honed."

"Speak for yourself!" She slapped him on the rear. Loren's jaw tensed. "At least I don't run from my job like your sister. Speakin' of who, why isn't this fella with her?" She toyed with Loren's collar as she spoke. "I know she's gone all washy on the psychopomp stuff, but—"

"Rika, stop!" Loren yanked himself free from her, visibly disgusted.

"Look, I ain't no Nadya, but a healer knows what a healer knows, and if this guy's not beggin' for your sister by nightfall, well. . . ." She batted her lashes. "You still owe me that kiss."

The heat was becoming oppressive. "What's she on about, Loren?"

"Nothing." Loren looked almost as sick as Osha felt. "Ignore her."

"Nadya, though? *Psychopomp?*"

Rika faced Osha squarely, abandoning Loren's body for a moment. "Miss Perala's our temple's most talented psychopomp. Or was, at least."

"What's a psychopomp?"

Loren shook his head. "Don't, Osha."

Rika didn't listen. "A thanadoula."

"What's a thanadoula?"

"Let it go," Loren pleaded.

"Oh, brother, don't you know nothin'?" Rika rolled her eyes. "I'm talkin' 'bout somebody who helps ya die!"

"Nadya doesn't do that anymore," Loren said. "She quit after—"

"Ya can't quit what you're meant to do, Lori! You of all people know that, always whinin' and complainin' 'bout it. Have you *met* yourself? You *wish* you could shut the spirits up! Ya do what ya do, whether ya get paid for it or not." Rika scoffed, incredulous. "You Peralas just don't like gettin' paid, I guess."

Loren sighed audibly, fingertips to temples.

"Look—" Osha was far too sick for this "—I don't care if Nadya *kills* people. I just want to rent a room. I have money. I'll pay."

"Rooms are free." Rika shrugged. "But so's the sickbay."

"A room, please." Loren's tone was stony. "Just get the key, Rika."

"Have it your way," she tsked. "I'll go scrounge it up. But don't expect me to come play nurse at midnight – you're on your own. My specialty's diagnosis, anyway, so my job's basically done. Besides, I got a party to be at." And away she went, veering and stumbling back through the wilderness in kitten heels.

Loren drew close to Osha now, voice hushed: "You sure you still want to play tonight?"

Osha rolled his eyes. "What do you think?"

So much concern on his face. "The healers are usually on to something when they talk like this."

"She's drunk!"

"Even still."

"I'm fine, Loren. I just had one or two or – I don't know." He rubbed his face. "I just had too much to drink. I need a nap, that's all."

"A nap." Loren seemed humored by this. "And then you'll go on stage."

"*Yes*, Loren."

"In front of a thousand wealthy socialites. Looking like *that*."

"Oh, screw off."

"I'm sorry, but—"

"Just go home, man. I didn't invite you, and—"

"Osha—"

"I can take care of myself just fine, so if you'd—"

"Ah-ha!" Rika was back again, and just as shrill as ever. "Would ya look at that! What'd I tell ya? His nose *is* bleedin'!"

Osha touched it again, fingers tingling, face not quite feeling like his own. And this time: a stream. A river. An outright waterfall.

Loren suppressed a grin.

"Guess I got ahead of myself, didn't I? Gotta rein in those predictions." Rika giggled. "Serves me right, gettin' zozzled on the job."

# SIXTEEN

The hostel was a small, dark cabin at the edge of temple grounds. Eight empty rooms spread like octopus arms from a hexagonal common space. Musty air, drawn blinds, complete silence. The perfect place to sleep.

Too bad about waking up.

Osha felt no better for the rest he got. Much worse, in fact. Yet he lugged himself out of bed, lured by distant echoes of "once in a lifetime" and "dream come true." Strange lyrics for this seasick rhythm – but the song was compelling enough, so he went with it.

He'd last seen Loren dodging Rika's advances, and found him again, alone, reading in the common room. Looking concerned. "Feel better?"

"Let's go."

Partygoers wove like ribbons through Valena's snowy streets, celebrations overflowing pubs and restaurants, pouring out of alleyways and row-house gardens. Dances and dinners and romantic liaisons sprung up alongside snowmen and snowball fights. People huddled for heat round warm laughter and steaming drinks, under lights by the billions: a shower of falling stars swaying to the inescapable thump of music.

Even the dead were dragged into the fray – every grave in town, from the nameless to the famous, showered with gifts. At the most renowned crypts, mounds of offerings rose up – pastries, candies, bouquets, paintings, photographs, and especially money. So much money heaped on the dead, the stray coins became a hazard, sliding over icy patches, threatening to derail streetcars.

Thoughts of corpses under his feet made Osha sick. Everything did. The whole cacophonous world tugged at his stomach like a fishhook, yanking it up again and again toward his mouth. It took focus to keep it down, but he managed, swallowing it hook and all.

Relief would have to wait. He could get his pills after the show.

And there would be a show.

No matter what.

Old, grand and no less extravagant than the Barsaminas themselves, the theater stood behind open gates, wrapping pale yellow arms round its courtyard, embracing a half-frozen fountain and absolutely anyone looking to celebrate.

It was hard to tell how big the lobby was in the crush of guests. The lighting was dim – nothing but the low luminescence of candles and string lights. Shadows stretched and throbbed with life. Old men shuffled cards, young girls gossiped. Children wove between wobbly legs, knocking people down, spilling drinks. Unmarked gifts circulated, to be opened by whoever happened to have them at the tolling of a bell.

Two broad thresholds opened into the auditorium, flanking an impressive, almost liquid staircase, spiraling toward a domed ceiling – a gut-twisting whirlpool. A balcony encircled it on the second floor, packed with nearly as many people as the downstairs. All gleefully bombastic.

Loren shot Osha a sympathetic glance. "I feel ya, kid. I hate places like this."

The walls were closing in, but they pressed on, squeezing between warm bodies, cold desserts and hot drinks. Toward the stage.

And what a stage it was.

Lush, red velvet drapery hung from intricate, spider's web woodwork. The cosmos itself spread across the concave ceiling, sparkling jewel stars inlaid by the hundred. Never had Osha performed amid such decadence. He'd never had the chance – nomads weren't welcome in high temples, gated communities, or even upscale brothels. Their concerts took place in parks and alleyways, on beaches, around bonfires, in the sinking stomachs of abandoned houses.

A woman was singing now, all silk and lace and lipstick, illuminated by swirling snowflake lights, her backing band drenched in darkness. The music was eerie and hollow – quiet – but Osha could still pick out its threads from the tightly woven chatter around him.

He would sing, too. His whole body protested, but he would. He had his guitar, though he didn't need it. The Barsaminas had supplied many things, all complimentary. Food, drink – even violins, evidently. There were more instruments scattered across the stage than Osha could count. He took stock of the bounty around him: broad trays of treats made the rounds, drinks floating overhead on platters, balanced by some magic Osha could never in a lifetime master. Loren accepted a glass of wine. Osha declined.

People trickled like tears down the steep staircases, pooling in the undulating orchestra pit, a churning sea of dancers. Loren and Osha followed suit, making their way between plush seats, past young lovers with feet kicked up, through mobs of squealing teenagers. Lower and lower, until, quite abruptly, they were stopped.

"Don't you take another step, Oloreben! We've got requests!" Iza stumbled out of the side seats, glass in hand.

Osha sighed.

Loren slunk back and away, out of the aisle.

"No drink?" Iza grinned, broad and rosy as she drew near. "Aren't you gonna loosen up that tongue of yours before having a go?"

"Not tonight," Osha said. "Feeling a bit all-overish."

"Ah, what else is new." She rolled her eyes. "Just don't let it stop a good show."

"How are things at my house, Iza?"

Iza's smile twisted with irritation, but remained intact. "Boring. A complete yawn. You're not missing a thing. I mean, do you see *me* there?"

Osha didn't get a chance to respond. Gabris appeared and butted between them – looking even more like Julis with his hair gone wild. Planting a kiss on Iza's neck, he turned to him. "So glad you could make it, old boy!" He paused then, eyes on Osha's empty hands. "Has no one gotten you a drink?" Arm shooting up, upsetting Iza's feathery headband, he bellowed: "Drinks this way! For the star of the show!"

Iza elbowed him. "Osha's opted to pass on the celebrated Barsamina hospitality. Says he's not feeling well." She adjusted her hair with a pout.

"Well, that's a shame." Gabris frowned at Osha. "Just don't let it stop a good show."

"That's what I said!"

Gabris kissed her again, knocking off her headband entirely. "Great minds think alike."

All this clumsy, rolling chaos had Osha second-guessing his plans yet again. He'd known more bearable nausea at sea.

"Gabi, you lush!" Iza pushed him. "How early did you *start*?"

"It's justified!" Gabris shot back. "Just getting here, all the way from Anatine? That's no small feat these days. And to see Osha Oloreben play! *Osha Oloreben*! Which reminds me – those notebooks of yours?"

Osha nodded.

"Impressive songwriting, I must say."

"Thanks."

"But Nadya had us know that you needed some lyrical help."

Osha took a breath and let it out slow, pushing his innards back down, away from his throat.

Gabris didn't care. He didn't know the danger he was in, standing so close. "I hope you don't mind that I penned a few verses myself."

"No, it's great," Osha croaked. "I might change a line or two, but—"

"Don't!"

Osha startled.

"At least give them a try!" Gabris insisted. "If you don't like them after that, then by all means. But give 'em a whirl, won't you? Just as I wrote them, next time you're on air. Don't you think that's fair?"

"Sure."

Gabris raised his glass. "Only fair."

Osha glanced at Loren. He clutched his own drink close, jaw set.

"What are you going to play tonight?" Gabris leaned in, a swaying tree in a storm. "If you don't mind me asking."

"I was thinking—"

"Play 'Farewell, Everything,' won't you?"

"Actually," Osha tried again, "I—"

But Gabris was begging: "Will you just play it for me? Special request? I so rarely make it down here."

The singer was closing her set now, giving her voice over to one final gossamer wail. Osha wondered, briefly, what color Julis would call it. Then the room exploded with applause.

"Your turn!" Gabris lunged at him. "Get on up there, old boy!" He looked less like Julis, behaving like this. "Show us what you're worth!" Less like Julis all the time.

Holding tight to the neck of his guitar, Osha let Gabris usher him down the aisle, across the dance floor, up the steps, and onto the stage. Squinting in the spotlight, he sought out Loren's eyes, but couldn't find them. Countless others looked on, though, some expectant, some humored. Some sickeningly drunk. Some distressingly sober.

There were digmen in the crowd: two women and a man, quite close to the stage. Rigid in their gray uniforms, impossible to miss amid the tumbling scarves and dresses of the soft, colorful locals. The officers marked a low point in the room, a sinkhole of energy. Any who came in contact with them fell somber and still.

Osha closed his eyes, waiting in the dark as the other musicians prepared themselves. He was beginning to think this was a bad idea.

A very bad idea.

But it was too late now. The band began to play. Without warning, the music rose up and coiled around him, shimmering and dulcet, a mellifluous noose on his neck. He could barely breathe. Helplessly, he looked at the other musicians. They just smiled.

He knew the song. He just had to concentrate. He tried to place his fingers on the strings, but they wouldn't cooperate. He opened his mouth to sing, but could only cough. And cough. And cough.

A great, greasy nausea forced him back, away from the microphone. Away from the audience. Off the stage. Waves of people crashed against him, laughing and singing, dancing and drinking. Only the band seemed to notice him down there, drowning. The drummer's worried eyes clung to him, her mouth moving in a disordered way, contorted and anxious.

Something was wrong. Something was immensely wrong.

Loren emerged then, phantom from the waters, and gripped his arms. "We have to go." He steered him roughly through the bodies, through smoke and broken glass and sticky, crumbling desserts – and into pain. Excruciating pain.

A clarion cry pierced the rippling music: "He's getting away!"

Up they climbed, up a mountain of stairs, pushing others aside, slicing through conversations. Loren was really rushing him, pushing and pulling and not caring that Osha was out of breath, not caring about the rage under his ribs or the claws in his chest. They barreled past Iza's father – a face Osha knew from the paper – red now, and sweaty, topped with a ridiculous cake of a party hat. Arguing: "I told you, officer! None of them are nomads!" Shouts sloshed and slurred. "I paid you good money for this!"

Osha was gagging.

They reached the lobby without slowing. Loren shoved him toward the exit, but a surge of digmen poured in to block their path. "Upstairs. *Now*, Osha."

On they went. Osha tripped as they clambered up the broad staircase, wheezing, acid in his chest, but Loren kept a firm grasp on his wrist. He could see the digmen below, swarming army ants, silence blooming out wherever they stepped.

Loren could dislocate an arm with that tugging.

Beyond the overhang, the upstairs hall was mostly empty – a quiet tunnel of conversations, lovers' spats and secret kisses. Loren dragged Osha past it all.

Something was alive in his body, teeming and hot. His lungs flailed to rid themselves of it, but coughing only led to retching. "Stop, Loren!" He gasped. "I'm going to be sick."

"It's a party, kid," Loren shot back. "You wouldn't be the first."

Loren's legs stopped at the end of the hall, but his arms kept going – prying open a window, reaching out into the night. It was a straight drop to the courtyard below. "Damn it."

Back down the hall they sped, trying doorknobs, dead-ending in bathrooms and storage rooms. Finally, behind a stained-glass door, within a cluttered nest of costumes and props, they found an exit. Beyond a swamp of satin and tulle and ribbony reeds of dance shoes, they found a way out. Loren yanked Osha through and slammed the door behind them.

Osha wrenched himself free and staggered across the balcony – over polished stones and hammered silver accents – to vomit over the edge. Lucky that the alley below was empty.

"Get a hold of yourself, kid." Loren looked appalled. "We need to get out of here!"

Osha shook his head, wiping his chin. "I don't know what's happening!" The pain was getting louder. Screeching. What color would Julis call *this*? He gestured at his stomach, his chest, unsure where to even point. "It hurts!"

"Shh!" Loren clamped a hand over his mouth. "Keep it down, man!"

Osha started to cry.

Loren's face softened, eyes darting around the balcony before settling back on Osha, wide and serious. "It'll be alright," he whispered, letting his hand drop. "Don't panic."

"You don't understand!" Not that he did.

"Breathe, Osha. Relax. We need to think."

*Think?* Osha would have laughed, were he not being boiled alive, scalding and shivering all at once. "Get Nadya." He couldn't feel this bad with Nadya – not with her narcotic ease. "She'll help."

"Nadya?" Loren sounded stricken. "Oh, man." He pulled away, visibly rattled. "This is bad."

"What's happening to me?"

"Like I would know!" He was angry.

"Don't get angry!"

"I'm not!" He was *furious*.

"I didn't do anything!"

"You could've just gone to the healing quarters and we wouldn't be in this mess!"

Loren began to pace. From one end of the balcony to the other, he hurried, peering into abyss after snowy abyss. An anxious shadow, tumbling through the frigid night. Osha couldn't watch. His eyes burned, like everything else. Like a building ablaze, organs screaming at the walls as the fire spread. It took all he had to muffle the cries. "What are we doing, Loren?"

"Leaving." He scowled. "I thought this would be a fire escape."

God, if only.

Loren's gaze lingered on Osha, blinking frustration and fear – until suddenly he brightened. "Your guitar strap!"

Osha touched his shoulder. He still had his guitar. That was a welcome surprise. Its subtle presence was nothing compared to the pain. So much pain, Osha didn't know what to do with himself.

"Unhook it and hang it between the bars," Loren directed.

"What?"

Loren's hands were on him again, unbuttoning the strap from the neck of the guitar. Its weight lifted, leaving Osha lopsided. Meanwhile, Loren crouched low, dangling the strap over the side of the balcony, anchoring the instrument against the balustrades. "We'll get closer, at least." He straightened, frowning at his work. "Shouldn't break any bones." Hoisting himself over the banister, he lifted the loose end of the strap and tugged. "Hope it holds."

Osha watched in horror as Loren fell. Floundering toward where he'd just been, solid and dependable in the prickly night, he found him hanging in the dark, swinging side to side – once, twice, three times – then edging down to the bottom of the strap. Dropping to the ground, maybe five feet below, his fall broken by a thick drift of snow. He smiled. "Come on!"

Osha whimpered. "What am I supposed to do?"

"Just do what I did! Hurry!"

Slowly Osha knelt, insides scraping as he bent. He took hold of his guitar strap without much trouble, but climbing outside the balcony was a process. Arms and legs trembling. Open air spinning.

"Do it, Osha! Come on!"

How much worse could it get? If he fell, at least he'd get to lie down.

He let himself go, barely holding on as his arms whipped straight. Hand over hand, he lowered himself, clumsy and groaning, until he was dangling at the very end.

And then it struck him. "What about my guitar?"

"Who cares about your guitar? Get down here!"

Osha clung tighter. "My guitar's up there!"

"Let it go, Osha!"

His whole body was shaking. "My guitar!"

Loren's hands were back, tugging in their frantic way. And just as soon as they yanked him down, they were pulling him back up, dragging him through the alley, pausing only for Osha to double over and vomit yet again. Deep maroon against the white.

Osha wiped at his eyes, tears on lashes making chaos of the festive lights around them. Skin so tender. "I've been poisoned!"

"By who, *Nico*?" Loren shook his head. "Trust me, kid, he wouldn't do that to you."

"You sure?" It certainly seemed like something he was capable of.

"Now's not the time for this." Loren pressed a palm to his forehead. Gentle, for once. "We gotta keep moving. You're burning up."

Like he needed to be told.

They reached the streetcar just as it arrived, but riding wasn't much easier than walking. It was work to sit up, work to breathe, work to fight the sickening city as it flashed its savage lights through the windows. Little eclipses on repeat – black and bright and black and bright – increasing in speed as they clacked and clanged over the hills. Osha was a bonfire now, yet the blistering heat did nothing to warm him up. Sweat dripped like ice down his back.

A sticky, red rain began to fall – staining his scarf, seeping between his lips. A handkerchief appeared, but he wasn't sure what to do with it. Loren's fingers danced around his face, but Osha couldn't understand what he said.

Finally, Loren pressed the handkerchief to Osha's nose himself.

And Osha closed his eyes.

DENIAL

# ANGER

BARGAINING

DEPRESSION

ACCEPTANCE

# SEVENTEEN

There was a chair and a table beside the bed, and a small dresser across from it, under a full-moon looking glass. White curtains enclosed it all, and beyond them moved a mutating cloud of slow, mumbling silhouettes.

Osha propped himself up on his elbows, searching for his reflection in the mirror. Seeing was a strain, given the vibration of the rain. The metallic ring of the gutters jerked the whole room about, but Osha managed, pulling his face from the melee after a few hard blinks. His eyes looked bruised and swollen, but at least they were where they should be.

Slowly, sound and sight and smell found their places as well.

He dropped back onto the pillow.

The pain had evaporated, but it had taken something of him with it. Memories were missing. An endless night, smashed to disparate bits: heady incense, soft voices, tender hands. Fevered gasping, bloody sheets, insurmountable confusion. His body had been returned to him, dressed in a clean blue robe – but time had been scattered to the wind.

Relief wasn't a big enough word – it lacked the lust, the neediness with which he now courted it. Yet relief wasn't all that he felt. Fear was there too, hanging like the drapes around him, cold and heavy. Dividing him from the life he knew.

The curtains parted, letting in even more fabric. His shrouded visitor startled slightly, meeting his open eyes. "You're awake." A woman's voice.

"Where am I?" Osha's own voice had never sounded so hoarse.

"The temple." A priestess. Of course.

"This doesn't look like the temple." Osha moved to sit up, but the woman stopped him. Gently, oh so gently. It seemed she used no force at all. Her touch was simply *convincing*.

"Don't move too quickly," she whispered. "You still need rest to heal." Her hands moved to his head, slipping through his hair, catching only slightly on the knots. "You look so much better already."

"How long have I been here?"

"Five days." One strand at a time, she worked the matted embroidery of his waves, delicately untwisting the knitting. Fingers probing, leaking through his skull, flooding his brain. He would've drifted off, if not for—

"Five days!"

"You slept, mostly."

"For five days? Did you drug me?"

"Not heavily. You've been quite cooperative."

He certainly felt drugged. The buzzing, bubbling syrup moving through his head, sliding down his neck, his back, his arms. *Cooperative*. Who wouldn't cooperate with this? The soft, rhythmic murmuring, the familiar warmth of her touch. . . .

"Nadya?"

The woman's eyes smiled. "No. But I can get her for you."

"No." Osha let his eyes close, tingling oblivion seeping through him.

After a moment, the priestess pulled away, leaving Osha adrift on summer waters, warm and sweet and melodious. "I'll be right back."

She floated out and back again, fabric rustling, this time trailed by three more veiled faces. All in the same crocheted caps, same gray-violet mantles, same pearl beads. All spoke softly. All touched like feathers.

They cleaned him, washcloths dripping minty, clearing his skin and lungs – but not his head. He was wandering the mammoth-tracked taiga in midnight dusk, bonfire smoke in the trees, mesmerized by distant songs, celebrating a different solstice. A child again. And all the while, he was massaged. Reassured. Given water. Cool, fresh water – down his parched throat, over singed organs and aching bones.

Melting into the bed, he muttered: "What happened?"

One cool hand touching his cheek, two dark eyes filled with earnest concern. "You know what happened."

"No, I don't."

"Yes, you do."

"No, I don't."

"We can't treat what you won't name."

"But I don't know what it is."

"Yes, you do."

He couldn't move a muscle. Not a single finger. But something swirled under his skin now, a budding energy, a new desire: to push them off of him, to run away and never come back. But all he could manage was a low, drowsy, "No. I don't."

"Yes. You do."

He did know. Of course he knew.

He'd spent countless nights awake in bed, dreading it. It had followed him to school, polluted his friendships, invaded his dreams. He'd wasted years bracing for it, like a punishment. But it had never been more than an idea. Nothing but a plague of misunderstandings.

Until recently, that is. When the doubts crept in. When nosebleeds kept him from Nitic's shows. When nausea kept him from drinking and dancing. From Julis.

And ultimately, from all the other nomads as well.

Osha tried to believe this was all he had to lose. Late nights, parties, unending travel – it had simply worn him out. He was just tired. He just needed a break.

Because the alternative was insane.

Never playing with the Sobinis again was insane. Never returning home or apologizing to Faia: insane. Never holding Julis sober, kissing him with conviction, admitting how much he wanted him – never being brave *for once in his life*: insane, insane, insane.

Being devoured from within: utterly, unimaginably insane.

This thing couldn't have stowed away all this time, hiding inside of him. Waiting. How was that possible? The very *reality* that allowed for such a thing was insane.

He'd go insane just thinking about it.

He tried to recall the booklets the doctors had given him, the pamphlets that came with the pills, but he'd worked long and hard to blot out those memories. After those first panicked, petrifying months, he'd stopped paying attention. He simply couldn't sustain the terror. Not without good cause. Not when he continued to wake each morning, strong and whole. Not when he had Faia to face. Poor Faia, for whom paranoia sprung eternal.

Forgetting hadn't been easy in that house. Hawkishly, his mother had monitored him: a strict curfew set, temperature taken nightly, his every blink and breath diligently tracked. And how he'd raged against it, skipping school, smoking cigarettes, mixing with people that made her cringe. As the years wore on, their living room skirmishes grew into a full-blown war. His mother wielded an arsenal of checkups and blood tests, time and again drawing from the doctor those same predictable words: "Still dormant! Longer than any patient I've ever known!"

Osha's only weapon was irreverence, but he used it pointedly. He left behind a treasure trove of medication when he ran away, a castle of boxes at the back of his closet – all the doses he'd managed to skip. One final, terrifically rude gesture aimed squarely at those who cared about him.

But things were starting to look different. Right before his eyes, the walls he'd worked so hard to build were crumbling. Stony memories hit the ground and split, fragmenting. Taking on entirely new shapes.

*His poor mother.*

His shelter in the taiga rains. The love his father never gave. She'd taught him to sing picking mushrooms, told him stories in the garden, filled his childhood with poems and paintings and bouquets. She'd gotten sick right along with him. Lanestabra had been her first home, and that city would punish her for ever daring to leave. It would reduce her to bones and anger – just like him. All the horror and rage and despair and disgust – she'd felt it just as keenly as he did. Each and every time a needle went into him, it pierced her, too.

She'd never been the enemy. She'd only been worried about him.

Dying.

An agonizing death.

In a foreign country.

Alone.

Osha could barely breathe. "This isn't happening."

They shushed him, these cloaked phantoms, pouring their idiot sympathy down upon him.

"This can't be happening." He said it louder, hoping for a nod, some sign of agreement. Right?

Nothing.

"Go away."

They turned their invisible faces to one another, shaking their muslin heads. Absurd as children dressed as ghosts.

"I said go away!" Osha threw their hands off of him, at last cracking through the shell of their spell. "Leave me!"

"We're here to help you. Next time—"

He kicked at them now, sheets flailing. "Get away from me!"

"If you would—"

"I'm leaving." He sat up straight, swinging his legs over the side of the bed, chest heaving. Room spinning.

"Please, just let us—"

"Enough!" Hand on his forehead, he steadied himself. This was no time to faint. "Go!"

They gave up. Drawing back in unison, mist on the wind, they bowed their heads— "Very well." —and left.

Being alone didn't change things, though.

He was dead either way.


# EIGHTEEN


It was still raining when they brought Osha his clothes, but the sound didn't bother him anymore. His mind and vision were back to normal.

His legs, however, were all but useless. For five days (*five days!*) he'd walked no farther than the toilet, less than a dozen steps from his bed. Now he teetered, unaided, down a long hall, into the large, open space where Loren was supposed to meet him. Loren, who'd been called against his wishes. Loren – his requisite escort out of there.

It looked more like a city plaza than a room. All types of people lingered there, dry and warm beneath the domed glass: temple students in long dresses, priests and priestesses in ornate cloaks, and others – hobbled patients, worried visitors, starry-eyed seekers high on the great mystery. They lounged on benches, beneath trees bent by the windows above.

Loren was waiting as expected, his dark, frizzy head easy to spot in the veiled crowd. Together, he and Osha ventured down yet another corridor and out into the cold, soggy day. Slinking alongside buildings, below well-placed overhangs and balconies, they made it all the way across the temple's campus without getting wet.

Once they crossed the gates, though, they were on their own. Even with Loren's umbrella, they were soaked by the time the streetcar arrived.

For several blocks, there were few sounds beyond the trolley's rattling: the squeal of its doors folding open and closed, the whine of its wheels on the tracks, the drumming of the rain on its metal roof. Osha didn't mind. He would've been fine never speaking again.

But Loren felt otherwise. Hesitantly, he broke the silence: "Nadya can help you, you know."

"You told Nadya?" The volume of Osha's response surprised them both. It rolled around the little car, waves in a cave, echoing and exploding against the walls. Jarring the other passengers.

"No," Loren said softly. "But you should."

"There's nothing to tell."

"Look, Osha, I know how sick you are—"

"*Were.*"

Loren looked askance at him.

"Do I look sick?"

"Yes. You look terrible."

Osha turned away from him.

"Why are you denying this, Osha?"

"I want a second opinion," he grumbled. "Don't you guys have any real doctors here?"

"We've got all kinds of people with opinions. Including my sister."

"Don't you tell her a goddamn word."

Loren looked like he'd been slapped. "What's wrong with you, kid? Don't you realize how serious this is? Would you honestly rather d—"

"Stop."

Loren stopped. That was a pleasant surprise. Perhaps he had some decency, after all. He was certainly handling this better than anyone in Oclia would. No fear, no ridicule.

Still – Loren, of all people. Why did Loren have to know?

Why did *anyone*?

"Don't tell a soul, Loren."

He nodded.

"No one, you hear me?"

"Yes." Loren's eyes remained fixed on his hands.

The streetcar crested the ridge and turned north – toward every place Osha had ever called home. Toward diseased marshes. Toward arctic bogs teeming with parasites. But it was Valena's bay below them now, uncontaminated and clean. Seamless against the dimming sky. Osha's view was broken only by the gnarled tops of wind-swept trees.

And a fly. A small black speck, skittering across the damp window.

A bug.

A dirty little bug. How easily they could slip into things, unnoticed. How ready they were to *infest*.

Osha scratched the back of his hand. Then his neck.

The fly lifted off the glass, dancing around the car before landing on the seat across from Osha. A man was sitting there, lost in a newspaper, oblivious to the lurking pest edging ever closer.

Closer.

*Closer.*

Osha lifted a foot, stretched his leg across the aisle, and smashed the fly with his heel.

The man looked up in a frenzy, flurry of paper falling to his lap. "Can I help you?"

Osha swallowed, shrinking back. "There was a bug."

The news flapped back up, a graffitied wall over which the man scowled.

The fly lay on the floor, dead.

Osha scratched one arm, then the other. Then both, all up and down.

Loren touched his hand. "Relax, Osha. Take a breath."

He did as he was told, but his arms remained fixed, wrapped around himself in a cold, comfortless hug.

"I'm going to move in with you."

"What?" Osha gaped at Loren in shock. "No."

"You're going to need someone there."

"You're overreacting."

"Am I?"

"I'm hardly alone out there. My house is never empty."

"You can't trust those people." Loren spat the words fast and hot, hissing bullets. "Even if you told them everything. They don't care about you."

"And you do?"

Loren didn't answer that.

Osha started scratching again. His legs, his sides. "You can't move in if you're going to cause problems."

"I'm not the one causing problems."

"You're the reason I lost my guitar."

"I also probably saved your life."

"I wasn't that sick!"

"I'm not talking about that." Loren spoke through clenched teeth, almost too low to hear.

"What, then?"

"It doesn't matter. I just—" He shook his head dismissively. "I can't pretend I don't know this about you." He gestured vaguely at Osha's body, as though its very existence was the problem. "I can't do nothing. I either move in, or I tell my sister."

"Fine." Osha sighed. "Move in then. Just don't bother anyone." Turning his back on his new roommate, he added: "Especially me."

# NINETEEN

If Loren found Waiter House as strange as everyone else did, he didn't show it. He merely looked around to orient himself, glancing across the dark bay to say: "That's Shipwreck Beach." And that was all.

They were drenched from their walk, and the rain wasn't letting up as they stepped inside. It thundered against the house with ferocity enough to rattle the windows. Scattered throughout the front room, dozens of candle flames quivered and twisted, struggling to keep time with the storm's impossible rhythm.

"Does this place have power?" Loren asked, pulling off a dripping boot with a soupy pop.

"Of course it does. It must be out from the weather." The house was freezing. Smelling of wood-rot. The banister of the staircase was splintering. Paint, peeling. Only the eclipse was unaffected. It had tightened, of course – the glittering moon taking a hungry bite from the sun now. But the piece hung even, clean and smooth amid the disheveled decay. "It's usually nicer than this."

Iza's voice snaked toward them then, slipping through the glowing frame of the kitchen's closed pocket doors. "If Polon would just hurry with those bootlegs, we wouldn't be in this mess. Said he recorded three shows last week, but I haven't heard a peep."

A deep, familiar cadence rose in response: "If you ever left Valena, you'd see things aren't so easy elsewhere. The recordings are coming. You just have to be patient."

Loren froze. "Who is that?"

"Gabris and Iza. Your sister's friends. *My* friends."

Osha moved to show him, but Loren grabbed him, wet hand on a wet shoulder. "Don't."

"Why?" Osha pulled back, a cascade of drops rolling off him, raining to the floor. He'd kicked off his shoes already, but his coat was still buttoned to the throat. Soaked. "And why are we whispering?"

"Just wait a minute." Loren cracked one of the doors, less than an inch. The kitchen table was ablaze with candlelight, and surrounded by people. So many people. Some Osha knew, some he didn't.

Iza was slumped in a chair, stocking feet on the table, arms crossed. "Well they better, 'cause we can't do this forever. I'm worried sick, you know that? That damn foghorn blaring away – they're sure to pick it up. And relying so much on a stranger? Whose idea was that anyway?"

Standing behind her, devilish in the candlelight, Gabris smirked. "I believe it was yours, darling."

"Well, he was more than willing. Too willing, really. Who's to say that dim dope thing isn't just an act? What if he's a spy?"

"Come now, Iza." Gabris dropped his hands onto her shoulders. "Don't be dramatic."

Iza shook him off roughly. "I'll be just as dramatic as I like!"

"Please, Iza," a woman interjected. "He's the last thing we need to worry about."

It was Nadya. Nadya, of all people. That explained how Osha could stand any of this. All he wanted was to eat and cry and be alone with his house – Iza's party and Loren's presence should have been unbearable. But anything was bearable around Nadya, apparently. She looked even smaller than usual, flanked by two giants, dark in starchy coats, faces unsmiling. Around her neck, she'd wrapped a scarf – one of those rambling numbers that trailed behind women in the streets, collecting sticks and leaves. Breath visible in the chilly air: "If anyone's being deceitful, it's us. He's just a kid."

"So's my little brother." Iza sneered. "You wanna know how *he* spends his free time?"

Across from her, Holic's face gave way to deep dimples. Osha had never seen him smile so fully. It was a little unnerving. "Iza, your brother would be quite the asset himself if he had any discipline. But let's focus. The ambassador will be in town in a matter of weeks. A rally of our very own! Miss Perala here informs me it will be at the temple, in the main courtyard." His smile broadened all the more. "Rather cramped quarters, but it will be an honor to hear him speak in person. A rare opportunity."

Two women giggled. They leaned side-by-side at the kitchen counter, wild-haired, chomping gum, nails lacquered and shining in the candlelight.

"Settle down, girls." Iza raised a hand. "You're turning into sadists."

"You would too," one of them spat, "if you saw what's happening in Nitosha."

Osha was lost. He loved Nitosha. Colorful little Erobian town. Two record shops, three bookstores, and a plaza rimmed entirely with pubs. Best clam soup in the province, to boot. He and Julis had deemed it heaven. "What's going on, Loren?" he whispered.

"Shhh."

"Come on, I haven't eaten all week. I'm starving."

He must have said that too loud, for the kitchen grew as still as a photograph. Holic's cheeks reverted to marble. The gum girls stopped their chewing. "Who was that?"

Loren glared at him. Osha turned up his palms and shrugged.

Nadya rose and moved toward the door, that low, soothing pulse preceding her, embracing Osha before she even greeted him. Peering through the crack in the door, she met him eye to eye. Lashes fanning lashes, they blinked.

"Hi, Nadya."

She stumbled backward. "Osha!" Turning to the befuddled faces behind her, she shared her findings. "It's Osha."

Holic's brow fell. "Must he *always* do that?"

Iza's lips moved soundlessly as she looked at Nadya, but their message was clear: "Not now."

Osha slid the door open fully, rainwater spraying from his sleeve as he waved. "Hello, everyone!"

Gabris alone waved back. "Good to see you again, old boy."

"You as well."

"Sorry about what happened at your show."

"It's no big deal." And he meant it. No sense pursuing a career anymore. Like he'd said to his mom a thousand times, why bother trying if he was just going to die?

The urge to cry came on fast.

With an apologetic look for the others, Nadya slipped an arm around Osha's back— "One moment." —then turned him around, back into the main room. "Where have you been?" She whispered. Delightfully tingly, her tone. "It's been days."

"Here and there."

After closing the door behind them, she studied his shivering form. "Osha, you're going to catch your death!" Removing the infinite bounty of her scarf, she set to work drying his hair. Voice all but lost in the soft, aquamarine fabric, she asked him, "Did they hurt you?"

Standing so close to her, Osha could hardly recall what "hurt" even meant. All the aches in his body had completely melted away. "Who?"

Nadya paused, squinting at his face. "No one," she said. "Your eyes just look a little bruised." She shook her head. "Must be the lighting."

"Well, why don't you turn on the lights?" Osha reached toward the wall and flipped the switch. Beams burst starry from the bulbs, shooting down the walls, spilling onto the floor. The whole house kicked on in a churning fit of thumps and hums. The metal bars along the baseboards began to tick, heating up. A chorus of joy and relief rose from the kitchen as the walls groaned and sighed around them.

Osha smiled.

Nadya didn't. She looked scared. Gathering as much fabric as she could in her small hands, she clutched the scarf to her chest. "There hasn't been power since the solstice."

"That so?"

"How did you do that?"

He shrugged. "It's my house."

Nadya's head tilted then, sights set on something beyond Osha. "Loren?"

Loren had retreated to the entryway, and looked like he was about to leave. "What's going on, Nadya?"

"Just seeing some old friends," she said. "Would you like to join us?"

"You know my answer to that."

"Come, don't be like this. Everyone is welcome here, right, Osha?"

Loren took a slow, deep breath and, as far as Osha could tell, didn't let it go.

"It's alright, Loren. These people visit all the time." Looking from one steely face to the other, Osha forced a grin. "No one's been killed yet." His humor was lost on them. "But you can always change your mind, old boy. You don't have to move in."

"You're moving in?" Nadya's jaw dropped, eyes dancing around the room like she'd lost something. "You can't move in here!"

"I most certainly can," Loren said. "And I will. First thing in the morning. You think you could help me with my things, Osha? Or do you need more time to recover?"

Osha elbowed him.

Nadya didn't even notice. "But Loren, this house—"

"I know all about this house. It sounds fizzing." Loren smirked. "And I'm not going to disrupt any morbid plans your friends might have while I'm here, if that's what you're worried about."

Nadya scowled at him. Violently. It was the darkest expression Osha had ever seen her make. A single, icy wave rolled off of her, hitting Osha's bones with a metallic clang before her ethereal seas calmed once more.

"No worries, Nadya. It'll be great, having him as a roommate." Osha only said it to break the tension. He certainly didn't believe it.

"And we know it's not safe to live all alone," Loren added. "What would happen if Osha were to get hurt? Or fall ill?"

Osha scratched at his wrist.

Nadya was biting her lip. Almond eyes aching. But still bubbling, still warm. "Can I talk to you outside, Osha?"

"Oh, brother." Loren crossed his arms. "Here we go."

"It's alright, Loren," Osha assured him. "Can't get much wetter than I already am."

Then, safe in Nadya's surreal little shroud, he stepped back outside.

# TWENTY

The chill cut through Osha's skin, fat raindrops smacking icy on his bones. The gnarled tunnel of branches overhead lifted and dropped like huge, gasping breaths, the forest flapping and slamming around them.

Beyond the thrashing shrubbery, Valena winked and blinked with its million radiant eyes. But all the howling and raging of the weather – or his body, for that matter – was quelled by the woman at his side.

Into the swirling soup of shadows, Nadya led him. Into clumping blue grass, toward the water, until the view spread out full and satisfying before them. The spires of the temple could be seen, lit from below, a silver spot on the skyline. Vertiginous staircases spilled toward its glow, dark rivers on the city's twinkling hillsides.

The foghorn groaned.

For a long time Nadya didn't say anything, and neither did Osha. Instead, he studied her: quilted coat, soft maroon tights. From her ears dangled silver and topaz, jingling and musical in the tempest. A plum purple flower barrette clung to curls already damp and matted. And along her lashes, long and dark, she wore tears: a glittering film over smooth brown irises.

Osha liked all that he saw but that.

He reached out – "Nadya?" – but she beat him to it, throwing herself into his arms in one sweeping burst. His knees went so weak, he nearly collapsed.

"I'm sorry! I'm sorry." She was sobbing.

Holding her like this was smothering. A plunge underwater. A swamp in which he was happy to drown. Nothing could touch him here. Not even his own wretched blood. "At least now you're getting Loren out of your hair." It seemed like a nice thing to say.

"Is that what this is about?" Nadya drew back, pulling her magical marsh with her.

"No, of course not." He offered a paltry grin.

"Oh, Osha." She took a quivering breath, drying her face on a sleeve. "I have to apologize for my uncle. For Gabris, and that party. For everything."

Mutely, he shook his head. Shrugged.

"You shouldn't have to worry about my problems."

He wasn't sure what she was talking about, but it didn't matter. He could feel her sorrow. Her tension. Fear, even. And none of it sullied the waters, so who was he to mind? "We're friends," he told her. "I'm happy to worry if it helps."

She turned to the view, small-smiled and sad-browed, the blinking lights of far-off boats dancing in her eyes. "I don't like this house."

Now that bothered him. He frowned.

Chewing her lip, she added: "I don't like the thought of Loren here."

Osha bristled. "He's a grown man."

"I know."

"He can make his own choices."

"I know."

"And you have no right to judge my house. You're never even here."

She went back to chewing her lip.

The wind ran circles round them, wild and rabid, but Osha could have stood there all night. Drenched in Nadya's miraculousness.

"There's just so much we don't know about each other." She spoke softly. An indoor voice, collected and calm. At home in the elements. Perhaps she made herself just as numb as she made him. "I do trust you, Osha. But Loren's all I have."

"He's just moving in for a while. It's not a death sentence."

Nadya smiled again, a smile so much like the rest of her. Hypnotic. Alluring. Demanding: "Why did you leave Oclia?"

"It's just a bunch of tundra," he said. "There was no reason to stay."

"What about your family?"

"You're not the only one with shoddy relatives, Nadya."

"Tell me about them."

"Alright." He drew a breath, but no pain escaped Nadya's medicine. Angry bodies, angry weather, angry memories – nothing could remain *that* angry. "My dad was a violent drunk," he began. "Ruined my sister's brain before she could even talk. Mom's a hypochondriac, on top of that. And her mom was a religious zealot – no one was good enough for her. My favorite uncle killed himself. My aunt could barely support my cousins. We were poor and cold and hungry and I hated my life." He turned his palms up, catching wayward raindrops. "How's that?"

Nadya looked horrified. "I'm so sorry, Osha." Such distress, and he hadn't even told the whole story.

"I thought you knew!"

A full catch of emotions, flailing in fishing-net eyes. "How could I?"

"You knew everything else!"

"Only what the spirits told me. And you can't push with them. They share what they will on their own time."

"Well, your ghosts certainly—"

"Spirits," she cut him off. "I don't talk to ghosts, and you shouldn't either. You never know what to expect from ghosts."

Osha shrugged. Semantics.

"Either way." Nadya shivered slightly. "I see why you left. It's no wonder you worked so hard on your language lessons."

"Lessons?" he snorted. "Language is easy." A common thread ran through the islands, one that Osha recognized early in the virtual quarantine of his youth. The nomads understood it, too, and the Union was all but built on it: once upon a time, long ago, the whole archipelago spoke the same tongue. The centuries had eroded it some – provincial independence, a dash of isolationism, a pinch of foreign immigration to taste. It was a mouthful at times, but each "language" was no more than jargon. "The accent is the hard part. But I understand everything."

Nadya raised a brow. "Everything?"

"I like to think so."

"You're a long way from home, Osha."

"Well, I do miss a word here and there," he confessed. "Psychopomp, for example."

She straightened at that, a ripple in her aura. "Psychopomp?"

"And thanadoula. What's that mean?"

Nadya looked down again, shrinking in every way. Each soothing tendril retracting, leaving him cold. "It's a type of healer."

Osha squinted at her. "And aren't you one?"

"Not anymore." Words quick and short. "I prefer my work at the apothecary."

"Why? You're a natural healer, if I may say so." Whatever a psychopomp did, this tranquilizing buzz couldn't hurt.

"I don't want to talk about it."

"Aren't we getting to know each other here? I answered your questions." She wouldn't meet his eyes, but he couldn't take his off of her.

Mind scurrying about, looking for excuses to keep her near. Hungry for her company, even as she stood right in front of him. Soft cotton clouds dip-dyed in despair. Despair enough to match his own, were he able to feel it. "Come on. For Loren's sake."

"A thanadoula only works with the dying."

He nodded.

"They lessen their pain and help them pass over peacefully."

"And?"

"And it gets old," she said dismissively. "It's just not very rewarding."

A colossal squall bore down then, nearly knocking them both over. The trees groaned and swayed, unleashing a shower of sticks with the smattering rain. Nadya drew close, once more slipping her arm around his back. "We should go in," she said. "This is getting dangerous."

"It's fine." With her so near, *everything* was. Even her callousness. Even her rejection. *It gets old.* Her opinion didn't matter – it didn't lessen her impact in the slightest. The crack of a branch cut through the roaring wind, and Osha watched it fall, a grin exploding on his face at its bomb-like thud. "Don't you think it's kind of exciting?"

"Not if we die out here."

"We'd be lucky to die from something like this."

She drew back, quizzical. "Are you alright, Osha?"

"Never better." Osha pulled her back to him. She didn't resist. In fact, she leaned in, heavy against his bony frame. Like he was strong. Like he wasn't about to faint from sheer euphoria.

He wanted to devour her. Swallow her up. Keep her within him, always, forever.

She rested her head on his shoulder, hair tickling the side of his face. "You know when you've met someone special, Osha? Someone just different enough that they wake you up and make you see the world with new eyes? And you want to be around them all the time?"

Osha felt his cheeks grow hot – thankful for the veil of night, thankful that Nadya's eyes were occupied with other things. It was a real struggle to keep the smile out of his voice. "I suppose so."

Nadya pulled away slightly, just to look at him. Lips parted, she studied his face. He'd lied to her, and she must have known: he had no experience with love. Affection, yes. Innocent desire. Julis's restrained touch. But not really love. Not until then, at least. Bones gelatinous, heart racing – what else could this feeling *be*? He didn't mind her age or religion or choice of home décor. He didn't mind the raging storm or his rumbling belly or the strangers in his kitchen. He didn't even mind dying.

Though it really was terrible timing.

"It's a rare and precious thing," Nadya went on. "A fragile thing."

He leaned a little closer, savoring her breath against his skin. Rarely had he been so bold with Julis – not without a drink or two – but Nadya was plenty intoxicating on her own. And what did he have to lose now?

"Times have been hard," she said, "for far too long."

Closer. Licking his lips. Hungry.

"But you've brought so much happiness to—"

Closer.

"Your nose!" Nadya's eyes went wide.

Osha pushed her back, hands rising to his mouth as the torrent overflowed. "Oh, come on!"

"It's alright. We should get back anyway."

Rain mixed with the blood, a red lake in his palm. He cursed, but not in a language Nadya understood. She just watched him, ever-patient, ever-compassionate. He forced a smile, but his words could barely squeeze past the knot in his throat. "Is this the happiness you were talking about?"

"Oh, Osha, no." She approached him now, hands outstretched. He backed up, but she was persistent: fingers on his face, radiating warmth. "You're so much more than that silly nose. Loren's so lucky to have you."

"Loren?" He was lost.

"You have no idea what you've done for him. You're the first real friend he's had in years. He's cheered up so much since knowing you."

"You're talking about Loren."

"He's never left home, though – and I do wish it wasn't for here. But if he wants to live with you, there's really nothing I can do to stop him."

And here Osha thought his heart had sunk already.

"Just remember he's sensitive, Osha. Far more sensitive than he lets on. He doesn't trust just anyone, but he trusts you. Promise me you'll take care of him."

# TWENTY-ONE

It was Loren who took care of things. Loren, who made the appointment with the doctor. Loren, who dragged Osha there when the time came, defying his protests, asking if he really wanted a second opinion at all.

Osha couldn't take care of anything. He couldn't even answer that simple question.

The doctor's office lay behind a patch of graves so thick they had to tiptoe – an unfortunate aesthetic for a clinic, made worse by the complete lack of a waiting area. The door opened directly into an examination room, no different than the ones Osha had known in Oclia. A shelf of reference books. A narrow bed. A wall of gleaming torture devices.

He turned to leave immediately, but Loren had a firm grip on his arm.

"You must be Mr. Oloreben!" The doctor was a round man, nearly as broad as he was tall. Thin hair, slicked back. Little spectacles and soft, friendly eyes. He stood behind a cluttered desk – a veritable museum of trinkets and pictures, most crafted by small children. Family photos on the wall. A roaring fire in an open hearth.

These comforting touches were lost on Osha. He glanced out the window longingly. The view was just a pile of headstones.

"This is Osha," Loren spoke for him. "I was the one who called earlier."

"Ah, yes. Loren. I remember. But enough formalities." The man made a grand gesture of checking his watch. "I do have a rather busy afternoon, so I suppose we should get straight to business. Mr. Oloreben—"

"Osha." His mouth felt dry.

"Osha. Please, take a seat." Osha moved with Loren, toward the sofa beside the fire, but was stopped. "The bed, sir."

Of course. The bed. He remembered this well – rough linen, stench of ethanol, sense of impending doom. He wanted to weep.

"Your friend here shared little beyond than that you've been ill. So please, Mr. Oloreben—"

"Osha."

"Osha. Tell me what's been troubling you."

"I should say, first—" Osha faltered, steeling himself against his words. "I may already know what's wrong with me."

"You're here for confirmation."

Osha sucked in a breath. This was even harder than he'd expected. He should have had a drink first. "So, when I was a kid, up in Lanestabra," he stammered, "I had an accident." His tongue felt like lead. "In a marsh. My thigh was cut, and the water got into the wound."

The doctor nodded, brow furrowed. But he said nothing.

"A contaminated marsh," Osha elaborated.

No response.

"I've had a prescription for the infection ever since."

Still, the doctor said nothing. He simply tilted his head.

"But for some reason I didn't need it until recently."

The doctor shook his head. "I'm afraid you've lost me. Are you saying your troubles originated with the water?"

Osha was thunderstruck. "You don't know what I'm talking about?"

"No, Mr. Oloreben—"

"Osha."

"I'm afraid you'll have to provide a little more information. Where did this accident occur?"

"Lanestabra," Osha repeated. "Oclia."

The doctor's face brightened now, a light switching on within. "Ah, yes. You're a *northerner*." He said the word as though that in itself was an illness. "I see. And what are your symptoms?"

Osha shifted on the bed. He started slowly, self-consciously, but the dam soon gave, and out it poured – in all its grim, gross glory. His eyes darted nervously between Loren and the doctor as he spoke. Loren's face was tender, flickering concern in the coppery firelight.

The doctor just looked confused. "What was the name of this affliction again?"

"This isn't familiar to you?"

"This isn't something I've encountered in Rimolee, no. But," his finger rose with his tone, "I've always harbored a fascination for your northern diseases. The permafrost epidemics of the Great Thaw most especially."

Osha scratched his arm.

"So tell me, please, what is your term for this?"

"It translates poorly," Osha mumbled, fingers digging into his wrist.

"Try me."

He couldn't. "I'm sure you know of it." Everything itched. Everywhere. "It's from the Thaw, actually. Mostly controlled since they fenced off the bogs, but the fences are getting old and—"

"Oh, of course!" The doctor bounced like a human ball. "Bog bugs!"

Osha grimaced, fingernails scraping down his neck.

"You call them bugs, correct?"

He nodded, claws at his chest.

"Why, that doesn't translate poorly at all!" The man clasped Osha's shoulders gleefully. A little painfully. "And what a condition! What a treat to meet someone so *infested*, as they say. *Bug-ridden*." He chuckled. "What an opportunity!"

"They're not *actual* bugs," Osha said firmly. "And I'm not positive that's what I have."

"Of course, of course. Confirmation." The doctor stepped around him, toward his collection of violent little implements. "What an opportunity," he repeated.

Osha looked to Loren for help, but Loren did nothing.

The doctor returned with a stethoscope. Could have been worse. "Let's have a listen, shall we?" He leaned close, smiling wide as he lifted Osha's sweater, pressing cold metal to his chest. "Ah, yes. There they are. There's that crackling you read about. You can really hear them, gnawing away like wood beetles. And to think, it's not even their active phase right now!" He rose again to his full height. "Would you like to listen? They're truly fascinating!"

Osha glared at him. "It's an infection. It's not a *they*."

"Of course. How entirely unprofessional of me." He removed the stethoscope and carried it back to the shelf. "I'm going to conduct a simple test, now. It won't hurt much – especially compared to what you're up against."

Chiming metal and clinking glass played along with the man's words, but Osha didn't look. His face felt swollen. The pressure in his throat was enormous. He was going to burst.

The doctor came back again, this time with a full syringe. "You're young. I imagine your blood clots well enough," he said. "But let's see how easily those veins burst. Roll up your sleeve, please."

Osha extended an arm and watched as the doctor pierced him. Needles had long since stopped bothering him. Cloudy blue liquid shot through the glass, dull pressure in his forearm. Under his skin, it unfurled like a skeletal leaf. Almost beautiful, for a fleeting instant. Quickly, though, the veiny pattern lost definition, collapsing into a shapeless, bruise-colored stain.

"As I suspected," the doctor said. "The walls of your veins are very weak. Very weak indeed." He withdrew the syringe roughly. "Those bugs are making quite the feast of you. Incredible!"

The man ambled back over to the shelves, and this time Osha's eyes followed, vision blurred. "Doctor, I don't think I need any more tests." Monstrous struggle, getting those words out.

"I completely agree with you. I do believe we have our answer. But might I ask: tell me again how old you were when you contracted this?"

"Twelve and a half."

The doctor raised his furry brows. "Mr. Oloreben, if I may be so frank, had you truly contracted this at twelve, you'd be long dead."

"I know." Osha clasped his hands together. No sense clawing skin off over imaginary itches. Insects weren't really creeping over his body.

No. They were *inside*.

"Well, I suppose there are greater medical mysteries in the world." The doctor shrugged it off with a smile. "Now if you don't mind me, I'm going to take a moment and—" He lifted a new syringe, filled with the same fluid now pooling in Osha's forearm – and injected it into himself. "Mmm," he smacked his lips, looking satisfied. "Like honey! Could you taste that?"

Osha shook his head, more in horror than response.

"And look at that!" The doctor continued to grin his chubby, buttery little grin. "My arm is certainly no worse for wear."

Osha's throat was raw. "Why couldn't I taste it?"

"You know how bog bugs wear down the veins. The elixir simply broke through the walls before the flavor could reach your tongue."

He couldn't breathe. He should have been more prepared for this. He'd had years, after all. He'd been lectured about it, forced to read about it, asked to think long and hard about it after stumbling home from the docks at night, drunk.

The doctor laid his hands on Osha's arm, as though to examine the stain, but instead, quite unexpectedly, pinched him.

"Ow!" Osha yanked his arm away. "Are you crazy?"

"Indeed I am not!" He chortled. "Merely conducting another test! Look again at your arm."

Osha lifted his hand, exposing the faint shadow of a rapidly developing bruise. Darkening like a photo, right before his eyes.

"See, that should not have happened," the doctor remarked pointedly. "You can pinch me if you'd like, to check—"

"No." Osha rolled his sleeve back down.

"Now don't be too upset with me," the man chided. "You're still in the early stages – you'll heal up just fine from that. Give those bugs a few feeding cycles, though, and hemorrhaging will be a *much* bigger issue. But for now—"

"Thank you, doctor." Osha climbed to his feet. The last person he wanted to cry in front of was this buffoon. "I have all I need to know."

"To the contrary, Mr. Oloreben! It's most urgent that we set up a second appointment. I'm sure we can—"

"No, thank you."

"Mr. Oloreben, this is not a condition you can manage on your own. It will be difficult to obtain the proper medications, and a terminal diagnosis like this—"

"Come on, Loren."

Loren's voice was small. "Osha, maybe you should listen."

"Mr. Oloreben, it would be wise—"

Osha didn't hear the rest. He left alone, slamming the door behind him.

# TWENTY-TWO

Living with Loren wasn't all bad. He kept the place clean, steered clear of the guests, and his orchids really were a nice touch. But beyond that? The fussing was ceaseless. He denied Osha cigarettes, alcohol, heavy lifting and sharp objects. He invaded his room nightly to tally what remained of the pills – and for all the bad dreams Osha was having, none were as nightmarish as that countdown.

Only when Osha was on air did Loren give him space – and plenty of it. He'd lurk about at times, listening from his bedroom door, but he never came too close. So the station became a fortress. Osha doubled, tripled, quadrupled the length of his program, leaning heavily on Nadya's contributions for variety. Maintaining the mood could be challenge – something about the narrowing eclipse, the subtle darkening of the house, made him anxious. But Nadya's lyrics had little in common with what was on his mind. They provided ample opportunity to let go, to drift off with the melodies, to weave and loop and layer the sounds. Sleepwalk the hours away. Skip the pesky death pangs and go straight to nonexistence.

The songs were catchy, too. Visitors would request the same one twice or even three times in a row. It became a game for everyone to try their hand at songwriting, throwing out new lyrics for each round. The voids in his repertoire became a playground, a nonsensical jungle gym of verbal wit and whimsy.

*"Live as though your life is long"*

"Written like an epitaph!"

*"Time's only measured in a song"*

"Still waiting for the final laugh!"

He knew the joke was on him. What a fool he seemed to them, singing such silliness – an idiot foreigner, a naïve little kid. Probably didn't even understand. But he did understand, of course. He just didn't care. He had no career to consider anymore. No future.

Rarely did he stray from the piano. Iza had conjured up a guitar for him, some cumbersome thing from the theater, but he didn't like it. His previous one had been small, just a parlor guitar, and the perfect fit. This replacement was a full jumbo, and it dwarfed him. Made him feel small. Weak. Fragile.

"My guitar is at the theater, too," Osha insisted. "If you could dig this up, why can't you find mine?"

"How am I supposed to know what you did with that thing? I can't even tell you what happened to *me* that night." Iza's face was ever-open, ever-innocent – but she wouldn't make eye contact. "In case you didn't notice, Barsamina parties are hardly austere."

"Just tell me the truth, Iza!"

"Don't pop a vein, Osha. Whatever's gotten into you has—"

"*Nothing's* gotten into me!"

"Clearly, *some* kind of bug's crawled up your sleeve." Iza's word choice was even worse than her attitude. "That's a perfectly fine instrument and, frankly, you've been less than gracious in accepting it. That old clunker of yours was almost beat clean through anyway. You should be thanking me."

"Could the digmen have it?" There had certainly been a lot of them at that party. "Could it be at their headquarters?"

"Bunny, that's the last place I would check if I were you."

Osha hated her.

He hated everyone.

He hated the chain-smoking guests and the hushed conversations he wasn't welcome to join. They'd talk over his soundscapes, chatting through his melodious dreams. Dry laughter and gossip, relentless as the weeping and wailing of the foggy bay. Worst of all was the way they looked at him when he asked for quiet. Like he didn't belong there.

*They* were the ones who didn't belong. This was *his* tomb.

Nadya was never among them – ever – but he hated her just the same. For *always* being there. When he woke up in the morning, when he fell asleep at night. While he slept. He couldn't shake her. Her face, her voice, everything about her repeated like a song in his head. And that *feeling*, that radiant, intoxicating feeling – life was an open sore in her absence. A wound in which she festered like a second disease.

His pills did nothing for that type of ache.

In fact, they were losing their effectiveness against aches of all kinds. Waves of pain lapped at Osha, day in and day out. He refused to overmedicate, though, cautiously rationing what little medicine he had – and it cost him. Some days, even eating was a task.

He'd been warned, though. Thanks to punishing classmates and his mother's paranoia, he'd spent years pondering (in great detail) the nature of agony. He knew discomfort well enough – his own father had broken his nose, after all. Twice. And worse still were the man's attempts to repair it. But this was different. This was a boiling vat of urban lore in which Osha cooked up a scalding batch of agliophobia in no time. Of all the medical pamphlets he got, he only really read the one on narcotics: a full catalog of drugs, waiting at his beck and call. With a perverse awe, he pored over it. Wondrous that he had access to such things. Terrifying that he might ever need them. Medications for a mammoth. Shots to knock him out cold.

"Idle hands," his grandmother would say, ever urging him to keep busy, distract himself with music and study, baking and cleaning, self-improvement – anything to avoid literal and figurative hell. But she died when he was sixteen, taking her reminders with her, leaving him to the wits of a nervous sister and a panicked mother. No moral guidance. No tortuously perfectionist goals. Just terror.

And the succoring promise of narcotics.

He'd always assumed, on some level, that oblivion would be there should he need it. And at times it was – in music, in the nomads, on the road. With Julis, in his bed. With his books. With his body. Smelling shapes and tasting moods, singing in teal and mauve. Kissed and caressed and constantly reassured: "You're safe with me. Your past is past. You can relax."

Now, however, in the unsettling glare of reality, Osha's pain-management options were feeble and few: rage, mostly. Resentment. The same coping skills he'd mastered back in Oclia – where "safe" was a foreign concept.

Waiter House did what it could – replacing tea with wine behind Loren's back, drugging the water. A glass or two soothed the burn in his chest. A long bath left him nearly catatonic. The temperature fluctuated to meet the needs of his skin, and the walls hummed lullabies as he cried himself to sleep.

If only he could layer them like blankets: Waiter House's love, Nadya's warmth, and his medicine's magical capacity for postponing the inevitable. In a bed like that, he could drift off peacefully.

But he was stuck with Loren. Death was going to hurt.

He felt his worst away from home, but restlessness was an affliction in itself. So to town he'd go – and whenever he did, the violinist was waiting. Same spot, same intrusive, lovely sound. Didn't matter the time of day or the weather. It was as though he never left. The old man would greet him with a smile, a nod, but never stop playing. He never asked how he was, even as Osha's skin thinned, rings around his eyes increasingly pronounced. He never asked about Waiter House or Osha's new guitar. He never said anything at all.

Osha hated him, too. And doubly so, for making him move.

In his new spot – a speck on a brick wall, a sniffling rake in the shadow of the provincial bank – no one stopped to listen. Maybe his hands had grown too shaky. Or his voice, too raw. Or maybe he'd just been damned to obscurity. An earlier death than expected, with hell being that behemoth of a guitar. He fought with its bulk joylessly, stomping bell-clad boots in a rage he could only hope was mistaken for percussion.

No one noticed. No one cared. No one even looked at him. Even on the rare occasion that someone slipped a bill into his hat, it happened quickly, in silence, with downcast eyes.

Pity money.

Osha didn't save his earnings. There was no reason to. He blew it immediately on the strongest drinks the café had to offer: teas spiked with vicious, blistering liquors. With eyes boring like knives into the violinist's back, he'd drink them one after another after another. Nevermind that they burned a hole through his innards – he'd drink till he couldn't remember why his stomach hurt to begin with.

And it was thanks to those cocktails that he finally drew a crowd. Cyclists stopped, pedestrians transfixed – never had Osha amassed an audience like the one watching while he smashed Iza's guitar. Splintering its oversized cavity. Snapping its neck. He slammed it on the curb until his trembling arms couldn't lift its remains. For an encore, he turned on his bicycle, kicking it weakly, lungs heaving up the metallic taste of blood. And then he exited stage right, boarding the streetcar for the North Woods empty-handed.

He didn't need to play, anyway. Didn't need the money. Waiter House would take care of him.

The bicycle was waiting when he got home, propped against the front porch, patient and forgiving. The guitar, however, remained in the gutter. It didn't belong to the house like the bike did. It wasn't like the broth simmering on the stove. Or the thick blankets piled on the bed. Or the piano or the wine or the glistening eclipse.

It wasn't like Osha.

# TWENTY-THREE

The herbalist lived at the edge of downtown, yet so far from any roads it felt like the middle of nowhere. The path to her house was long, and so narrow that Osha and Loren had to walk single file, brushing stone walls and garden gates all the while. At the end lay an island of shrubs and brambles and wet, matted grass. And within that, a cottage – weathered, sunken and bedecked with lawn furniture.

Waiting on that creaking porch, they could hear the bay: maritime chimes and groans, disembodied boat-songs. Osha was in no mood for music, but Loren hummed along. "Liven up, kid," he urged him. "You're not out of luck. Raissa's the most respected practitioner in the city. Even temple healers turn to her."

An old woman opened the door then, homely and plump. So plump, in fact, it was hard to imagine her squeezing up the alley to her house. Perhaps she never left.

She smiled at Osha like an old friend. "Nadya's brother, I take it?"

The fragile optimism Osha still carried dropped to the ground and cracked. Sighing, he gestured to Loren – to his wild hair and full lips, earthy skin and celestial eyes – all things he shared with his sister.

"That would be me, Raissa." Loren corrected her.

"Oh, of course! I should have recognized you!" She looked embarrassed. "It hasn't been that long, has it?"

"About twelve years."

"Oh. Well, in that case." She faced Osha once more. "Then who might this young man be?"

"This is my friend Osha, from Oclia."

"Do forgive the confusion, Osha. It's been a long time. Loren here used to work for me, you know – pulling sacred plants straight from his neighbors' yards! Damn fools thought they were weeds!" She laughed at that with relish, like she'd committed the perfect crime. Smile lingering, she looked Osha over, head to toe. "You're the patient, then?"

"I'm not a patient. I just have a question."

"Of course." She nodded deeply, almost bowing. "Do come in."

A light breeze swept over them as they entered the house, walls rustling like linens on a clothesline. Heart-shaped butterflies by the thousands clung to the woodwork, perched on the furniture, folding and unfolding and flitting about. A flurry of spring petals, pink and orange and yellow, paving every inch of the disheveled front room. Wings on Osha's face and neck. Sticky little legs, clinging to his hands. Creeping on his skin.

Loren squeezed his arm. "It's alright, Osha. They're just butterflies."

"I keep them for their cocoons, their wings – their everything," Raissa explained. "Wonderful garden compost. Used to sell it at the market, but that was years ago." She chuckled again. "At least I think so. Can't say I remember my own age anymore."

She sat them at the dining table, cleared away the butterflies with an irritated wave, and served up a tray of tea and dried fruit. Down, again, the butterflies descended, as surely as dust. Landing on Osha's fingers, shoulders. The rim of his teacup. There'd be no drinking *that*.

The old woman settled in across from them and smiled. "Now, Osha, I'd love to hear what you have, ah—" she chose her words carefully, a twinkle in her eye "—concerns about."

From his coat, Osha drew a small pouch. "I was wondering about these." Opening it, he loosed two of his pills. He'd only wanted to bring one, but Loren thought it would take four or five to get the information he wanted. Two was a compromise.

At the rate he was taking them, two was a full day of his life.

Raissa leaned over them, braid slipping from behind her and onto the table – knocking a pill to the floor.

Osha leapt up. "Careful!"

"Oh, there I go again." Raissa bent to retrieve it.

Slowly, Osha lowered back into his chair. "They're not easy to get."

"These pills are from up north." Loren said. "They're for an illness that we don't have here. Do you think you can figure out what's in them?"

"Goodness!" she exclaimed. "It's been a long time since I've done that sort of thing."

Osha shot Loren a glance. Loren replied with a subtle shrug, more with his eyebrows than anything else.

"Why haven't you asked your sister about this?" Raissa held a pill up to the light. Osha was sweating, watching her clumsy hands with such precious cargo. "Nadya knows far more about alchemy than I do."

"She's got other things on her plate," Loren said.

"Ah, yes." Raissa nodded, rolling the pill between her fingers. Smelling it. "With the wedding coming up, I can imagine."

Osha shot Loren another glance. This time, Loren avoided his eyes.

"Such a sweet girl," Raissa rattled on. "She'll make a lovely bride."

Loren's response was quiet. "The wedding's postponed, actually."

"Oh, no spring ceremony?"

Loren shook his head.

"Summer, then!" Raissa clapped her hands together. "I do believe I was married in the summer! At least I think so. Perhaps it was fall. Hmm. . . ."

"Miss," Osha cut into her reverie. "The medicine."

Her hand fluttered beside her head like another butterfly. "Oh, yes. Do forgive me." She stood, daintily placing each of the pills in her palm. "Give me one moment. I'll find my mortar and pestle to grind these up."

Osha winced.

"I'll be right back." And off she toddled, into another messy room.

Osha erupted. "Nadya's engaged?"

Loren looked just as troubled by it as Osha was. "Nadya's engaged."

"To who?"

"He's been, um, out of town for a while."

"How did I not know this?"

Loren shook his head, butterflies alighting on his curls. "It's just not something we talk about much."

"Engaged!" Osha's chest hurt.

They fell silent, the rabble of butterflies thickening, blizzard-like around them. From where he sat, Osha could see the woman in her kitchen, sifting through bags and boxes – everything piled on everything, spilling from open cupboards, tumbling off the shelves. She sang a little tune as she rummaged, large hips swaying in time. At last, tossing that skinny, frizzy braid back over her shoulder, she declared: "Found them!"

She returned to the table with a copper platter. On it, alongside the dreaded mortar and pestle, were several paper packets and a motley assortment of ramekins. "Now, let me tell you first off, I already know what the main ingredient is."

Osha perked up.

"They crushed up very easily, and the smell was so familiar."

He nodded.

"I couldn't quite place it, but I just knew I'd worked with it before."

His toe began to tap. "Yes?"

"Then I realized it wasn't anything I'd ever prescribed but – of all things! – something from the garden. Perhaps I should prescribe it, now that I think about it. Quite nutritious, really. Plenty of iron."

"What is it?"

"Why, it's blood."

"Blood." He hadn't held onto much hope, but it still stung to lose it.

"Well, blood *meal*, I imagine. Mammoth, most likely. Good for anemia, I've heard – and wonderful fertilizer." Raissa dipped a finger into the mortar, smearing the dark powder about, rubbing it between her fingertips. "Unmistakable smell! But such a strange texture. Those little things you had, those, those – what were they called again?"

Osha openly rolled his eyes. "Pills."

"Pills, yes. Your pills. Solid little things, weren't they? Yet with next to no effort they've become as fine as ash."

"Grinding things tends to do that," Osha growled.

Loren elbowed him.

"I do have these." She gestured to the packets, unperturbed. "A pinch of this and a pinch of that might spell a chemical reaction of sorts. That's the best way to learn what the admixtures are."

Loren feigned enthusiasm. "Let's do it."

Tearing the corner off a package, she met Osha's eyes: "Brace yourself. Sometimes these can be a bit intense." Tipping it into a ramekin, she loosed a cloud of dust, then tossed a pinch of medicine on top. It was true the texture wasn't what Osha expected. It was smooth, chalky, fluffy even, staining her fingers. "And now the water." She lifted the kettle from beside their teacups, now all but lost beneath the butterflies, and poured.

Nothing happened.

"What does that mean?" Loren asked.

"It means, um. . . ." She fumbled with the packet, squinting at the writing. "It means there is no Dimova smoke-weed in it."

Osha scowled. "Dimova smoke-weed doesn't even grow in Oclia."

"I suppose it wouldn't." Raissa looked slightly bemused. "Is that important to consider?"

"This is an Oclian drug."

"Oh, goodness me. You did say something about the north, didn't you." The woman laughed, bosom rising and falling as she leaned back in her chair. "I'm not sure how much luck we'll have with these, then!"

Osha rubbed his temples. "What do you mean?"

"Well, they're all from the desert, just over the mountains. I went on pilgrimage, ages ago. You know how youth is – always swept up in some religious fervor." She winked at Osha, like he'd understand. "Found these in the healing quarters at the High Temple and, ah, slipped a few into my purse, if you know what I mean. Don't think anyone missed 'em." Giggling again, girlishly, she elaborated: "This isn't all I took, either. They've got quite the collection of odds and ends over there. Don't think I could've started my practice without them!"

"So these are useless," Osha deadpanned.

"In a word, yes," Raissa replied. "Pity, I so rarely get to experiment like this. I was really looking forward to it. Oh well." she folded her hands in front of her, somehow laying her arms down without causing any winged casualties. "I'm afraid I can't help you."

Osha drove his palms into his eyes, elbows hitting the table, not caring how many bugs he killed. Loren's hand came to rest on his back, but it was no comfort.

"I wouldn't worry too much," Raissa assured him cheerily. "I'm sure the other ingredients are only secondary. And you can find a good iron supplement just about anywhere."

# TWENTY-FOUR

Osha said nothing on the walk back through town. Nothing on the streetcar. Nothing as he and Loren slunk past the dark storm of digmen swirling round the North Gates.

Loren eyed the officers warily. "I wonder what's going on?"

But Osha said nothing.

Nothing, until they were deep in the woods, far from anyone who might hear. And then he yelled. Flailed. Thrashed. Kicked at the gravel and tree trunks, cursing in Rimolean, Oclian, Sagoman – he didn't know what he was saying. He could hardly even hear.

"Don't give up yet," Loren pleaded with him. "I know someone else—"

"No!" Osha turned on him now, a mindless beast. Heart racing, half-blind, panicked and snarling: "No more of these idiots!"

"I'm only trying to help."

"Two pills! Two!" Osha shook his hand at him, fingers poised to pick him up by the nostrils. "I lost two pills to your *help*! You, with your moronic counting! You should know what that means."

Loren took a step back. "I'm sorry."

Osha took a step forward. "*You're* sorry? You don't even know what sorry *means*."

Loren took another step back. "I know."

Osha lunged at him, grabbing his shoulders, shaking him. "No, you don't know! This is *my* life, Loren, not yours! *My* life! My *life*!" He thrust him away. Turning his back, he gave way to tears.

Clouds moved above them, bulldozing the sun, muting the patchy forest light with shadow. Everything the same: cold and dull. Osha rubbed his chest, tight and aching as he sobbed.

"We can figure this out, Osha."

Osha didn't turn around.

"This isn't our last chance."

He glowered at the lifeless duff, the mindless rocks.

"Even if you have to go back north."

Now Osha did turn around. "Back north," he spat. "Oh, yes, it'd be *much* better to waste away there! Treated as a pariah. Dumped in a sanitarium like trash!"

"Just to get more medicine!"

Osha's chest was burning, and the flames were spreading fast. He clawed at his sweater, panting. "Back north!" His stomach caught like a matchstick. "While you and your sister live your long, happy lives – with whatever perfect ass she's fallen for!"

"Please calm down, Osha."

"Oh, come on, Loren." Osha stepped toward him again, and this time he didn't back away. "Calm down? You brought me to the best people in this whole damn city and they could do *nothing*. It's *over*. I'm nineteen years old and my life is *over*!"

"It's not good for you to get this upset."

Osha yanked his collar, wheezing. "You don't know what's good for me." Shaking. Sweating. "You don't know anything."

"Osha." Loren's voice was hardly a whisper. "Your nose is bleeding."

Osha punched him.

It was a shock to them both. Osha watched in horror as a thin trickle of red crept down from Loren's nostril. Loren touched it in disbelief, then broke a grim smile. "And now mine is, too."

"I'm sorry." The forest grew darker.

Loren adjusted his glasses – largely unscathed, but definitely out of place. "Do you feel better now?"

Osha shook his head.

"You're making yourself sick." Blood was running freely down Loren's face now – just as it did Osha's. "Don't you want my help?"

Osha could barely breathe.

"*Think* for once, Osha!"

He couldn't. He bent forward, hands on his knees, gasping.

"Or are those bugs eating your brain, too?"

Osha vomited – a torrent of tea and resentment on the gravel. On moss and matted leaves. On Loren's shoes. "Damn it, Osha!" Loren stumbled back, groaning and shaking his feet. "Forget it. I'm done." He threw his hands up and turned to walk away.

"Loren, stop! I can't breathe!"

But Loren kept going, tossing his words like a scarf over his shoulder: "Good luck with that."

Slowly, Osha lowered himself, gentle on the sharp ground. Pins and needles filled the air – piercing his lungs, stabbing tiny holes all around him. Black pepper in his vision. Electric sparks in the canopy. Snapping stars over Loren's face.

Loren – who'd come back to tower above him, solid and stoic as a tree. Extended arm like a sturdy branch. "Come on, get up."

Osha rose and teetered, leaning heavily on his friend. His only friend. The only person he had left. The only person who'd still have him.

"I hate you, Loren."

Loren smiled. Still bleeding. "Not as much as I hate you."

# TWENTY-FIVE

Three times, Osha tried to douse the fire, and three times, he threw up his pills. He didn't have it in him to tally what he'd lost, but knew it was too great a gamble to try again. His head was clear enough to understand that. And then some.

Without the temple healers to sedate him, awareness was merciless. The fever did little to dull the pain. The haze of sleeplessness brought no relief. It wasn't the first time his body had defied him – his crooked nose and stunted stature were hardly empowering, and the whole sleepwalking thing had been a disaster. All told, though, it had been a decent enough contraption: a warped but workable little radio whose music he should've appreciated, now tyrannized by a truly cringe-worthy melodrama. And he, a captive audience. No way to change the station. Nothing to do but listen.

Waiter House, at least, tried to keep the volume low. Pitchers appeared at his bedside, glasses filled and refilled on demand. Keeping the water down took focus, but his efforts were rewarded – an hour or two of relative ease, deep breaths, cooling embers. But there was no tempering the worst of it. No numbing that phantasmal itch. The cold-boned terror. The dizzying despair.

The gargantuan task of staying sane was his and his alone.

On the bright side, no one came to visit. He could moan as loud as he wanted.

Loren tried to help, too, though Osha couldn't imagine why. There was no reason to mop his sweating brow when his whole body was drenched. No sense cleaning blood that just kept boiling – bubbling over onto shirts and sheets. Coming up from his stomach. Discoloring the toilet water. Yet clean, Loren did.

And as he cleaned, he talked. Odd phrases, odd topics. Forests spilled out of him, in vivid detail. Streams and shrines and summer. Mammoths and mountains and mushroom hunting. Concerts and parties, as well. Late nights with the nomads. Nitic and Ivra, Neta and Pia. Julis, exquisitely described. Unnamed, yet undeniable. His large hands, his warm face. Smiling voice and woodsmoke smell. Dreamlike, these visions

Loren painted. Osha couldn't help but get lost in them. Lost in Julis's madcap ideas. Lost in his sketches and poetry and wit. Lost in the green of his eyes.

But Julis wasn't with him now, and never would be. No drinks, no kisses, no laughing to the point of tears. These were only Loren's words, doled out in stilted, broken sentences. Like a list.

A list of all that Osha had ever loved.

Osha didn't give much thought to how Loren had gotten his memories. He was in no position to care. Any disjointed recollections – stolen or otherwise – were preferable to the present. He couldn't remember being so miserable in his life.

There just had to be better ways to die.

But this is what he got.

This is what he got for lying to his friends. Lying to Julis. Lying to himself. For cutting all ties and taking off alone.

For leaving Lanestabra. For abandoning Faia to the abyss. His sudden absence must have been quite the shock, and she didn't take shock well. She'd take it as violence, and play it on herself like some horrible song. Never aimed at the proper audience. Never their father or the neighborhood bullies. Never him. No. She kept her cuts and scars and rooftop edges all to herself.

This is what he got for hitting her, just like he hit Loren. In a claustrophobic fit – hemmed in by his mother's demands, staring down the barrel of a lengthy bout of fasting and blood tests – he punched his helpless baby sister in the face. And he ran away the very next day.

To this.

This is what he got.

Death, to avoid becoming his father.

His mind ran circles around it, thoughts pounding relentlessly in time with his guts, but he couldn't go home and apologize now. He could hardly even get out of bed. Not that he needed to – the only place he wanted to be was the temple, and that was a lost cause. Every time he asked about it, Loren's answer was the same: the forest was barricaded by digmen. No way in, no way out. Something about a manhunt. Osha didn't care about the details. He stopped listening at "impossible."

He lost track of the days. Sometimes it rained, sometimes it didn't. Sometimes Loren was with him, sometimes he wasn't. And from time to time, through the window, he heard the officers – scouring the beach, shouting about foghorns and airwaves. But he didn't think much of them.

Until they were in the living room.

He'd been sleeping, lightly, drunk on cold water and wet rags. Loren had gone off somewhere. Maybe the other room, maybe outside. He didn't answer his calls. Didn't come to help him stand – slowly, cautiously, careful not to black out.

"Loren?"

No reply.

Just the digmen downstairs, southern accents strong. Veering into Sagoman at random. Bouncing back to Rimolean almost violently. "It should be right around this (*nonsense*)." Pure linguistic chaos. "Based on the foghorn (*nonsense*)." Nauseating to take in. "(*Nonsense.*) I don't get it."

Osha didn't get it, either.

He crept toward the door, hands along the wall, swimming his way through swirling fever foam into the loft. To the edge of the balcony. The eclipse pulsed steadily, waves of light pushing against him. Gripping the railing, he looked down.

And there they were. Pacing. Looking lost.

Waist deep in floorboards.

Cut clean in half.

Osha squeezed his eyes shut, clinging tight to the physical world. Arms shaking. Toes curling. Solid things, all around him. Yet when he looked again, nothing had changed. Two young digmen, guns slung over their backs, pointed hats on their heads – cut smooth as ships through the floor, passing through furniture like empty air.

How high was his fever?

"Can I help you?"

They didn't seem to hear him.

Had he already died?

He took a few deep breaths. In with strength, out with pain. In with calm, out with ghosts. *Out* with them. "Excuse me, sirs?"

They didn't even look up.

Alright, then.

One step toward the stairs. One step onto them. Step. Step. Step after quivering, dizzying step. Lower and lower, pausing now and then to steady himself, to rub his eyes, to stare at the men below – closer all the time, slimy smiles spewing broken jokes, voices cold. No legs. Arms swinging in the cellar.

Finally, he was there with them, bare feet firm on the solid floor. Standing right between them. Unseen. One of them wandered in the direction of the bay, floating down as though with the slope of the land, until only his head was visible. Then he turned around with a grin: "Maybe they have an underground bunker. Just like (*nonsense*)!"

The other chuckled, swaying smoothly through the boards – "(*Nonsense*)!" – then followed, wading into the deep end as well.

Passing right through Osha's legs along the way.

He was going to pass out. Staggering forward, he held tight to the back of a chair. Wooden frame. Woolen fabric. Dust in the air. Sturdy walls. These were all things he could touch. Things that would respond.

The digmen moved on, outside. Through the window, Osha could see them walking away: full-form, boots on bending grass. Footprints in the mud.

He pinched himself. Not too hard, but God did it hurt. A decidedly undreamlike sensation.

So he went after them. Teetering to the door, he opened it and stepped onto the porch. Thick white sky. A bay of wretched cries. And ah, yes – he had no shirt. Drenched in sweat, bloodstained and chafing, he'd torn it off some time ago. Hours? Days? It didn't matter. What mattered was that it was freezing. "Excuse me, officers!"

They didn't turn around.

He dragged his feet farther. Yet another set of steps. One by one, legs shaking, nearly toppling. Then at last: barefoot in the wet grass. Earth squishing, vibrating, alive.

He was real.

This was all, somehow, very real. And with each step through the sopping lawn, all the more so.

Because he was catching on fire.

Like a veil, Waiter House slipped off of him. All his armor, sliding down like rain on a windowpane. A snake shedding its skin. Comfort and safety falling to the ground. And down he went with it. Naked and raw. Desperate to re-dress his wounds. Wounds he hadn't even felt until that moment – ice in his bones, flames in his flesh. Gnawing, cramping, knotted innards. Screaming tyranny. Utter and absolute rebellion. He wailed.

They heard that.

"Who's there?"

Oh, come on – guns, now? Pointed at him? In his state?

"State your name!"

He should have expected this. He knew it was coming. It was in all the old pictures – terrifying history books schoolmates left open on his desk. Sanitariums stuffed with writhing, bleeding, sobbing animals. All-consuming agony. He was bawling like a baby.

"Your name!"

"Osha!" A wonder he could speak at all, but guns were known to work lesser miracles.

"Osha Oloreben?"

How was this not a dream?

Loren appeared then, mad and wild-eyed, yanking him up. Tearing him limb from limb. "What are you doing? Are you crazy? Get inside!"

But Osha couldn't move.

"Get up!" Loren was dragging him.

This nightmare couldn't be worse.

Then a shot rang out.

He stood corrected.

The bullet blew past him, a handful of hurricane, typhoon in his hair, and ricocheted off a porch post, blasting through the siding and into the house.

Then a second shot. A different kind. A flash of light, crackling over his skin, burning through his eyes. A photograph. While one digman reloaded, the other had the nerve – *the psychopathic audacity* – to take a *photo*. Osha had hardly a dozen pictures taken of him in his life. But yes, let's immortalize *this*.

Loren heaved. Osha's back hit the steps, pain rattling through his spine, sharp and ringing – but quick to dissipate. Lifting off in tiny bubbles as Loren pulled him up the stairs. Floating away. Popping. His head went light and woozy.

The gun fired again, but missed dramatically. One more bullet through the side of the house – leaving not a trace. No sign of the first bullet, either.

The digmen were spinning around themselves. "Where did they go?"

Loren's touch felt lighter, though nothing in his demeanor changed. "Come on, Osha! Get up!"

Osha braced himself and rose, barely upright a second before Loren shoved him through the doorway. Then down again, on all fours. Vomiting onto the floor. Blood on the boards like water on wool. Absorbing.

Loren slammed the door and Osha fell back against it. "They tried to shoot me!"

"Well, you shouldn't have gone out there!"

"Oh my God, Loren!" He was crying again. Or still? Either way. "This hurts so much!"

"I know. You've been saying that."

"No, I didn't know!" The floor was clean again. Dry now, stainless. "I didn't know at all." All that Waiter House did for him – the soft air, the tender melodies, drugs in the plumbing – how ungrateful he'd been. "I can't go outside!"

"And you shouldn't!"

"I *can't*, Loren!"

"I don't want you to!"

A strange pressure stepped in then, something thin and new between Osha's fingers: a cigarette. Already lit. He drew on it hungrily. "How do you live like this?" Oh, sweet smoke. No idea what plants. Didn't matter. "Digmen everywhere!" Another drag. "Out for blood!"

Loren's smile was thin. "You might have worse luck than me, kid." He patted Osha on the shoulder and stood. "Let me get you some water."

Yes, water! Loren moved off toward the kitchen, and Osha relaxed. Another drag. This was better. Not ideal, but better.

Fleetingly, the officers reappeared. Their top halves, that is. Both guns drawn now, held in shaking hands. "They have to be (*nonsense*)! With (*nonsense*) like that (*nonsense*) he should be dead!"

Another drag. Another drag. Another drag.

Then they left, voices drifting off into the trees.

Another drag.

Vanishing into their world.

Another drag.

Leaving Osha alone in his.

# TWENTY-SIX

However much time had passed, it was enough for Osha to give up on recovering. And yet – somewhat monstrously – he did. He woke one sunny morning to find the world calm and still. Eyes clear, body light and cool.

Relief descended like a fine dusting of snow – scattering with a sigh only to settle again, thicker. Heavier.

Loren wasn't in the room, but his voice was nearby. Angry. So many walls and closed doors made it hard to hear the exact words, but there was definitely an argument.

Not even a minute of peace. Osha closed his eyes again.

". . . with those damn songs . . ." Loren was shouting.

". . . you know it's complicated . . ." It was Iza. Iza was back.

". . . gonna get him killed . . ."

". . . since when are you . . ."

They were drawing near, Loren climbing the stairs: ". . . and you don't even care!"

Iza close behind: "Who says I don't? A person can care about more than one thing at a time, you know!"

The bedroom door swung open and shut. And there stood Loren, even tenser than usual. "How are you feeling, Osha?"

Osha remained flat on his back. "Better."

"Really?"

"They reopened the woods, I take it."

Loren nodded. "You heard Iza."

"Such a beautiful voice," Osha smiled. "Music to my ears."

Loren snorted. "I think you're still sick, kid."

Osha took to the task of sitting, the room swaying along with him, and gestured toward the door. "What was that about?"

"It doesn't matter," Loren grumbled.

"It sounded like it did."

"Don't worry about it. You've got your own problems." Loren eyed Osha, hands on hips, appraising him like an object he might purchase. Scowling as he hunted for defects. "What are you going to do now?"

Osha lifted the water glass from his nightstand and took a sip. Plain, somehow. Missing a flavor he couldn't quite recall. Something small. A floral bitterness, as vague and subtle as everything else in his memories. It all seemed so far away now.

"I don't know." He scratched his arm. "Apologize for punching you?"

Loren almost smiled.

Osha scratched the other arm. "Thanks for staying with me."

"It's not like I could have left."

"You're too kind."

Loren wasn't humored. He repeated himself, firmly this time: "What are you going to do, Osha?"

Osha looked away from him, out the window, at bare branches trembling in the blustery sunlight. Twiggy, helpless things – not so different from those that grew near his mother's home, barely surviving in small pockets between buildings. At least three died each winter, and the replacements never fared much better.

"How long would you have at home?" Loren asked. "With the right medicine?"

Osha shrugged. "A couple years. Five, tops."

"And without?"

He sighed, eyes falling to his hands. Over the knuckles of one spread a spectacular bruise, a tender rainbow that would make playing any instrument a challenge.

He deserved it.

"Osha?"

He didn't answer.

"Have you ever seen anyone die, Osha?"

He scratched his chest.

"I have." Loren came closer, looming overhead like a gathering storm. "And I don't want to do it again. It was a bloody nightmare, Osha. It was brutal and horrific and their body became *meaningless*. You'd think there'd be something left, but there's not. It's *gone*."

Osha was dumbfounded.

"You can talk to as many spirits as you want, but hear me when I say they're nothing. Not compared to life. Not compared to a living, moving, thinking person. They're *nothing*. When you die, you are *nothing*."

Was this some kind of punishment? "What are you saying, Loren? Does it look like I need this right now?"

"You need to go home, Osha. You'll die if you stay here."

"I'll die either way!"

"You don't have to!"

"What difference does a few years make? They wouldn't be fun, I can tell you that much."

Loren took a breath, shaking his head. Quiet, at least for a moment. And then: "Just think about summer, Osha."

Osha rubbed his eyes – almost too sore to touch. "What about summer."

"That sweet, heavy air. Swimming. Freezing water, fresh river smell." He was doing it again. The *listing*. "Ripe berries, wild on the vine, baked in the sun." Just rambling. "And the birds – explosion of music, every dawn." Far less comforting, now that Osha felt better. "Though the sky's never too dark. The sun's never far away." Decidedly uncomforting, in fact.

"Why are you doing this?"

Loren ignored him. "And the beach! Hot sand on your feet. With your sister, in the—"

"How do you know I have a sister?"

That stopped him. "I . . . um . . . Nadya told me."

"What are you doing, Loren?"

"I'm trying to level with you, kid. You can see another summer – but not here. Not like this."

"What do you care? You get rid of me either way."

"Damn it, Osha!" He was mad again. "That's not what I want! That's not what *anyone* wants! People care about you, and you're throwing your life away!"

"I'm being eaten alive!"

Loren sighed. Wordlessly, he moved to the foot of the bed and sat. Head down.

"I feel good here, Loren," Osha said. "Just let me die in peace."

Loren's voice was small: "You don't have to die yet."

"Go to hell."

The silence stretched and yawned, filling the room, spreading into the trees beyond – leaving Osha with plenty of space to think. About pain. About death. About Faia, unable to even watch him get a shot. How poorly she'd handle seeing him like this, beaten and bruised and bedridden. And yet the thought of never seeing her again – it was confusing. Distressing.

And Loren's secret weapon, apparently.

"You have people that love you, Osha. Think about your family."

Yes, think about them. How he'd fought them, wrecking their dreams, robbing them of peace and happiness. And now look at him: destroyed by his own delusions. How would they respond if he showed up now, crawling home to die? Would they even take him back?

"They'll take you back."

But did he want them to?

"I won't help you anymore," Loren said coldly, eyes hard. "Don't you want people who will?"

Osha couldn't look at him. "I'll do what I need to do, Loren."

"Good. Then you'll leave tomorrow."

# TWENTY-SEVEN

The train was scheduled for dawn, so Osha made sure to shower and pack that night. All the bloodstained towels had vanished, replaced with clean ones, fluffy and dry. But beyond that, Waiter House didn't offer much assistance. A one-way ticket to Sabelso cost him nearly every cent he had. He'd hoped the house would leave a little money in his pockets, but it refused. It didn't provide any clean clothes, either. There wasn't even food in the kitchen.

It was almost like it was mad at him. Like it didn't want him to go.

The first steps out the door were patently terrifying, but there was nothing to worry about. Not yet, anyway. Boarding the streetcar brought a new wave of panic, and approaching the train station felt like a funeral march. One step farther from comfort, one step farther from ease. One step closer to peeling off his own skin. Nothing to protect him. Nothing to pacify him.

For now, though, he was relatively pain-free. Damn near normal, in fact.

Hopefully he wouldn't get sick on his trip.

He tried not to think about it. Fear wouldn't help him any. He needed optimism. Just an inkling of trust that this might work out, that he might buy himself some time – or at least some relief.

Going north didn't have to be so bad, either. He didn't have to rush all the way to Lanestabra, surrendering his newfound liberties. To drink and dance and be merry. To freely hold another man's hand. Or simply spend time outside. He could linger on the South Coast, where Oclia's wizardly doctors would lull away the horror without the added torment of sub-zero temperatures. He could stroll the clean streets of Oradai, eat eel, sip coffee – that bracing, bitter brew northerners made possible with glass houses, just as Rimoleans did with their own sacred plants. How he'd afford it was a mystery, but stranger things had befallen him than unexpected money. He just had to have faith.

At the very least, he could lounge in the serenity of Mosmist Beach, where legend had it he would always feel good. There, it was said, nothing bad ever happened, and everyone fell in love.

It was there that Julis first held him. First traced his face with his fingertips, first pressed those cardamom lips to his own. They'd only known each other a few weeks then, and their bands were about to part ways – but they resisted. Barefoot in the sand, they dug in their heels. It was too fast a friendship to break. Too electric. Too easy. Having spent his life as a monster or a music box, Osha finally felt like a *person* with Julis – understood in a way that thrilled and baffled him. So they locked together and fought their fate, trying their best to melt. To become one being. To remain intact.

The nomads did as nomads do, though, and he and Julis would go months without touching. They wrote often, entrusting their intimacy to rogue couriers and traveling salesmen. But such lengthy separations made it easy to lose the plot. Even when they were together – dancing at the same parties, sleeping in the same bed – they heated and cooled like the seasons. The giddiness, the ardor, the mystic anarchy of Julis's mind – it should've hatched an embarrassment of love songs, but instead it bore doubt. Paralyzing doubt. Between Osha's feeble frame, his moods and his meanness, there was precious little to like. So he was never quite sure what Julis wanted. Never sure what he *himself* wanted.

Only when their tender touches began to bruise him was he sure of anything at all. Julis would not be part of his life after that. Julis would *not* be part of his death.

Nor would he be part of this trip. Osha put him out of his mind.

He arrived at the station on time, exhausted and hungry, but the train was running late. He took to wandering then, through the perpetual petals and ash of downtown. Nearly no one was up yet – just a small procession of cloaked priests, haunting with their torches in the morning mist. He meandered through the shuttered shops of the market, palming enough change for a cup of tea and a pastry, if nothing else. But not one eatery was open. So he continued his chilly stroll, making his way to the end of a pier. And there he waited, pink sky folded above and below, reflected in the rippling bay.

On either side, boats clanged and groaned, knocking together, forever bullied by the briny water as it churned. Under the dock, between the boards, Osha could see crabs. He watched them crawl over one another, clawing at the barnacles that paved the thick posts. Sea stars, sun stars, anemones. The tide was very low; it was unusual to see the bottom.

"I wouldn't jump, if that's what you're thinking."

The words were soft, but gruff – and all around him. At first, Osha couldn't tell where they came from at all. Like a disembodied voice calling just as he fell asleep, they could have come from his own head.

But they didn't.

They came from the old violinist – standing on the pier just a few feet behind him, smiling.

Osha tamed his shock quickly. "Why would I jump?"

The violinist raised his brows. Humored, concerned, incredulous.

"Even if I wanted to," Osha motioned toward the water, "that wouldn't kill me."

"Sure it would." The man moved closer, joining him at the edge of the dock, peering into the water with one of those indefinable expressions of his. "Not the fall, no. But you'd be surprised how tangled you get in the ropes under those boats." He smiled at Osha again, a strange twinkle in his eye. "I would know. Fell in once myself after one too many."

Osha didn't press the issue. "I'm surprised to see you here," he said instead. "I didn't think you ever stopped playing."

"Ah, I'm not quite the worker bee you think I am." He chuckled to himself, but it wasn't lost on Osha that he held the violin even then.

"So what are you doing here?" Osha asked.

"Following you." The old man was looking right at him, yet still his voice didn't quite match his mouth. The acoustics of the pier, maybe? Sound carried differently over water. "You're heading home, I take it?"

"Just left, actually."

"No, no," he waved a hand. "Not that home. Your *real* home."

Osha tensed.

"May not be my place to say it," he went on, "but I think you're making a wise choice. You still have time, and Waiter House isn't going anywhere. It'll be waiting – as it does – if you happen back by."

Osha's tongue felt numb.

"Can you play the violin, son?"

He swallowed. "A bit."

"Here." The old man held out the instrument. Beautiful little thing, polished and gleaming, beaming in the soft pastels of sunrise.

Osha didn't move. "You want to hear me play it?"

"I want you to have it." The man said.

"What?"

The old man shook it at him, insistent. "What's it take for you to understand things, boy? Take the damn violin! It's yours."

"What about you?"

"Look, I know you don't have much money, and your guitar's in pieces. You're gonna need this if you expect to get anywhere."

Hesitantly, Osha reached out. Touched it. The violinist released it the moment his fingers wrapped around the neck. "Attaboy." The man drew back. "She's been a good friend to me, that ol' thing. Take care of her."

Then he turned to leave.

"Wait," Osha called. "I don't understand. What will you do?"

The violinist glanced over his shoulder. Wide grin, glistening eyes. "You really are slow, aren't you, boy?"

He must've been.

*Osha Oloreben.* The man said it without even moving his lips. *I've been dead for years.*

DENIAL

ANGER

# BARGAINING

DEPRESSION

ACCEPTANCE

# TWENTY-EIGHT

It took three days, zigzagging between the mountains and the coast, to reach Sabelso – and each one was dreadful. Osha languished in a rickety third-class car, bone-cold and tormented by the relentless whine of the leaky windows. Hair was falling out, little black strands raining down, loose in his eyes, tickling his face. Forcing him to all but sleep in his hat, just for some peace. And there was no distracting himself. Stupidly, he'd brought no paper to write on, and the train's jerking undermined every effort he made with the violin.

To top it all off, he felt awful, and his quest for comfort – sit, stand, pace, repeat – earned him nothing but uneasy looks from other passengers. Throwing up wasn't just repugnant in that tiny bathroom – it was humiliating, as time and again he'd emerge to rows of disgusted eyes.

He was heading north again, all right.

He missed Nadya.

He hadn't bothered to say goodbye to her. Or anyone else, for that matter. But he had Faia to look forward to. Sweet Faia would forgive anything, whether he deserved it or not. She simply didn't have it in her to be mad.

His mother, however.

Good God, he didn't want to go home.

The train wound round sleeping volcanoes, each snow-capped peak another jewel on a necklace strung together by the tracks. The slopes were interchangeable to Osha: nameless, stony enigmas that eventually gave way to lower passes, dark and dripping with moss. And lower still, to pillowy hills cradling green, marshy pastures. Then, finally, the wiry fingers of inlets could be seen, shimmering bays filling out their watery hands.

Osha leaned against the damp windowpane and watched it all, the shadowy gleam of his sunken eyes reflected back at him, batting lashes.

The whole world, the whole way, was muted by a smothering fog.

Over the intercom, a woolly voice announced the stations as they approached, but Osha recognized none of them. The nomads had stuck to the old roads – overgrown highways tying gutted ghost towns to teeming cities, rarely crossing Union rail lines. Here and there, passengers disembarked, stepping into misty mysteries. Some glitzy, with gusts of noisy, smoky air billowing through the open doors. Others lonely: tiny wooden structures marooned in the monotonous countryside.

New passengers boarded to refill the vacant seats. For the most part they sat in silence, faces buried in books and newspapers. It was especially quiet with digmen on board, and the farther north they went, the more frequent that became – gray coats milling casually, clogging the narrow aisle, clustering near the luggage rack to chat while everyone else held their breath. Even the stewards kept their eyes down in their presence, busying themselves with ticket stubs and travel brochures.

Sabelso made its grand appearance in the haze of dawn, sparkling at one end of a viaduct so long and low it seemed the train became a ship, slicing smoothly through the choppy waves. The bridge was brand new, silver and beautiful: a gift from the Pan-Archipelago Union.

The train slowed as it made landfall, slinking between hilly orchards, vineyards laced with fine ribbons of mist. It curved around the city, spiraling to its center, and jerked to a halt in a wide plaza. Lusty lanterns dotted the square, caressing themselves with spindly, wrought-iron tendrils – dazzling, through the wet windows.

Less dazzling outside, though. Just cold.

Dozens of people poured out of the train there, crowding Osha at the doors, bumping and banging into him. They scattered evenly across the plaza and disappeared, the din of luggage and murmuring quickly swallowed up by the whispering air, leaving him alone with his bruises.

The train gave a sigh and indifferently pulled away.

The abandonment was abrupt, and the morning frigid. Osha wasn't sure where to go, but the chill forced him to move. If he wanted to get home, he'd have to make money anyway. So off he went, hoping Sabelso's braided maze would take him to the park blocks. To an audience.

The city took on a luster as he walked, sun burning through the fog and bringing the streets to life. Everyone in town had a foot (or a whole leg) in Sabelso's pearl industry – and consequently everything from telephone booths to private homes were studded with bay-born treasures. Even the sidewalks boasted wealth, pearls paired with beach glass and polished stones in elegant designs. And the cemeteries – for there were proper cemeteries here – featured pearl-encrusted graves, tombstones dripping like half-melted candles.

Osha loved this city. In the summer it sang, merrymakers clogging the streets, stumbling from garden parties to pearl dives to smoky pubs. Sabelso was a crossroads for the nomads, and the reunions that bloomed in the park blocks kept the mood celebratory. Lost loves rediscovered, new babies met, stories exchanged. Bands swapped members at midsummer, vying for new talent like recruiters for a sports team. Osha had considered joining others: the Filonas, the Copolos, the Balestros. *Julis* Balestro. His scrambled senses and bookish ways had never endeared him to that carnival life – and his perennial invitation to run away together pulled on Osha like a magnet. But Osha wasn't about to trade his whole family for one man, enticing though he could be. He never left the Sobinis. He sang with them every night, right here. Hot and happy in the jubilant tumult.

But it was awfully quiet now, and unnervingly empty.

It was early, though.

Salt air heavy in his chest, Osha paused at a view – a high balcony on a bluff, overlooking the sparkling bay. He could see Erobia from there, just across the water. A glossy new train line stretched toward it, hopping haystack rocks and grassy outcrops – but didn't reach quite as far as he'd hoped. The tracks ended abruptly, skeletal and twisted against the netting of sea-sky, jagged shards over the tides.

Broken. Violently broken.

Guess he'd have to take a ferry.

He caught his breath and moved on, not stopping until he reached the tree-lined terracing of the park blocks. But even that place was empty. Few cars were out, and even fewer bikes. Any pedestrians passing did so in total silence. No old men with bird seed, no paper-peddling youth. Definitely no street performers. That wasn't the only thing off, either: the surrounding buildings – the city hospital, the police station, the notorious Hotel Kavan – were festooned to the hilt with flags. Great, smothering banners draped over the windows, triple-forked snake tongues striped in the same shades of peach and sunset orange as the officers' ribbons. And all the way up the hill, to the steps of the provincial capitol complex, Osha saw more of the same.

This was not the Sabelso he remembered. This was the victim of some bizarre kidnapping, tied and gagged in broad daylight for all to see – with digmen guarding every corner lest it try to escape.

"Oh well." Osha sighed. This wasn't his destination, anyway. Pulling the violin from his bag, he offered it a smile. "I've never been too good with your kind, you know," he confessed. "But I'll do my best." Hat off and at his feet, he lifted the instrument awkwardly. One stroke, then another, just to check the tune – and away he went. A lot of legato with zero vibrato, but he was rusty. He hadn't played a violin since . . . well, since the last time he was here.

If this was indeed Sabelso.

He wasn't oblivious to the stares of others. Slack-jawed, some of them. Terrified, almost. True, this wasn't his strongest instrument, but it was a song he knew well – one he'd played countless times on the radio. Yet it must have sounded awful, for he'd hardly started before being stopped cold. Whistle trilling. Voice demanding: "Alright, enough!"

"I'm sorry, I—"

Hands on him now, spinning him around – "Just who do you think you are?" – he was forced face-to-face with a surprisingly small digman. No bigger or older than himself, and wearing an identical look of shock. "Osha?"

"Neta?"

"You came back!" She jumped up and down, hands clapping. Horrifically dressed, but otherwise the same. Same cropped, golden waves. Same nails, same lips: red as they'd ever been. Even the uniform felt familiar – the old fisherman's getup she'd donned wasn't so different. A coat with brass buttons was just a coat with brass buttons.

And Neta was Neta.

She collected herself quickly, ironing flat that moment of glee, adopting the same controlled poise as everyone else. "It's prohibited to play that here, sir."

"Oh, come on. I'm not *that* bad on violin, am I?"

Neta's face was stony. "Don't taunt an officer of the Pan-Archipelago Union."

Osha laughed. "An officer!"

"Your list of violations is growing, Mr. Oloreben."

Osha faltered, smile dropping some. How serious was she? He didn't know how to proceed.

But Neta did. "Pack your things. You're comin' with me."

They moved much faster than Osha's lungs liked, even with Neta's limp. It wasn't a bad limp – hardly noticeable most of the time – but her spine never let her move quite like others. No scrambling up mountainsides or plunging into caves. What she lacked in posture, though, she sure made up for in posturing. The crook in her back lent her the air of being just a little bit *better* than everyone around her. A certain tilt to the chin. A subtle lean. Coupled with her striking looks, she cut quite the intimidating figure.

And all the more so in uniform.

Taking a cue from those around him, Osha kept his wheezing quiet. Whispering: "You really an officer now?"

"If you can't beat 'em, join 'em."

In silence, she steered him away from the park blocks, past the No Name Club (boarded up), past the butcher shop (not open), past the Belz Café (crowded, but entirely with digmen), and toward the Central Bank – or what had once been the Central Bank. Its grand pillars had collapsed, half the building spilling out into the street. Officers crawled like insects there, wheeling carts of money and pearls out of the rubble. A teeming hill of poisonous ants.

Neta smiled and nodded as she passed. "Morning, Luca."

"If it isn't little Neta!" One of the workers paused, tipping his hat. "What have you got here?" He eyed Osha with palpable distrust.

As if Osha's lungs needed more stress.

"Accident." Neta shook her head with a tsk. "Hit and run, can you believe it? This fella here took quite the wallop – still gettin' his wits about him. Just takin' him in for a report."

The digman stepped away from his cart, closer, hands coming to rest on the barricade's heavy chain. Eyes narrow, he squinted at Osha. Up and down. Slowly.

Osha rubbed his chest. *Breathe*, Oloreben. In and out. You got this.

"Say. . . ." the man blinked. "Don't I recognize this guy?"

That's it, Osha was going to pass out.

"This kid?" Neta looked Osha over and shrugged. "Hell if I know. Can't even get his name. He had quite the whack on the head back there."

The officer leaned closer. "Is that right?"

"Yep." Neta grinned. "So we better ankle, before he forgets his age, too."

"Wait, though, Neta—" The man straightened, snapping out of the reverie Osha had dragged him into. "About the other night. You still haven't answered my question. Forgive me for being so forward, but—"

Neta cut him off: "I'd rather kiss your sister, Lu."

The digman's face went red.

"I mean it, too." She reached over and patted his arm. "Give her my number, will ya?"

And off they went.

"Pull yourself together, Osh," Neta whispered, the bank safely behind them. "There's no need to panic. I got you."

"I'm just a bit winded." At least they were walking downhill.

"Catch flies – you're scared as a kid at a cliff dive." She studied him briefly, suspiciously, much like the digman had. The *other* digman, that is. She adjusted her hat. "I'd expect more from someone like you."

Osha snorted. "What's that mean?"

"Just figured your position called for a little bravery, ya know?"

"My position?"

"Keep it down." She hushed him. "We'll talk about this later."

She pulled him through an open door, the dim dankness of an empty pub stamping out the morning light, and led him toward a corner table. Far from the entrance, far from the bar. The sea air followed, mingling with the stale, sticky beer smell in a way that would have reminded him of Neta had she not been sitting right there with him. As it was, he didn't need reminding.

"You want a drink?"

"I don't have any money."

"I'll pay." From one gray pocket she pulled a wad of bills, and along with it – quite by accident – a small pouch. Floundering to put it back, her tan cheeks blushed just as bright as her lipstick.

It wasn't hard to guess what she was hiding. She smoked it day and night, the flick of a match forever lighting those mismatched eyes of hers – one green as grass, the other brown as dirt.

She pulled herself up, grinning across the room at the bartender.

The bartender did not return the gesture.

"Don't worry about it," Osha told her. "I'm good."

"Food then? What do you want?"

"I'm not very hungry."

"Not hungry?" Neta's jaw dropped. "Are you sure you're Osha? Am I with the wrong kid?"

"I haven't been feeling well."

"That so?" She shook her head. "Well, it serves you right. I *told* you not to leave us like you did."

Neta had little sympathy for the infirm. She'd made a career of dodging discomfort, after all. Being addicted to painkillers was just fine by her – so long as she didn't run out.

"How are you feeling right now, though?" she pressed.

Osha shrugged. Aside from the full-scale military occupation? "Not bad."

"Then have a drink."

She ordered him a warm, spicy brew, and at last he began to relax. Relieved to be sitting, relieved to be with someone he recognized. *Mostly.* "So, tell me—" he gestured at her uniform "—what's all this about? When did you become an officer?"

"When I *applied*, that's when." She smiled proudly, swirling her drink in her hand. "They can't get me if I've got them." She darkened then, meeting his eyes squarely. "But you hear me, Osha. They can still get *you*."

Osha smirked. "And why would they want to *get* me?"

She cocked a brow. "That music?"

"It's illegal to play music now?"

"*Yours!*" Osha wanted to defend himself, but Neta plowed on. "Don't worry, though," she said. "As long as you're with an officer, you won't be suspect. Just stick with me and everything'll be berries."

"I appreciate the offer, Neta, but I've got to get home." Osha took a long drink. "I don't have much time." Loaded words, those. Itchy. "I'm flat broke, but if the Sobinis are heading north I—"

"Shh!" Neta glanced around. Another smile for the bartender. "You can't just drop names like that."

"Drop names?"

She leaned close then, voice low: "Are the Sobinis still around?"

"Why wouldn't they be?"

Neta turned her eyes to the door, to the cold, stoic world beyond. "There's no nomads here, Osh. Maybe at the lake village, but not here."

"What happened?" Osha asked.

"Just go to the lake." She still wouldn't look at him.

"Come with me."

She met his eyes again at that, tapping the ribbon on her chest. "I got work to do, buddy. And you've already given me more than enough cause to arrest you."

This was just too strange.

"Listen, I got a little place in the Warehouse District." She fished out a notepad – an official one, the kind on which tickets were scrawled and crimes reported. She scratched down an address. "Stop by when you get back."

"I told you, I'm heading north. With the Sobinis, if they can help," Osha said. "I may not be back."

Neta took a sip, licked her lips, and smiled. "You'll be back."

# TWENTY-NINE

Even in Osha's state, it was only a few hours' walk to the lake. Energized by Neta, driven by hope, and (most of all) fortified by booze, he sang his way along the old, shaggy roads, winding through the dead brown landscape. The wild wisteria groves were just knots now in the winter, lacy maple stands missing all their frog-foot leaves. It was cold. It was muddy. It was passenger pigeon territory, and they could be heard, distantly, ominous and grating in the still air. Ghastly in mass, good for nothing but an easy meal. But Osha didn't mind. Neta had sent him off with a full flask, a roll of bread, and a small bag of smoked salmon. And it was necessary – the vines that once gave him plump, dark berries now bore nothing but thorns. The snowmelt stream, however, tasted fresher than ever, and heading out to a ghost town was a treat in itself.

Many ghost towns were new, abandoned only recently by farmers siphoned into state-run communes, rewarded with subsidies and rail access. But the lake village predated the Union – by quite a bit. It went all the way back to the floods, to the rash of settlements forged by refugees, lost and landless, marooned by fire and water and disease. Disparate people, lumped together and thrown to the wolves by the ruling classes on account of race, money, ideology – they nonetheless found themselves in one another. Found family and pride and music. Courage and freedom and movement. In time, they became something cohesive. Something inspired and whole, at least in Osha's opinion. They became nomads.

And they were usually around here somewhere.

The village itself was fantastically unstable – collapsed roofs sprouting trees and moss, rotten wood beams encased in mushrooms. Not a single window had glass in it, not even broken. Flood marks could be seen on the structures, cryptic notes jotted down by history. The cabins all reminded Osha of Waiter House, steep and slanted, rising from the earth so naturally. They huddled around a wide, grassy expanse like mountains over a valley. There'd been a road there once, and a little plaza – but time had made a meadow of it. Its rowdy past, swallowed up and gone.

Much like Osha's, evidently. There was no sign of anyone anywhere.

He picked a house and climbed its steps, took a seat at the top, and absorbed his surroundings. The afternoon sun splattered over decaying rooftops, dappled and shifting as the breeze toyed with the trees. Osha had a sliver of the lake in his view, visible between two sunken cabins – but its blue wasn't very pretty right then, nor was the trickle of the creek very soothing.

What was he doing out here? In the middle of nowhere? All alone? No one could help him if he got sick here. No doctors in these woods. He had to consider things like that now. How could he have been so foolish?

He pulled out Neta's flask. Empty. Well, that answered that.

He considered crying, but instead picked up the violin. At least he could play out here – and he could cry anywhere. As far as he could tell, self-pity hadn't been outlawed.

He plucked at the instrument a bit, but it wasn't very satisfying. He'd seen others throw themselves into the violin, bodies twisting, faces contorted, possessed as they drew from its strings demons and gods and broken hearts. But Osha wasn't that type of guy. He liked guitars and pianos and drums. Things he could beat on.

He reconsidered crying.

But whispering distracted him.

"Is he a digman?"

"No way."

"Look at his coat, though."

"It's too dark."

"He's too loud. Go tell him to stop."

"*You* tell him."

Osha stood and turned around, scanning windows, picking apart the dense, viny forest. He saw no one. Back down the stairs, into the grass: still no one. The calm was so deep, in fact, he almost thought he was imagining things. Raising the violin to his chin, he set the bow to the strings and pulled out one long, smooth note. Then paused.

Nothing.

So he began to play. His old favorite. 'Farewell, Everything.'

That did it. Two children spilled out of the house next door, frazzled and frantic. "Stop! Stop!" Their voices were low, but they may as well have screamed.

Osha dropped his arms to his sides, defeated. No matter where he went, he couldn't finish one goddamn song.

The children beckoned him closer, but when he stepped forward they backed away. Scrambling back onto their porch, they cowered in a corner.

"I'm not going to hurt you," Osha promised.

They shushed him.

One of them – a dirty, androgynous little thing – finally edged toward him. Took a breath. Touched his arm. Tugged his sleeve. "Come inside."

Osha followed them through the threshold – straight into the shock of a wall-to-wall crowd. Dirty faces, disheveled clothes. And then darkness, total and complete. Doors closed. Windows boarded as they were, he couldn't see a thing.

But he could hear.

A nervous murmuring rolled through the room, with one voice rising above it. A woman, quite near to him. She leaned low and whispered to the children: "He's not an officer?"

"I don't think so."

"And he's alone?"

"Yes."

Her clothing rustled as she rose to her full height. Osha could make out little more than the gleam of her eyes. "What are you doing here?" she asked him.

"Trying to get home."

"Shhh," she chastened him. "Lower your voice. Where do you live?"

"Oclia."

A low laughter rippled around him. "Bless your heart, child," the woman said. "You can't get there from here."

"I have to."

Osha's eyes were adjusting, unwrapping the woman before him. She was in her sixties, maybe seventies. Nearly a full head taller than him, thick hair pulled back in a braid. "Why were you playing that song?"

Osha shrugged. "I thought I was alone."

"You're with the resistance." It wasn't a question.

He almost laughed. "The resistance?"

"What is your name?"

"Osha."

A collective sound rose up now, some strange blend of groaning and gasping that was punctuated by one very familiar voice: "Osha!"

A small spark in the dark. "Nitic!"

The reunion was dampened by a full chorus of shushing.

In the unfolding room, Osha could see movement – a lone giant, pushing his way through the faceless mob.

"Osha, the musician?" The old woman asked.

"Yes, the musician!" Nitic brought on yet another wave of shushes, but ignored it. Seizing Osha roughly, he planted one firm, bristly kiss on each cheek. "It's been far too long!"

Phantom whispers circled them, quick and slick as swifts. Dive-bombing them. "Osha Oloreben!" "Did anyone see him arrive?" "Get him out of here!" "He'll get us all killed!"

What a time to be drunk.

"Take him, Nitic," the woman ordered. "Anywhere but here."

# THIRTY

"Osha, Osha, Osha!" Nitic's voice rang like gunfire as he led Osha into the trees. If all that hushing in the dark had been for secrecy, their cover was decidedly blown. "I can't believe you're here! How did you find us?"

"Neta. She—"

"Neta?" Nitic glanced over his shoulder, heavy black brows rising. "Did you say Neta?"

"Yeah, she—"

"Is she in Sabelso?"

"Yeah. She's—"

"You don't know how good that is to know, man! I have so much to tell you!"

Osha gave up on doing the same. "I'd love to hear it."

"No." Nitic shot him another look. "No, you wouldn't."

Something wasn't quite right with him. He was thinner. Haggard, almost – an interesting spin on such a large physique. He'd always had a regal air, pronounced all the more in Osha's worshipful eyes. He'd known of Nitic for years before meeting him, from the radio, from bootlegs and magazines – and ultimately from other nomads, as curiosity pushed Osha beyond his insular upbringing. He remembered well his nervous joy, meeting his idol in person. The elation when Nitic said he had potential. The maniacal, desperate eagerness to be taken under his wing. To run away with his band. It was like falling in love.

But now his hero looked tattered. Days without a shave. Dark mane short and uneven. Wild-eyed as he stomped through the underbrush, through mounds of detritus that had once been houses. He led Osha across the creek on a plank of wood – which he then lifted and stashed behind a bush. "Nobody's gonna need that."

"You sure, Nitic?" The creek was no idle thing at that time of year. It bordered on river status, in fact.

"Nah, it was just for me. None of them come back here."

He looked ravaged. It had only been a couple of months, but Nitic Sobini could've aged a decade.

Not that Osha had fared much better – fingernails splintered, hair falling out. Soon he'd be a hobbled old man himself.

Maybe they both had bugs.

The forest opened suddenly, unnaturally. A park or garden had been there once, but now there were only weeds. The gray sky pressed heavy on the field, chilling it, dampening its colors. Yet what colors they were! A chaotic patchwork of dried flowers and beads, patterned canvas and cloth. It was easily the largest collection of nomad wagons Osha had ever seen. His eyes went wide. "How many people are here?"

"Not too many now. There were more before."

"Before?"

"Sit down." Nitic pointed at a chair – one lonely chair, crooked in the dirt – and went to work untying the flaps at the back of a wagon. "You're gonna want something."

Osha sat, spying glass under the wagon as he did so. A bottle.

No, three – five – *eight* bottles.

Osha stopped counting. "Is this the medicine cart, Nitic?"

"Sure is." He roped up the sides, inviting in the dull light. Dozens of jars met the day there, gleaming from little shelves along the walls, yoked at their necks with labels and dates.

"I'm kinda tipsy already, to be honest."

"You are?" Nitic lit up, black eyes sparkling. "You got any left?"

"Afraid not."

"Damn." He sank again. "Man, I need a drink." Taking a seat on the back of the cart, he lifted a jar. "These ol' things just don't do the trick."

Osha had never seen him like this. Not once. Not when his partner left him. Not when Ivra threw his fiddle in a lake. Not even when he lost his finger to a spider bite – though he (and everyone else) certainly lost sleep over that one. "What's going on, Nitic?"

He scrutinized the bottle in his hand, uncorked it with a shrug and took a swig. "Just waitin' to die."

*Did* he have bugs?

He took another drink. "You remember that guy from *The Melody Review?*"

"Of course." Friendly fellow. Thick glasses, flat hair. Aging-before-his-time and childlike enthusiasm in equal measure. "What about him?"

"So he came out, what, a week before you left?"

"Around that." It was nine days. Osha was just beginning to feel sick when the journalist showed up – his third bout of "flu" in three months. He decided to stop traveling after that. They weren't far from Valena, and he'd heard they had a good lamb stew there. He figured that would help.

He'd been wrong on all accounts.

"Well, that little ass showed up again," Nitic spat, "a couple weeks later, with a whole grip of digmen. Said they were comin' to check on 'structural integrity' or some crap like that. Claimed the ghost towns weren't *safe*. Said they were there to *protect* us. And that damn journalist wouldn't even look me in the eye. Just like everyone else – only likes our music, if that. Our music and nothing else about us."

"Come on, old boy, it's not that bad."

"Easy for you to say!" he snapped. "Listen to you! You're no nomad, you know that, *old boy*? You can play at it all you want, but you'll never be one of us. You don't know how this feels."

Osha had never been the target of Nitic's temper. It stung.

"Rejected by everyone!" Nitic barreled on. "Pushed out of society! Hunted like vermin!"

"Hunted?"

"Those digmen, Osha! Those goddamn digmen!" He lifted the bottle for another sip. "They're arrestin' us in bloody droves! *Enslaving* us on those railroads, those suicide bridges – or just killing us outright, makes no difference to them."

Osha was speechless.

"We don't fit into that lofty little vision of theirs. If you don't pay taxes, what good even are you? If you don't leave a paper trail, if you can't be *tracked*. . . . But you know all of this."

No. No, he didn't.

"Anyway. I got a story for you, Osh." Nitic turned away, rummaging through the cart, looking for something.

Not far off, a flock of passenger pigeons took to the air. Thick swoosh, dulled by the trees, roaring like the ocean. Terrible squawks at a crescendo. Then down again, somewhere else in the wooded thick. Invisible but very present. Foreboding.

Nitic held up a bottle, revealing the deep mahogany of a rich wine. "This one's for headaches. You're gonna have one without it."

Osha took it without hesitation.

And many others, too.

"Took this when they chopped off my finger. Trust me, it helped." Nitic was rambling. "This one's more for chronic stuff – bad backs and all. But why not?" Increasingly excited as he went on. "And this one's for childbirth! That's gotta be something. Take a shot. Take two!" Like he wanted Osha to go blind. "How you feelin'?"

"Alright."

"You need more."

A reunion *was* cause for celebration, he supposed. So celebrate he did. After five or six samples, his head was swimming. Nomad medicine certainly hadn't lost its edge.

And Nitic showed no signs of stopping. "Bottled tears! This one's great. You don't have to feel your own sorrow – it's like somebody else did the crying for you!"

Osha tipped it back: lump in his throat. He couldn't guess the ingredients in any of these. Some were bitter, some were sweet, some so spicy they stabbed like pokers through his nose. Overall, though, remarkably palatable.

At last Nitic stopped, hands coming to his hips. "You good now?"

Osha smiled sheepishly. "I'm good." With a pharmacy like this, he wouldn't be in such a hurry to get home. The bugs that so plagued him were now no more nettlesome than fruit flies.

"Good," Nitic said. "'Cause I have something to tell you." Osha settled in, curiously watching as Nitic took a slow, full breath and let it go. "Everybody's dead."

Osha's smile fell.

"So that jackass from *The Melody*? Guess I can't really blame him. He got it bad, too – called in just for talking to us. Knocked about for our location – had a big ol' shiner. But still. That goddamn rat. He could've lied, but he didn't.

"Of course, we're hardly the first. They've been burnin' our towns for months. Claimin' it's for our own good, claimin' no one's there when they do it. But people always are. *Always.* Half of 'em don't make it out. And the others, well – we took in so many escapees, our band nearly tripled! That's why you see all these wagons here.

"But everybody's gone now, so."

Osha licked his lips. "What do you mean *everybody*?"

Nitic took another breath, opened his mouth, gestured limply, but said nothing.

The pigeons rose up again.

Down again.

"It's, um, it isn't easy to say this," Nitic fumbled. "They had a thing for me, those digmen. Probably 'cause of the interview, what with Mr. *Melody* there. Kept callin' me a bigshot. Fancied me a real radio star. Decided I was too big a name to tamper with or something. So, I, um — well. You can see for yourself, I'm still here." He forced a grimace-ish grin. "So not *everyone*."

Pigeons up. Pigeons down. Closer now.

"It's easier to say 'everyone,' though, I'll tell you that. Easier than saying what actually happened. Trust me, I don't wanna tell you scat about that — but you should know. You of all people should know. After all you've done for us."

All he'd done? Osha had never been so icily aware of how little he'd done in his life. He hadn't been there when they needed him. Hadn't been there for anyone. He'd been lazing in luxury, pampered and waited on, playing joke songs and eating pastries. So self-absorbed he didn't even read the news.

"Some are still alive, I'm sure." Nitic continued. "Taken away, though. Not dead yet. Maybe. But maybe not. Just as well. Soon enough."

Pigeons.

"The ones they left are definitely dead, though. About a dozen, I'd say. Not all family, but some. Ivra. Timo. Pia." His voice broke. "Pia's kids." He took a moment. "But some of those folks I hardly knew." His eyes were wet. "And call me what you will, but it helped." He blew out sharply, almost whistling. "Call me a monster, Osh, but it's just easier to watch strangers die."

Osha didn't want to hear it. Or see it. It was like watching his father cry. Not that he'd ever done that — his dad wasn't one for remorse.

"They lined 'em up in the commons." Nitic's gaze drifted, face draining as his mind traveled back. "Had 'em tied up, standing like a wall in the grass. Everybody but me. And they were just pattin' me on the back, actin' like old chums. Making me watch.

"One by one, they did it. One by one like dominoes. And they were all lookin' at me. No blindfolds. Eyes on me, each one, as they fell. And some of 'em didn't die right away." He ran his hands over his head. Aggressively. Agitated. Twitching. "There was a lot of blood, man. A lot of pain. And those dogs just laughed. And told me to laugh, too."

"Good God, Nitic." The forest was spinning.

"They shot one of the twins before Pia – just so she could watch. I've never heard screaming like that in my life."

Osha wiped his face. Why did he have to know this? What was he supposed to *do* with this?

"And then it was Pia. And she looked at me, just like the others. And those dogs had my face, and they took my mouth like this, and they made me smile. And they said, 'look, nomads really *are* carefree. Next he'll be singing.' And that was the last thing she saw."

Osha wanted Nitic to shut up.

"Then there was no one left but her other kid."

*Needed* him to shut up.

"That's when they put the gun in my hand."

*Don't say it. Don't say it. Don't say it.*

The passenger pigeons were up again. Treetops, stirring. Air, thickening.

Nitic was bawling. "They shot her first, Osha, I swear they did! They left her screamin' and covered in blood. I was shakin' so bad I couldn't even hold the gun, but they kept shoving it back at me sayin', 'Don't you care about your family? Look at her! Put her out of her misery!'" He threw back his head and wailed.

The flock broke through the trees, branches snapping as they spilled into the clearing. Ink and tar, they poured over the daylight. Darkening the sky. Blinding. Deafening.

*Thank you, God.*

Nitic's mouth kept moving, chest heaving, eyes leaking. But all Osha could hear was the tumult of crunching static – thousands upon thousands upon thousands of wings beating. The sky positively shrieked.

The wind picked up. Feathers rained down. Sticks and pebbles. Dirt and bird scat.

Nitic carried on, oblivious. Somewhere else entirely. Somewhere Osha did not want to go.

Then blackness. Like a lid slammed down, the clearing closed. Wagons lost under a blanket of birds.

Osha's hands came to his ears. The noise was horrific. He'd never liked it, but now it hurt: little beaks driven deep into his ears. He clenched his teeth.

Nitic took no notice.

Slowly, the river thinned, growing shallow. The sky flickered back in little stars. Then clouds on a high wind. Then a milky mountain stream, flecked with squawking debris. And finally, a broad, clear lake, foggy and still. Silent again, save for Nitic's terrible talking.

Osha didn't want to uncover his ears, but he did, of course. Sticky palms. Blood. He wiped it away before Nitic noticed – not that he would.

"—nothin' but nightmares now," he was saying. "And that's it. That's what happened." He ran his large, brown hands over his face, his hair, his neck and shoulders. Eyes on the empty sky, he fell silent.

The silence lingered for a very long time.

"I'm sorry, Nitic," Osha finally offered.

Nitic came back with a shrug, pulling a pipe and a pouch of herbs from his shirt pocket. The continuing calm was broken only by the spark of a match. One big puff for the last Sobini standing.

"What about the other bands? The Balestros?"

Nitic grunted. "Julis is fine, last I heard. Don't worry 'bout your little boyfriend."

Normally, Nitic's tone might have bothered Osha. But he was beyond caring now. Miles beyond. "Where is he?"

"I'm sure he's hiding, too."

Osha buried his face and cursed. Nomad curses. He couldn't look at Nitic anymore, but closing his eyes was no better. Pia was waiting there, behind his eyelids. Pia, with her long, smooth hair like Faia's. Gentle, dreamy Pia, who he'd so loved. In the orbit of her sweet little girls, she'd waxed esoteric about stars and planets, drawing up a chart that explained his soul with surprising accuracy. She'd had less success reading his palm, though – said he'd live a long life. Find lasting love. Become a father.

Now neither of them would see the future.

There was something else going on, though. Something decidedly different than grief.

Hadn't he just seen them?

Back in that house, before the doors closed and submerged them in gloom – hadn't Pia been there? Hadn't Ivra? He could swear they had been.

"Who are you with now, Nitic?"

"A couple refugees from Erobia. Activists. A lawyer." He nodded as he spoke, as if this were news to him as well. "And their kids, of course."

"And?"

"And. . . ?"

"There were at least thirty people back there."

Nitic narrowed his eyes at him. "Did I give you too much medicine?"

Osha wasn't sure what to make of that.

Nitic went on without him. "Found a house out here the other day," he puffed, "down the lake a bit. Surprised I never saw it before. It's just a little cottage, but still. Been spending a lot of time out there. Gets nicer every time I visit. Probably movin' in there soon." Puff. "Not been feelin' too social."

"A house?"

"It's really somethin', Osh. I can actually relax there. Like my troubles just drift away. Never thought I'd want to settle down, but I'm starting to get it. Warm sheets. Hot soup. A couple times I even found some mead. There's probably some now that I've said that – that place always seems to know what I want. Wanna head over and check?"

"No." Osha's head was shaking. Pounding. "Don't you have anywhere else to go?"

"Why the hell would I bother?" Nitic looked shocked. "You heard what I just told you." Outright offended, in fact. "How else can I live, Osha? How can I go out there – into the world – now? After *that!* How can I *live*, Osha? Tell me! How!"

Osha had no answer.

Nitic collected himself, drawing again on his pipe, leaning back. "Nobody's safe out there, anyway," he muttered, ragged face vanishing behind the smoke. "And things are even worse in Erobia. You wouldn't believe the stories I hear. Not that I could go there, even if I wanted to. Resistance blew the viaduct, and no boats are gonna cross that strait." He took another frustrated puff. "I'm stuck."

The whole cocktail of concoctions flowing through Osha could only pad against so many blows. "Stuck," he repeated. "What do you mean?"

"I mean *stuck*." Nitic tilted his head, as though for a different perspective. "Could be worse, though. No one can find my new place, that's for sure. And even here in the village, we got farmers bringin' us food. As long as they don't get arrested, we can hide forever, am I right?"

"Do you really have to hide?"

"Of course! These people got warrants out for their arrest! We're talkin' full-fledged resistance members, man! Why do you think they've heard of you?"

"Heard of me?" Osha pressed his chin to his palm, unsteadied by confusion. "Why?"

"Who are you trying to kid, Osha? *Farewell, Everything*?"

"What's that got to do with anything?"

Nitic's puffing grew incessant, nervous. "It's catchy, man. All your songs are. Real popular with a certain crowd, if you know what I mean."

"I don't know what you mean."

"Oh, come on. Drop the act. I'm on your side."

"My side?" Osha's brain was buzzing. "Look, Nitic, obviously I missed something. I've been a little preoccupied."

Nitic smiled. "And what is it you've been up to, Osha?"

Electric shocks, all through his head. Things clicking and locking into place. Things he should have connected before. "Is this why I can't play in Sabelso?"

Nitic nearly dropped his pipe. "You played in Sabelso?!"

"What do you think? I'm a musician!"

"Musician!" Nitic leaned forward, squinting through the smoke. "Ya know, I'm also a musician, Osh. But I don't sing 'Farewell, Everything' on Rebel Radio."

"Rebel Radio." Each word struck like a boulder. His thoughts took to running, racing like hell away from them. Away from everything. He'd had enough. "This is nonsense. That's impossible." His words tumbled out, choppy but resolute: "I'm a musician. That's all. A musician."

"Are you joking?" Nitic's voice was really rising now. "Do you have *amnesia*, man?"

"Alright, listen." Osha took a few breaths, gasping for clarity. "This is what happened: I met some people in Valena with a radio station. Just a little station, hardly ever on – just some stupid daytime drama, and I played at night. It wasn't *Rebel Radio* – it wasn't anything." His eyes bore into Nitic's, insistent. "It was just for fun."

Nitic laughed, roaring and rattling through Osha's bones. "Fun! *Fun!* That 'little station' is part of something *huge*, Osh! Rebroadcast all the way to Erobia! How do you think the resistance networks, man?"

This had to stop. He was going to pass out.

"Either you're feeding me a line, or someone pulled some serious wool over your eyes." Nitic surmised astutely, tapping the ashes out of his pipe. "But you are what you are. And people love you, man. It's nothin' to feel bad about."

"Oh God, what was I *doing*?" Osha clutched at his chest, recognition thundering through him. "I let them rewrite my songs! Were those coded messages or something?"

"Osha!" Nitic was in stitches now, doubling over. "Only you!" He shook a finger at him. "This could only happen to you!"

"It's not funny!" This had to be a bad dream. "Stop laughing!" Why wasn't he waking up?

"Alright, fine." Nitic straightened, smoothing his sweater. "Seriously, then – what you're doing's for a good cause. I'm proud of you. Plus, you can really hear my influence, you know? Got a copy of your record a while back, and on that third track—"

"Record?"

"Just that little bootleg floatin' 'round resistance circles. It's good, man! You're really coming into your own! As your mentor, I gotta say—"

Osha burst into tears.

Nitic froze.

He didn't care. He couldn't stop. He was out-and-out blubbering, and it didn't matter why. The Sobinis. The resistance. That old standard, death. The tidal wave crashed without rhyme or reason, washing away all those strange brews, sweeping up his memories and scrubbing them to a shine. Every radio broadcast, every request. Every prompted word, every nonsense lyric. Every disjointed conversation, overshadowed by illness – loneliness trumping logic. Pain beating out common sense.

And death so close now, he hardly had time to mourn his friends.

Nitic eyed him warily, refilling the bowl of his pipe. "Do you want more bottled tears?"

Osha dried his face, throat aching. "Who all thinks this about me?"

"The resistance." Nitic's tone was gentle.

"And?"

"Any nomads that are left." He struck a match, adding brightly: "You're our pride and joy."

"Anyone else? Any officers? The goddamn ambassador?"

"Settle down, Osh," Nitic cooed through the smoke. "It's alright. They might know your voice, but they can't know what you look like."

Yes they could. "Oh my God, Nitic." And they most certainly did. "They took a photo!"

"Who did?"

"Those digmen!" Osha's chest was caving in. "They took my goddamn photo!" Slowly, now: inhale, exhale. He held out a hand. "Can I get some of that, Nitic?"

Nitic passed the pipe. "Listen. If we go to my house we can—"

"No." Osha puffed hungrily. No empty comfort, no peaceful denial. No easy death. No more houses. "I need to go home."

"Come on, now." Nitic looked concerned. "You don't have to run and hide." Concerned, but not understanding. "Just stop singing those songs and you'll be fine."

Smoke in. Smoke out. Rhythm steady, heady and sweet. "You have to help me, Nitic."

"Stay with me a while. My house is—"

"Just get me across the border."

"You gotta let this go, Osh. It's not possible."

"Is it, though? Even with just us two? We can't catch a ride with a fisherman or something? The mail boats? Surely, the post goes through."

The look on his face wasn't promising. "What's the rush, anyway? This'll all blow over soon and—"

"I have bog bugs."

Nitic's brow fell. "What?"

"I said I have bugs, Nitic."

His eyes narrowed to beady little gleams. "No you don't."

"Yes I do."

"You *can't.* You can only catch that up north."

"I had it before I left."

Nitic leaned closer, voice raising: "No, you didn't!"

"Yes, I did."

Nitic slapped the pipe from his hand and onto the ground – herbs flying loose, smoldering in the duff. "Then what the hell are you smoking for? You trying to kill yourself?"

"I'm already dying."

Nitic grabbed him by the shoulders and shook. "Don't say that, man! You're young! You're strong!"

"You're hurting me."

Nitic let him go. "Goddamn you, Osha!"

Osha rubbed his arms, watching his friend collect his pipe. Nitic brushed it off, tapping out pine needles and dirt, and slipped it back in his pocket with a sigh. Then a smile. "We got this, Osh," he said softly. "With the right drugs, you got years, right?"

"Only if I get home."

"Then we'll get you home."

# THIRTY-ONE

They stayed the night in the meadow. Nitic insisted his house would be better, but Osha didn't want it. He hadn't a clue what to do with Nitic's news – those balls of terrible truth he'd been forced to juggle – but he knew it wasn't time for elation or sedation or any other *-tion* Nitic's house might provide. It just wasn't right. Sabelso was strangled by an occupation, and his friends – the only real friends he'd ever had – had died in pain and terror. He could suck it up and do the same. Wasn't that the sort of sacrifice a resistance member would make?

Besides, he wanted to sleep outside, smoke and stargaze, pretend nothing had changed. And he mostly succeeded, barring Nitic's sleep-talking – begging for mercy just before sunup.

The nomad cars still ran, but they were far too conspicuous to drive. Even unhitched from their florid carts, they screamed in color, just begging to be seen. So Nitic and Osha walked. Early in the morning, they set out, tired, cold and slow. And on foot, they slipped easily into town – heads down, through the dump. It was staffed almost entirely by prisoners, many of whom might have recognized Nitic. Or Osha, for that matter – whoever he'd become. But they managed it unnoticed, suffering nothing but the awkward shame of freedom.

A worthy prelude to fear.

Nitic had never liked cities. Too many rules, he felt. Distrustful glares, angry demands – these were his allergies. So a full-on military presence had him in hives. He avoided the digmen like a skittish animal, taking backstreets and alleys, cutting through parks – going so far out of the way that they got lost looking for Neta's apartment.

And fretting all the while. "You alright, Osh?" "You tired?" "Why are you coughing?" "Did you get hurt?" "Is that blood?!"

Not that there was anything else to say. Reminiscing was prickly, and there was no future to speak of. Singing was fine in the woods, but not in the city. And Osha didn't feel much like singing anyway. Not after the mess it had gotten him into.

Neta's patio overlooked the rail yards – or so she'd claimed. But Osha couldn't see any patios when they arrived there: just yawning awnings and tracks, winding off between warehouses and canneries, vanishing in an unchartable sea of concrete. It didn't look like a place anyone would live. Or even want to live.

It certainly didn't *feel* hospitable.

It felt *sad*.

Sadness flooded the tracks, in fact, drowning the whole train yard in smothering melancholy. Like no sorrow Osha had ever known. It introduced itself eagerly, though – rising from the ground, snaking up his legs, ensnaring his heart. Demanding to be felt. Osha looked to Nitic for an explanation, but Nitic didn't seem bothered by it.

He was just bothered by him. "What's wrong? You've gone all pale."

"I'm fine."

"Well, act like it then. You're stressing me out."

They were almost there, so on they went. Over a low brick wall, down a short ladder, and onto the tracks.

Straight into paralyzing despair.

Physical, it was. Like hands. Pleading and pulling. Holding him in place.

Nitic was oblivious. He strode casually, down the center of the rails, to where the roof gave way to open sky – stopping only to call back: "Come on, man! Get to Neta's before you fall apart!"

Osha slogged after him, but the sorrow was deep and getting deeper. He could practically hear it now – *could* hear it – weeping and wailing, with not a soul in sight. Just Nitic, tapping his toe impatiently. So Osha kept his head down, fought the urge to cry, and pushed toward him.

Until he reached the photos.

Portraits at his feet. Hundreds of them. Duplicates, triplicates – up to a dozen of each. Spiraling around themselves like a blooming kaleidoscope. Curled and scarred, abused by the weather, by the grind of trains above them. They stared up from the filth, into his eyes. Frightened. Suffering.

Looking up brought no relief – they were everywhere. A whole lake of photos, and Nitic a twitching island in the center.

"What is it, Osh? You alright?"

"These pictures!" None of these people were alive anymore, that much was clear. The gravel and oil stains – the air itself said that plainly. Countless people, sobbing all around him. Osha wiped his eyes. "What happened here?"

"You don't know about this either? Where have you *been*, man?"

Osha mustered a shrug. Dying was embarrassingly self-involved.

"Story goes—" Nitic moved back toward him "—there was a protest here. And all these people were trying to block the Unionists from passing through. From getting up to Erobia to fight."

Osha knew where this was going. There seemed to be a trend in Nitic's stories.

"But the trains just kept going."

He wished he hadn't asked.

"And these pictures here – it's a commemoration. They put 'em right where the bodies were." Nitic hopped from one rail to the other as he spoke. "Nice gesture, I guess." Back and forth, as though trying to keep warm. "They did give their lives for us – whatever that's worth."

With a sluggish horror, Osha realized what Nitic was doing. He was being respectful. He was keeping his boots off their faces.

Unlike him.

He staggered up onto a tie, a new wave of grief rolling through him.

"People come every week, with a new photo each time. A bit risky, if you ask me – but that's resistance tradition."

*Resistance tradition.* The only weekly tradition Osha ever had was eating sweet bread and reading prayers – resentfully, at that. Some hero he was.

He couldn't even listen anymore.

But Nitic wasn't done: "You can count 'em, too, to see – eight, nine, ten. Ten weeks ago, this happened. 'Bout a month after you left."

Osha's chest ached. With each shallow breath, something tore just a tiny bit more. His gaze fell on a photo of a girl, not much older than himself. Hair loose and shimmering, almost stirring in the breeze. Cheeks ruddy. Lips parted. *Breathing.*

She blinked.

All ten of her.

Osha gasped.

Eyes back up. Back to the banality of the warehouses. Back to dull, ugly cement. "Enough of this, Nitic. Let's get out of here."

Nitic cocked a brow. "Show some respect, Osha. These were some of your biggest fans." And with a grim smile, he added: "They were only doing what you asked them to."

# THIRTY-TWO

Neta's home was inconspicuous, secretive even – barely a box on a warehouse roof, hiding atop two rickety flights of stairs. But its view of the bloodbath below was unparalleled. A row of columnar shrubs guarded the rooftop's edge, but did nothing to block the misery wafting up from the tracks. Nothing to obscure the gleam of the sun on the glossy photos. Nothing to dissuade Osha from his new conviction: to die just as miserably as he could.

It's what he deserved.

His grandmother had held the notion that *piety* could stave off misfortune. *Goodness* could keep disease at bay. And maybe she'd been right. It was only after causing pain that he felt any. Only after hurting Faia did he hurt.

And he wasn't dying until he went on air and ordered death.

Neta was herself when she opened the door. No pomp or regalia. Just an unwashed waif in a loose sweater. She didn't even say hello. Not that they did, either – no one said a word. Neta and Nitic just stared at one another, on and on and on.

Osha began to feel he should leave.

"I'm happy to see you, Nitic," Neta finally said.

"I am, too."

"Are you alone?"

"Aside from Osha."

"Oh, Osha!" That broke the spell. "Come in, boys."

Her place was as small as it looked – a cramped little studio, kitchen like a hallway – yet unexpectedly lavish. The furniture was plush. The cupboards (perhaps unsurprisingly) embellished with pearls. A full wall of glass opened onto the concrete beyond – but even that seemed more attractive when viewed through the window's graceful, polished frame.

The tracks weren't part of that picture, either.

The heady spices of nomad cooking hung heavy in the air, out of place among such finery. But welcome.

"So, when did you move in here, little cousin?" Nitic ran his fingers along the doorframe – the same woodwork as the window, the bathroom and closet doors, and even the kitchen cabinets: chiseled cherry waves, curling into themselves like stormy seas. "Quite the place you got."

"Just one perk of the business I'm in." She winked at Osha.

Nitic glanced from Neta to Osha and back again. "And what business is that?"

She puffed herself up, chin raised high. "You're looking at a full-fledged officer of the Pan-Archipelago Union!"

Nitic's jaw dropped. "So you've joined them?"

"Well, I—"

"To hunt your own people like animals!"

Neta crossed her arms. "Come on, it's not like that."

"Then what is it like?" Nitic's temper certainly wasn't slowed by grief.

"What did you expect me to do?" Neta raised her voice as well, not one to be outdone. "Just be a sitting duck—"

"You had a family, Neta! Remember them?" Nitic was fuming. "And did you use your backward authority to help them in any way?"

"I didn't know, Nitic!"

"How could you not know? *Everyone* knows! You knew when you *left*! Why else would you have chosen *this*?"

"I didn't know the *specifics*!"

Osha edged back toward the entrance, placing a hand on the door handle. "I'm just stepping out for some air."

"Just go!" Neta waved him off. "I shouldn't have you here anyway."

"Now what is this?" Nitic roared. "You *invited* him here!"

"I didn't think it'd turn into a screaming fit!" She was shouting just as loudly as Nitic now, a shrill soprano to his deep baritone. "I have neighbors, you know!"

"And what are they gonna do?" Nitic shot back. "Call *you*?"

Osha turned the knob and stepped out, unnoticed as he collapsed into a fit of coughs. Whether from disease or frayed nerves, he couldn't be sure – but any excuse to get out was fine by him. The fight raged on, easy to hear through the closed door, though drowned out somewhat by his coughing. Hardly relaxing, though – splitting open at the chest, overwhelmed by the taste of blood. It wasn't just his lungs, either – his nose had joined in, too. He fished a scarf from his bag, held it to his face and – wheezing and bloody – sat down on that haunted patio and waited.

He could hear the sobbing from the railway, even with the shouting, even with his rasping. How had he driven those people to do *that*? And the nomads, for that matter – taken away, murdered in front of their families – could he have prevented it? What exactly had he *done*? Just how much blood was on his hands?

A lot, as it turned out. He wiped them on his pants – they were dark enough, it didn't show. Not that it mattered. Everyone already knew what he'd done.

Everyone but him.

If he'd even *once* thought about the world around him – if he'd just *one time* read a newspaper – would he have been such a fool? If he hadn't been so hooked on avoidance. Drunk on Nadya. High on Julis.

Sweet, innocent Julis, who he'd also hurt.

Osha's family would not have approved of them. No holy book condoned their kisses. No passage blessed their tangling limbs. Never mind Julis's soft voice. His feminine eyes and lips. Never mind the coterie of masseuses and midwives who'd raised him with a woman's touch. He was a man, in spite of it all. The only son of seven, but a son, nonetheless. Tall, dark and scholarly. Bearded, more often than not. And Osha wouldn't change him if he could – though he'd been taught (with warranted suspicion) that men weren't meant for other men.

Not that he was urged toward women. It would've been a waste to prepare him for sex. It was work enough, preparing him for death.

So he met Julis unschooled. Knowing nothing of passion or touch or love. Nothing of desire but unworthiness. Nothing of his body but flaws. And Julis didn't understand. Optimist that he was, he simply didn't get it. Couldn't fathom the feral beast he stroked. Couldn't grasp why it would pull away. Why it would hide. Why it would leave.

Osha deserved his pain. He was a cruel, selfish murderer, and he should've died long ago. Alone, quiet, unknown. Not like this, taking the whole damn world down with him. He deserved every iota of agony this disease could deliver.

His breath soon came back, smooth and easy. He didn't want it.

Neta and Nitic returned, too, in typical Sobini fashion. Smiling. Laughing, even. As though nothing was wrong at all.

"Whoa, there." Neta startled at the sight of him. "You know your nose is bleeding?"

"Oh, is it?" He forced a grin. "Am I allowed back in there?"

She looked him up and down with a grimace. "Not sure."

Nitic spoke up then – "Oh, come on!" – though he looked just as uneasy. "This is *Osha*, for the love of God! Be a friend and *hide* him already!"

Neta shook her head and turned back for the door. "Just clean him up before he comes inside."

Nitic took Osha's hand and yanked him to his feet. Fast. Leaving him dizzy. "Is this gonna be a problem, Osh?"

Osha shook his head. "Just don't tell Neta."

"You sure?"

"I'm fine."

"'Cause I'm not doing this, you know. I'm just helping you across that border. I'm not cleanin' up your blood, you got that?"

"I got it."

"I mean it. I'm not takin' chances with this one."

Osha sighed. "You can't *catch* this from me, Nitic." In hundreds of years – *thousands* of cases – not once had this spread between people. Yet somehow this fact had never sunk in. With anyone. When Osha cut himself cooking, even Faia kept her distance. "That's a myth."

"Whatever you say." Nitic twitched. "Just don't *die* on me. I've had enough friends bleed out recently. I don't need to see you like this, too."

"I know."

"So stop bleeding, then!"

Osha's nose obeyed, surprisingly, in rather short order, and he was clean and ready in time to eat. Those two long walks – to the lake and back – had done wonders for his appetite. He even ate seconds. Spinach and brown rice. Pumpkin soup and spiced beets. And the rare, savory divinity of roast chicken. Valena had been so oppressed by vegetarianism that not even Waiter House could conjure up much meat, but now Osha's plate positively overflowed with it.

Neta looked smug. "And you always said I couldn't cook."

For dessert, she pulled out an official Pan-Archipelago Union suitcase. Nitic rubbed his hands expectantly as she unlatched it, revealing her secret little laboratory: a razor blade, a glass tube, a chunk of singed wood. Several small jars, some full of liquid, others with a dark resin paste. And finally, in five separate pieces, that beautiful monstrosity of a pipe.

Neta assembled it nimbly, like playing a familiar instrument. "You gonna join us, Osh? Since you're not feelin' good? Does wonders for my back, ya know."

"Well, I—"

"He's fine," Nitic cut in. "Just needs a good night's sleep."

"Actually, I—"

"No." Nitic glared at him. "Are you nuts? In your state?"

Osha gave up. It wasn't worth it. He liked the thought of drugging his pain away. He liked it a lot. But he didn't like the thought of those drugs wearing off. And besides, he'd earned what he had coming – what he was already feeling, in fact, creeping out from between his ribs.

He rolled out some sleeping mats and tried to make himself comfortable, watching from a nest of pillows as the room filled with smoke. The smell tugged at him, pulling him toward wild, messy memories. Dark woods and open parks, alleyways and barrooms. It'd been a game for the Sobinis to ply him with their medicines, to see what he wouldn't do, to define his nebulous limits. And Osha had been more than willing to play along, doing almost anything to escape his mother's echoing voice. Her nagging, her questioning, her fear – no matter how far he traveled, he just couldn't shake it. And it made him crazy.

But not crazy enough to smoke what Neta smoked.

And now he never would.

Just like he'd never see Sagoma. Never swim at Tida Cove. Never dive at the Cavri Cliffs. Never climb a volcano or smoke real tobacco. Never learn to sail or play a cello. It was infinite, what he wouldn't do.

Not once had he been with a woman – or a man, though he'd had the chance. Hell, he'd hardly even been with *himself*. Thoughts of being eaten alive had ways of invading these situations, and they were never very helpful. They'd slipped between him and Julis like a funeral shroud.

Had he even really *lived?*

He watched his friends smoke in silence. Hat off, little hairs dropping, skittering down his neck like spiders.

Spiders could lay eggs in his ears now, for all he cared.

Night fell, a bitter chill blowing in through the cracked window. Neta shut it tightly, but Osha still couldn't play the violin. "Trust me, I'd love it," she assured him, "but these walls are thin as paper. It's so I can hear folks comin' with those photos. I'm supposed to lock up whoever does that – it's part of the lease. But I don't work much after hours."

Her wink was lost on Nitic. "You do work, though," he snapped. "You work, and it's—"

"Stop, Nitic," Osha cut him off. "Life's too short for this."

He let it drop. Grumbling, he rolled onto his back, and they lay quiet below the glass. Crystalline and clear, stars clustered overhead in hollow wisps – hazy cosmic smoke at the chimney tops, frozen and scentless.

"Might be the city," Neta sighed, "but it's still a good view, am I right?"

"Fizzing," Osha replied.

"Fizzing?" Neta turned to him, a wry smile on her lips. "What even happened to you, Osh? How'd you get wrapped up with that scene in Valena, anyway?"

Osha kept his eyes on the sky. There weren't as many stars here as in Valena, and there was certainly no Nadya. But aside from that, he'd just as soon forget the whole city. "What scene?"

At his other side, Nitic began to hum. 'Farewell, Everything.'

Neta reached across and flung a pillow onto his face. "Keep it down, you," she growled. "I could arrest you if I happened to hear that."

Sandwiched between them, Osha was feeling very small.

"Really, though, what happened?" Neta pressed.

"I don't want to talk about it."

"Ever humble Osha." She sighed, stretching her arms with a yawn, folding her fingers behind her head. "One of these days you ought to take some credit for your work, ya know. You should be proud. Most northerners only care about border control. But standing up for *us?* That takes some gall."

Yet again, Osha wanted to cry. At this rate, he could make weeping a second career. Or a first, since singing wasn't a viable option anymore. "And how have I done that?"

Neta scrunched up her nose at him. "Alright, the modesty's getting a bit hard to swallow. You broke half the Balestro band out of jail!"

"I what?"

"You can drop the cover, Osh. I'm not in uniform right now."

"That song of yours, Osha," Nitic explained, "the one about the storm? You were plain as day about how to get outta that prison."

Nadya had practically written that one start to finish, its verses so laden with local colloquialisms that Osha had barely understood it. The wordplay was fun, though, and the melody had a lift, so to speak. An up-tempo pop that took his mind off his woes.

"Well," Neta hedged, "there *were* resistance members there. But before you got involved, nomads weren't ever part of those jail breaks. And now the Balestros are free, thanks to you. Laizo and Clesa. Julis! Like he didn't love you enough! If that 'singing in pastel' nonsense impressed him, imagine *this*! You saved their *lives*, Osha. You're the only one who gives a damn. No one else in the resistance cares about us."

Nitic glared at her. "They all care more than *you*, though."

"Based on what?"

"Based on your job!"

"Haven't you heard of changing the system from the inside?"

"That only works for the motivated."

Osha interrupted now, monstrously tired of everything. "With all that's happening to you guys, why wouldn't the resistance care?"

"Why would they?" Nitic sneered. "They're city folk. No high ideals are gonna change that. They think we're all criminals. They think we're made of *dirt*." Nitic studied his hands appreciatively. "Just 'cause I've got such a nice tan."

Osha's mind flashed back at that, to Perala House. To Uncle Nico and his twisted commentary – talking about appearance and inheritance like it had any connection with morality. No two resistance members looked alike, though – but *all* of them tricked sickly travelers into playing controversial songs on illegal radio stations. "This is bigger than that,

Nitic. It can't just be about how you look."

"Like hell it can't!"

"But that's insane!"

Nitic offered Osha a smile. "See, no one else says it quite like you."

"What I don't get," Neta cut in again, "is how you keep gettin' away with sayin' it." She shook her head. "Like you could sing for the ambassador himself and walk free."

Nitic snorted. "He might even dance."

"Especially to the songs about him!"

Osha buried his face in his hands. "I sing about *him*?"

Neta and Nitic went to pieces with laughter.

"Just don't get yourself killed, Osh." Neta patted his arm, but it was hardly reassuring. "I like having you guys around."

Nitic shifted on his mat. Osha was done for the night, ready to close his eyes, fall asleep, forget the world. But Nitic had other plans. "Osha's gotta get home, cousin," he said. "We're heading north just as soon as we can."

"No," Neta groaned. "Not this again."

"Maybe sooner, if you know any shortcuts."

"I don't know nothin'. You fools are on your own." Neta rolled onto her side, draping an arm over Osha's chest. "You should stay here."

Osha shook his head. "I can't."

"Why? Why can't we all just stay like this?" She snuggled close to him, soft hair against his neck. "We need each other."

"I'd love to stay, Neta. Really, I would. But I have to find a way back home."

"Well, you're cozying up with the wrong kid then," she murmured drowsily. "You gotta call your resistance pals if you wanna get to Erobia."

Osha rolled onto his side, turning his back on her, closing his eyes.

"Besides," she went on, toying with his thinning hair. "It's not what it was up there. Even if you got across the strait, you'd never make it to Oclia alive."

"Stop scaring him," Nitic hissed. "Osha's gettin' home just fine."

Neta yawned. "Osha's doesn't have a home." Sleepily, she nestled closer. "He's one of us."

# THIRTY-THREE

Osha awoke to the sound of his own moans.

Pain stretched out around him – smooth as a blank canvas, waiting for detail, begging for definition – covering the whole damn world. And deep within it he existed. A tiny thing. A worthless thing. Hardly capable of taking in air.

His sleeping mat was covered in blood.

His friends fluttered and flapped, pecking at him for words he didn't have. He shook his head, again and again, dizzying himself so they might understand. But it didn't seem to help.

Neta was shouting. Nitic was shouting. "Bugs, bugs, bugs." They beat the word back and forth like a ball.

"Call a doctor!" Nitic demanded.

"Are you kidding? You know what happens if he's caught here!"

Neta wanted them to leave. Nitic pulled Osha from the floor, shoved a rag over his face, and dragged him toward the door.

His things, though – he needed his things. His hat, his violin. "My bag," he managed. It wasn't clear if Nitic heard him.

They staggered downstairs, into morning light, noise, movement – mind-scrambling chaos. "You can't do this, Osha! I told you not to do this!" Nitic dragged him through the streets, past digmen, past children, past alley cats. Onto a streetcar.

Then sitting, at last, sitting.

Piece by piece, Osha found himself. Teeth chattering, eyelids like sandpaper. Trembling limbs. Death in his bowels. It *had* to be death – bubbling into his chest, hot and cold. Seeping into arms and legs. Poison.

Nitic touched him everywhere, but there was no comfort in it. He gripped his hands, his face, his shoulders – trying to make him still. "People are *looking*, man. You have to calm down."

He couldn't, though. He was kicking at the floor, desperate to get out. Out of this body. Out of this structure fire. He took it back now – everything he'd promised about penance and sacrifice. Honoring his friends, paying for the pain he'd caused. He took it *all* back. He was a coward and a hypocrite and a liar, and this wasn't war. This wasn't meaningful, and he wasn't heroic. This was hell. And maybe he did deserve it, but he wanted out. He wanted out *now*.

Yet Nitic held him to it. "Get yourself together, Osh!" Face drained, eyes crazed. "You haven't been shot!" Osha's blood gushed just the same, though. "Why are you doing this to me?"

A damn fine time for your trauma, Nitic.

The streetcar circled near the water, rising and falling with the yellow dawn waves. And beside the sea: a cemetery. Pink and pearlescent. A sweeping bay view. A fine place to be buried. What luck, dying in Sabelso.

But they didn't stop there. They were going up. Through the twisted veins of the city. To the park blocks. And there, Nitic lifted him, bruising his underarms as he hauled him outside. Into pulsing greenery, punctured by plazas. Stones and staircases swirling up to the capitol fortress: spires like a city of knives atop Sabelso's highest hill.

Osha vomited onto the sidewalk. Mostly blood.

Nitic pulled him close for a moment. Tears in his eyes. "I'm sorry, Osh." Then he pushed him away. To somebody else. Someone who helped him through a door. Led him to a sofa. Told him to sit.

Like he could do much else.

The morning light dimmed – dulled by windows of turquoise glass, chippings of aquamarine – and the growl of street noise was overwhelmed by human suffering. People surrounded him here, in various states of disarray. Some moaning, some crying. Some somber and still.

None of them were Nitic.

One was trying to talk to him.

Osha didn't understand. "Where am I?"

"You're at Sabelso City Hospital." They held a clipboard. A doctor. Maybe a nurse. On their white cloak: a triple-looped ribbon. A digman? "What is your name?"

"Osha Oloreben."

Wait, wait, wait. Should he have said that?

It was too late to take it back. It was scratched down and out of his hands. "And what is your chief complaint today?"

"I'm dying!"

"Do you have any conditions that—"

"Bog bugs." He dug his nails deep into the cushion beneath him, teeth clenched. Naming the pain only fed it.

"Bugs?" That was scratched down, too. "We'll arrange a bed. Wait here."

Where did they think he was going to go?

He looked at the people around him. A man with blood in his hair. A crying mother. A screaming baby. Osha doubled over and groaned. It was allowed here.

Doctor Digman wasn't gone long. Osha was helped to his feet and guided to a hallway. Infinite. Endless. He could barely stand, yet was expected to walk forever. Step after step, he stumbled, leaning his full weight into the stranger at his side. The walls wouldn't support him any – they were made of fabric. Limp, white fabric, hanging from the bars and pipes that crisscrossed the ceiling. Maybe plumbing pipes, maybe ventilation. Either way, this was no hospital. This was a warehouse.

"You'll have to keep up, Mr. Oloreben," said his human crutch. "Our wheelchairs are all in use. You're fortunate to get a room."

"Room" was a stretch – less than two feet of standing space, but Osha didn't care. He was done with standing. He collapsed onto the cot, grabbed the pillow and squeezed. Curled on his side, he rocked with it, slow-dancing cheek to starchy cheek.

Someone new came in then, tall and stiff in a sharp coat. Carrying Osha's bag. Astonishing to see it there. The man held it up like a severed head, delivered a short, trite eulogy, and shoved it under the bed.

Next came another clipboard. More questions. More demands. Osha told him to go, to come back after he'd slept, but the man just wouldn't cooperate.

"Speaking like that is forbidden."

"Like what?"

"Like that. This is government property. Our national language is the only one tolerated under this roof. Deviance will have you forced from the facility."

Osha pulled his wits together, which didn't take long – he didn't have many left. He'd been speaking his own language. His native language. The language of not having to die like this. "I'm sorry," he managed, in the language the man spoke. Not the language Sabelso spoke – the language Sagoma *wanted* them to speak. How in God's name was he supposed to keep track of this?

"Sit up, please."

These were profoundly unreasonable requests.

Osha's arms were lifted, his sweater removed. An oversized, grayish thing slipped on in its place. Lying on his back, he watched the same transformation befall his legs: shapeless, loose-threaded pants – pants someone surely died in – tied to his waist with a drawstring. At the foot of the bed, a roll of sheets was unfurled. Pulled over him like a coffin lid.

"We can't do much for your condition," the man said. Eyes on his clipboard, he started talking about drugs. Others shuffled into the linen cave, with rolling carts, metal trays, polished instruments and jars. Each had something to say, but Osha couldn't hear anymore. The words were mashed to foreign babble, voices drowned out by the screaming pain.

At least he could cry in his own language.

# THIRTY-FOUR

His dreams were crushing. Bombs dropping. Buildings burning. Bones breaking. Yet waking brought no relief. Osha's eyes opened wide, but his body wouldn't move. And all around him, ghastly figures. Blanched and bellowing. Circling close. Icy fingers on his face, he lay frozen as a corpse.

Until – quite suddenly – he wasn't.

With a wail, his arms and legs went flailing.

The room was empty. There were no ghosts – just curtains, drawn shut on all sides but one. And where they opened: a table. A pitcher of water, two pills on a platter.

And a man.

He sat in the neighboring bed, propped up by a stack of pillows, watching with a wide grin. "They really doped you up, didn't they?"

Osha stared.

"Unless there's another reason you're at fisticuffs with the air." He winked. He was around Nitic's age – ten, maybe fifteen years older than Osha – but possessed a boyish countenance that made it impossible to know. Large, dark eyes. Dimples. Hair stamped with a streak of white, but full. Wavy. Swept back like he was running free, even while stuck in bed.

Both his legs were in casts.

Osha rubbed his face. Gently. It was tender. "I'm confused."

"Well, I'd call that an improvement. How are you feeling, old boy?"

Osha thought a moment, mind and body having some trouble meeting up. "Um. . . ."

"Ha! Believe me, you're doing much better. I have to say, I was pretty worried about you."

Osha sifted through his memories – untangling, sorting, slowly piecing together a coherent story: Neta, Nitic, the streetcar. A vague horror gripped him. "Is it over?"

"Depends what's ailing you."

"Am I dead?"

"I certainly hope not! That'd leave me in an awkward position, now, wouldn't it?"

Osha frowned at the curtains – so threatening, just moments ago. But there were much more frightening things than sheets. What remained of his life, for example.

"My apologies," the man offered. "Let me introduce myself. Padin Kors, of Anatine."

"Osha Oloreben, of—"

"Osha Oloreben?" The man's jaw dropped. His whole face transformed, in fact, melted by some inexplicable, unearthly shock. "*The* Osha Oloreben?"

This conversation was exhausting. Osha was sweating.

"What an honor!" Padin drew himself up, leaning toward him, eyes wide. "Polon Larami."

Why did that sound familiar? Osha swallowed. "Excuse me?"

"My name. Polon Larami."

"How many names do you have?"

He laughed. A full laugh. A free laugh. "Forgive me. But you should know as well as any what we're forced to do these days." Osha's face must have been quite vacant, for the man then added: "Because of the war."

Osha repeated him. "The war."

"But *comrade*." He said it fervently, as if it meant something. "Your contributions to the movement . . . your work. . . ." He fumbled for words. "I must say, it's a true privilege to meet you."

Osha sighed, thoughts blown on his breath like strands of a spider's web. Weaving them back together was no small feat, but another triumphant connection was rapidly made.

Ah, yes. The resistance.

"Why are you here, Polon?" Osha asked, eager to change the subject.

Polon gave him quite the look. "I broke my legs."

"Oh." Osha nodded. "Of course."

The man sank back, hands behind his head, eyes on the ceiling like something he could read. "Got trapped at the temple when Nitosha fell. Three whole days, buried in the rubble. Pitch-black darkness. Voices all around, but nobody could hear me. Worst thing I've endured – worse even than prison. But every cloud has a silver lining." He smiled at Osha. "I'm here, aren't I?" Another wink.

Osha didn't get it. What was so great about here?

"Ferried down on a Union boat, no less. A Union boat!" Polon snorted. "With much ado, I might add. A PR move, of course. A photo-op for the ambassador. Rimolean raid victims, 'rescued' from the Erobian rebellion – or so it was spun by the papers. Makes no difference to me, though. Got me across that strait – that's all that matters."

Oh. *Ohhh.* He'd crossed the strait. Didn't Osha need to cross the strait? "You crossed the strait."

"On a *Union boat!*" He said again, louder. "They took me for a *priest!*" More laughter. "I was beginning to think I'd die in Erobia. Never get home, never see my fiancée. End up with 'Padin Kors' written on my grave! But now—"

"Wait, wait." Osha tried to sit up. Tried, but failed. Pummeled by dizziness, brains like pebbles in a wave. "Wait." He swallowed. "The Union took you across the strait?"

"Ironic, I know." He chuckled. "It was a medic ship. Only for the ill and injured, of course. Our Union would never take pity on, say, the hungry or persecuted. But wounded children make for good publicity, am I right?"

"What—" Osha wasn't sure what to ask. "If—" What had those doctors *given* him? "When—" If he could only think! "Do you speak Oclian?"

"Afraid not, my friend."

Osha sighed. Regrouped. Focused. "Can I get on that ship?"

Polon scrunched up his nose. "Can't see why you'd want to. Rimolean hospitals are a much better option, at least at present. Things are not well up north and—"

"I'm going to Oclia."

For a moment, Polon didn't speak. Lips parted, wordless. Looking hurt. "But comrade. Your services are needed *here.*"

Osha sighed again, heavily. "I'll be back."

"Well—" Polon eyed him uncertainly "—in that case. Yes. Simply show the nurses your papers, and they'll arrange your passage."

Papers. "I need papers?"

"Just your Oclian passport."

Osha's heart sank. "And if I don't have it?"

"Well, then you won't have much luck, I'm afraid. But that's not important. You can—"

"Yes it *is.*" Osha tried sitting again. "It *is* important."

Polon frowned at his casts – thoughtful or disappointed or annoyed. "If it truly is," he said, "perhaps my fiancée could be of service. She has a certain knack with false identification. How much time do you have?"

Oh God, what a question. "I don't know."

"I'll send a request with Comrade Coresh. He'll be leaving here soon, I'm sure. But the others—" He shook his head. "Yara took such a blow, I fear she'll never wake. And Phressa, as well. Conscious, but can't remember her own name!" He darkened, lips curling into a sneer. "There's no healing in this world. Not without justice. Not without freedom." Then the shadow lifted. He grinned. "But I don't mean to bring you down. We've so many reasons to look up! The Union, for one – footing our bill here." He laughed again, aggressively. "We're almost even now. Almost, but not quite. Not after what they did to me in prison." He shook it off, drawing a breath. "But tell me, comrade: what's your story? What left you in such a state?"

The sudden absence of Polon's voice was jarring. "What?"

"What brings you to this lovely establishment?"

No sense hiding it. "I have bugs."

Polon sat up at that, snarling: "Did they do this to you?"

Of all the reactions Osha expected, that was not one. "No!" That was true no matter who Polon was referring to.

"They do that, you know." Polon relaxed a bit, but his eyes still burned. "Infection's just another weapon to them. You've heard about the refugee camps, I'm sure. So much disease."

Osha looked down. He was no war victim. He was just a fool.

"Either way, my condolences." Polon's voice softened. "It's . . . *wounding* to learn this about you." His words were sincere. "You've done remarkable things, comrade. Immeasurable good has come from you. Without your communiqués, we'd be lost. And coded within such inspiring songs! What your music does for morale! You're a true hero."

"How long till your legs heal?" Osha fought the conversation's current once more.

"Oh, any day, now. I can already walk on them – with a cane, of course. Just waiting for the casts to come off, and then I'll be heading home. At last!" Polon's eyes glazed over. "To my beautiful fiancée!" Color in his cheeks. "It's been far too long." He looked drunk. "One hour with her, and I'll be good as new. I tell you, that woman could breathe life into the dead. Such sweetness! But you know how it goes. A handsome lad like you? Surely, you have someone like that in your own life."

"Not really, no."

"Well, you're probably the wiser man. Your heart's with the cause, after all – certainly more than mine. Ah, I'm just a fool for love." He sighed, gazing up at the pipes. "Wasn't much older than you when I met her. I'd been working with her mother – and now, *that* woman! *Married* to the cause. Absolutely fearless. Smuggled papers from the ambassador himself! But the dogs caught on, of course. Sniffed her out and killed her right in front of her children. Her *children*! Stuff of nightmares, I tell you. Rattled her son to the core. He'd been so full of life, too. Just loved nature. Talked to plants like old friends. But after that he wanted none of it. No friends, no fun. Let alone politics! That boy shut up and locked like a safe. Pushes love away. Replays loss like it's all there is.

"Depressing, that's for sure. But I promised not to drag you down.

"His sister's the one that matters, anyway. All that matters in the world!" Polon gave another sigh, a sleepy delirium dusting his eyes. "No kinder, gentler soul has walked this earth – yet she's a fighter all the same. Taken to our cause like a lioness. She won't fail her mother's memory, you see. Death's her business. The dead are as living as we are to her – and it keeps her honest. Committed. To the ancestors. To the cause. To her patients! My stars! From what I've heard, death's a slice of heaven with her. She's got a way with that energy. Channels it, they say – straight from the other side. If you don't make it up north, comrade, I highly recommend it. She's bliss for people like you." He smirked. "Certainly makes me hope I go first, if you catch my drift. But I'd never tell *her* that."

Osha stared at him. Flickers in his brain. Fireworks.

He knew this story.

"Forgive me, I'm rambling. Been cooped up here far too long! And it's just . . . I've waited so long." Polon drew himself up again, reaching toward his bedside table. "You should see her. A picture's worth a thousand words, after all. Or so I've been told." He shuffled through papers and envelopes, eventually pulling out a small photograph. He and Osha had to stretch to pass it between them, but they managed. "Perhaps you've met. She operates from the same city as you."

The photo shook in Osha's unsteady hands, but the image was clear: an alluring woman with a soft smile. Smattering of freckles. Thick, dark curls, loose over narrow shoulders. "Never seen her."

"Yet another tragedy. Believe me when I say hers is a rare and bottomless heart. You couldn't possibly imagine such warmth."

But Osha could imagine. Easily.

It was Nadya.

# THIRTY-FIVE

Polon was right about one thing: there was no healing in that world. Not in the Union. Not in Sabelso City Hospital. The air was rancid. The beds were stiff. The hour was a mystery, daylight dulled by the flags on the windows, forever flapping with the wind. The doctors and nurses had no time for compassion, and the curtains did nothing to dampen the moans of other patients. A grating song of terror and tears played on a loop, day in and day out, without end.

Yet whenever Osha's own voice rose to join that chorus, a dark-haired nurse appeared with a syringe. However recent his last shot, she never failed him. His arms went black with bruises, but he wasn't about to turn her away. Those gleaming trays, heaped with potions and pills, were as marvelous to behold as a holiday feast. There were drugs for pain, drugs for nausea, even drugs for that hideous itch. When coughing overwhelmed him, the nurse brought a balloonful of enchanted air. Just two deep breaths, and death wasn't half bad.

It was magic. Miraculous, old magic. *Chemistry.*

God bless the geniuses who retained this medical wisdom. Bless the historians who saved it from the murk of memory as floods and fires devoured all else. Bless everyone who made it possible for this sorcery to find its way into Osha's brittle veins.

God bless narcotics.

Osha had never been very religious, but life looked different from a hospital bed. Maybe his grandmother had been right. Maybe something *was* watching. Maybe if Osha showed enough reverence, some ethereal being would step in and make sure to keep the drugs flowing.

Until the very end.

Please.

Amen.

The same nurse who brought the holy offerings was also in the business of clean sheets, warm blankets for frozen limbs, and damp rags for bloody, sweaty faces. A thin woman with a hard jaw, she didn't smile or speak much – but when she did it was in Rimolean. Osha didn't know her name, though she appeared with increasing frequency. For each visit paid to Polon, that black-haired angel would check on Osha three, four, even five times.

"She *knows*." Polon trusted no one.

But Osha wasn't convinced. "If anyone here knew, we'd both be under arrest."

"Maybe we are. The food here's no different than in prison, believe me."

He did have a point. They were prisoners, in a way. Osha was chained to his bed by a dizziness that scarcely allowed him to sit, let alone stand. Depending on what he'd been dosed with, at times he couldn't even talk. And worst of all was the peculiar humiliation of using a bedpan.

Polon just laughed it off. "We're comrades in more ways than one! I've barely left this bed in weeks – I'm sure you can imagine what that means."

Osha didn't find it very funny.

But he didn't complain. Not about the chill in his bones. Not about the blood from his nose – or ears or eyes or anywhere else. Not even about the perfumed letters his cellmate received from a woman they both loved. Not even loneliness would tarnish his grace. He had to be grateful. He had his piety to prove. What would become of him should the syringe angel deem him unworthy?

He'd soon find out.

Polon was asleep when the nurse came to judge Osha's holiness. No witnesses as she scrutinized him. No one to vouch that he'd done all he could. "You haven't been eating," she scolded. "You should at least try. You're dangerously anemic."

"Anemic." Osha snorted. "Lady, I'm dying."

"And it's my job to fight that."

"No, it's not. Look at this place. It's your job to keep me quiet, at best. And you've done wonderfully, trust me. But you can't save my life."

"I'm well-aware," she snapped. "I'm quite familiar with your condition." Icy, that voice. Not what one would expect from an angel. "You're not the only patient here who has it."

"What?" Not *once* had Osha heard those words. Not in Oclia. Not anywhere. It was rare enough to become infected, let alone survive to make new friends. The only companions he'd found were in books, stories of the Great Thaw, the Marsh Plagues – back when no one knew the cause and sanitariums were packed to the brim. History – that's where his comrades were. Monstrous though it was, Osha took an odd comfort in imagining them all – crying and bleeding and losing their minds, just like him. Made him feel less alone.

But he wasn't alone now. Someone else was going through this, too. Right now. Under this very roof.

"There have been several cases recently. There was an outbreak at the Bridge Camp."

Osha's heart was racing. "Can I talk to them?"

The nurse turned her back to him, pointlessly smoothing the curtains. "Only one is still alive."

For a second, Osha felt let down. But why would he wish this on anyone else? He'd already hurt his mother, his sister, several dozen activists and God knows who else. Just how cruel *was* he?

The woman faced him again, bony and rigid. "You're on the wrong side of this conflict, Mr. Oloreben."

Polon was right. She *did* know.

"I'm not on anyone's side," Osha said.

"That's not what I mean." Her voice was quivering. "You're in the wrong province. There's nothing anyone can do for you here."

"That's why I'm going home."

She shook her head, wiping an eye.

Osha glared at her. "Don't tell me I can't."

"I've been trying for months." She drew an unsteady breath. "They let diseases cross borders, but not their victims." Pursing her lips, she stiffened. "But I don't need to tell you this."

A dim realization took shape as Osha looked at her. Something about the lines creasing her forehead, the tension in her shoulders. Familiar, all of it. And terrible to behold. "Who's the other patient?"

He had no reason to ask. He already knew the answer.

But the nurse answered just the same: "The other patient is my son."

# THIRTY-SIX

"Sagoma denies the outbreaks. Denies involvement, denies they're even happening. But you've read the reports. It doesn't matter the number of victims, so long as one or two are resistance members. Doesn't matter who else gets sick."

The nurse had found him a wheelchair – a child's wheelchair, but he was small. Especially now. Thinner every day. Sitting up took strength, and coping with her pace was a challenge, but this was a journey he wanted to take. Through soupy corridors and billowing sheets. Past wild-eyed men, weeping women, creatures so wounded they hardly looked human.

The other patients slept, mostly, or stared slack-jawed at the ceiling – dying, slowly but surely, from boredom.

"We left Nitosha in the fall, during the raids, but before the passage closed. Thought we'd stay in Anatine, but we never made it. Got held up at the camp when they found the water issue. It would've been easy to infect the tanks – we only had two, shared by a hundred people. . . ."

It wasn't hard for Osha to keep track of what he heard, but nearly impossible to respond. He'd been given a whopping dose of *something* before embarking. Not that he'd been in much pain. "I feel I should warn you," the nurse had told him, "my son is somewhat . . . further along."

"These were refugees of war, mind you," she carried on now, "so open wounds were par for the course. Over a dozen people fell ill within a week. I was the only nurse. I couldn't do anything on my own. So I brought them here. And here's where I stayed."

Osha's questions were blown from his head before he could ask them, fluttering off on the hard breeze, pressure heavy on his eyelids. He knew, abstractly, that they weren't going fast – that she was being gentle, taking corners with particular care. But try telling that to his body.

"My son had no symptoms for a month. But it's progressed quickly."

By the time they stopped, Osha was drenched in a freezing sweat. Not the best first impression.

"We have no children's ward," the nurse said. Pursing her lips, she added, "But you can't be picky with free care."

She lifted him from the chair and walked him through the fabric, into the dim room, toward a little wooden stool beside the bed. Osha fell onto it, taking a moment to center himself before facing the woman's son.

The boy's gaze was fixed on the ceiling, hair mussed by a nest of pillows. A child – no more than eight, though his face wore the wear of someone much older. Bruises devoured him, alongside bandages, blood and open sores. One sunken cheek: eaten clean through.

*God bless sedatives.*

"He's blind." The nurse fanned her fingers before her eyes. "His sight went just last week."

Of course he was blind. The whites of his eyes were shot with red, pupils blue and cloudy.

Osha's own eyes were on fire.

"You there, Mom?" The boy's voice was dry, croaking.

"I'm here." She moved around the bed and took his hand. "I brought you a visitor."

"Who?"

"Osha Oloreben."

The boy smiled broadly. "Osha Oloreben?" Unnerving to see joy on that face. "Really?"

Osha spoke up: "It's true."

"It's him! Mom, it's actually him!" It was a bit too much for the boy. He erupted with coughs, blood spattering from his mouth, spraying Osha's sleeve as he reached out to comfort him. Gulping for air, Osha stroking his hair, the shadow of unlived years fell over them like a quilt.

Then, gruesomely, his smile came back. "Why are you here, Osha? Are you here to fight?"

"I'm a patient, actually," Osha replied. "Like you."

"Were you wounded in battle?"

Osha turned to the nurse for direction, but she wasn't looking at him. Or her child. Or anything at all.

"As a matter of fact, I was." Why make the kid feel worse? "It was quite the skirmish."

"You're so brave," the boy whispered. "Was this in Erobia?"

"It was." He nodded pointlessly. "In Nitosha."

"I miss the north. I was born up north."

"Me too."

"You're kidding!"

"I wouldn't lie." Osha grimaced, glad the boy couldn't see him.

"Are you going to play anything for me?"

"I have nothing to play with. I had a violin, but I, um, lost it in battle."

"Well, I like you on piano best, anyway. I was learning the piano, too. To be just like you."

Osha bit his lip, eyes on the hole in child's cheek. "I'd say we have a lot in common."

"Mom let me stay up late for your shows." Life in those eyes, even now. Unnatural. "You sound just like you do on radio."

Osha couldn't keep this up any longer. "So, then—" he tried to change the subject "—you want to be a musician when you grow up?"

Wait.

Oh no.

Osha cringed.

The boy didn't notice his misstep. He was distracted – face contorted, labored breath replaced by a low, protracted whine. His mother leaned in then, waking from some quiet nightmare. Hands on his face, she shushed him until he relaxed, eyes dropping to half-mast.

The boy looked dead.

And his mother: wide awake. "You have to help us, Osha."

"How?"

"Tell them to hold their fire. A weeklong truce – nothing more. Just so people can travel."

"I can't do that."

"Yes, you can. Comrade—" (*Here we go*) "—if anyone can, it's you."

Osha shook his head. "Ask the guy with the broken legs. Maybe—"

"No." She darkened. "You listen, Oloreben." Teeth bared, she hissed at him: "You may not have long, but I have to keep living in this world." Cold fire, chin trembling. "I don't get to turn my back and die."

Osha looked toward the hall, eager to get back to bed.

"How can you watch my son suffer and do nothing?"

He turned back to the boy. Purple on his little chest, barely visible above the hem of his shirt. Festering scabs near his mouth. And in that wounded cheek – was that movement he saw?

He felt sick. Sick on top of sick. "I can do one thing."

The nurse wheeled him back to his room, but he probably could've walked. Anger was one hell of a fuel. Anger that, at thirteen, had him collecting beetles just for the pop, the crunch of exoskeleton, the gory explosion. At fifteen, compelling him to smash his mother's tea set to the floor. And at seventeen, pushing him to the brink of madness, cracking his household with a seismic force before running away in shame. Always so futile, this rage. Growing but never maturing. Never *doing* anything.

What it needed was purpose.

Polon was awake when they arrived. He eyed them suspiciously as Osha knelt to retrieve the bag under his bed. It rattled tellingly as he lifted it – his pills were still inside. There weren't many left, but they still outnumbered the years that child had lived.

The nurse startled at the sight of them. "How did you get those?"

"There aren't a lot. Less than a month's worth." He held the bottle out to her. "Here."

She took a step back. "You can't be serious."

"Your son needs them more than me."

She shook her head.

"I'm going home," Osha said.

Her head didn't stop. "You won't make it. Not without those."

The room dimmed, the nurse falling behind a sheer, red veil. Osha blinked once, twice – and down each cheek rolled a fat, sticky drop. He let them fall. His vision cleared. "I'm not who you think I am. I don't deserve these. Just *take* them."

He shoved the jar at her, and she accepted in mute shock. For a long moment, neither could do more than stare at the bottle in her hands. "Oh, Osha," she finally whispered. "How can I—"

"Go." He turned his back on her. Tired of her desperate face. Tired of her wrinkled brow. Tired of mothers with sick children.

Tired of people thinking he'd done *good* with his wretched life.

"Please, Osha—"

"Go before I change my mind!"

# THIRTY-SEVEN

The nurse didn't come round again. Osha was left to same rotating staff that cared for Polon. Drugs came when they came, not when he wanted them, and no extra blankets were offered. Time sharpened, along with his temper. The hours were long, rocking in filthy sheets, humming through pain, hair falling in chunks, mad at the world.

Memories beaded in his sweaty head, and not happy ones. No joy could shine through this murk. Osha could only pity his past self. How stupid he'd been to believe in happiness with *this* waiting for him. Plotting a future with Julis like he had one. Talking Faia down from rooftops, bandaging her self-inflicted wounds, hiding the knives – like life was even worth living. He was nothing if not a thorn in their sides. He'd have broken them both by staying, just as surely as he did by leaving.

He'd found his eclipse again, at last, in totality – but it wasn't magical or beautiful. It was just dark.

Increasingly, Osha's prayers strayed from the meddling God of his family. Their new target was death. And death was surprisingly quick to answer. It didn't make a personal call, though. It sent couriers: the directors of the hospital, two large men with prominent Union insignia.

"Osha Oloreben? Get your things. You're leaving."

Sagoman words. He'd have to focus.

Polon had given up trying to talk to him, turning instead to that pile of asinine love letters, reading and rereading them as Osha gasped and groaned just feet away. But now he snapped out of his reverie. "You can't kick him out! He's a sick man! It's your civic duty—"

"This is no business of yours, Mr. Kors."

"It's alright, Po—" Osha caught himself just in time. "Padin."

"This is illegal!" Polon ignored him. "He'll die out there without proper care!"

"We understand this situation far better than you."

Polon struggled with his heavy casts. He was trying to get out of bed. "If you understood the situation at all—"

"It's alright!" Osha repeated firmly.

"You know why they're doing this," Polon huffed. "It's because—"

"Padin," Osha laid a hand on his shoulder, both to hold him down and hold himself up. "I wish you luck with your travels. And please, send my best to your fiancée."

But Polon wasn't listening. Eyes wide and wild, he shouted: "OSHA OLOREBEN IS BEING ILLEGALLY EVICTED FROM THE HOSPITAL!"

And then he began to sing. At the top of his lungs, he bellowed it out: 'Farewell, Everything.'

Osha lunged at him. "Don't! Are you crazy?" The men gripped Osha's arms, pulling him back and into the hall. The song continued, though, so different in Polon's deep vibrato. The quiet build-up like a threat. Chorus no longer a cyclone of anguish, but a declaration. An indefatigable cry. An anthem. Julis had called it blue, dark blue, *too* blue – but it was surely a different color now. Osha hardly recognized it at all.

And like the accident it'd been written for, the song followed him. As he staggered down the hall, curtains were thrown back by those who carried the tune. Kisses were blown as he passed, tissues thrown, fists raised. They sang powerfully in their broken voices, from deep in their shattered bodies. It was deafening.

One director prompted the other on ahead. "Call headquarters."

Osha was led into a room. A real room, with real walls and a door. The chanting dulled as that box closed around him, but he could still hear it – crumbling into a cacophony of shouts and jeers.

Then the sudden bite of gunfire.

Osha's heart nearly stopped. Polon's probably *had*.

Julis always said that song needed a splash of red.

He searched desperately for something to vomit into. Next to nothing in this small space: a wooden desk, a telephone, the narrow sofa on which he sat. He spotted a wastebasket and tried to stand, but the heavy hands of the director held him back.

So he threw up on the floor.

The man staggered back in disgust, but Osha had no sympathy for him. He should have known better. This was a hospital, after all.

Not that it felt like one then.

The door opened onto silence. In strode two digmen – the older of them bedecked in a type of regalia Osha had never seen. He dismissed the director with a flick of the wrist. "You may leave."

"Sir, this patient has yet to complete the release forms to—"

"Do I look like I care?" He spat. "I said get out of here!"

Osha turned to the director: "My things—" But he left too quickly. And the digmen stayed. "You're not gonna need 'em."

They were going to kill him.

Just as well. Osha sighed, planting his chin in his palm.

"Call him," the head officer ordered.

The younger man took a seat at the desk, gleefully accepting the challenge of getting through to "him." Wires plugged, unplugged, and replugged into the phone's switchboard. "Oh, he isn't there? Well. . . . Yes. . . . Yes, alright then. . . ." The rattle of the receiver being lowered and lifted was giving the commander a twitch. His subordinate offered a tense grin: "Sorry. I'm on hold." And on it went. "Yes, transfer me. . . . A private residence? Yes, it's very important. . . . Would you be so—"

*Wham!* Explosion of pain. The room went black.

Blood gushed torrential from Osha's face, left eye absolutely shattered. Slowly, his vision opened, raw and red – and strikingly one-sided – revealing the looming commander, rubbing his knuckles with a smirk. He'd gotten tired of waiting. Osha gaped at him. "Why—"

The fist found his stomach this time, and Osha pitched forward, choking. Gasping. Vomiting again.

"What do you mean *why?*" The digman growled, poised to throw another punch.

"Please!" Osha begged. "I'm in enough pain!" There had to be better ways to practice Sagoman.

The digman bent low, studying Osha like a roadmap. "Just who do you think you are, northerner?" Hands clasped behind his back, he began to pace. "What kind of monster brings this filthy agenda to a *hospital* of all places? Corrupting the most vulnerable!"

"I'm sick," Osha panted. Hair falling like feathers. "I'm a patient."

"A likely story."

"Sir," the younger man pointed toward the receiver. "I'm having trouble hearing."

"Sorry." The commander smoothed his coat, his ribbons and buttons and braids. "It can wait."

Osha dropped his head between his knees, closing his eyes. It'd been an hour since his last injection. Not half what the black-haired nurse had given, but it did take the edge off. This would hurt a lot more later. If they'd just hurry up and finish him off, they could all get on with their merry lives.

Or at least the officers could.

"Yes, yes." The telephone chatter carried on. "Put me through, then." Finally: "Sir? Am I speaking with the ambassador?"

Osha looked up. Was he understanding this? This had to be a joke.

Like a rodent, the commander scurried toward the desk. "Give it to me! Give it!" Like a toddler. "No, no. Better – put him on speaker." He glared back at Osha. "Our *friend* should hear this."

The younger man did as directed, and soon the ambassador's voice came through, mid-sentence, full and unmistakable. "—have a little time. My niece has prepared a lovely meal, haven't you dear? Alright, now. What seems to be the trouble?"

"Regarding your request for information on Osha Oloreben."

"Ah, yes. What news do you have?"

"Sir, we've captured him."

"Captured him? Osha Oloreben?"

"He's in custody at Sabelso City Hospital, where he's instigated riots among the patients."

"Riots?" The ambassador snorted. "I have a hard time believing that."

"Sir, Osha Oloreben is a powerful—"

"I know who he is." The man sounded moody. Much less polished than on the radio. "Put me on speaker. I'd like to talk with him."

"It's done, sir."

"Mr. Oloreben, can you hear me?"

It took Osha a moment to respond – or even grasp that he *should* respond. "Yes?"

"Good, good. And how are you this fine day?"

He scraped up a cumbersome little sentence: "I've been better."

"Have they hurt you at all?"

The digmen stared at him, and he stared right back. Blood dripping down his face. "A little."

The ambassador's voice rose at that, hardening: "Rest assured, these officers will be penalized for their misconduct."

Osha's breath caught. "Excuse me?"

"Forgive me for not issuing a statement on your behalf sooner." The man's Sagoman was clear and slow, making sure he was heard: "I didn't realize it would come to this. I'll wire an announcement immediately."

The confusion was dizzying. "I don't understand." At least he was well-practiced at that phrase.

"Your underground work is very much appreciated, but I believe now it would be prudent to go public with your contributions to the security of our Union."

The commanding officer spoke up at that: "Sir, you cannot mean this." He clearly didn't know what was going on, either.

"Agent Oloreben is one of our most cunning infiltrators." Flagrant madness, yet the ambassador claimed it in the same buoyant, confident way that he claimed everything else. "Were it not for the information encoded in his broadcasts, my niece wouldn't have known of yesterday's attack. I have this man to thank for my very life."

Osha clung to his seat, room spinning.

"Impossible!" The commander exploded. "The disruption he's caused just by being here—"

"Officers," the speaker chided, "there will be insurmountable marks against your standing if you fail to follow my orders. You will release him at once."

"Yes, sir."

"And, Mr. Oloreben – one more word for you."

Osha cleared his throat. "Yes?"

"Do take care of yourself, my lad," he said in flawless Oclian. "I hate to imagine you holed up in some dingy hospital. You know the key to health is a good, hearty round in the outdoors. Or have you already forgotten our conversation?"

# THIRTY-EIGHT

The outside was jarring. Osha had forgotten how bright it was, how full of movement and laughter, noisy paper vendors, clothing boutiques, café debates and drunkards. And to think, just days before it'd seemed so stoic.

Blood and vomit soiled his clothes, but they were the only ones he had. No one had retrieved his things for him. The rush to get him out of the hospital had been too frantic, even after he was pardoned for his "crimes." But, like it or not, pity had often been his meal ticket – and a few kind souls offered him change just for sitting on a park bench, pallid and beaten. And he wasn't even asking for it.

He'd been issued new papers – special ones – stamped with an ornate seal, affixed with a small badge. But they protected him from all the wrong things. He was virtually above the law, yet had no shield against his own flesh. What good was amnesty when doctors thought him too disruptive to treat?

Most devastating, though, was his new nationality: he was officially Rimolean now. In spite of his protests. In spite of his pleas. War had its logic, and there was just no arguing with it. So that was that.

They'd smiled as they sent him out into the cold. "Happy birthday," they'd said. The date on his visa matched the one on the calendar, apparently. He'd made it to twenty.

He slunk away when the drugs wore off, into an alleyway, and spent a freezing night moaning in a pool of blood. Longing, illogically, for Julis's arms. He'd always been so patient when Osha couldn't sleep. Patient with his dark moods, patient with his dread. Patient even with his fearful, failed attempts to make love – fully crippled by thoughts of *this*.

Now *this* was all he had. He'd just have to hug himself.

No one paid him for that performance. Human sympathy could only encompass so much. But he was beyond caring what people thought. He had the abyss to contend with.

He felt a little better in the morning. He could stand. He could speak. It took a gargantuan effort to focus, but he needed to. He had to find a way to Erobia. He had to fight this thing while there was still time.

Hope was a hard habit to break.

So, weak and winded and shaken to the core, Osha set off for the Warehouse District. The occupation was nothing compared to the army of bugs reigning over him. Not only were the digmen tame by contrast, they were helpful – following their directions, Osha made it to Neta's without ever laying eyes on that miserable rail yard. He'd had enough grief.

Yet there always seemed to be more.

Neta's door was open when he arrived – hanging sideways, torn from its hinges – so Osha didn't have to knock. He just walked right in. Broken dishes greeted him, shards among loose paper, knickknacks and ash on the floor. The sofa was where he remembered it, but the chairs had been knocked over, upholstery ripped. Stabbed, it seemed. A pair of scissors lay on the rug between them.

But the violin was nowhere to be seen.

Osha trudged through the wreckage, toward the bathroom. The violin wasn't there either – or his shoes or hat – but his reflection was. Half his face, consumed in blue. Left eye even more swollen than he'd thought. Dried blood on everything. In all of his life, he'd neither looked so bad, nor *seen* anyone who looked so bad. That it was even him there, skeletal and swaying in the mirror, was nearly unfathomable.

"Neta?"

No one was home.

Gingerly, he washed his face, then made his way back to the main room for the scissors. Out of all this chaos, there was one thing he could control. One small pain he could alleviate. He chopped his hair to the last half-inch. Matted and cowlicked, it was nonetheless an improvement.

Cramping and drained, he sat on the sofa to regroup. There was no one here to help him. No one to get him north, to get him drugs, or even get him a cup of tea. Looking from one ravaged chair to the other, he didn't see a single friend.

But he did see blood. A dry puddle near the closet door. A smeared streak on the floor. A clump of golden hair. For as long as he could, he resisted the urge, the pounding desire to look up. On some level, it had already registered. On some level, he knew. But his mind pushed back. He didn't want it.

He didn't want to be there. He didn't want to be in Sabelso, or Rimolee, or the Union. He didn't want to be anywhere in the world.

But he still existed, appallingly. So he looked up. And with a slow and irreversible finality, he saw it. A bullet hole. Smack in the center of the door.

What were Neta's words? In the bowels of his memory, sunk in a swamp of suffering: *You know what happens if he's caught here.*

Neta was dead because of him.

Polon was dead because of him.

Countless resistance members, dead because of him.

For all he knew, even Faia was dead because of him.

He was wailing. Stomping his feet, clawing at himself. His body resisted, pain shrieking along with him – but there were ghosts inside of him now, and they would howl even if it hurt him.

He was the one who should have died. Should have stayed in Oclia and kept all this death to himself. But he'd clearly struck a deal. Somehow, someway, rage-blind and life-starved for just a few extra years, he must have made some awful trade – and now there was hell to pay. He could've died innocent, but no. Now there was blood all over his hands, and not just from his nose.

Osha's legs lifted him, dragging him to the closet very much against his will. With similar autonomy, his fingers rose to touch the splintered wood. Door slightly ajar, his trembling hand pushed it closed. Almost.

Something stopped it. A suitcase. *Neta's official Union suitcase.* Breathless, Osha bent to unlatch it. And there they were: painkillers.

Painkillers! Enough to last for weeks, as far as Osha knew. His mind raced through the process, trying to remember what to do. So many blades and resins, such disjointed paraphernalia. But it wasn't too complicated. He was a devotee now, after all – he knew how to dole out sacrifices, how to offer them to the gods. He knew how to twist the five silver pieces together into that snake-like contraption Neta so loved.

She wouldn't need it anymore.

"Who's there?"

A man's voice. Stony and cold.

Osha turned to see two digmen. Two guns pointed at him.

"What do you think you're doing?" They demanded.

He recognized one of them. A memory dimmed by brutality, by pain and loss and baffling revelations. But a recent memory. Only a week old, give or take. He'd flirted with Neta, that man, baby-faced and blushing outside the bank. Neta had called him Luca.

Luca adjusted his gun.

Osha snapped the suitcase shut and rose to his feet, lifting it along with him. "Where's Neta?" Only then did he realize he was still crying.

"Who?"

"What do you mean *who*?" He was bawling, in fact. "One of your officers!" My, was he distraught. Shouting at men with guns? He didn't know he had it in him. "Who you probably shot right here in this spot!"

"We'll shoot you, too, if you don't cooperate. Papers. Now."

Osha's lips curled, tears drying on the hot breeze of rage. He fumbled with the fabric of his shirt pocket, drawing out the nonsense of his new identity, holding it up for all to see. "Osha Oloreben."

The digmen glanced nervously at one another, a pair of flickering lightbulbs. But they didn't lower their weapons. "Put down the suitcase."

"No."

"We know what's in there. That's contraband stolen from the—"

"So?"

"So hand it over."

Osha stepped past them, suitcase firmly in hand.

Their gaze followed, guns like hands on a clock. "Neta was a thief and a traitor."

Osha pushed the remains of the front door aside. "And am I?"

They looked to one another again, angry at their uncertainty. "There are penalties," they blubbered, jabbering something about "order" and "lawless nomads." Useless words and they knew it.

"I'll be on my way." Osha turned his back on them. Then paused. "But one more thing. *Luca*." He met his eyes, smiling at the alarm he found there. "Next time, don't *kill* the girl you want. You'll never get far like that."

The digman's jaw dropped.

Osha stepped out through the door.

# THIRTY-NINE

A trip to the docks yielded nothing. Osha spent over an hour there, shivering in the spray of the waves, accosting sailor after sailor, to no avail. Each conversation went exactly the same: "Take me north!" he'd beg. "Anywhere!"

"You're mad," came the reply. "Do you know what you're asking?"

"Yes! I'll pay – just get me there!"

"I don't feel like dying today, kid. You're on your own."

The shrill notes of rejection left Osha's ears bleeding. He had no choice but to give up.

The northbound tracks were just as broken as he was, but he went to the train station anyway. There, he could at least keep dry. Under arching glass canopies, he could lay on a bench and rest.

But he didn't even get to sit down.

Any other day, he would've been shocked by what he saw on the platform – but he was all out of shock. He was out of responses entirely. No more moans, though the bugs kept eating him. No more tears, though his friends were still dead. He was resigned to this reality.

Resigned to the happy child waving at the station. Calling his name.

It was the boy from the hospital. Like Osha, he still wore the clothing he'd gotten there – disheveled, loose and gray. But unlike Osha, he was grinning, ear to ear. The pills seemed to have given him a second life.

Osha waved back, though something didn't feel quite right.

Then again, what did?

The boy turned away from him, toward the woman at his side. At first, Osha didn't recognize her: hair down and unkempt under a pointless little hat, wiry silhouette in a long, brown dress. The boy tugged on her sleeves, shouting and pointing. "It's Osha, Mom! It's Osha!" His voice was echoing all around them.

His mother was distracted, though, flipping through train passes and papers. Distracted enough that Osha's greeting startled her.

"Oh, God, Osha! Your hair! Your face!" She openly gawked at him, eyes flooding with tears. "What have they done to you?"

"Just look at that blood on his shirt!" The boy gushed. His own face was smooth now. Bandages gone, wounds healed. Those little pills worked miracles. "He's definitely seen some action."

Osha shrugged. "It happens."

What was it that seemed so strange?

"I'm glad to see you." The woman's voice had been steadier at the hospital. "I must say, it's a relief, after what happened."

"I was lucky."

"Yes, you were."

They stood in silence for a moment, the boy beaming up at him, worshipful.

"I'm leaving Sabelso," the woman finally said. "They've reopened the gates to Anatine. I'm going there. I need a change." She sniffled. "Where are you going?"

"Nowhere." Osha shrugged again. "I'm broke."

"Oh, Osha." She unsnapped the purse from her belt and plunged in a gloved hand. "Take this." She handed him money. A lot of money. Enough for any train ride, and then some. "You've been so generous. It's the least I can do."

"Thank you."

"And also—" She knelt and began rummaging through her bags. When she stood again, she was holding the pill jar. "I'm afraid I have to return your gift."

Osha took a step back. "No, no, no." But good God, did he want them! He crossed his arms, fighting the impulse to snatch them, to swallow them all right then and there. "I can't." The little boy looked so vibrant now, gazing up with such life in his eyes. How could Osha take that away from him?

The woman drew a breath, voice quivering as she asked him: "What good will they be to me?"

"They're for your *son*," Osha reminded her.

"Osha." She spoke coldly now, struggling for composure. "My son is dead."

Something inside Osha dropped – rapidly – down from his throat, to the pit of his stomach. Something icy and leaden. "What?"

"Do you see him with me? You think I'd leave without him?" Her teeth were clenched, but her words were clear: "He's *dead*, Osha."

The little boy kept right on smiling, eyes glued to him.

That child had been blind.

Osha shuddered. "I'm sorry." A wave of nausea rose and crashed, loud and mean and violent. The platform lurched and tilted, but there was nothing to grab onto. No anchor to still his stomach. No buoy lest he fall. There wasn't even a boat – just a dirty boardwalk, dropping precipitously to the tracks.

An engine was fast approaching, battling its own weight to slow, wheels screeching, whistle shrieking – much like Osha wanted to.

He wasn't as resigned as he'd thought.

"That's my train." The woman laid a hand on his arm, steely even in her gloves. "Please," she whispered, holding out the medicine. "Take care of yourself."

Osha took the bottle wordlessly.

"I'll keep fighting," she promised. "All the more, having met you. You'll live on, Osha. Through the resistance, you'll live on."

Osha swallowed, measuring his words carefully so as not to scream or vomit or pass out: "I'm not dead yet."

"Forgive me." She looked down, blinking hard. The train stilled, settling with a thunderous sigh. "My son—" The woman wiped her eyes. "His suffering's over. I'm just so sorry that you—"

"The doors are opening." Osha pointed to the train.

She turned to see. "So they are."

The nurse didn't say goodbye before boarding the train. She didn't even look back. But her son did. He grinned toothily and called out – one last echoing cry before disappearing through the door: *Keep up the good fight, Osha! Freedom or death!*

DENIAL

ANGER

BARGAINING

# DEPRESSION

ACCEPTANCE

# FORTY

Osha didn't have much when he boarded the train for Valena. His things had waxed and (mostly) waned on his trip north. He'd lost clothing, friends, all hope for survival. But since leaving the station and accepting his fate, everything had settled. Sensibly. Memorizably.

1 Union-issued suitcase

2 bleeding nostrils

3 weeks' worth of pills

4 articles of clothing (all currently on him), and

5 silver tubes that joined together to form an elegant, elaborate pipe

It was raining and night was falling and Osha was ferociously relieved to collapse into his soft, warm seat. Suitcase on the luggage rack, feet propped up, he felt almost good. With the nurse's money, he'd bought a first-class ticket, and still had plenty to spare. She'd given him so much, in fact, that he had a hard time believing her plans. "I'll keep fighting" seemed more like code for the opposite.

The resistance loved codes, after all.

Either way, Osha was to be pampered on this trip.

A blanket awaited him, folded neatly and tied with a ribbon. It served to cover his filthy, ghoulish costume – something everyone on board appreciated. A kind-faced stewardess brought him vegetable soup, and a cup of tea to wash down a pill. His health had been on a steady incline that afternoon, with the help of his medicine. No more bleeding. No more sweating. Only a deep, throbbing tenderness – absolutely everywhere.

After the stewardess took his dishes, Osha unfolded his seat into a bed, pulling shut a wall of drapes around him. Closed off from the aisle, he watched through the window as Sabelso's glittering lights faded on the horizon, and quietly cried himself to sleep.

He didn't wake till morning, as the train lurched to a halt. One of those small country stops, nondescript and forgettable, seemingly detached from signs of life. Osha opened his curtains for breakfast, only by chance seeing who was boarding. A kid. A short, plump teenager, not a day over fourteen. His dark face dimpled as he smiled at those around him, at odds with his aesthetic. He carried an identical suitcase to Osha's, and – as one would expect with such baggage – wore the costume of a digman. Placing his luggage on the rack, he locked eyes with Osha.

Then he headed straight for him.

"Junior Officer Ivo Vorshet," the boy announced, taking a seat across the aisle. He extended a hand. "But call me Ivo."

Osha nodded, unwilling to fold back his blanket for a handshake.

Junior Officer Ivo Vorshet looked disappointed, but recovered quickly. "Where are you heading today?"

This kid was downright perky.

Osha cleared his throat. It had been hours since he'd said much more than "thank you" – though he'd said that with glorious frequency. "Thank you" for a pillow. "Thank you" for a warm, fresh roll of bread. "Thank you" for a small cup of wine. "Thank you" for a weighted, herb-filled eye mask to help him sleep (and, no doubt, to cover his disfigured face). "I'm going to Valena," he answered.

The boy seemed taken aback. "But aren't you Osha Oloreben?"

Osha stared at him for a very long time before answering. "I suppose so."

"Don't you think you're running a risk?"

Osha coughed. It stung. "What am I risking?"

"Your *life*, sir."

Again, he could only stare.

The boy began to squirm. "Of course, I'm sure you know the danger. Who am I to talk to Osha Oloreben this way?"

Staring.

"Please forgive me."

Osha coughed again. "Don't worry about it."

"You mean it?" The boy gave a huge sigh, possibly his first exhalation of the whole conversation. "That really means a lot to me, sir. See, it's only my second week on the job, and I'd hate to make a bad impression. I was lucky to even get hired."

"Well, you seem like an upstanding officer."

He blushed. "*Junior* officer." Even with skin as dark as his, the red in his cheeks was unmistakable. "And it's Ivo. Just call me Ivo."

Osha turned away from him, toward the slow pull of bleak pastureland as the train forced itself into the foothills. But the boy didn't look away from him. His eyes bore down tangibly, each twitch in his thick suit louder than the one before. As his fingers took to tapping, Osha shot him a glance. "Can I help you with something?"

Ivo recoiled. "No, sir."

Osha faced the window once more.

"Well – actually."

Now it was Osha's turn to sigh.

"Would you be honest with me, if I asked you something?"

"Do I look like a liar?"

"No! It's just—" He looked around the cabin for words. "Do you think someone like me could be a *real* officer?"

"You're a bit jumpy."

Ivo grimaced. Magnificently, at that. Better suited for the stage than the military.

"You're young, though." Osha softened his tone. "I'm sure you'll grow out of it."

"Thank you, sir. You're a true inspiration." The boy relaxed. "See, the boss doesn't think a brown kid can even do the job. It's like I have to work twice as hard just to—" The boy withdrew suddenly, horrified by some perceived misstep. "I'm so sorry. I know I shouldn't complain."

This again. Perfectly good bodies, condemned on account of their *complexion* of all things. Osha drew a ragged breath. "Why did you take this job?"

No hesitation: "To be of service to this great Union."

"You—" (cough) "—you're putting yourself in harm's way for people who don't even respect you."

"I'm only a courier," Ivo said quietly. "I'm not in harm's way."

"But you will be." It wasn't particularly easy, breathing. "And for what?"

"Sir, I am a patriot. I believe in Sagoma. I believe in unity. And most of all, I believe in the old vision. You've seen how lost this province has become without history to guide it. Surely, you agree that our cause demands some sacrifices."

"You don't think some things—" (gasp) "—should just be forgotten?"

"You can't run from the past, sir." Ivo looked confused. "It stays with us whether we want it to or not. And if you don't face the parts you don't like, they'll eat you alive."

Osha tugged at his shirt collar, panting.

"You can't sleepwalk through life," he went on, "unconscious of the story you're part of. Unaware what your actions mean in the grand scheme of things." Such lofty rhetoric from a kid. He'd obviously listened well to the ambassador's speeches. "It makes you vulnerable. Sleepwalkers are known to get hurt, sir."

(Wheeze) "I'm aware." Osha wanted to pull the drapes.

"But me, sir – I'm future-minded. I've got my eye on the past so I can walk toward that blazing horizon without tripping on it!"

"I don't need a lecture on this," Osha snapped.

"Sorry." Ivo blushed once more, looking down. "It's just – you're a good man, and I'm certain you feel the truth in my words. See, I may not like how my superiors treat me, but my heart's in the right place. I'll prove them wrong. And our Union will be all the stronger for it."

Osha said nothing. The train picked up speed, scenery disappearing almost as soon as he saw it: a flock of sheep clustered under a tree, a churning river, a lonesome cabin.

"Sir?"

Osha coughed.

"I mean no offense."

"None taken."

"You're truly a hero of mine."

More coughing. A mouthful of blood. He swallowed it, disgust undisguised.

"And a hero to us all, after warning of the assassination plot. Though, if you want to hear my theory, I think—" He stiffened suddenly, eyes wide, mortified. "I'm sorry – *do* you want to hear my theory?"

"Of course," Osha lied, tired of his life.

"'Cause really, who am I to share my silly theories with the likes of Osha Oloreben?"

"Just spit it out, kid."

Ivo leaned across the aisle, drawing close, voice little more than a whisper. "I think the ambassador gives information to the resistance *himself*. There are defectors among them – and infiltrators, like you. And he had to know an assassination attempt could only benefit the Union. I think it was all *staged*." He pulled away then, smiling to himself. "Just look how strong the Union is in Valena now. And how weak the resistance."

Osha could barely pretend to care.

"Still, though." Ivo shifted uncomfortably. "I wouldn't risk it if I were you. The underground *is* active there, if small. And your wanted posters are all over the province—" he grimaced slightly "—not that you're *wanted*. But still. What if they recognize you?"

"Would they?" Osha pulled an arm from below his blanket, pointing at his swollen eye. "Even like this?"

"Well," the boy thought carefully. "Maybe not. Especially with the haircut. But I did. True, I saw the passenger list, so I knew where to look – but still." So much blushing. "I have to admit, you're smaller than I expected. No offense."

No bother. His looks hurt a lot less than these splintering coughs.

"It's just that you seem larger than life."

"Do I."

Ivo stared into nothing, brow furrowed for a moment. "What if they capture you, though? Interrogate you?"

"I have a good alibi."

"Of course you do. How could I have thought. . . ." Ivo berated himself yet again. "Forgive me."

A steward passed through. Osha held out a hand to stop him. "Cup of tea, please."

"Right away, sir."

Ah, first class.

As the man hurried off, Ivo continued to fidget. "Um, Mr. Oloreben? Might I ask, if I may, how did you get that?"

Osha pointed to his eye again. "This?"

He nodded.

"Let's just say there's a lot of fighting up north."

# FORTY-ONE

Ivo Vorshet disembarked at the very next stop. Lifting his luggage from the rack, he held it up for Osha to see. "Classified information here!" he stated proudly. "I deliver important messages, too – just like you."

Then he left, and Osha got back to the business of being coddled.

He took his medicine in full doses, three pills a day, always with a sumptuous, if small, meal. Appetite was a fickle thing, but knowing these were among his last meals compelled him to eat. They were decadent, too. Fruit and goat cheese with honey, egg scrambles, warm sourdough sandwiches. One dinner was even *Oclian-themed*: seaweed salmon, noodle soup, vinegar water, and bean pudding – with the wrong kind of bean, but close enough. On small wooden platters the food was served, three courses at once, so he could have dessert first if he liked. True opulence.

He locked himself in a bathing stall to wash his hospital clothes – drying them on a heated towel rack while he enjoyed a long, indulgent shower. Refreshed as he could be, he made his way to the dining car and borrowed a book from the library. The selection was small, just a couple shelves, but Osha had never seen anything like it on a train.

Not that he'd seen showers and heated towel racks on trains, either.

He'd never ridden first class. Never lounged on the soft, fat cushions of the viewing cars, where he could read or doze or watch the stars through rounded windows as they climbed up the mountains and into the sky. If the train was the last thing he ever knew, he'd be perfectly happy – and he made that clear to whatever god might be listening. Let this lavishness be his grand finale.

Not even his grandmother had prayed so fervently. He was becoming a regular zealot.

But his prayers were ignored. Death didn't pick its victims from first class.

It hung around, though. Osha caught its reflection each time he passed a mirror – and never more sharply than when he finally opened his ruined eye. His face was slow to deflate, and by the time the swelling subsided enough for him to peer out, he was already used to the lopsided darkness – and it was a shadow that didn't lift.

It took him a minute to understand. In that little bathroom, his eye certainly *looked* open – bloodshot and deformed though it was. And yet the left side of the room remained dark. He ran his fingers over his lashes, pushed the lids apart as much as he could stand. Yes, it was wide open. But it saw nothing at all.

He could have been angry. He could've cursed the digman that hit him, the doctors that diagnosed him, the billions of gluttonous ancients that cooked the world, loosing this plague from the ice. But why bother? What was one lost button when the whole suit was wearing out? Soon, he'd have to throw the whole thing away.

A bevy of officers boarded at Anatine. A gray huddle at the door, arms drawn. Osha couldn't see them if he faced the window, so he faced it. Blindness, perhaps, had its perks.

A fine time to die, sick of the world.

It was dawn when they reached Valena, just like when Osha left. The digmen disembarked alongside him, but scattered quickly, leaving him alone with that wretched, wailing fog. He lingered on the platform, legs trembling, head spinning, suitcase heavy – until curiosity dragged his feet to a small kiosk. A wall of timetables, train schedules, the occasional local event. A play at Barsamina Theater. An ad for a gardener.

And wanted posters.

Just three: a murderer, a rapist, and him. The photo was cropped, Loren's hands barely visible as they pulled him from the camera. Hair matted, eyes bulging, face strained – it was an unflinching portrait of a suffering man. A frightened man. A man who'd just been shot at.

He looked good. Much better than he looked now. Sepia suited him, the blood on his face easily mistaken for shadow.

A gloved hand slipped into view then, blocking the poster. Tearing it down. Crumpling it up. An officer. "Sincerest apologies, sir." He bowed curtly and walked away.

Osha sighed. What a life.

He wandered toward his streetcar stop, where he'd once played and sang and believed in the future. The vendors were setting up. Taffy was being pulled. Commuters rubbed their eyes, steaming drinks in hand. But he was no longer part of this world. Half-in, half-out, just like his vision.

He savored the air, regardless, that sweet aroma flooding the intersection: rolls and wraps and cakes of bean paste, berries, nuts and cheese. He made his way to the pastry cart without thinking, raising his hand to wave without looking up.

Though he really, really should have.

But it was too late. He was right there, now, not two feet from the vendor. Two feet from her tense shoulders and the fingers crawling over them – creeping slowly, quivering, sliding up and down her neck. Knobby, green and rotten, tangling in her hair. And just behind her, a contorted, ancient face, hissing in her ear: *So soft . . . such beauty. . . .* A warped and wounded old hag, dry-leaf words tumbling and crackling on her frigid breath. Osha could feel it from where he stood. Like ice.

Surely, the pastry clerk was aware of this. The lines of her face, her dull glare – she knew. Osha had never seen her smile, not once in months. No telling if she could *see* the dead woman, but she was undeniably, inexorably, horribly aware.

He was moving away without meaning to. Step after backward step. Staggering. Then turning around entirely, desperate for something soothing. Something solid. Something less dead.

But there was no escape.

Everywhere he looked, milling through the morning crowds, were people who simply should not have been there. He'd seen them before, brushed against them on his way up from the train station. That brown-haired gentleman. The girl in the blue dress. But he hadn't *really* seen them.

"Are you well, young man?"

Osha startled. It was alright, though. The woman speaking now was alive.

"Fine, thanks."

"You look like you've seen a ghost."

He turned from her, fixing his eye on the streetcar stop. It wasn't far. It wouldn't take long to get there. He'd only have to pass seven, maybe eight dead people, flitting above the streetside graves like they lived there.

Well, maybe not *lived*.

He took a breath, tucked his chin, and waded in. Slowly at first, then faster. A few of them reached out, fingers cold and tingling under his skin – but he made it. Smashed shoulder-to-shoulder with the living, aching and bruised, he boarded the streetcar. Suitcase in hand, he could almost pass for a businessman. Only his stained hospital clothes, broken face, and irrepressible look of terror gave him away.

As it was, people were staring.

One woman in particular wouldn't take her eyes off him. Hair unkempt, makeup slithering in streaks, she outright glared.

Osha wasn't embarrassed, though. He was too distracted by the bullet hole in her neck.

*What's in the suitcase?* Her voice was choked with emotion. And blood.

Protectively, Osha pulled it close.

*He's in there, isn't he?* He shook his head, but she wouldn't have it. Throwing back her head, she roared: *You have his ashes!*

"No, no!" Osha rose on instinct, stumbling into other passengers as he backed up. Like scandalized dominoes, they fell away from him.

*I know you have him.* She pointed at the living. *And so do they.*

"They can't even see you," Osha whispered. "You're dead."

Her head dropped, lips curling up into a snarl. *Give him back!*

She lunged at him.

"No, no, no, no!" Osha raised the suitcase like a shield, but she dove right into it. *Through* it. Into nowhere, leaving Osha alone before his captive audience.

They gave him plenty of space as he returned to his seat.

"Apologies," he offered uncertainly. "It won't happen again."

And it didn't.

Not inside the streetcar, at least.

Outside, however, Valena's dead lined up for a hero's welcome. The whole city overflowed – matted and wet, flickering and fiery, twisting and screaming and splashing against the streetcar in waves. Osha did his best to avoid the windows, eyes down until they reached the North Gates.

And there, he plunged into the woods without a backward glance.

# FORTY-TWO

Waiter House glistened like a gem in the trees. A dirty, mossy gem – but a gem, no less. The stairs cracked under Osha's feet as he climbed them, wood rotted, railing warped. He paused on the porch, listening for any voices beyond the ivy overtaking the walls. There were none.

The sun was rising higher, mist quieting as it dissipated. A light wind stirred the fresh, dewy green: tiny flowers budding in the grass, red shoots sprouting from dark soil. It was almost spring here. Already. His birthday had only just happened, and yet spring.

Pity he couldn't enjoy it.

He turned his back on life and opened the door.

The house gave a sleepy yawn as he stepped inside. A musty aroma – tea and smoke and old perfume – dampening the sweetness of Loren's orchids. The flowers watched as he dropped the suitcase and kicked off his slippers, the symmetry of their colorful faces a little too human.

The furniture was sullied, the floors stained – but the eclipse still beamed. Just a sliver of sun remained, and from its shrinking light blew an almost musical chill. A tinkling, like the chime of tiny bells. He'd heard it before, with Faia, that long ago afternoon. He'd always wondered if he'd imagined the sound, so meek and subtle. But here it was again. Real.

As real as Nadya Perala, sitting right there on the sofa. Alone. Radiant. Gaping at him. "Osha! What are you doing here?"

He sank into a chair across from her, into the warm, bubbling pool of her presence. Sore limbs growing light. "It's my house." She didn't look half as pleased with their reunion as he was. "Last I checked, at least."

He noticed Loren now, too – hanging in the kitchen door like a coat. Osha offered a smile, but didn't get much in return.

Maybe they'd been fighting.

Nadya kept her eyes on Osha. "What happened to you?"

"I took a little trip." He was in no mood to reminisce. "Is there any tea? I could use a cup."

"The stove won't work."

No matter. The relief pulsing off of her was really all he needed.

"There's no water, either."

"What are you doing here, then?" Osha turned toward Loren. "You don't have to stay here like this."

"I know," Nadya spoke for him. "No one comes anymore."

"Aside from you and Loren," Osha corrected. Loren's books were on the table. Orchids, still scattered through the decay.

Loren said nothing. Sunken, head hung, skin all but drained of color. Strangely disheveled, too – not even wearing his glasses.

Must've been one hell of an argument.

Nadya also avoided his eyes. "Loren. . . ." She turned her gaze out the window, toward the lush verve of the forest.

Osha shook his head. He didn't have time for these two. He stood and moved toward the kitchen. Loren stepped aside to make way, brow furrowed in concern. One hand raised as though to touch him. Fingers reaching out. "Don't," Osha snapped. "I'm fine."

Loren drew back, looking hurt. Shocked, even. As though he expected a happy reunion. Mutely, he followed Osha through the door.

"Did you say something, Osha?" Nadya called after him.

"No." He tested the sink faucet, and out came water. Clear and clean and at his service. "You sure you don't want tea?" Kettle on the stove, little flames alive below it. Cabinets stocked, almost to overflowing.

"If you can make it—" Nadya rose "—I'll drink it."

Osha shot Loren a glance. "Loren?"

Loren just stared at him.

"Loren," Nadya murmured again. Taking a seat at the dining table, she pressed her chin to her palm. "Loren left when the others did."

"Left, did he?" Osha smirked at her brother.

Loren's mouth hung open.

"Things have been rough here. The riots, the occupation. . . ." Nadya sighed. "He went east to stay at the High Temple."

Osha narrowed his eyes. "And?" Why wasn't Loren saying all this?

"He'll come back when this all blows over, I hope."

"Come back?"

"From the High Temple."

"You telling me he's still there?" He almost laughed. "I'm not *all* blind, you know."

Nadya blanched. "What do you mean?"

"Come on, you can tell what happened to my eye."

She swallowed. "Well, yes. And it looks dreadful. I would love to know what happened."

Osha snorted. "I bet you would." She probably already did, in fact, with informants on both sides filling her in.

"Osha, what's going on?"

Not that her lies bothered him much. Not now. Not with her rippling aura washing over him.

"Please don't be cross," she cooed. "So very much has happened since you left."

The more she focused on him, the stronger the waves. Rolling with increasing speed, all but knocking him down. He'd forgotten the intensity of this feeling. As potent as any drug in Sabelso, and then some. He could hardly fill the tea strainers.

"I've been trying to care for your house. I come as often as I can." She looked around helplessly. "But I can't seem to do for it what you did. Maybe when Loren gets back—"

"What is this *about?*" Osha looked from brother to sister and back again. This was the most bizarre version of the silent treatment he'd ever witnessed.

Nadya looked down. "I'm sorry."

Loren drew closer though, face unreadable. Curious, perhaps. Or frightened. Or outright horror-stricken. He was trembling. Quaking and quivering in the strangest way. Like a candle it seemed, casting an uneven light into the kitchen. Almost like the eclipse.

Or a ghost.

*Exactly* like a ghost.

Osha staggered away from him, knocking over his teacup.

"Are you alright, Osha?"

He kept edging back, clasping the counter for support. "Nadya, *where* is your brother?"

"I told you. He's at the High Temple."

The kettle started to whine.

Loren was steaming. *You can see me, can't you?*

Osha turned and fled.

# FORTY-THREE

As it turned out, the end of life wasn't so different from the beginning: caught up in minutia, textures and smells. Vexed by limbs and bodily functions. Inconsolable sobbing. Frequent naps.

Unless Nadya was there, Osha rarely left his bed – much less his room. At most, he paced, heavy and slow, carving out small channels through which his tears could flow. No worries over water damage – Waiter House mended itself just as surely as his body didn't.

He made no music, though instruments still littered the loft. He couldn't stand being near the radio, and the whole vile contraption remained as well. People must have left in quite the hurry, leaving so much behind. How were they supposed to wage war in comfort and safety now?

Ultimately, he covered the station in a sheet. Just one more phantom. Of many.

Rain brought the rage – disembodied shouts and threats, echoing through the trees. Wind brought the weeping of women. And fog, of course, brought the ships. Two, sometimes three of them. Burning. Slow-sinking, blazing torches. Perhaps there'd been a collision – an incident in the rocky shallows. Osha couldn't know for sure; the disaster was old, something time really should have cleaned up by now. But it repeated and re-repeated, with the idiot redundancy of a skipping record. Passengers, crumbling from the decks like dry cheese. The smack of lifeboats on the water, the screams, the cries – they kept him up at night.

And a silent bay wasn't much better. In the calm, corpses floated like litter, bloated in the glittering sun, life vests tattered, hair splayed around them. And Shipwreck Beach: strewn anew with its ancient debris.

Osha tried to keep the curtains drawn, but again and again he'd find them open.

*You're killing my orchids. They need light.*

Loren was the only house ghost, but he was inescapable – following Osha from room to room, into the dark of his eyelids, even his dreams. But at least he wasn't counting pills anymore.

He had other demands.

*When are you going to tell my sister?*

"When you tell me how you died."

*It's not important.*

"Does Nadya know?"

*That's irrelevant.*

"Why can't she see you?"

*I'm no guiding spirit. I'm just dead.*

"Then why are you here?"

*Look, I'd leave you alone if you would listen! Nadya wants to help you, but you have to ask. It won't work if she forces it. Just swallow your pride and tell her, for everyone's sake. No one wants to see you like this – and you're hardly hiding it.*

Loren was right about that. No sweater could disguise Osha's skeletal frame, and Nadya had surely heard him coughing and crying and talking to the walls. She was a priestess, after all. She knew. She was just being polite.

But Loren was wrong about Osha needing help. He didn't want it. He didn't deserve it. And, frankly, when it came to Nadya, he didn't trust it.

*You have to forgive her, Osha.*

"You don't know what she's done to me, Loren."

*Yes, I do. And she didn't mean it.*

"She didn't mean it? Manipulating my lyrics? Making me an outlaw!"

*Blame Iza, blame Holic – but don't blame my sister.*

"I should blame you! You could have just *told* me!"

*I didn't want to get you involved.*

"I was already involved!"

*Fair enough. Take it out on me. But go easy on Nadya. She doesn't take advantage of her patients anymore. Not on purpose, at least.*

"I'm not her patient."

*Oh, you're her patient, alright. Whether you like it or not.*

Again, Loren was right. Nadya came almost daily, and not once did she ask him to break the law. She asked nothing, in fact. She kept entirely to herself, staring at the bay, watching the bodies drift like she could see them. It was Osha who used her – seeking her out, thirsty for relief, guzzling her rarefied waters. They didn't speak much, and it wasn't clear why she kept visiting. But Osha wasn't about to question his anesthetic.

He ate his pills like candy, steeling himself as they dwindled. Jaw locked, lips sealed. With only one day of rations left, he still didn't say a word.

Instead, he retreated to the cellar, uncorked some wine, and prepared for battle.

And that's where Nadya found him, half a bottle in, head in his hands.

"At least use a glass, Osha." She unhooked two, the hanging rack shifting and chiming along with her earrings. Taking the bottle, she filled one for each of them. "Now—" she placed one in his hand "—won't you please tell me what's troubling you?"

She was beautiful. Everything about her positively sang. Into his bones she burrowed, a humming vibrato that relaxed his muscles, loosened his heart. A melody to sink into. Thick bass, airy flutes, highs and lows closing around him, swallowing him, digesting him in the most spectacular way. He wanted to melt into her. To *be* her.

But still, he didn't tell her.

"I wish Loren was here. It's obvious that you need someone to talk to, and I know how close you were." She smiled faintly. "But you can trust me, too."

Osha could have laughed. So many things were wrong with what she said, he didn't know where to begin. So he started with the facts: "You talk to dead people, right?"

She cocked her head. "Ancestral spirits, yes." Tingling words, turning Osha's head to sand. "Why do you ask?"

"Does it get tiring?" He was slurring. Half a bottle was more than enough to topple his defenses. Especially with Nadya there, he was done for. "Do you ever get a break?"

Loren rolled his eyes, his whole form following like a spiraling wave. He regained shape quickly, though – much to Osha's disappointment.

Nadya looked thoughtful. "They only speak to me when I need them. When I call. Or if there is something I should know – like when I met you." Her hand on his knee. Shock waves. "What's going on, Osha?"

Loren's twisting, ethereal mass unleashed a barrage of *tell hers*.

Osha took a sip. "What about ghosts, though?" he pressed. "Not ancestors – just dead people."

Nadya kept her eyes down, gazing into the swirling red of her wine. "I'm not really bothered by ghosts. I learned long ago not to let them in."

Wonderful. "Tell me how."

*You don't have time for this, kid. You're too far gone.*

Osha hissed at him: "Who asked you anyway?"

Nadya stiffened. "What did you say?"

"Nothing." He grinned at her. Feigned a cough.

Eyeing him quizzically, she straightened. "Well, if you want to know," she began, "it's a matter of sensitivity. Of making yourself still, feeling out and understanding the peculiarities of a place or thing. It takes years of practice to really know what you're doing, and the spirit realm is not to be taken lightly. You encounter all sorts of unsavory creatures."

"You're telling me." Osha raised a glass to that, but Nadya didn't. She took a long, slow sip. "I wish we could go to the temple."

"Why can't we?"

"Oh, Osha, don't you know?" She looked at him like a stranger. "They took the temple. They made it the Union's regional headquarters." One more drink. "Tore down the greenhouses, burned all the plants—" and another, dripping a little "—the whole priesthood's hiding or in jail." She drew a breath, stilling the quiver in her voice. "Can you believe that?"

"So that's why you're here."

Nadya looked hurt. "Oh, Osha, no! I'm not hiding. I *want* to be here."

"Here? In this house?"

"With you."

He lifted his glass to block his grin.

*I told you.*

Perhaps all was not lost. Perhaps he could still know love. Dodge his doubts and go with Nadya where he'd failed to venture with Julis. Beyond fumbling hands and breathless confusion. Into the oblivion of oneness. Under Nadya's spell, his nerves couldn't stop him. His nerves weren't even part of the equation. He took a sip. Licked his lips.

*Get your mind out of the gutter, Osha. You're sick. She wants to help you.*

"But the plants are all gone."

Nadya shook her head sadly.

*It doesn't matter – she can still help. Just tell her.*

"What do you need, Osha?"

Osha faced her squarely, then. Took in the coppery gleam of her eyes. The soft pink of her lips. Leaned closer. Raised his brows.

*Oh my God, Osha, just tell her!*

"Screw off, will you?"

"Osha!" Nadya drew back, appalled.

"I'm sorry, I'm sorry." He grimaced. "I, um, guess I'm kinda drunk."

*That's the least of your problems.*

"Osha, what's going on with you?"

"Things have just been a little rough, that's all."

Nadya sighed, air going cottony around her, and tipped her glass back one last time. Slurping the final drops. "Likewise." Lifting the bottle, she squinted into its depths. Then frowned. "It seems our problems never cease. Now the bottle's empty."

"We'll just have to open another."

She didn't protest that.

They built a fire in the hearth – a big one – from wood that sprung eternal, just like the wine. Like the bread that appeared when they got hungry. The instruments, when Osha wanted to play. Or the laughter in their throats, as desperate to escape as they were. Laughing as Osha's life went up in smoke. Laughing as the world burned.

"This house positively spoils you!" Nadya declared, popping open a third bottle. "Pity, though, it won't do a thing unless . . . well. . . ." She trailed off.

"Unless what?"

"Nothing." Nadya beamed, a gush of tranquilizing warmth. "Who am I to complain about free wine?"

*Tell her!* Loren pleaded with him. *This is driving her mad.*

"I can keep all the secrets I want," Osha whispered. "She sure does."

"What are you muttering about, Mr. Oloreben?"

"Just that I always thought you were so pious," he said loudly. "But look at you!"

"Everyone has to forget their troubles now and then."

"I'll toast to that!" He threw his drink back: one swallow for those he'd hurt, one for the penance he'd pay, one for the black splash of nothing at the end. "Could be worse, though. At least you've got prestigious relatives if you really need help."

*Come on, Osha.*

"Is that what you've heard?"

"I've heard more than you think."

*You've got to be kidding me.*

"Have you now? And what about you, northerner? All these months, and I hardly know more than your name. What were you up to when you were away?"

"The usual. Running errands for the resistance."

*You guys are making me sick.*

"That's no job for someone in your condition."

"Well, I'm not always this drunk."

*Just say it! She obviously knows!*

"This is my last chance to enjoy life, Loren," Osha mumbled. "Just let me."

Nadya shook her head at him. "What *do* you keep rambling about?"

"This cellar's getting too small for me. Let's go get some air."

Osha wanted Loren to be housebound, locked in Waiter House's skull like the half-formed idea he was. But he followed them out the door, easily. Almost like he had no choice, in fact – a jellyfish on a hook, dragged from the sea against its will. Perhaps the whole *property* was his domain – and Osha wasn't about to leave. He'd just have to ignore him, even as that chill crept up his back. Encircling his body in unremitting *tell hers.*

He focused on the sunset. Beams of light cut between looming peaks, slicing the surface of the bay, drawing out glistening, violet blood. Little wisps of mist glowed fuchsia over the floating bodies.

Nadya plunged into the yard, bottle in hand. "I'm so ready for spring! I can practically smell it! It's just heavenly, don't you think?"

"It is."

"Then get down here! Let's take a walk!"

Osha shook his head.

"What are you afraid of?"

Surprises. Pain. Dead people. "It's too cold."

She tsked, making her way back up the steps. Setting the bottle aside, she took him in her arms. "I can keep you warm."

Osha's knees went weak.

*Oh, brother.*

She studied his face, curiously. "You've gotten too thin, northerner."

*Don't do this to me, you guys.*

"You need some blubber stew," she giggled, "like you have at home."

*Oh God, please stop.*

Her breath spread and shrank on Osha's neck, a flower opening and closing once again. And the vibration she gave off: almost violent, now. Every cell shook loose in his body, letting in the twilight chill to cool the burn, to sweep away the ashes of death. He could've passed out.

Instead, he kissed her.

*Come on, I'm right here!*

It didn't matter that she'd used him. That she'd lied. That her uncle was the ambassador and her fiancé a lion of the resistance. Polon was likely dead and soon Osha would be, too – and until then he needed her. More and more of her. He'd devour her whole, keep her in his belly: a medicine that never wore off. After all she'd done, she owed it to him.

Not that she fought it. Hands in his hair, fingers melting through his head, she pulled him even closer.

If only he could die right there.

The wine bottle fell, liquid blubbering out, a rhythmic splash on the porch boards. It rolled there a moment, like a bleeding wound.

Nadya looked confused. "How. . . ?"

Osha turned her face back to his. "It's just the wind."

Loren gave it a second kick, but his foot passed through that time. Pulsing and furious, but helpless. *Don't make me watch this! That's my sister!*

"Close your eyes, then."

And Nadya did.

# FORTY-FOUR

*What have you done?*

Osha opened his eyes. He was in his bed. Under shimmering blankets. Embraced by music.

Nadya.

Nadya was beside him. Still asleep, yellow morning light on her face, swaying shadows across her cheeks.

He drew back from her and rose, stifling a groan.

*What did you get out of that, Osha?*

Osha gestured toward the door. "Outside," he whispered.

*Are you trying to torture me?*

"We were only sleeping." On tiptoes, Osha crept toward the loft. The bitter, cold, Nadya-less loft.

*Sleeping? You call what happened last night sleeping? And you, in your state! You'll get her sick 'sleeping' like that.*

"Calm down, Loren. It doesn't work like that." Gently, he shut the bedroom door behind them. "Anyway, we didn't—"

*You didn't.*

Osha covered his face. "Did we?"

*She's engaged, Osha.*

"No, she's not," he grumbled through his fingers. "Not anymore."

*Not anymore?*

"Polon's dead, Loren."

*Dead? How do you even know—*

"It doesn't matter!" Osha threw his hands down. "How can any of this matter? You're dead, for the love of God! And soon I will be, too. So don't deny me this one last experience. I'd never done it, and—"

*Never?*

Osha shook his head. "It never really worked out."

*Then why did this have to?*

"I don't know." Osha sighed. "I don't remember."

*Listen to you! You hardly deserve the life you have left.*

"Look, I won't be able to do things like this for long—"

*Thank God.*

"Just let me know love while I can!"

*Love?* Loren drew back sharply. *You call that love?* A prickly thing now, sparking and snapping at the edges. *That's not love and you know it!* A bouquet of knives, spitting prismatic: *This is* death, *Osha!*

Osha felt nauseous. "What are you on about, man?"

*You're dying, and she's a thanadoula. That's all there is to it. You feel death in her, that's all. Death, coming through to lure you home. You've known love, Osha – you've known what it's like to be understood. The connection, the joy. This isn't even close. You couldn't care less about my sister. You're using her just like she used you.*

"I thought you *wanted* her to help me!"

*Just so she's not alone! So she doesn't lose her mind from grief!* He softened again. Foaming. Osha tried to look away, but it was useless. This stomach-churning display was inescapable. *Every day since I died she's gotten worse. That's why she visits you. That's why she slept with you. It's not love, Osha, it's a distraction! So she can forget about me!*

"So she does know you're dead!"

Loren swelled at that. *Don't ask her about it, Osha.* Inflated like a monstrous porcupine balloon.

"Like hell I won't! *You* don't tell me anything."

He sizzled now. Lightning all around him. A thunderbolt. *If you can have secrets, so can I!*

Osha swallowed.

Loren shrank and shifted, returning to his old shape. Papery and transparent. Apologetic. *Sorry for the outburst.*

"I just want to know love," Osha said softly.

*You'll have to look elsewhere, kid.* He mustered a smile. *There are plenty of fish in the sea – easily hundreds of bodies, just in that bay!*

"Those are rotting corpses!"

*And what are you?*

"I'm not dead yet!"

*What world do you think you're part of now, Osha – mine or Nadya's?*

Osha rubbed his temples. "Quiet, Loren. You're making me sick."

*Oh, I'm making you sick.*

"Look, I didn't even start this. Take it up with your sister."

*Like she'll talk to me. Temple folk don't mix with the unascended.*

"Unascended?" Osha pressed his eyes. "I'm too hungover for this."

*Hungover! You think this is a hangover?*

He glanced back toward his room. "I need a pill."

Nadya stirred when he cracked the door – a twang in an otherwise steady hum – but she settled again quickly. Osha padded past her warily, opened the nightstand drawer, and slid out the pill jar – pulling the cork with a pop. He froze.

Nadya rolled to her side, curls obscuring her face. Only her lips were visible, plump and mumbling— "I didn't want. . . ." —then falling still once more.

Osha let out a breath and turned the bottle over. One lonely pill came dancing out, twirling in his palm. Giving a bow.

The grand finale.

He shook the jar. Peered into its depths. Probed the lifeless flats of the drawer. Breath ragged, he dropped to his knees, checking under the bed, under the nightstand, all along the smooth, clean floorboards. "Where are they?"

*You took them.*

"I took them?"

*Well, what do you think happened?*

So this was it.

The trembling hit like an earthquake – he was going to lose his last pill if he wasn't careful. Scrambling for the bottle, he tried to put it back, but dropped the whole jar on the floor instead. *Bang.*

Nadya startled awake. "Osha? What happened?"

He shoved the pill into his mouth. Not that he could hide things now. The show was over. Everything was. Lifting the glass from the nightstand, he washed his life down, past the knot in his throat, into oblivion. Waiter House rushed in to refill his cup, the gentle song of a summer creek swirling off the rising water. But the jar remained empty.

Nadya's hands rose to her hair, struggling to free her eyes from its frizzy web. "What's going on?"

"I'm sorry." Osha folded his arms. "I didn't mean to wake you."

"Oh, Osha!" Hair aside, she met his eyes. "You're crying!"

"I'm fine." He took a step back.

"No, you're not." Pity oozed off of her, sticky. "Come here."

"I . . ." Another step, sucking in the air. "I'll be right back." And out he went again, straight through Loren on his way to the door.

*Ow! Don't do that!*

"It doesn't hurt you," Osha shot back, plowing down the stairs.

*You don't know how I feel.*

"You have no body!" Osha paused on the bottom step, the effort of his movements catching up with him. "You can't feel pain."

*But I still—*

"I don't care, Loren!" Osha smashed his palms to his eyes, lids bruising like overripe fruit. "Oh God! What have I done?"

*You took your last pill.*

"I know what I did!"

*It was bound to happen eventually.*

"Shut up, Loren!" Osha swung a fist at him, his arm passing clean through. He did it again anyway. And again. "You have nothing to lose! Nothing! I'm losing everything!"

*I already lost everything!*

"And a lot of good that did!"

*Believe me, I'd rather you went before me!*

"Well, try harder next time!"

*You want me to go, Osha? You want to die all alone? I can leave!*

"Can you, though?"

Loren said nothing.

"You can't!"

Nothing.

"You're stuck here!"

*Well, so are you!*

"Why?" Osha crumpled on the floor, croaking with sobs. "Why do I have to die like this?"

*You think you've got it bad? You wanna know how I died?*

"You don't understand." He wiped his nose, blood streaking down his sleeve. "You were never *dying*. You didn't have to wait and worry and suffer, on and on. But I do. I'm dying, can you grasp that? *Dying!*"

Footfalls sounded above, up on the loft. Nadya stood there, brows knitted, awash with concern. "Who are you talking to, Osha?"

He tried and failed to muster a grin – and words were no more forthcoming. He gestured helplessly, mouth agape.

"You're dying?"

He shrugged. "Sort of."

*You have to say it, Osha. She can't help unless you ask her to.*

Nadya chewed her lip, eyes bearing down. Anxious. Oppressive.

Osha slumped in defeat. "I'm dying."

"It's about time you admitted it." She let out a sigh, shaking her head at him. "You've got to be the worst liar I've ever met."

# FORTY-FIVE

Nadya needed supplies, and promised to be back soon, but pain wasn't known for its patience. In the dry-ice burn of her absence, even Osha's clothes hurt. It was too cold to go without, though, especially with Loren there – feathery and frayed and fantastically useless. He tried his old tactics, his strange, lengthy lists – but Osha's body was a windowless cell. He simply couldn't see out.

Again and again, he reached for his pills, like a falling man grasping for something solid. But there was nothing to hold onto. He couldn't even pray now. Any god that allowed this was clearly not to be trusted.

It made death less frightening, at least. A real wonder, the way that worked – in the right light, death looked like a holiday. And the light was glaring. Osha found himself begging for the dark. Pleading. Groveling.

Before an awfully small audience.

*I'm not going to kill you, kid.*

Loren dropped a cobwebby hand onto his shoulder, but Osha batted it back. "Some friend you are."

Waiter House was no help, either. It opened windows, softened sheets, offered water he couldn't hold down. Hardly a raindrop in a forest fire. A bouquet beside his deathbed. Unimaginable, how bad he'd feel elsewhere. He'd surely black out – if not die on the spot.

So he struggled to his feet. "I'm going outside."

*Osha—*

"I just need some air!"

*You don't know what you're doing.*

Loren couldn't stop him, though. "You don't know what's good for me!" Loren couldn't do anything.

But Loren wasn't the only one there.

*Here we are!* A woman cut in then – unmistakably dead, and right outside. *That's him, alright. I've heard him say that a million times.*

Familiar, that tone. All too familiar. Like things weren't bad enough. There'd be no going outside with *that* waiting for him. Osha covered his face and moaned.

Loren looked out the window. Then smiled. *You know her?*

"Tell her to leave!"

*No, I'm not going to be rude.*

Osha sat back down, trapped. Blood everywhere, stretching gooey from his face, red ribbons tied to his fingers. "I can't right now. I'm busy."

*Let's just see what she wants.* Loren leaned out the window, lifting from the ground as he did so, bracing against nothing at all. *You there! Down below! Can I help you?*

*Why yes, as a matter of fact you can. I'm looking for my grandson.* Crystalline, that voice. Unburdened by accent or language. Just pure, ringing meaning. *I take it he's here? Dark hair. Big eyes. Handsome, almost, if he ever took the time.*

*Yes, he's right up here.*

"Damn it, Loren!"

*Goodness, it's a wonder he's still alive. That boy never could tell up from down. It's no surprise he wound up in a place like this.*

Loren's legs kicked slightly, toes dipping into the wall. *Should I come down to let you all in?*

*Oh no, we can let ourselves in just fine. With your permission, of course.*

*Permission granted.*

"Oh, God! Loren, why?"

*Be a dear and let him know we're coming.* Delicate inflection, musical in a way – like the closing eclipse. *Oh – and do ask if he's been saying his prayers.*

Osha rolled his eyes.

*A more spiritual take would do him some good now. It's really all he's got.*

*I'll remind him.*

*You're a doll.*

Loren's face reappeared then, grinning. *Have you been keeping up with your prayers, Osha?*

Loren could laugh all he wanted. He had nothing on this pain – cranking up, it seemed, so as not to be outdone. Osha couldn't even speak.

*She looks nice. Nadya would like her. She's got that glow, you know? You can tell she's not earthbound.*

Osha closed his eyes. This was unbearable.

There was no hiding how wrong he'd been now. How selfish, how short-sighted. All those years, swearing he'd been misdiagnosed! He was about to get a real talking to.

He opened his eyes. And there was Mimi.

Mimi and Neta and Pia – the least natural combination in the world – tangled together as one. An unholy abomination.

The universe had broken.

*Good God, Osh. You're a mess.*

*I can hardly bear to look.*

*Now, don't let it get to you, dears. He needs this.*

They shimmered and billowed, crisp and clear, hot and cold coming off them in waves. Pia broke away first, splitting like a thread to run her fingers through his hair. *Oh, sweet boy.* Making dust of his skull. *I know it's hard. All change is.*

He wasn't breathing.

*Just relax, Osh.* Neta came forward now, taking his arms. Dissolving them, too. *Don't make it worse than it has to be.*

He was passing out.

*Really, though—* Mimi kept her distance, head shaking slow *—I hope you're learning a lesson from this.*

The pain vanished.

Everything did.

Not even relief remained – only warped and waving water, a thin black tar stretching seemingly forever.

*Can we speak honestly now?* Mimi was still with him.

They all were, bright pulses in the dark. Stars.

"Am I dead?"

*Goodness, not in the slightest! Always so dramatic. We just wanted to have a chat, and you seemed a bit distracted. And you hardly listen on the best of days.*

Loren stifled a laugh.

"What could we possibly chat about, Mimi? Just let me die."

*I'm afraid we can't do that, darling.* Pia smiled at him, gentle as she ever was. *You've been going about this entirely wrong.*

"How can I die *wrong*?"

The women laughed, stretching and weaving, wrapping him up with glee. Osha couldn't tell where or what he was, but he did what he could to get closer to Loren, pressing into the safety of his folds while the others unraveled around them. It turned out he *could* feel in this place after all. Things like fear and dread came readily. But he could also feel that Loren cared about him – fiercely, at that. And a good thing, too, because it sure didn't feel like their visitors did.

*Tell him!* Neta hollered. *Tell him about Nitic.*

*Oh, poor Nitic.* Pia sighed, blowing Osha about like a sheet. *Pity what happened there.*

"Is Nitic dead?"

*Oh yes, very. Suicide. Simply couldn't take the guilt. Sweet of him to worry so for me and the twins, but highly unnecessary. Not to mention foolish – just look what it got him! I can't say I'm surprised with you, but I expected more from Nitic. Pathetic, getting trapped in that awful house.*

"How can you talk like that, Pia?"

Her eyes bore down with blank bewilderment. *I see no reason not to.*

*We're here in your best interests, dear.* Mimi smiled at him. *It seems you've gotten yourself into a predicament. These room-and-board situations charge awfully steep rates, you know. Your little creature comforts are hardly free. Palliatives in the water. Sedatives in your afternoon tea. You think they're worth it?*

"I'm in pain, Mimi. This house is helping me. If I could just hold down some water, I'd get some relief. Isn't that better than suffering?"

*Spoken like a true addict. Just like your father.*

Neta shook her head. *That's no way to live.*

*You don't have to throw your whole soul away over a bloody nose,* Mimi scolded. *There are ways to soothe that don't involve traps like this – and they're usually far more effective.* She looked around the darkness – flashes of the house appearing, electric and fleeting, wherever she laid her eyes. *I mean, goodness – have you ever even found a record player here? There's no medicine for you quite like that. If this house really cared, it'd know that much.*

Pia tsked. *Nitic sure could've used a wine cellar like yours.*

*Try to have some sense, Osh.* Neta curled around him now, snake-ish and silvery. *Don't sell yourself so short that you lose death like you lost love.*

"Love? And who ever loved me?"

*Julis, you dolt! And they say romance is dead.*

Osha looked around, at a loss. *Everything* here was dead. "We were only friends. We'd just drink too much – it meant nothing."

*Nothing!* Neta's voice rippled through him. *You two were so in love it was embarrassing. Shacking up like a married couple, pettin' each other like cats. Nothing! No wonder you screwed it up, with that attitude.*

"I didn't want to hurt him. I didn't want to drag him into *this.*"

*You think he would've been bothered by some measly bugs? Julis "Grow Old With Me" Balestro? The man's a saint. Waited a whole year just for you to take off your pants! I've never seen anyone so smitten. He would've done anything for you. And you went and broke his heart, man – just 'cause you wouldn't listen to your own.*

"He didn't really know me. Things would have changed if he did."

*Oh, brother – you don't know yourself. Which is why we're here, so let's not get distracted. Julis is the least of your concerns now. You missed your chance. Your time's up. You blew it with life, Osh. Don't blow it with death.* She tightened around him, a vise on his head. *Focus! You've got an honest-to-goodness witch at your service*— Neta held up a hand: Nadya on her palm, beams of ecstasy shooting out like bullets. *A vessel. A channel. A direct link to the beyond. You're safe with her, under any roof. So why stay here?*

*Think about music.* Pia caressed him again, hair like tentacles. *When you sing, how you drift away! Your path out is well-tread, Osha. You know divinity. The planets themselves promised it to you at birth. Granted, they didn't give you much else – discernment, for one. Forethought. Self-awareness. But the cosmos can only help you now. Death is your time to shine! Why put these walls between yourself and eternity?*

Mimi swam forward now, dwarfing her companions, pressing down on Osha like a full moon. *You aren't trapped yet. You don't have to become like your little friend here, broken off from the natural ebb and flow, stuffed into this hole where he'll never grow or change. So, for his sake, get your things in order. He's given far too much for you to throw it all away. You've hurt that boy's feelings left and right – the least you can do is save the soul he's been fighting for.*

Loren had drawn away, eyes down.

"If I move out, what happens to him?"

Mimi looked him over thoughtfully. *That's for him to decide.*

"Can't he leave?"

*Not with the baggage he's carrying. You get stuck, holding onto such heavy things.*

"Baggage?"

*Shame,* Pia said, *like Nitic.*

*Or habits,* Neta added, *like that old man with the violin.*

*Or—* Mimi smiled sadly *—like your friend here, it could be—*

*Don't!* Loren surged and splashed around him. *Don't tell him! Please.*

*Very well. You've chosen your fate.* Mimi brushed him aside, slipping like paper between them, enclosing Osha completely. *Now, you, Osha: I've seen how you torture yourself. Such guilt over Faia and your mother. You've even turned this illness into a punishment – like some horrid atonement for imagined sins. Where on earth did you learn such silliness?*

"From you."

*Oh, gracious. I suppose you're right. How embarrassing! How little we know when we're alive!* She chuckled. *Anyway. I'm telling you now to do the opposite. Let it go. It'll make things so much easier, my boy. Just forget your family.*

"Forget them? Listen to yourself! Your own daughter and granddaughter! I abandoned them, in poverty, without a word. I could have ruined them! I don't even know if Faia survived!"

*Of course she did! Goodness, the things you worry about! Look at the pain you cause yourself. Had to pull you clear out of your body just to have a conversation!*

"I have bugs, Mimi."

*Excuses, excuses.*

"And I deserve the pain. I've hurt people, Mimi. My mother – your daughter. Is she alright?"

*She can handle herself just fine.*

"And Polon – is he dead?"

*Must you always assume the worst?*

"Neta, was it me? Was I the reason you were killed?"

*No hard feelings.* Neta shrugged. *Did wonders for my back, I'll tell ya that much. And besides—* she smirked, the twinkle in her eye overwhelming for a moment, like the flash of a camera *—you've already made it up to me.*

"How?"

*You'll see.*

*Nothing can happen that wasn't meant to happen,* Pia cut in, dancing around in that whimsical way of hers. *Everything is tied to everything else. Living, dead, big, small – we're all guilty. We're all innocent. Blame is an empty pastime.*

"But I am guilty! I am to blame! I can't die like this!"

Mimi bristled. *Oh, don't tell me I convinced you of that hell nonsense, too.*

"I can't die without trying to fix things."

*Well, of course not. Not yet, anyway. You've got a little entanglement here that needs to be resolved.* She winked at Loren. He'd made himself very small. *But you can't change everything. You must let go to move on. To resist is the only real hell.*

A shock jolted him as she touched his cheek. He took a breath.

*It's time for us to go.*

Flickering flames. Another breath. "No, not yet."

*Your little witch is coming.* Neta kissed his forehead. *You'll be fine.*

Osha was thrust into it now, into the growling grind of his organs.

Pia's lips found his cheek. *Good luck, sweetheart.*

Guts splintering. "Don't leave me like this!"

*I'll see you soon, dear.* Mimi patted his head. *Until then, do go easy on your friend here. He's given far more for you than you know, so try to consider his feelings. A bit of kindness might get you both out of this mess.*

"Don't go!" He was coughing now. Crying. Blood and blood and blood. "Come back!"

"I'm back, Osha. I'm back." Warm, solid, human hands – on his forehead, in his hair. Nadya! Pushing out the pain, little by little. Filling him up like a swimming pool.

Loren stood back, lacework and fluttering, as far from them as he could. Making more than enough space for Nadya to work her magic.

Without another soul in sight.

# FORTY-SIX

He must have been bedridden a week, but couldn't grasp even three of those days. Nadya handled him like the healer she was – easy on his bruises, carefully quilting him in extracts and rags. Pressing him like juice, out of himself and far, far away – set adrift somewhere not even Loren could visit. Shooting him clear to the moon.

And part of him never came back.

Even after recovering, he hurt when Nadya was away. Rather horribly, at times. Heavy and dizzy and perpetually nauseous, he couldn't muster a fraction of the energy he'd once had. And breathing was a thing of the past. Each smoldering breath kindled the twin terrors of urgency and despair – famous for driving sanitarium patients out of high windows.

So he strung up a noose, studied the height of the train bridge, dreamed of overdoses, drowning, even throwing himself down the stairs – but suffering hadn't made him less of a coward. He remained the same boy who ran from bullies, white-knuckled his way through windy days at sea, and beat sticks in arctic alleys to scare wolves that weren't even there.

The same boy who couldn't write home.

Oh, to be brave like Faia! How many ledges had he talked her back from – ledges he was too scared to approach? Yet she'd survived the shock of his absence. She'd adjusted. His wretchedness would never push her to the edge again. He could let go of her. He could let go of his guilt.

In theory, at least.

He mulled over Mimi's warnings, playing and replaying all he'd heard, trying to decipher the code. Trying to care. Eternity in Waiter House didn't look that bad from where he stood. Anything was a step up from this pain. Pain that made his movements slow, clouding his thoughts, sharpening his tongue. Besides, spiritual freedom might require nothing more than moving out. Perala House still stood, even if the temple had collapsed, and Nadya was all he really needed.

But that didn't help the Loren issue.

And Loren didn't help it, either.

He wouldn't say how he died. Wouldn't say what he needed. Wouldn't say anything at all. He made himself like glass, like dust, like dying firelight – but he couldn't disappear, no matter how he tried. He had to bear Osha's interrogations, his guesses and accusations, his fits of frustration. But he didn't have to respond.

"What secret is worth *this*, Loren?"

Nothing.

"How can I rest in peace knowing you're stuck here?"

Nothing.

"I'm trying to be kind, damn it! You're ruining it for both of us."

It may have been its own kind of suicide, caring about Loren, but he couldn't help it. So for the time being, he stayed. Hoping for the best – whatever that might be – and letting Nadya take care of the rest.

Earthly matters were her specialty. Eating and drinking, bathing and sleeping. She wandered their woodland pharmacopoeia, collecting plants, pricking his fingers and pressing crushed leaves to the wounds – looking, listening, waiting for some supernatural truth to descend upon her. Most of his fingers were marred to the tune of "not this one," but there were a few hits – and those were quickly mixed into medicines so thick and chunky, the mere sight made Osha gag. He ingested them nevertheless. Mustered a show of gratitude. Anything to keep her close at hand. She was the only medicine that helped.

And she apologized for that incessantly. "If only" this, "if only" that – the temple was never far from her mind. But Osha couldn't see what difference it would make. Not even vine tea could heal him now.

"It's not just about healing, Osha. The plants *guide* us. Show us how to *be*, how to live and die as the ancestors did. As we're meant to."

The ancestors were the last people Osha wanted to emulate. They'd sorted humanity on a color wheel. They'd set the world on fire. They'd done *this* to him. "You sound like a Unionist, you know that? Always digging up the past. Whose side are you on, anyway?"

"It's not about sides." Her smile was flat – the crescent shadows of the eclipse looked happier. "The plants are bigger than politics. Their wisdom is deeper." She sighed, brow furrowing. "Yet so easy to forget."

"So take your complaints to the people in charge. I'm sure you'd find someone to listen."

Her smile vanished completely at that.

Osha let it go. He got no pleasure from teasing, and was past needing redemption or respect – or whatever it was he might get from confronting her. In truth, there were times he couldn't even recall what he was mad about. Anything that forgettable wasn't worth risking her company over.

Little lesions were appearing on him, papery skin opening like the pages of a book. They were messy, and some festered. His thigh in particular demanded attention – right where the original wound had been, way back in those filthy swamps, at the very beginning.

It was time for the end.

When Nadya was away, he sorted kitchen knives, hunting for just the one to usher it in.

*Don't do this, Osha.*

"Oh, look who can still talk."

*Suicide won't get you out of here.*

Osha lined the blades up from longest to shortest. The obvious choice was the largest, but perhaps a smaller knife would go in easier. Serrated edges were definitely out. "And that matters to you?"

*Of course it matters. I don't want you to end up like me.*

"Then tell me how to get you out of here, too."

*Forget me.*

"Then forget me!" Osha snapped. "You haven't the faintest clue what I'm going through." The second-largest knife seemed to be the sharpest. "I have every right to do this."

*Look, I may not understand—*

"Clearly."

*—but you have ways to make this easier.*

"Oh, do I? And what would those be, Loren?"

Loren kept his eyes and voice low: *Whatever's in your suitcase.*

Osha paused. Straightened. "How do you know about that?" He'd completely forgotten himself.

Loren said nothing, but this time Osha didn't mind. Relief was waiting. It always had been. All this time, just up in his room. Devoured by his blind spot when he lay in bed – but mere feet away! A wave rushed through him, a raucous zest, a new youth.

He dropped the cutlery and headed for the stairs – Loren dragged along like a cat on a leash. "How could I forget?"

*That's not all you've forgotten.*

No bother. He remembered it now. "Why didn't you remind me?"

*Because I hate it, Osha. I don't want to watch you go like that – your brain all slow and sloppy.* He wavered. Like radio static. *But it beats stabbing yourself.*

Slow and sloppy didn't sound so bad. Osha found the suitcase right where he'd left it, knelt on the floor, and kissed it. "You're here! You're still here!" Solace, succor – happiness, even. A good death.

Or not.

Lifting the lid, Osha found no resins. No jars. No pipe. "What else did I forget, Loren?"

*Don't ask me, kid. I can't explain this.*

Osha stared at the luggage, but it failed to make sense. Thick folders, sealed letters. Rows of little boxes in paper and twine, marked with names and addresses on glossy, embossed cards. With quivering hands, he lifted one. Fought with the stringy bow. It would have been easier had he actually wanted this, but he didn't. He didn't want to open this mock holiday gift. To reveal the Union seal on the lid. To expose the thick gray ash within, pierced with bits of chipped, jagged ivory.

But he did.

And immediately threw it down.

He closed his eyes but still saw it, burning into his brain. If his memory was failing, it needed to fail a hell of a lot faster.

*Look at that! Dead people!* Loren hovered close. *Resistance members, I'm sure. The Union threatening the underground. What are you doing with this, Osha?*

Good question. The boy from the train flashed in his mind, smiling as he disembarked, suitcase held aloft. Important messages, indeed. This mix-up had surely cost that kid his job, if not his life. "It's the wrong one."

*No worries. It's better that these weren't delivered – no one wants mail like this. Still, it'd be nice if someone here had tagged along. I wouldn't mind the company. But I guess if you're murdered, you're probably out* avenging *or something. Bet that's why I'm stuck here, come to think of it.* He sighed. *Revenge and all.*

"What?" Osha gaped at him. "Are you saying you were murdered?"

*If you want to call it that.*

"By who? How? Why didn't you tell me this?"

*Well, it's complicated.*

"We have time, Loren! Maybe eternity if you don't explain soon!"

*I was shot, that's all. Happens all the time these days.* He gestured to the boxes. *It's no big deal.*

"No, this *is* a big deal, Loren. I want details."

*If you really want, I could just show you.*

"Show me?"

*May as well. My body's right outside.*

# FORTY-SEVEN

The plank lay at the north tip of the beach, where the root-riddled earth met the bay. Like a cellar door. Or a coffin lid. Warped and waterlogged, held in place by jagged stones, it was certainly well-camouflaged. No surprise Osha hadn't noticed it before – especially with all the bodies. Ghastly, bloated and slack-jawed, it seemed they would rise at any moment and close in. And he'd be powerless against them. The pain of the great outdoors was all but paralyzing. He could hardly stand, let alone run from the dead.

Yet he was expected to unearth a corpse.

*You can do this, kid. Don't be scared.*

"Why the water, Loren? Why weren't you buried normally?"

*Are you kidding? This is an honor! High priest stuff. After everything else, it was the least Nadya could do.*

"Nadya did this?"

*Who else?*

Osha glanced toward the house. How many hours had Nadya spent behind those windows? Gazing out at this beach? All those dreary afternoons. All those cups of tea.

She'd just been admiring her handiwork.

*You should do this before she gets home – unless you want her to see.*

He didn't. He didn't even want *himself* to see. But this was Loren, and Osha was determined to uncover his secrets. Uncovering his body was just part and parcel. He found a long piece of driftwood – for leverage, he thought, though it made a great crutch. Each step was a battle, a storm of hot pokers. There were tears in his eyes before he even started.

He had to do this quick.

So he went to work, rolling rocks off the damp wood, stones slurping and sucking in the wet sand. Cursing the whole while, he managed – until there was nothing left to move but the plank itself.

*Lift it slowly. I don't want you to break anything.*

"It's a corpse, Loren."

*It's my corpse!*

Osha lodged his branch under the wood, and in one mighty heave cranked it up and out of the way. It rose, teetering on its side for just a moment, then slapped down flat on the shallow water. Osha sank to his knees, wheezing. Relieved. Impressed with himself, to be honest. To do what he'd just done in his state? Quite the feat.

And his reward was a carcass.

Sea stars surrounded Loren's flaking hands, fingers neatly folded on his bare chest. Face half-eaten, eyes plucked out. All signs of a violent death expunged by nature's crude, insatiable hunger.

It reminded Osha of himself. "I wish you'd told me sooner."

*So you wouldn't have to see me like this?*

"So it wouldn't be so hard." His head was spinning. "This hurts."

*Serves you right.*

"What? Why?"

*The way you're looking at me!* Loren was swelling now, cloud-like, swirling. *Like I'm the grossest thing you've ever seen!*

"That's not you, Loren! That's a dead body!"

*I'm sorry.* Loren snapped back into shape, rubbery and self-conscious. *I just feel a little exposed.*

Osha glanced down at his remains: completely nude. "Well, you are."

*I can still use it, though. My body's not worthless to me.*

"Good for you." If only Osha could say the same about his own.

*With my bones, I could help you.*

"I don't need bones." He wiped his eyes. Red tears. "I need to go inside."

*Nadya was going to take them herself, eventually. Not that they'd work for her.*

"But they'd work for me?"

*We're talking, aren't we?*

Unfortunately.

Loren blew out long and slow, nearly depleting the light within. *I don't know much about it, honestly. Nadya's got all sorts of dead servants. They're old, though — lost their faces long ago. They claim to be family, but who even knows.*

"How could you help me?"

*I don't know. It's different every time.*

"Could you kill me?"

*I don't know, Osha!* Anger again, deforming him. *Why not take a hand and find out? The left one's barely even attached. Just break it off.*

Osha looked at the corpse. "Just break it?"

*How else are you gonna get it?*

Osha drew a breath and held it. Air was all he had to keep down the rising vomit. He reached down and dipped his fingers in – but the slimy crust of a sea star forced him back out. "I can't. I can't do it."

*It's just a body. You're in one right now.*

"I know! That's why I don't want to tear one up!"

*Just do it! Before Nadya gets back, come on.*

Osha shut his eyes and reached in again. Grabbed Loren's hand. Pulled. But something slipped – flat and gooey in his fingers. Unwilling to look, he dropped it, then groped back to where he'd just been. *Far* less flesh now. Skin had slid from bone like a glove.

Osha gagged.

His own hands were horrors now, soaked in death water. Decaying flesh, microscopic in all his little wounds. But he would do this. He would. For Loren. For himself. For whatever the plan was.

What was the plan again? "I can't do this, Loren!"

*Yes, you can.*

Clenching his teeth, he repositioned himself, this time taking hold of the whole arm – yanking and tugging and twisting. Water splashing around him, onto his legs, onto his face. *Water.* Just plain water. Nothing more. Not frothing human decay. *Water.*

Then at last, with a truly abominable sound, it gave.

Osha tossed it aside and sat back on the beach – wringing his hands, wiping them on his clothing. Bellowing. Snapping limbs from cadavers had never been a goal of his. He could have died very happily without it.

*Not quite orthodox,* Loren mused, *but I think it should work.*

Osha opened his eyes. At his side lay a full half arm, rudely torn at the elbow, fleshy and sinewy and rancid. "What now?"

*Now you clean it. Unless you want your room to smell more like death than it already does.*

# FORTY-EIGHT

Nadya was still away when Osha boiled the flesh from Loren's arm. Still gathering herbs or cleaning house or burying dead bodies. It didn't matter. As long as Osha had some privacy – and a tall glass of water – he was fine with anything. His nerves remained raw, but things looked promising. Loren did indeed seem empowered by his bones.

At the very least, he could move them. *It must be from all that experience – all those years of having them in my body. God, it feels good to touch things again!*

"You move the curtains all the time."

Loren scoffed. *That's easy.* His eyes were bright, so focused on his hands that his lower body disappeared. *But this!* With ease, he danced his fingers around – like soul and body had never parted. Larger bones, however, mostly fell to the floor. One even snapped. *Oh yeah, I broke that as a kid. Must've still been weak there. Guess it did kind of ache when it rained.*

Osha let him carry on, turning his attention back to the suitcase – but still couldn't make heads or tails of it. Dainty boxes of human remains. Wax-sealed Union folders. Letters addressed to honorifics like "chairman" and "general." The top one addressed to Nico Dov.

Nico Dov. Nico Dov. That seemed familiar.

*You alright, Osha?*

"Yeah." Inside and out, his head felt as furry as a cat.

*You sure?*

"No." He looked up again. "What am I doing, Loren?"

*Unpacking a treasure trove of classified materials. The resistance would* love *to have you on their side now.*

Loren sounded nonchalant, but Osha felt something heavy at play. It flickered in his mind like a fading dream. Some conflict of interest. Some great misunderstanding. Something he could almost remember.

*Osha, kid.* Loren drew near, dropping his digits one by one: a trail of fingertips to follow. *Am I losing you?*

"I'm fine."

*No you're not.*

"Given the circumstances," Osha amended.

Loren was unconvinced. *You do remember the resistance, right?*

"Of course I do." He was flailing, though. Grabbing at tail feathers as the birds flew away.

Loren hung on him like a frozen blanket, but Osha was sweating. *What happened when you went north?*

"They'd closed the border, so I couldn't get home." His heart was racing. "I stayed with some friends. I got sick. Spent a week in a hospital – and that's where I met Polon."

*And what happened to Polon?*

Osha was wringing the past out for all it had, but the dark wasn't giving up much. "What do you mean?"

*How did he die?*

"He died?" Osha shook his head. "Did he? Didn't Mimi say something about that?"

*So you remember Mimi.*

Osha bristled at that. "Of course I do! She's my grandmother! I lived with her for years." He rose indignantly, but the same shadows flooding his thoughts overflowed into his vision. Sending him stumbling.

*We don't have much time.*

Osha clung to the bedpost, feeling he'd done something wrong.

*You can't remember your own middle name.*

Yes, he could. Glancing around him, he found a handkerchief, clean and neatly folded near his pillow as usual. And there it was: O.E.L.O. Osha . . . he held his breath . . . Oloreben.

Panic.

"That's a trick question! There are two of them!"

*You can't even remember Julis Balestro!*

His throat was closing up. "You don't know what I know!"

*Yes, I do, Osha! I've always known!*

"Death's made you mad, Loren! It's *ruined* you!"

*You hated me when I was alive, too! You just don't remember!*

Osha squeezed his head with both hands, but there was no juice in that fruit. How wrong he'd been! How impossibly wrong! He'd even *feared* the wrong things. Pain and death weren't his enemies. *This* was.

Deep breaths, Osha. Slowly, now. Think.

Who was he, again? Osha Oloreben, born in the Oclian taiga. Protector of his needy sister. Musician, singer. Decent cook. Aspiring gastronome. Runaway, polyglot, honorary nomad. But beyond that, a reject. A virtual leper. Because there were bugs in him. Prehistoric bugs, revived by the same idiot ancestors that everyone else seemed to worship.

And they were eating a hole in his brain.

Nothing else mattered with a bombshell fact like that.

*Listen, Osha, I know you. I know you in ways that you'd hate. Every thought and feeling you've ever had around me, I know.*

"So you're psychic, too?" Loren was right. He did hate that.

*Not like Nadya. Nadya's different.*

"Obviously," Osha spat.

*Nadya's been trained. She can control it. I can't.*

"So all this time, you've been prying into my thoughts?" Exposing his hunger for Nadya. Digging out Faia. The things he'd shouted, the punches he'd thrown. The sheer embarrassment of being *himself.* "And not for healing or religion or anything else!" He'd never felt so humiliated in his life – as far as he remembered, that is. "All this time! Just for fun!"

*Fun! You think this is fun? You think I like knowing how you feel about me? Or the misery of strangers? Or the nasty, manipulative thoughts of Nadya's friends?*

Nadya's friends?

Loren softened. *Holic? Iza? Gabris?*

Osha started to cry.

*Osha, I'm sorry.*

He tried to turn away, to hide – but that wasn't possible.

And apparently never had been.

*It's all still in you, Osha. It's just your brain that forgets. All your feelings and experiences – the energy's still there. It always will be.*

Osha wiped his eyes. Skin like Loren's corpse. He could rub it clean off. "This ends now."

*No, Osha, please – you have to figure this out. You can't trap yourself like this. You won't be whole again.*

"Who cares!"

*You do! Do you like this?*

"No! Obviously no! I want it to be over!"

*Well, does it look over for me? It doesn't end, Osha.*

Osha glared at him.

*Let me help you. I'm sure I can do something. We've got my bones, remember?*

He looked down. Hands, raw and peeling. Joints aching. He had nothing left to lose. Not even his mind.

*Let me try. Please.*

"Fine."

Loren smiled. *We got this, kid.*

And with that, he disappeared.

Then reappeared as everything there ever was.

# FORTY-NINE

*Loren stood with Holic and Iza, at the edge of the temple's main courtyard. The celestial mosaics were swallowed now – by gray coats, banners, hundreds of shifting bodies. All of Valena, waiting to hear the ambassador speak. With no proper plaza, this was where the speech would be held. And this was where he would look for Nadya.*

*No simple task, in the maw of such energy. Drowning in sentiment, frazzled dreams, discordant fantasies, the nonsense of the masses – how he loathed crowds. Other minds twisting through his own, turning in such alien dances Loren could hardly call them human: it was maddening. And here the volume was only turned up. Pulsing. Demanding. Like each and every body in the plaza would burst. Hate and love and ambivalence, screeching like a cloud of passenger pigeons. A raucous din of unspoken words – with Holic and Iza the loudest of all. Terrified by what they were about to do. Even more terrified than he was.*

*For he had business of his own.*

*He'd had an argument earlier. With Nico. Nico, who'd come for his twisted parade, his dark festival, his grandstanding speech. Nico had a bone to pick with Loren. Loren, who'd claimed the Oclian rebel was, in fact, a trustworthy Unionist spy. Loren, who'd claimed to have recruited Osha Oloreben himself.*

*Loren, who wanted nothing of war whatsoever.*

*"You told me those codes served a double use." Nico had backed him into a corner, literally and figuratively. "But the past two weeks they've been gibberish to interpreters. Now the resistance knows my whereabouts to a T."*

*The tedious art of giving Osha's songs meaning for both Union and resistance was Nadya's burden – but Nico didn't know that. He didn't know Osha had skipped town, that Iza was managing bootlegged reruns however she saw fit. All he knew was his life was at stake – even more than usual. He was a smart man, though, and finding loopholes in his logic was never easy. "Osha's got another card up his sleeve, that's all."*

*"Prove it."*

*So Loren had come to the temple, to the ambassador's heady speech, arm in arm with the assassins. To draw attention to them. To mark them with his own familiar face. To show his allegiance by putting his own body on the line.*

*An allegiance that didn't extend beyond Osha. Osha, the innocent. Osha, who thought like him. Same pace, same rhythm. Wildly different content, but exact same melody. The only person Loren felt at ease with. The only honest person he knew.*

*Nadya, in theory, stood somewhere on that makeshift stage, black-masked like all the guards. Nico's extra eyes, looking for Loren as he looked for her. Poised to cry "fire," or even shoot if need be. Non-lethal bullets for her, of course. The goal was to capture the rebels – those coiffed and powdered masterminds – not kill them.*

*Plus, Nadya couldn't aim to save her life.*

*It didn't take long to pick her out. She was a full head shorter than anyone around her.*

*And unfortunately, so was he.*

*But he was wearing red. Nico's red scarf. Bright red gloves. He raised his hands repeatedly to his hair, up in the air, trying to draw his sister's attention. But the only people who noticed were already well-aware of him.*

*"What's with all the fidgeting?" Iza elbowed him. "Why ya gotta keep touchin' your face? You're makin' me nervous."*

*He'd lied to her, too. Said he needed a ride to pick up peat moss and fertilizer. How convenient that she was renting a car. And sure, he'd wait out the rally. Sure.*

*But the only thing he was sure of was that she'd kill him when this was over. If Iza wasn't in jail by the end of the day, Loren was as good as dead.*

*He pretended not to know about the gun. Feigned shock when Iza pulled it out from between her breasts, taking aim just as the ambassador took the stage.*

*A sharp crack. A collective shriek.*

*She missed.*

*And no sooner had she cursed her luck than luck abandoned them completely. Guards closed around Nico like flower petals, leaving one lone figure – the smallest on stage – to their shaky retaliation. Loren raised both gloves: a gesture of surrender, red-handed though he was.*

*And then came death.*

*He saw it coming, that tiny orb, spiraling from the smoky mass of coats, arching over the warping crowd. And beyond it, the eyes of the shooter went wide with horror.*

*It hit like a boulder, tossing him into the air. Life folded like an accordion: twenty times, Nadya dropped her gun. Twenty times, she jumped from the stage. Twenty times, pushing through the armored wall, through the crowd, through the glistening chaos. And twenty times, he drifted down, a feather afloat on a river of screams.*

*Dimly, he saw Iza, arms pinned behind her by a man in gray. Holic's boots scraping against the cobblestones. They were being arrested.*

*But he wasn't.*

*He was being pulled upward with a scalding vacuum force – sizzling through him, clearing his vision, turning the courtyard to crystal.*

*At last, his killer reached him. Black mask to bloody cheek. "Loren! Oh, Loren! I didn't want this!"*

*He couldn't respond. He couldn't even feel. He was detached, for once. Separate, for the first time. Just watching. Watching Nadya pull dripping, gauzy rags from his bulging eye. Watching sand and stones spill out, in awe. Had he been hit anywhere else, he'd merely be bruised – but his temple leaked life in billowing tresses.*

*More bullets were fired – real ones. Not that it made much difference.*

*Nadya lifted him, graceless and lopsided, shoulder blade piercing the wound in his head. Dark, frizzy murder curls, now wet with blood. "We have to go."*

*They limped through the pandemonium, a bird with a broken wing. Past snipers and breaking glass. Past naked plants, stunned by the cold. Through the crush of the courtyard's exits. Down shortcuts learned as children. Away from the temple. Away.*

*To a car. An official car. A clean car. Nadya wrapped his head in a long, soft scarf and shoved him in.*

*At last, she removed her mask. No longer the veiled priestess, done doling out another quick and painless death, she drove. To Osha's house. To Waiter House. No trouble finding it, no need for a guide – she knew her way around the underworld.*

*But she struggled to get Loren inside. She buckled under his rag-doll weight. He was nearly empty, though. Lighter than he'd ever been. Memories: packed up and sent off. His senses had flown. The last wisps of his life – gathered and stored at the bottom of his lungs – had hissed out and blown away.*

*Right along with his sister's sanity.*

*She dumped him on the kitchen floor, knowing full well she couldn't fix this with tea and towels. She could only sit in silence. Eyes on her brother as he twitched and rasped. As his limbs lost color. As his heart pumped doggedly into the void.*

*Until finally he stilled.*

*The kitchen grew cold.*

*It was hard, at first, to place himself in those surroundings. Standing now, on two feet, much like a living man. Watching his sister stroke once-Loren's hair, head on his chest, drenching him in tears. "I didn't want this. I never wanted any of this. I just wanted us. All I ever wanted was us."*

*He heard her words, but nothing else. No thoughts. No tune to carry the lyrics. She looked and sounded utterly mad. But was she?*

*Terrifying to have to wonder.*

*Eventually, she stopped. Drying her tears, she rose and disappeared, leaving him and his body alone.*

*Utterly alone.*

*He wandered up to Osha's room, but Osha was also gone – trying to get north, trying not to die as well. Loren scoured the room for signs of him, notebooks or papers on which he'd scrawled his morbid musings. A poetic spin on this puzzle. A map of death that he could follow. But his hands passed through whatever he touched.*

*Osha's echoes remained, though, strangely – like the drum of his thoughts had been pounded into the walls. Still audible to Loren, somehow, while all else was silent.*

*He went back to the kitchen. His body was stiff now, the hollow cavity of his temple modestly turned away, the upturned cheek deceptively clean and smooth.*

*The floor was a mess, though.*

*Nadya returned with her little bags, accouterments commonly seen at funerals. She cleaned the body, anointed it. Burned some mystical plants, said some mystical words. But nothing mystical happened.*

*Nothing happened at all.*

*"Go now," she whispered. A kiss for each cheek. "You're free."*

*Then she hoisted up the corpse and dragged it outside.*

# FIFTY

"Loren!" Osha was himself again. His gasping, aching, shivering self. "What the hell was that?"

*I went inside.*

"You went inside?"

*Like Nadya's spirits do.*

"Nadya does that?"

*I'm just trying to help.*

"You call that help?"

*You think I liked it? Your body is a* terrible *place to be, Osha.*

The room reeled around them. Baffling, these surroundings. How had he gotten back here? Where had he just been?

*Do you remember now, Osha?*

Oh, he remembered alright. He remembered Loren's ninth birthday, when his mother woke him early to watch the sunrise from a tree house she'd built while he slept. Pink over the rooftops with his dark beauty, soft-cheeked and warm. He recited poems for her in thanks, though he didn't need to speak — she knew his thoughts just as he knew hers.

He remembered Loren falling from that tree house years later. His mother wrapping his broken arm in rags soaked in pungent herbs, singing. The pain kept him awake, so she stayed up too – mining his mind, distracting him, reminding him of all of his favorite things. Plants and poetry and prose. And though it wasn't said, she herself topped the list.

She bought him his first orchid then – naming it, just as she named her own flowers. "It can't survive in the wild now," she'd told him. "The bugs that pollinated it are long dead. It's up to you to keep it alive. I believe in you."

He remembered those weekends when his mother disappeared, when he and Nadya slept at the temple like a relative's house. Watching Nadya surrender to her gifts – following the family path of palliative care, spirit-channeling and drug trips. But Loren was never too traditional. He ignored the voices in his head, honoring his mother with love alone. A love deep and strong as any sacred calling.

He remembered the men coming one night, waking him, showing him his mother, tied and gagged on her knees in the front room. He hadn't understood their lecture, the talk of fealty and family. But he understood the rage. The hate. The embarrassment at having been undermined so cunningly by a brown-skinned woman. A mere two generations from nomadism. Unfit for home ownership. A smear on civility. A bohemian. A rebel. A smuggler. A spy. A faithless whore.

Nadya's father was behind the bullets, though he didn't fire them. Politics masked the jealousy. The heartache. The loathsome fact that Loren existed at all. Two shots at once, both sides of her head – and all her scrambled thoughts went black. Her love, her sorrow, her regret: chunks of skull on Loren's shirt. Abandoning him to the brutality of life.

Nadya screamed, but he remained silent. Silent for months.

Loren looked pale now, even for a ghost. *What's happening to you?*

"I know—" Osha held up a hand, still struggling for breath. "I know how to help you."

Loren frowned. *I'm supposed to be helping you.*

"No, no." Osha pulled at his shirt collar. Talking wasn't easy, but his head insisted. "I know why you're still here. When you died—"

*Wait – you could see that?*

"You gave your life for me!"

*Damn it, Osha!* He went to pieces. Liquid marbles on the floor. Dewdrops rolling away. Mortified.

"Stop it! Listen to me!"

Loren drew himself together. *I'm sorry you had to see that.*

"Why, Loren?"

*It sort of . . . plays on a loop, I guess. It's awful, actually. Sometimes I'm afraid—*

"No – why did you do it?"

*It doesn't matter now.* He stiffened, flat and brittle. *What's done is done. But God only knows what you'll be wallowing in if you don't get out of here.*

Osha leaned back on the mattress and groaned. For the cramp in his guts, for the sweat on his forehead. For the house closing in on him.

For Loren, forlorn.

There'd be no leaving him now. Under any circumstances.

*So what do you remember, Osha?*

"It's not important." He sat up quickly. Temples throbbing. "I know how to get you out of here."

*Would you forget about me? Look at you!*

Osha wanted to shake him. Take him by the shoulders and rattle some sense into him. But he was afraid to touch him. Afraid to unleash the drama of loose brains and sobbing sisters once more.

Not that he could get it out of him. Loren was alive again, alive and well in Osha's tingling flesh. Flooded in to fill the dry pools where Osha's own memories had once been. "It's this war, Loren! This war you won't fight." Osha tried to level with him. "You may not like what Nadya does, but she's doing it for your mother. She's accepted her inheritance. She's trying to clean up that mess. She just wants a happy family."

*Then she shouldn't have gotten involved in politics.*

"She was born involved! Just like you!"

*I'm not my family, Osha.*

"Yes, you are! And until you admit it, you'll go nowhere!"

*Says the runaway!*

"And look what that got me!"

*Look what my sister got you! And other patients, too! People who needed her, sent out as bait — running errands, spying, risking their necks without even knowing! All 'cause her twisted comrades figured, 'Well, they're gonna die anyway!' That's why she quit her job, Osha. She didn't want to do that anymore. She didn't want to take advantage of suffering people. She's spineless, not evil. But then you came along, and just look what happened!*

Osha had no idea what he was talking about. Not one clue. His words banged about the dark like knocks in a haunted house. But now was no time to panic. The clock was ticking – the eclipse a bare sliver through his open door. Burning in his bones. "Don't you hear yourself, Loren? You care about this. You care about Nadya and other people. And you were born with the tools to make peace, but you won't use them!"

*Don't be a fool. Peace isn't possible. When in history has peace even happened?*

"How would I know? No one knows *anything* about history!" His lungs erupted with blood. Spasms, splitting him open.

Loren waited for it to pass, deflating as it carried on. Just as drained by it as Osha was. *Don't fight with me, Osha. You're running out of time.*

"I know." Osha hung his head between his knees, blood dripping to the floor. "That's why I have to do this now."

*Do what? End the war?*

Shakily, he stood. More coughing, torturous and gurgling. "Yes."

*Good God, you are sick.*

Leaning on whatever he could, he made his way to the suitcase. Classified papers. Private letters. Things Loren's mother would have made quick use of. Surely there was something helpful there. Something to appease the dead entombed alongside it, names gleaming on their little boxes, expectant and excited. Osha stumbled as he approached, legs nearly giving out, but someone caught him. Held him up. The sizzling infinity hands of an ascended spirit. Ms. Perala herself, perhaps – with her fire and guidance and wild affection.

But no.

*Do be careful, dear. Must you always be so reckless?*

"I'm sorry, Mimi. I'm in a hurry."

*Rush, rush. Will you never slow down?*

"This is important."

*Is this a bad time?* Pia was back as well, ribbons round his grandmother.

"Yes it is." Osha wrenched free from Mimi's grasp – a chill strong enough to hold him still, yet thin as water. He shuddered.

*But this is the time we have.* Pia seemed baffled. As though her mystic, cosmic schedule was the only one in existence. *It's time for you to come.*

Osha looked to Loren, but found no clarity in his face. No comfort, no explanation, no congratulations on finishing this last hellish chapter of life. His face was hardly vacant, though: sorrow, distress, alarm – these glittered crystalline all over him.

Osha glared at the intruders. "Give me a minute. And you say *I* rush."

Mimi blocked his path like a curtain. *It's time.*

"I said not yet!" He pointed at Loren: sullen and brittle, limbs like branches in fall. "He died for me!"

*Sweet of him, wasn't it?* Mimi's smile was thin. *Let's go.*

"No. Let me fix this." Slowly, he bent, lifting the suitcase, careful not to spill its contents. Cradling human remains to his heart. "Don't worry, fellas," he cooed. "We're gonna make this right."

Pia wrapped around him now, a cyclone of hair and pity. *You're so uncomfortable here, you can't possibly think clearly.*

*Oh yes,* Mimi concurred, *bodies are never level-headed. Let's have you step out a moment to talk this through.*

"I'm fine." Osha pushed through them, into the loft, toward the radio equipment. "I won't leave like this." They followed closely, bright and shimmering with annoyance. "I'm not done yet."

*But Osha, you should be happy!* Pia's voice rose rolling, rippling under his skin. A thundering wave of nausea. *You've finally lost enough to join us.*

Osha pulled the sheet from the radio, setting the suitcase beside the console. "Lost?" Aside from blood, strength, sanity: "What have I lost?"

*Self-loathing, mostly,* Mimi answered him. *At last, you can bear your own weight. Can't even remember it, in fact!* She giggled, girlish and threatening.

Osha faced them squarely. "Are you doing this to me? Are you making me forget?"

*Heavens no! Those little parasites are working just fine on their own. You've been well-warned of this symptom, dear. But I suppose you wouldn't recall!* Mimi laughed outright now.

*Perhaps we steered them a little,* Pia confessed with a shrug. *It was this or your hearing – and wouldn't that be hell for an audiophile like you?*

"This would be hell for anyone!"

*Then why not leave it all behind?*

Osha cleared a space around the microphone. Scattered papers, scratched-out scripts, forgotten knickknacks: onto the floor. Taking his seat, he lifted the first envelope. Nico Dov. Nadya's uncle. The ambassador. What kind of mail did he get?

*Are you not done with this?*

"I said no."

Mimi frowned. *This boy Loren is nothing but an anchor. If you attach yourself to him, there's no helping you.*

Nonsense, that's what Nico received. Absolute nonsense. A dissection of some mystifying poetry. A code. But if Osha was good at anything, it was translating things.

Pia pushed between him and his work. *Do you remember Nitic, Osha?*

"Of course." Sort of.

*He's caught in a spiral, you know – like your friend here. Circling round the day he shot my daughter. Reliving every instant. Every shove, every taunt and jeer. The cries of his family, begging him for help.* Osha wouldn't look up, but Pia found a way into his eyes, cupping his face in her starry grasp. *Without an intervention, he'll go mad – forget he even has a soul. Mutate into a demon. Or weather! Or worse!*

Osha was dripping sweat. "I'm staying with Loren."

Mimi tsked. *I shouldn't be surprised. You've been like this since the beginning. Only lost souls end up in these death hotels.*

"It's called Waiter House."

*I don't care what you call it. You've made a poor choice – as usual.*

He flung the letter down at that. "Like you're so free! Listen to yourself! You're not ascended. You're just as trapped in your ways as anyone else. Same old words – even the same face!"

*Just a mask so you'll recognize me.*

"Why do you even care what happens to me? I'm just a vestige of your mortal life, too, you know."

*Humanitarianism, my boy. At my core, I am an altruist. Why else put myself through such moral rigors as religion?*

"Well, maybe you're wrong. For all I know, this house is a good thing. It'll give me some time to think – to *actually* let go, rather than end up a hypocrite like you." Oh, yes, these arguments. There was no telling what he'd forgotten, but he sure knew what he remembered. "Where do you get off telling me to give up my attachments? You haven't given up yours. You're just as dogmatic as ever."

*True,* she agreed, surprisingly. *It takes a lot of living to really know how to die – and I'm nowhere near finished. It's not easy, breaking free from the human mind. Just listen to the living! You'd think they were the most powerful force in the universe, the way they carry on. Like they can make or break history!*

"They can, Mimi. Just look what they did to me." Osha held up his hands, stained blue with bruises, encrusted in wounds.

*Darling, we're not saying people are ineffectual.* Pia brushed his hands away. *They just think a bit much of themselves. Like their developments are permanent, their worldviews complete. Like they have* control. *But they didn't create those bugs any more than they brought on the floods.*

*Yet they'll take the credit.* Mimi chuckled. *Like they can cause earthquakes!*

"Earthquakes?"

*Earthquakes, Osha.* Pia said it emphatically. *And dramatic ones at that! Forced the nomads to the mountains. Deformed the lowland. Sank whole cities! I didn't see them myself – spent the floods as a tree down south, so.* She paused a moment, thoughtfully. *Not that time's strictly linear – I suppose I could still give 'em a whirl.*

Osha's head was spinning.

*Then again, maybe not. It was rather hellish for a time – and I'm not quite the masochist you are. Sweet Osha, always with the agony!*

Nauseating, these words – with such lustrous, liquescent movements. He couldn't take much more.

*It's admirable, don't get me wrong. Brave of you—* Pia smiled, scrunching her nose just a little *—but I'll take my lessons in smaller doses.*

Mimi stroked Osha's head. *Humans have nothing on the power of nature.* Caressed his cheek with flaming fingers. *This poor body of yours has taught you that much. Things are so much bigger than anyone can realize – living or dead. So do go easy on us. We all forget from time to time – you're not the only one.*

Pia circled his back, pins and needles. *We're only trying to help you, Osha.*

*And we're doing our very best,* Mimi added. *It's just that the human brain has got . . . well . . . let's call them claws.*

*Oh yes.* Pia nodded. *It's quite addictive.*

Sickening, all of it. Osha closed his eyes to their leapfrogging, whirlpool waltz. But it didn't help. They danced just as happily in the dark.

*Still, I'm not ready to do it again.* Pia smirked, a glint in her eyes. *So who says we need to clean our closets just yet? I for one am in no mood for another round.*

*Oh, heavens, no!* Mimi scoffed. *Let me rest these old-soul bones.*

*I'm still surprised by Neta – diving back in so soon!*

*She did have spunk, didn't she?*

*Never one to back down from a challenge.*

"Neta?" There were three of them last time, weren't there?

Pia answered by morphing into a clear glass version of an entirely different person. Blond bob, red lips, glowing chimera eyes. Twirling and laughing, even her voice had changed: *I'll be a writer next time. Make people think – grasp some nuance for once. And a dancer! Perfect posture, not an ache in me!*

To Osha's horror, Mimi joined in. Twin spirits spun around him now, tittering and terrible. *My new mom's no nomad, but at least it's in her blood!*

*Here's to the madness of grief! The only way to get her in bed with my father!*

They collapsed laughing, melting, a formless pool of midnight sky.

Osha stared at Nico's letter, trying to still his stomach. Whoever Neta was had set sail, out of his memories, off somewhere far, far away. And as disturbing as forgetting was, watching these mutating cosmic creatures was worse. He needed them to leave. Their senseless, maddening diversions had to go. He had work to do.

*Don't fear amnesia, sweetheart.* Pia rematerialized, herself again, relaxed and breezy. *It's something we all go through eventually. Neta took it like a champ.*

"I don't care about Neta."

*What a thing to say about your daughter!*

"I don't have a daughter!" *Did* he have a daughter?

More uproarious laughter.

He dropped his head to his hands. "Just go! I don't have much time."

*No, child, that you don't.* Mimi drew close again, arms around him. *At least you're finally being honest with yourself.*

Osha glanced at Loren – quiet all this time. Scarcely a flicker in the corner of his eye.

"I want to help my friend, Mimi."

*Suit yourself. But don't cry to us later. We're awfully busy, you know.*


# FIFTY-ONE


*You've lost your mind, kid.*

"You're welcome." Osha lifted the letter and tried to read again – carefully this time. Without distraction.

Mostly.

*What are you even doing?*

"Shhh."

*You should have gone with them.*

"Will you stop?" Osha slammed a hand down – then drew it back with a gasp. Cupping it tenderly, hoping nothing had broken. "Just let me concentrate."

*You've got nothing left, Osha. How are resistance codes going to help you?*

"Resistance codes? Nico Dov is with the resistance?"

*Over his dead body!* Loren almost laughed. Moving closer, he blanketed Osha in a chilly mist. *Union code-breakers sent that. It's a transcript.*

Osha stared at the papers in his hand. A spare list, an unprefaced maze of words. Epitaphs, rain clouds, history – disjointed terms falling in line beside dark references to bank bombings and arms smuggling. A slender linguistic waterfall, cascading meaninglessly to the end of the page.

*So you've forgotten your own songs, now?*

"What do you mean?"

*These are from your songs. You sang these lyrics.*

"*I* did this? Why would I have given my songs a double meaning?"

*Triple meaning, technically. A different message for each side – plus what you* were actually *saying.* Loren smiled sadly. *It wasn't your idea.*

Osha sighed. Nothing to be done about it now. "Make yourself useful, Loren. Help me out here."

*I don't know what you're trying to do.*

Osha knew some link had snapped with Loren's death. Nadya's thoughts were closed to him now. The whole world's were. But Osha wasn't very worldly these days. There was still something between them. "What kind of mind reader are you?"

*Fine.* Reluctantly, Loren drew even closer. Glacial water on Osha's arm, gently pointing his finger, running it over the words. *These are the lyrics that Iza had you sing. And this is what they meant to the resistance up north.*

"Has the meaning changed?"

*I doubt it. Not if they're sending this to the ambassador now.*

"Then this is perfect! The ambassador never got this, so he can't understand it. Maybe no one in Sagoma can."

*I wouldn't know. You're my only link to life, kid. You're all I got.*

Osha sat back in his chair, distracted by that. Confused and intrigued and increasingly uncomfortable. The joints of his fingers were beginning to swell. "Why me?"

*Like I enjoy it so much.*

Osha drew a breath. Sat forward again. "Look, if you want to get away so bad, help me do this."

*This? This is my ticket to freedom?* Loren was unimpressed. *The same coded broadcasts that got me killed?*

"You abandoned your sister to this mess and not once helped her out. I'm sure that's why you're stuck here. You could've found a way to make things better, but you didn't."

*And this radio fever dream of yours will save the world.*

"Oh, forget it. I'll do it myself." Osha went to work flipping switches. Then, with a pen (handy how these things just *appeared*), he underlined whatever seemed useful. Nothing about attacks or violence. Nothing about money or territory. Movement, yes. Movement for those poor souls at the border. He didn't remember much, but he remembered them. Like at a dam, they'd pooled – pressing uselessly at a political wall, hungry for northern drugs. That desperate nurse and her son.

Yes, movement. A ceasefire. That's what everyone needed. So goods could be shipped. So the mail could pass through.

*That'd have to be quite the ceasefire.*

"Who asked you?"

*You asked for my help.*

"I un-asked."

*Listen, Osha—* somehow, Loren came even closer *—if you're really going to do this—* half inside of him, prickly and cold *—you'll have to call on real people.* He flopped Osha's arms about like a drunken puppeteer. *You can't just suggest something at random – you have to command it. Issue an order. Give a directive.* Dead weight, his fingers wrinkled the letter, pushing it about. Loren was making him turn the page. *There are pseudonyms here.*

"How do you know that?"

*I've seen letters like this before. There's always a list of names at the end. Resistance changes them all the time, so the code breakers are constantly updating. Like here – see? There.* Loren flung Osha's hand down like a dead fish. *Padin Kors was finally found out. That took a while. And Xobel Mara – that was Nadya.*

Osha's head was throbbing from the effort this took. He was already regretting the decision he'd made – the choice to stay. To endure. The bugs were starting to swarm now. Ideals were weak little things against a plague of locusts. Especially naïve, impulsive, inchoate ideals.

But he was chained to this. He could either pull Loren out of the bog or fall in after him.

Loren's meddling was helpful, at least, clumsy and cold though it was. No visions came with a partial occupation, no mental tyranny – yet it did seem to dull the pain. He was helping him, taking what he could of his suffering. After all he'd already done! How could Osha ever pay him back? He could barely even read.

*Don't lose your nerve, kid. You may as well try.*

Osha had slumped down without realizing, curling around his churning insides. Bracing for the firestorm.

*We have everything we need here – somehow. Beats me the luck you have, but you do have a way with accidents. So let's do this.*

Osha straightened. Took a few breaths.

*What have we got to lose?*

There certainly wasn't time to hem and haw. He was dying right then and there.

Osha lifted the headphones. Fought sloppily with the wires. Put them on. Cranking the main knob, he was hit by a blast of whining feedback – then silence, vast and welcoming. He was on air.

"Hello?" He paused.

*Go on.*

He drew away from the microphone. "You think they're listening?"

*I'm sure someone's tuned in. Can't promise it's who you want, but I guarantee you have an audience.*

Osha cleared his throat. "Pardon the disruption of your regular programming. This is Comrade Oloreben, broadcasting live from occupied Valena, with a very important message."

Loren all but laughed. Tickling inside of him. *This is nuts! You've no idea what you're doing!*

Osha leaned back again. "Yes, I do."

*You don't have a clue. Just let me do it. I know what to do.*

"Do *not* possess me again."

*I know what's going on in your head, Osha. It's not much.*

"Oh, shut up." Osha leaned back in. "I can no longer turn a blind eye to the cost of this conflict."

Loren snickered. *Blind eye.*

"Too many have suffered. Too many have died, often senselessly. Families, torn apart. The struggle is honorable, and our cause is true. But there comes a time when we need to consider how much is too much." Reaching into the suitcase, he lifted one of the ash boxes. Reverently, he read the name: "Faron Felso. My friend."

*What in God's name are you* doing, *Osha? How high is your fever?*

"I want to say something nice about him," Osha whispered.

*About who?*

"About Faron."

Loren blinked like a moth-ridden lantern. *You're gonna pretend you knew everyone in these boxes.*

"Yes."

*You want to end a war by making people feel bad.*

"That's not all—" A bolt of pain cut him off, shooting through him head to toe. Leaving him breathless and charred, wiping lava tears with corrosive hands.

*Whatever you need to do.* Loren shrugged. *Try to make sense of your stupid life.*

Osha ignored him, focusing. "Faron's passing is a tragedy for us all. In a world where honesty is so rare, Faron was exceptional, and—"

*Don't go overboard, now. You're lying. Keep it vague. No one will believe you otherwise.*

Osha paused, unsure how to proceed. "I . . . um . . . trusted him."

*I'm afraid I've heard more compelling speeches.*

"Faron is gone now, thanks to this conflict."

*Guilt trips are useless with these people.*

"His blood is on our hands."

*This is going nowhere.*

"Will you just be patient!" Osha shook Nico's letter angrily. "I have the codes!"

Every. Single. Word. Echoed in his ears. He'd said that directly into the microphone.

Loren blanched as only the dead can. *That's it, I'm going in.*

And in he went. Flicking off the light in the room, flaring up as a torch from within. A waking dream. The frank absurdity of a night terror.

Nico was there, hissing words like Loren heard at his mother's death. Suspicions, accusations, demands. He was merely a figurehead, a poet, an *ambassador*, yet commanded a power through charisma alone that was unfathomable. People loved him. Even people who hated him loved him. Loved him so much, they forgot he was essentially impotent.

Authority you can't define can't be defied.

Loren had to do what he said. He had no choice.

And Osha watched. Still existing somehow. Someway.

He'd found a patch of mushrooms, once, with Nitic and Ivra. They were days away from the others, having lingered in the city for Nitic's interviews. They were tired. They were hungry. They were cocky and jejune and foolish. They ate the mushrooms with abandon – and for somewhere between two hours and two-hundred years, it felt just like this. This half-dream immersion, like the fabled moving picture shows of old. It seemed whatever Loren touched, he touched. Whatever Loren did, he did. But did he *really*?

Osha pulled away from Loren's memories, naturally. Nervous and repulsed, knowing exactly what was to come. The visions pulled away from him as well, taffy stretching thin and flaccid.

Yes, he did exist. And if he really concentrated – physically condensing, balling up, drawing hard boundaries around what little he could control – he could hear himself speaking.

Or was it Loren?

He didn't understand the words he used. He couldn't hear them clearly. Muffled, they came, vibrating through the crowded temple grounds, pulsing through each person. Iza's little gun, quivering. What was he saying? Something about the weather? Something about traveling in fall? Something – whatever it was – in absolutely perfect Sagoman. Sagoman! He'd never heard such words in his voice, rolling and rich, a lovely liquid ocean of an accent. No sharp stutters, no slipping on ice. Lush, warm and easy. Like summer.

He *must* have been talking about the weather.

It was overcast when Loren was killed. It had sprinkled before the rally and the air was still humid. Especially with all those people around.

Iza fired – jumping at the sound, like she thought it would shoot quietly. From his safe distance, Osha watched the uproar unfold, the senseless chaos of chance, the unspeakable horror of inheritance. And while he watched he made himself even smaller. Listening.

". . . for too long, history has been intertwined with our. . . ." Voice like a distant chime. A pleasant tenor, light and gentle, if racked by coughs. A fine voice for a singer. He'd never appreciated it. But he'd never heard it speak Sagoman like a native, either, rolling with someone else's inflection. Never heard it from the outside. Never with Loren's ears. And Loren's ears, apparently, could listen to it all day.

He seemed far less charmed by *using* it, though. He was suffering in that body.

Both bodies.

*I didn't want this, I didn't want this.* Nadya was crying into Loren's matted hair.

That poor woman. Osha felt no magic in her now, no narcotic force that pulled him to her, convincing him she was safe. Beautiful. Irresistible. No. She was old – well into her thirties, gray invading her curls. He'd always known, of course, of all the time she'd amassed before him. But somehow he'd never *seen* it. Never seen her sorrows – etching wrinkles in her brow, making her slouch. Sorrows that poured like a fountain over Loren's dying form.

All Osha could feel was pity. He couldn't even fault her for all she'd done to him. All those things, all that . . . what was it?

He let himself go again, popping like a bubble, diffuse and drifting through Loren's troubled past. And there, in the murk and heartbreak, he found them: his own memories, still intact, thoughtfully stored and curated in Loren's sturdy mind. A biography. A whole library. Everything Loren had intended for him to find before.

Osha gathered all the memories he could carry, shrinking down, safe and small, to put them away. Even if his head was leaky, he had other places to stuff them. His stomach. His heart. Formless, feeling places. All that mattered with memories was emotion, anyway.

Nadya kissed Loren's face, lips warm and smooth on his bulging brains. She was used to death, had come to love it even: an intimate adventure, a sacred space in which she felt privileged to tread. But this was her brother.

She was no miracle worker for those she shot.

It was raining when Nadya dragged the body outside. Through the window, Loren watched the bay, fanned and pockmarked by the drops. Strange waters. Whole towns, under those tides, forgotten, now peopled by nudibranchs and bioluminescent algae.

And ghosts – swollen and stiff and just as shocked as he was that death came on a spectrum.

Then it ended.

Loren pulled back, leaving Osha alone in his body.

His vicious, violent body.

*Cry if you have to. You're off air.*

Osha didn't want to. He closed his eyes and steadied himself, breath after searing breath. And Loren waited, silent and still against the windy eclipse, until Osha spoke: "Thank you."

*I didn't do much. Said to issue fake IDs – medical excuses for those stuck at the border. Said to ask Nadya for the paperwork.*

"In Sagoman?"

*So more people would understand.*

Loren's face was straight, but a small happiness danced in his eyes – pride, perhaps in knowing he'd done right at last. Or recognition that Osha had found himself again, deep in the folds of his death. That he was whole again.

Either way.

"How do you feel now?" Osha pressed. "Redeemed? Free? Anything?"

He shook his head.

"But that was perfect. That should have worked."

Loren turned up his palms, at a loss.

"Well, crap."

# FIFTY-TWO

Nadya returned at nightfall, with a big bag and a satisfied smile. "You wouldn't believe the plants I scrounged up for you! I can't believe I got my hands on them."

Osha watched from the sofa as she moved through the front room and into the kitchen, humming and happy. Lit beautifully by the blazing ghost ships outside. He'd come downstairs to be near the fire – preferring the one in the hearth to the one out the window.

*I'm surprised she goes into town at all. It can't be safe—* Loren snorted — *being a traitor to* both *causes.*

Breathing was a real task now, but Osha kept at it. He had to. He'd solved nothing. "She comes here to hide, doesn't she?"

*Mostly. But helping you relieves some guilt.*

"What will she do when I'm gone?"

*Good question.*

Nadya poked her head out of the kitchen now, breezy and beaming. "Were you talking to me, Osha?" Words so sweet amid the guttural screams of the drowning.

"No." It took effort to speak, to raise his voice so that she could hear. It was much easier to talk to Loren. By magic of rotten arm, Loren didn't seem to care if Osha whispered or shouted. There were certainly perks to grave-robbing. "How was town, Nadya?"

"It's been better." She frowned. "But I won't bother you with details. You don't look well. Shall we go upstairs?"

"And miss the eclipse?"

Nadya squinted above the fireplace. The moon's ravenous inhalation had swallowed all but the barest glint of sun. Osha could feel its suction, the cold vacuum that once pulled disconcerted giggles from his throat. All around the room, those telltale waves of light rolled and roared: the dry sea in which he and Faia had clung to one another, years before, resisting the riptide. Nadya's forehead creased. "I really think you should—"

"No." He fell into a coughing fit. Nadya drew near, but he gestured for her to stay back. And she did, chewing her lip as he bloodied his hands.

"Osha, really—"

"No," he said again, firmly. She flooded through him, as she always did – waves over the pain, washing it away. But he wouldn't let it distract him. He would not grow lazy with relief. "Tell me, Nadya—" still, this took an awful lot of strength "—do you still work for the resistance?"

*Good God, Osha, what are you* doing?

"The resistance?"

"You're with the resistance, right?"

Nadya stared, slack-jawed. Clad in a thickening red sheen.

"Or is it the Union?" He blinked back the blood, eyelids scraping. "Forgive me, it's so hard to keep track."

*You can't be serious, Osha!*

"What are you talking about?"

"It's funny, really, what the resistance made of me – when here I'd prefer the Union take over. Build some tracks so I can get home." More coughing. Gasping. Groaning.

*Now? You're honestly doing this now?*

Nadya reached for him, but he pulled back.

"And all because of this place! Fitting, I suppose, for a death house."

*Come on, enough.*

She was petrified. A wild current in her waters.

"People *did* die, Nadya. Because of Iza and that goddamn radio station. Because of me. *Polon* was shot because of me."

*Stop, Osha!*

Nadya took a step back, into the flickering glow of the ships. Toward ghosts watching empty lifeboats drift away. The blood drained from her face. "Polon."

*You don't even know if that's true!*

"Shot," Osha repeated. "Because of me."

*You're being cruel.*

"How do you know about Polon?"

"I'm dying, Nadya, not stupid!"

"He was killed?"

Osha turned away from her, struggling for composure. Her sedatives were losing some effect. Hard to tell if that helped or hindered his cause.

*Why are you torturing her?*

"Osha, I couldn't stop what happened with you. I tried." She was crying. "I didn't want this. I didn't want any of this."

"That's what you said when you killed your brother, and did that change anything?"

*Don't you dare bring me into this.*

Nadya was struck dumb. Crying ceased, fingers glued to her cheeks.

"You think he wouldn't tell me?" Osha rasped.

*You think you have to* avenge *me?*

Osha turned to Loren now. "I don't know! Maybe I do!"

Nadya took several stumbling steps back at that. "What are you saying, Osha?"

*This can't help either of us.*

"Well, nothing else did!"

*Like we tried much!*

"Like we have time for more!"

"Osha, stop! I don't know what you're doing! I don't know what's going on!"

Osha braced himself on the sofa and rose, eyes fixed on her. "Loren needed you." He managed a weak, wobbly step toward her. "But you left him for violence and war!" And another. "You chose death over love!"

She followed his lead like a dancer, edging away bit by terrified bit. "What happened to Loren was an accident, Osha. A terrible, terrible accident. You don't understand the trap I was in."

"You're a hypocrite, Nadya! A selfish, petty—"

*Osha, stop! This isn't the answer!*

"You have to help, too! Show her what she's done to you!"

Nadya's eyes had never been wider.

*She's not learning from this. She just thinks you're crazy.*

"Don't let her live this down!"

*I don't want revenge!*

"But maybe you *need* it!"

"Osha, calm down. You're in pain. You're sick." Nadya was sobbing now. "Now's not the time for this. It's complicated. It's my family. It's my mother and my father – and I can't change who they were or what they did. But I have to honor them. Please understand, I'm trying to do right by them. I'm trying to fix things."

"By reenacting their failures? Or using the dying to do it for you!"

Nadya buried her face in her hands. "I had no choice, Osha."

"Holic and Iza are rotting in jail. Loren's dead. And you come here to hide." He continued to close in on her. "Taking advantage of a dying man." Hunched and shaking and bloody. "You're a coward."

Another coughing fit. Blood on the floor.

The water came on in the kitchen. Then the lights. *Is this what you want, Osha?* Loren stood at the switch, flipping it: up and down, up and down. Then to the cupboards, opening one after the other. *To torment her?* Slamming them. *Will this get you to stop?*

"Put your heart into it, Loren!"

Nadya stumbled back, slamming into the wall, chest heaving.

"See how angry you've made the dead?"

*Oh, for the love of God, Osha!* Loren shut the water off. *Talk about a low blow.*

"You don't understand!" Nadya's hands were clasped at her chest – shaking, violently shaking. "You don't have to live like me. You don't have to make the decisions I do. You get to—"

"I get to die."

She shook her head. Sheer panic. "That's not what I mean!"

"Yes it is." The pain was ratcheting up now. Really ripping into him. "Do you envy me?"

Fear had cut Nadya off from her medicines. Fear had cut her off from God. And, consequently, Osha was cut off, too. Her mouth was moving, but he heard nothing. Not Loren, not the cries from the bay, not even his own moans. The tearing in his guts was deafening.

Oh, the things fear could do.

"Go, Nadya."

"Osha, please—"

"I said go!" He turned his back on her and stormed into the kitchen. Driven by the pain itself. Straight to the knife rack. He drew out the sharpest one. "Get out of my house!"

"Osha!"

*No, Osha, no! This is way too much!*

"And what happened to you?" He pointed the knife at Loren. Shook it. "Was that not too much?"

*Put it down, Osha.*

Nadya trembled at the kitchen door, ashen – the blush of her cheeks gone with her anodyne mystique. Tired eyes. Creased brow. Small voice. "Tell him I love him." Soaked with emotion. "Kill me if you must, but tell him I'm sorry!"

*You're way too sick for this, kid. Drink some water. Take a nap.*

Turning the knife toward Nadya, he studied her. A frazzled, frightened woman. All alone in the world.

"Please, Osha."

She wanted death. Wanted it like a lover.

Loren tensed, balling up. *I really hate to do this, but—* He shot into him. The room flooded with his death, but Osha fought it. With everything he had, he fought it. Fought the truth he found there: the clear fact that Loren had forgiven his sister. That there really was no need for retribution. Yet still he remained, along with the mystery of why. And Osha couldn't press the issue now – he was locked in battle. Holding onto the knife took monstrous effort. Superhuman strength. His arm was growing heavy, fingers like wet clay.

At last it dropped, blade clanging upon the floor.

Loren stepped out, electrified and cursing.

Osha was no better off. "Never do that again!"

*Believe me, I won't!*

Nadya clasped her hands, pleading: "Osha, listen—"

He thrust a finger toward the door. "Go!"

"Please—"

"Now!"

A thin crescent from the eclipse lit her hair. Dying light on her shaking head. And then she left.

Leaving Osha alone with his pain.

# FIFTY-THREE

*So that was a brilliant idea.* Loren flapped like wings about his head. *What the hell's the matter with you?*

Osha swayed, mute for a moment, dizzy with dying.

*You want to go through this without her?*

"She needed to go." Precariously he bent, lifting the knife, nearly falling right on it as he struggled back up. "She'd try to stop me."

He turned for the stairs.

*Where are you going?*

"My room."

*For God's sake, Osha, leave the knife!*

He paused at the steps. "You have no right—" Coughing. "You—" More bloody coughing.

*Will you just think about this?*

"Think about this?" Two stairs. "Think about this?" Two more. "I spend every waking moment thinking about this!"

*There has to be another way. You can't give up now! You can't!*

Osha paused for breath. Looked the ghost in the eye. Resumed his walk.

*I died for you! Does that mean nothing?*

"There's nothing left to do, Loren! I can't fix this!"

He made it to his room. Sitting on the bed, knife in hand, facing the mirror. One last moment with this body. It'd served him well, for the most part. It'd been a good body. It had shown him beauty, drenched him in music. Ate its way through three delicious provinces. He'd basked in warmth, shivered in cold. Melted in Julis's arms. He'd had a good run.

He studied his face now, his choppy black hair, his blue-white skin. Eyes sunken, deep wells ringed in purple. A skull. It was time to let it go.

Lifting the water from the nightstand, he took a queasy sip. "I'm going to kill myself."

Loren was silent.

Osha held the knife to his wrist and pressed, deep between the bones, and drew it all the way to the gleaming tip – for nothing.

He tried again.

And again.

He couldn't break the skin. Couldn't slice at the right angle. Couldn't *something*. The blade was too dull. Hands too unsteady. Body too weak.

He hurled the knife across the room – through Loren and into the wall before clattering to the floor. But the despair was short-lived. Pain was full of ideas.

"Your bones, Loren!"

*What about them?*

"That arm is sharp – the broken one. You can hold it."

Loren flickered. *I don't want to.*

"Please, Loren!"

*I'm not going to kill you!*

"Why are you putting me through this?"

*Suicide's not the answer!*

"It's not suicide if you do it!"

*Please, Osha, there has to be another way!*

"You're just scared of being stuck here with me. I get it. I wouldn't wish myself on anyone either, but if—"

*Osha, stop it. I don't hate you. No one hates you like you hate yourself.*

"I don't hate myself."

*Yes, you do! You think you're unworthy of everything! Love and comfort and respect. You deny everything good in you to the point that you're hardly aware of yourself at all! You can't even hear your own music! You push away those that want you. You think your own family hates you. Your sister worships you! Your mother would happily die in your place! Yet you're so certain of rejection, you can't even fathom being loved! It's like you traded common sense for talent – you speak all these languages, but can't understand what people are really saying! Damn it, Osha, I've bared my soul to you – you've felt exactly what I feel, and you can't even* grasp *it!*

Osha's ears were ringing. "Grasp what?"

*That I'm in love with you!*

That did it.

That was the answer.

Loren exploded like a firecracker, a shock of light from his feet, sizzling up through his head. Sparking and sputtering and radiant. Starry.

Impossibly beautiful. The whole spiraling cosmos funneled through him, a fantastic tumult of wonder and concern and clear, distilled love. Free.

"Oh my God." Osha covered his face. "Are you kidding?"

*I love you, Osha. I've loved you this whole time. You can be a real ass, don't get me wrong – but I can't control who I love any more than you can. And to see you, to meet you in the middle of this war – you've no idea how hateful it's made other people. You wouldn't believe their thoughts. But you! You go around with this wonder, this trust. And your music! You're beautiful, you're talented. You're magical, and you can't even see it! If you'd just let love in! As bitter as you act, on the inside you're still good. And too many people are the opposite. That's why I never told you about the resistance. That's why I protected you in secret. I couldn't stand the thought of seeing you corrupted. Knowing you were dying was bad enough. I had to keep you innocent.*

"Touching eulogy, Loren." Pain was no sentimentalist.

Loren spread over him, a clear night sky, radiating a tingling chill that burned to Osha's very bones. *I know I'm not who you want. And I wish I could give him to you, just to see you happy. You're no one's burden, Osha. You're not the inconvenience you think. People love you. So I can't risk you getting stuck here. I hate watching you suffer, but I just can't chance it.*

"Listen—" Osha rubbed his eyes, unwilling to face the timeless, unyielding wisdom coursing through Loren's celestial form. "You're one of the best friends I've ever had. And this is all very sweet, believe me. But Loren, really – I'm not worth it. I'm selfish. I'm ugly. I just drew a knife on your sister. There's more reason to kill me than not."

*And you say you don't hate yourself.*

"Will you just kill me already!" Osha was drenched now, sweating and bloody and unbearably nauseous. "You're free, Loren. You figured it out." Pain like liquid metal, dense and acidic. "Do it quick and move on."

Loren wavered. He felt it, too. The bugs were eating them both.

"Come on, old boy." Osha spoke softly now. Slowly. "Be a friend."

Loren said nothing, but it didn't matter. He was moving. He bent over the bones, lifting the longest of the broken shards and raising it above Osha's crumpled form. Osha held out a wrist. This was it. The eclipse was closing. All he knew was coming to an end. He shut his eyes.

*Why would this be any sharper than that knife?*

"What?"

*What makes you think this will work any better?*

"I don't know. You can at least hold that."

*I'm not sure how hard I can press.*

"Just try and see!"

Loren took the semblance of a breath, glittering, every imaginable color rippling through him. Then he went to work.

It hurt. "Good God, Loren!"

*I'm doing my best.*

"Ow! Not like that."

*It's just not very sharp.*

"Stop it! You're bruising me."

*This is stupid.* Loren pulled back. *I'm not doing this.*

Osha lay back on the bed, splayed like the splash he'd make under the train bridge if he had real guts. But his guts were useless, knotted as they were. It took healthy guts to do what he wanted. Committed guts.

"Stab me."

*Excuse me?*

"You heard me." Osha sat back up, surprised he hadn't thought of it before. "Look at that thing. It's a *dagger.* Stab me in the chest with it. In the heart." He clambered to his feet – much too quickly. A black wave crested and crashed, tossing him into the bedpost, helpless as the room reemerged.

Loren watched with a promising blend of sympathy and remorse.

"Please, Loren."

Without warning, Loren struck. Bone hitting bone with a malicious thud before bouncing back.

"Ah!" Osha pitched forward, doubling over the mattress. "What is wrong with you?"

*I'm doing what you told me to!*

"That hurt! Go easy on me."

*I can't! I'm supposed to be killing you!*

"What kind of killing was that?"

*Alright, look. If you want this to happen, I have to stab you somewhere soft, like your stomach.*

"Fine." It was fine. His stomach may as well have had a knife in it for months. Osha was almost willing to stab it himself.

Almost.

*Osha?*

"What?"

Loren drew himself together, solid and opaque. A blinding ray of violet white, a thick smear of burning moonlight. And then kissed him. Charged and sizzling – a jolt down Osha's spine, branching through his limbs. A moment of peace, an instant of release. Love like he'd always wanted, genuine and safe, cool and fresh as snow on his lips. And like snow, it melted there. Loren blurred and faded. Osha reached for his shoulders, his face – any part of him – but his arms found only open air.

*Remember that I love you.*

"Loren, *please*." Osha no longer knew what he was begging for.

*Alright.* Loren nodded. *Let's do this.* Smile soft, eyes swirling. The infinite depths of his fully dead face graced with sincere tenderness, he thrust the jagged bone into Osha's middle.

That worked.

Osha fell to his hands and knees, unable to draw a single breath. Blood soaked through his shirt, poured onto the floor, a dark lake on the wood. Waiter House was not cleaning it up.

*Wait, Osha!* Loren flitted like flies on a corpse. *It's still – I have to pull it out.* Crisp as a dry leaf, ink-pen lines around a swirling fog. *Lean back, Osha. Lean back.*

Osha flopped to his side. Some creature – some massive, midnight octopus – took hold of him then, reaching up through the floorboards, trapping him in its undulating shadow-band tentacles. Suction, powerful suction. The whole world pulled inward. The moon had at last swallowed the sun. The eclipse was at totality.

Rapidly, he went down: one screaming swoosh to pitch-black seafloor. And the darkness slammed shut like a door.

# FIFTY-FOUR

*Emptiness. Hollow silence. Echoing black.*

*Then, one by one, tiny pinpricks of light. Slowly, they emerged, thickening – snowy stars peering through a luminous cloud, shining all around him in an immeasurable dome. He was under it and in it and spread upon it like melted butter, sinking into its mesh even as he admired its beauty. Cold, swirling, impossible midnight.*

*And music.*

*Music didn't just rise up above the silence – it was the silence. It was the dark, it was the light. It was everything. Humming and chirping and buzzing like a vast jungle of insects, building a radiant symphony, a brilliant explosion of immaterial diamonds, shades of gold and white and clear blue that had no names in any language. Burning through him, dissolving him, obliterating him. Opening up the truth.*

*Warm, loving, bittersweet, crushing, orgasmic truth.*

*Truth beyond facts. Beyond passenger pigeons and woolly mammoths – revived in laboratories before the floods. Beyond earthquakes collapsing a thousand square miles. Beyond moving pictures and airplanes and ten-lane highways. Beyond a world that had many times known itself in completion, grasped every material boundary and detail – only to forget, again and again. Relearning, re-creating. A myriad of trivialities were aglow within him like an electric bulb – irrelevant. Those mysteries were not real mysteries. There was a truth that extended far beyond history's riddles. Truth was a word that the human mouth never got right. Truth was a word that wouldn't translate.*

*Truth.*

*No troubles here. Only the barest sense of self. And at the same time, the grandest. A broken dam, a rushing river of connection, the aquatic fire of oneness. Screaming love, deafening purity: around him, through him, as him. Heartbreaking, glorious, melodic pulsing: around him, though him, as him. Everything, the real everything, not the dirty colorless physical grit of life, but light, meaning, sempiternal mists of sizzling perfection: around him, through him, as him. Pleasure, annihilating pleasure: around him, through him, as him.*

*This was how it was meant to be. How it had been, in the beginning, when all things were one churning crush. Before the universe exhaled. Before he forgot that he was the ground and the sky and the furniture of his house, the food he ate, the dreams he had, the songs he sang, the words he heard, garbage, art, dead things, other planets, other galaxies, other dimensions, the plastic he dug for in the dirt. He was everything. There was only one thing.*

*And the only possible response was gratitude. Oh, to be part of it!*

*His grandmother was there, somewhere, everywhere, right in front of him. No face, no body – a scented candle, a colored flame, a familiar spot in the ecstatic tumult. She pulled him close. Steam in steam, complete immersion. Nothing but love.*

*A dark kernel of guilt pierced him then, separating him somewhat. A stone in a lake. A small, solid, impossibly heavy fleck of ash amid brilliant flames.*

Faia?

She'll be fine. Everyone will be.

*The guilt dissipated, bubbling up and out in a tidal gush – something like tears, shimmering and fluttering, rippling away through the oily effervescence. Everything was as it should be. War, suffering, chaos: all just as it needed to be. A cryptic series of lessons meant to bring you closer to* THIS. *There was no other way. It could be sad. It could be confusing. But it couldn't be wrong. Nothing could be that wasn't meant to be. Nothing happened by accident. Nothing was a mistake.*

*All anyone could really do was love.*

*He felt other ancestors there, spiraling back through the coil of time. Icy cities capped with colorful domes. Dirt-road begging and penny-show peddling. Desert dancing, singing to the very God his grandmother trained him to fear. But there was nothing to fear here. It didn't even hurt, having to part with his long family line – thousands of souls coming through his own, telling the same stories, dreaming the same dreams. He could let them go. He could let every physical particle of Osha Oloreben go.*

*A weight was lifting – a weight he knew intimately. A weight he'd always felt but never noticed. Leaving him with nothing. Fantastic nothing. Just tumbling air and tangled time and blubbering forgiveness. The weight was gone. He was nothing. He was dead.*

*And he'd never felt more alive.*

*Another surge of love from his grandmother. A disembodied smile.*

Now you know.

*And she released him.*

He took a breath. Then another.

He was breathing. Lying on the floor, in Waiter House, blanketed in thick, woolly quiet.

Was he still dead? Was he trapped here? Was this it for him?

He lay still, scanning himself. Searching his thoughts. No repeating horrors, no reliving his violent demise. Nothing running circles through him but glorious, liquefying oblivion. Bells in his bones. Unspeakable beauty.

He moved to sit, but something caught him: a pain in his side, a fishing hook. "A wound," Osha muttered, trying to fill the confusion with something certain. Looking around at all the blood, he nodded. "A wound." A wound wouldn't still hurt without a body, would it? And the ground was so solid underneath him. He reached out slowly, touched his bedsheet. Felt it.

He was alive.

Loren's bone lay beside him, smeared in berry glaze like a barbarous little pastry. Gingerly, Osha pulled up his shirt to explore what it had done to him. It had changed him, that was absolute. It had changed everything. He had an open wound now, raw and ugly – and from it spilled all of his illusions.

He hooked his fingers on the bedframe and pulled himself to his feet – but he didn't really need the support. His head was clear. His legs were steady.

As a matter of fact, he felt fine.

For a long time he faced the mirror, gaping at his equally mystified reflection – unable to look away from a million years of family, all singing through him at once, guiding him, making him who he was. Four billion years of evolution, fourteen billion years of existence. What a stunning creature he was. The flush in his cheeks, the shine in his eyes – even the ruined one seemed less mottled. Still blind, but somehow blind with *clarity*.

"Loren—" he paused, unsure that it was safe to say it "—I don't think I'm sick anymore."

But Loren was gone.

DENIAL

ANGER

BARGAINING

DEPRESSION

ACCEPTANCE

# FIFTY-FIVE

On the first day of Osha's second life, he was cautious. He showered delicately, careful not to aggravate the hole in his stomach, then bandaged himself with gauze, encircling his waist like a hug. Tender. Gentle. How rough he'd been in the past. Brutal with himself. Insensitive with objects. Careless with the universe.

He opened windows, letting in the sweet spring breeze, losing track of time. Eating slowly, savoring the experience, not quite able to trust his nerves – expecting a relapse, but receiving only rapture. A hundred unique flavors. Textures startling, as though he'd never eaten before. Spice and richness and doughy comfort. One tiny morsel of everything in the house.

None of it was replaced.

He couldn't find much to wear, either – just the old, tattered things he'd left Oclia with. But he couldn't complain. There were no relentless shipwrecks, no bodies in the bay. The eclipse above the fireplace had frozen at totality, collecting dust before his very eyes. Beyond the nagging ache in his middle, he had no pains. Life lay before him like a vast, warm plain: a summery path in a blooming meadow, beckoning him forward.

The universe was love and everything that had ever been imagined was within him.

On the second day, he felt stronger. Strong enough to go into town. Stronger than he'd felt in weeks. He rode in just after dawn, under clouds heavy with life-giving rain. The squawking of crows, tires crunching on gravel, wind whistling against him – all of it, music to his ears. He rested when he needed to, his wounded belly sore, his lungs still tired. But it was fair, the deal he'd struck with his organs: he would take care of them, and they would take care of him.

And take care of him they did – pulsing like the city's throb, breathing like the trees, keeping perfect time with the rhythm of life.

Valena itself, tattered and beaten and harassed by the sea, was stupefying in its glory. Dazzling. Resplendent under the dark sky. Wood and brick and glass, drawn from the bountiful earth, advanced through millennia, expertly assembled by countless unsung heroes. The work put in, the process, the *history* – how had he never noticed it? He'd helped nomad scavengers scour old dumps, dredging up artifacts that easily predated the floods. He'd seen antiques revived by chemicals and careful hands, and returned to the land of the living. But he hadn't appreciated it. He hadn't understood. Production, distribution, artistry! Pain and exploitation, profit and enjoyment: psychic links on an endless human chain.

In mute awe, Osha made his way downtown. Past the swaying, clanging streetcar. Past people, vibrant and vivacious. Luminous in their billowing cloaks, color and light ballooning in his vision.

Oh, vision! Miraculous vision!

Diligently, his right eye brought him the vivid luster of life, the bustle of bodies and blood. But his left one – his left one was even more marvelous. From the physical fray it pulled shimmering auras, glistening stardust fires burning around each and every person. No two were alike and yet – beyond the occasional blot of pain – their bodies played little role in their differences. Age, sex, color of skin: silly and inconsequential. He saw mood. Spirit. Soul. Sunshine joy, inky despair. Temple mystics – unmasked yet unmistakable – shrouded in sizzling mantles of violet white. Even the digmen, cloudy under black umbrellas – and out in *droves* – were beautiful in their own way. Not frightening now; they themselves were the frightened ones. Foreigners, most of them, lost in this strange land – at odds with their jobs and longing for acceptance. Blue and red and gray. The petals no longer littering the streets had been replaced by a veritable human bouquet.

And not one person he saw – with either eye – was dead.

Now and then he was bumped by those around him, but it didn't hurt. Didn't cause his skin to swell and darken. So odd, though, that they didn't all just melt together. In so many ways they mixed and mingled, bleeding into one another, streamers trailing and tangling – pulling so strongly that Osha nearly lost his footing. He'd do what others did, go where others went, feel what others felt – without meaning to at all. Yet these bodies all remained confoundingly separate. Infuriating, really. He had to bridge that gap.

So he spoke.

Never had he had such a collection of chipper greetings at his disposal. They bubbled up like a spring, splashing into the street with the rain. "Beautiful day for a walk!" He accosted people.

"You crazy, son? It's pouring."

"Lovely weather we're having!" Again and again.

"Bless your heart! Way to cheer up an old woman on a stormy day."

"Fine day to be alive!" He meant every word.

"If you say so."

The lack of enthusiasm stung a little, but he shrugged it off – striding the streets with gusto, heart pumping healthy for the first time in months. Possibly years. He skipped over garbage, wet newspapers, matted paper bags. He jumped in puddles. He ran, just because he could. Not far, though – no farther than where he'd busked for pennies – before a wounded twinge stopped him. But it was a meek ache. Timid. Stepping forward quietly, courteously requesting that he not overdo it.

Yet.

Rain drummed cobblestones and rooftops, trickling between the notes of tenacious street performers – the few who withstood the digmen typhoon. Sweet, sacred musicians! Harbingers of heaven. Osha stopped to listen. Old, familiar songs, heartbreaking melodies. Only after a singer shot him a glance did he realize he was crying. But self-consciousness wasn't what turned him away. He wasn't embarrassed at all.

He was hungry.

Starving, in fact. All the hunger he'd lost to disease raged now, all of it at once – a pleasant pain, a purposeful pain. Pain that inspired, driving him forward.

To the pastry cart.

Had he remembered what he'd seen there, he probably wouldn't have gone, yet there he was: staring down the rattled gaze of the vendor. She appeared alone now, but it was clear that she was anything but. Terror rippled around her, lightning in clouds of exhaustion. But he wasn't afraid. Not today. In fact, he wanted to take her hands. Kiss her cheeks. Take her in his arms and sing death away. But in a world where people frowned at smiles, the embrace of a stranger was decidedly unwelcome. All he could offer her was spare change and a growling stomach.

He bought five pastries with money he'd gotten from a mourning mother, and wept as he ate – for her and her poor son. For the pastry clerk and her unshakable ghost. For all the suffering he'd seen, lives lost to war, to the illusion of separateness. Devastating, that they couldn't see the truth, that the entire vast universe had once been the barest kernel, spirit and form clenched together as one. Everything, together. And for all the transformations – the deaths and rebirths and bouts of amnesia – they always would be.

And God, didn't it feel good?

The temple folk seemed to understand. And nomad astrologers, inviting planets to live inside of them. Psychics, madmen, children – they all knew, on some level. Anyone who moved past matter, who stood back from the tedium and minutia of life and looked at the whole – they could see that each and every thing was exactly the same. The Union, the resistance, the past, the future, the living, the dead, beauty and trash, the pastries he ravenously devoured. Glorious, cannibalistic existence! He could have passed out from the pleasure.

Pleasure! Not just the absence of pain, not just relief. *Pleasure!* The likes of which he hadn't known since Julis. Yet here he was, flushed and buzzing, the whole world his lover. And if Julis was with him now!

Oh, *Julis.*

Gentle Julis, lost in the horror of this lying world. Out there, somewhere, watching everything he'd ever known dissolve. Hiding. Afraid. Brilliant, beautiful Julis, who already knew the wondrous colors Osha only now saw. Who spoke endlessly of history and art. Who restored antiques with his own trained hands.

He deserved nothing but love.

Osha had to find him. *Had* to. If he didn't, he'd never stop crying.

He headed home at dusk, his bike a crooked coatrack hung with produce and sweets. Waiter House seemed a bit rundown then, moss creeping up the shingles, porch splintering. Some of the furniture was missing, but the piano remained. Other instruments too – piled by his bedroom door, desperate to be heard. They'd reached for him in his sickness. He'd heard them scratching the plaster as he sizzled and sobbed. Now he would play them all: the little wooden percussion set, the drums, even the flute, which he had no idea how to use. He'd play the mandolin, that old, peculiar creature of Iza's. It wasn't too unlike the guitar. He could figure it out, bring it to town. He'd need an income, after all. The house clearly wasn't giving any more handouts.

Sleep was impossible. Like a child before a holiday, he tossed in his bed. Then paced the floor. The stairwell. The front room. And finally, outside, under the crisp, clean moon glow. Darkness swirling, teeming with microscopic movement, particles dancing to melodies of frogs and crickets, hooting owls, rippling tides. He gulped the smell of blooms and brackish water, so heavy in the air. He lay on the pebbles and shells of the beach and stared at the infinite stars. And they looked right back, icy light showering upon him, into him, through the very marrow of his bones.

"Thank you, Loren," he whispered to the sky. "I love you, too."

By the third day, Osha was afraid his energy would drive him mad. Was this truly how it felt to be whole? Had he really taken this for granted? What things were possible with a body like this? Quivering with life, positively frantic to heal. He could join the resistance, planting bombs like trees. Or the Union – translating communiqués in every language he knew. He could find the surviving nomads and continue south – to the bottom of the archipelago, to the Nameless Province, where subterranean villagers would slit your throat for stepping on their rooftops. And he could join even them, sharpening knives and hunting unassuming tourists.

But why do any of that when he could bathe in moonlight and love the world?

He didn't care how this had happened. Perhaps he'd bled out the sickness as the ancients had with leeches. Perhaps there'd never even been a sickness, but instead some Oclian spirit, some evil taiga ghost, released like helium from his gut as he popped like a balloon. Perhaps he'd been healed by love. It didn't matter. It only mattered that he was alive. Wide awake and swollen with gratitude and utterly, indisputably alive.

Only one thing weighed on him, and a trivial thing at that: the puddle of blood on his bedroom floor was not drying. Not sinking beneath Waiter House's skin. It was unresponsive to soap and water, and outright ignored towels. It simply refused to be absorbed. Osha pulled a rug over it, and it didn't soak through. Didn't even discolor the rug's rough underside. It did nothing at all.

Osha could respect its dedication. Impressively persevering, that blood.

But he'd prefer not to see it.

# FIFTY-SIX

On the fourth day of Osha's second life, there was a knock at the door. Just as the afternoon sky dropped low for another spring shower, a short, quick rapping came – immediately followed by the turning of the knob. Someone with confidence. Someone who assumed he wouldn't answer.

Someone who knew about the house to begin with.

Osha had been eating: winter squash baked with kale and eggs, sautéed chanterelles with goat cheese and red hot peppers – all purchased at the market, as Waiter House's food had started to rot. He took a mouthful with him, chewing as he made his way across the living room, chewing as he marched into the entryway.

Nadya jumped back.

"What do you want?" Still chewing.

"I . . . I just wanted to check on you." She looked distraught. "I know I said it before, and I know it means nothing, and I know there's no—"

Osha waved it all away, finally swallowing. "Forget it, Nadya. I'm over it."

She looked downright terrified. "Over it?"

"I overreacted."

"No," she replied meekly. "You really didn't."

"Come inside if you want to talk so much. You're letting in cold air."

Nadya stepped forward slowly, giving Osha a wide berth as he reached around to close the door.

"I'm not going to hurt you," he assured her.

Her brief, nervous laugh lapsed into something of a cringe.

"You want any food? Tea? I'm baking some bread right now – smell it? Haven't made sourdough in years, but I didn't forget a thing! Like riding a bicycle. There's an incredible baker at the market – you know, the one with the beard? He gave me the starter. Says it predates the floods!"

Nadya eyed him uncertainly, a still figure against the wall. "You went to the market?"

Osha nodded. "Why?"

"You haven't gone out in weeks."

"That's not true. I just went out this morning."

She was silent a moment, watching as he checked the oven timer, lit the stove, pulled down cups. Then at last: "How are you feeling?"

"Great," he replied, no hesitation. "Never better."

"I don't understand."

He paused his dance through the kitchen and offered a shrug. Then on he went – filling the kettle, thankful that Waiter House still had water. The power was already out in a few rooms. It'd be sad when the utilities shut off completely. Sad, and soon. "Relax, Nadya. Have a seat."

Nadya looked as though he'd suggested she set fire to her own hair. She sat, though, stiff and self-conscious.

Osha joined her at the table and resumed eating. No spectral warmth came from her now – he had no need for medicine. Instead, it was a dull, muddy blue that hung over them. A once-glistening shroud now caked with sludge. Guilt. Shame. Remorse. Feelings Osha knew all too well. How Nadya had managed to dizzy him with bliss while feeling such misery was beyond him.

"What do you have there?"

"Just some eggs and things," he mumbled. "Sorry there isn't more." He drew himself up, dabbing his lips with his napkin, clearing his throat. "And really, I'm sorry I kicked you out. That knife thing – that was pretty rude. But the tea should be ready in a minute."

Nadya shuddered visibly.

Osha took another bite. "So, what have you been up to?"

She drew in a breath.

The kettle began to whistle. Osha rose, but kept his eyes on Nadya. "Well?"

"Collecting plants."

"Not for me, I hope."

"Yes and no. . . ."

"Don't waste your time." Osha poured the hot water, hands steady. Nadya openly stared, the air around her heavy. A strange blend of sorrow and bewilderment. Like she didn't know him at all. He smiled. "I never deserved it. You saw what a jerk I was."

"You were sick."

Osha set Nadya's tea down in front of her. "That's no excuse."

"No, you were *very* sick." She shook her head. "You seem so different now. And your eyes look so. . . . What happened to you, Osha?"

Loneliness – that's what she felt. The same loneliness that had driven her to his bed, keeping her there as he slowly died. And to think, he'd wanted her all for himself, to isolate her all the more. The things pain had done to them! Gently, he touched the back of her neck. She didn't move. "Thank you for taking care of me." Fingers sliding down to her shoulders, he leaned down and kissed her cheek.

She drew back with a gasp.

He burst out laughing.

"I don't understand." Her confusion was morphing into something closer to anger.

Affection was impossible in this world. No wonder people felt so lonely.

Osha moved away from her, returning to his food. "You thought I'd be dead, didn't you? You've got that little bag with you." He'd seen its contents in Loren's memories, spilled out on the kitchen floor: herbs and oils meant to sanctify a corpse. "I know what's in there." He was laughing again, unable to restrain himself. "You're here for my body!"

It was fun to watch her squirm, flustered and frightened, gaping at her own possessions in horror. But he soon had his fill of her distress, and turned back to his plate. "It's very thoughtful of you—" he took another large, sumptuous bite "—but wholly unnecessary, I assure you."

"Are you better, Osha?"

He smirked. "What do the spirits say?"

She looked away from him, brow furrowed.

"What about you, Nadya? How are you?"

"I . . . um. . . ." She shook her curls a little bit, trying to free herself from whatever thoughts ensnared her head. "I'm fine."

"You sure?"

"I am." She smiled. "And actually, I have news for you."

"News you didn't think I'd live to hear?" Osha chuckled to himself, stabbing his eggs.

"Polon's alive," she said. "We're meeting in Sagoma next week."

Osha was happy for her. She needed something to fill that void. Didn't everyone? All these lost souls, clinging to each other so as not to float away. Poor, sweet people, searching for a love they've always known. A love they've always been part of. A love they forgot to feel.

"It'll be nice to be near my family. I have no one here, now." She cleared her throat. Shifted in her chair. "Plus, the resistance is making strides down there that—"

Osha's smile fell. "You're moving near your family to *fight* them?"

"I'd like to make peace, Osha," she said softly. "And anyway – how can I quit now, after what you've asked of me?"

He took another bite. "And what would that be?"

"Thanks to your little radio stunt, I'm positively swamped in requests for fake IDs."

Osha leaned back, setting his fork aside. "People heard that?"

"Of course people heard it! *Everyone* heard it!"

His cheeks went red. "The Union?"

She nodded. "The codes were all current – both sides knew exactly what you intended. The Union's just as prepared to ferry the sick as I am to provide the papers." Her expression clouded somewhat, gaze growing distant. "But I'm honestly quite surprised by it all. I didn't know you understood so much."

"Must be a shock, after working so hard to keep me in the dark." Osha was tired of this conversation. Tired of the whole senseless conflict. Violent and garish. Boring. Not to mention complicated – all things considered, he'd probably have to change his name.

Like a true resistance member.

Nadya looked down. "I'm sorry, Osha. I've done you wrong. I've done so many wrong. But for once, thanks to you, I can do something good. I can help people. I can put life before politics." She sighed. "I wish I could be more like you – neutral and free. But I can't abandon this conflict. Not until it's over." Her voice was strained. "I have to fix it. I know I've done a terrible job so far, but maybe – with your help – I can do better. You're much more cunning than you let on."

"And much more retired." Osha went right on eating. "I won't be a part of it."

"Osha, do you know the power you have? The Union opened a border passage specifically at your request."

"They what?" He gawked at her, blindly scraping his plate for food.

"It's tightly regulated, of course, but it did lessen pressure from the opposition. They didn't want to seem inhumane – not after your broadcast. People trust you, Osha. On both sides."

Osha rolled his eyes. He'd *definitely* have to change his name.

"Please don't be cross. I'd like to make amends."

"Do whatever you want." He frowned at the empty plate. He didn't like being harsh, but he had a new life now, and it would be a better one. His middle names would make a fine alias – he had two, after all. And he remembered them. He remembered everything. "Just forget about me."

She burst into tears.

That was a surprise.

"I'm sorry, Osha! I'm just so sorry!"

He took a deep breath.

"If I could turn back time, I would—"

If she didn't stop crying, he'd start too.

"—I would've never wrapped you up in this. I would've done everything to prevent it! Everything!"

"Well," Osha said loudly, drowning out Nadya's sniffling as best he could. "At least there's an open passage now, am I right?"

"There is." She nodded. "You've saved lives, Osha."

"That's fizzing!" He spoke all the louder. "That's nothing to cry over. At least one good thing came of us knowing each other."

Nadya felt about for a handkerchief, digging through the pockets of her coat, coming up empty-handed. Waiter House provided nothing, so she drew the hem of her dress to her nose, blowing into the lace. "Actually—" she sniffed "—there's something else."

"Whatever it is, know I'm not joining any cause." He stood firm. Even with her sorrow making a knot in his own throat, his mind was made up: "Let's just pretend we never met."

Her eyes refilled. "I understand."

"So? What is it?"

"Nothing." She shook her head, looking down. "It doesn't matter."

Osha stood, taking his dishes to the sink. The water was hardly a trickle now. He sighed.

"Might I stay a while? Just for the night?" Nadya looked dejected. "It's raining so, and soon it will be dark." Tiny and tired and gray. "And I have some things I'd like to ask you."

"Like what?"

"Well," she began, "for one, I didn't even know you could speak Sagoman."

He smiled at that. "I can't."

"You can't?" Slow, nervous laughter. "But – how, then?"

Osha shrugged.

Nadya looked him up and down, once again disturbed by the mere sight of him. "Well, you certainly fooled me," she said uneasily. "Osha Oloreben, you fooled everyone."

# FIFTY-SEVEN

It was a good thing Osha hadn't died, because Nadya had an awful lot to ask him. Not that death necessarily killed her conversations, but still – the questions were endless. Strange and personal and altogether unnecessary. Questions about his childhood, his family, his culture. Questions about his own ancestors.

"Why do you want to know all of this anyway? Is it somehow useful to your cause?"

His mistrust made her teary. "You're making yourself dead to me, Osha. At least let me honor your memory."

Occasionally, she'd ask about his health, eyes narrow, head cocked. And though she of all people would understand, he simply couldn't find the words for what had happened to him. Couldn't bear to define it. Wouldn't burden it with language.

A delicate fear crept in, meanwhile, as she dissected the superficial crust of his life – that he'd lose the understanding he'd been granted. That with too much worldliness, the elation would fade. That he could unremember eternity. Worse yet, he felt guilty for wanting to be alone. Guilty for growing tired of her fractured energy. And when it came to things like truth and love, guilt was a master thief.

But some of this guilt wasn't even his. Nadya's own shame flooded the house like a river. Perhaps she only needed vine tea: a holiday party with the ancestors, a nice long chat with the dead to yoke her back to the cosmos. But that wasn't an option anymore – and Osha was too swept up in her emotional cyclone to think of alternatives.

He could hardly even tell where he ended and she began.

So he let her question him. At least it helped him find himself.

She let him question her, as well. It was true that she'd come for his body, she confessed, but not just that – she'd also come for his home décor. Loren's orchids meant more to her now than ever, and she collected them as they talked, stuffing them two-by-two into the city car she'd parked outside. Theater instruments also found their way into the mix, as did the bag of herbs she'd left behind. Those herbs – abandoned and ignored since Osha's fleeting death – brewed up a particularly strong cup of tea. Such concoctions were the crux of the psychopomp business. "They'll put you right to sleep," Nadya said, "peacefully and painlessly." Scrutinizing him, she added: "I really thought you were ready for them."

So she'd been planning to kill him, too. Osha was touched.

Nadya tired early and wanted to sleep. Most of the furniture had disappeared, so Osha offered up his own bed. With her eyes firmly shut, he was free to tend his bandages, appraising the old collage of bruises fast fading from his skin. It felt like years since he'd been sick. Everything he'd ever known – everything but the boundless, melodic amalgamation of the cosmos – had paled like a long-ago dream.

Pleased with his body's progress, he sat before one of the last remaining objects in the house: his desk. And there, in a muddied, wrinkled notebook, he began the frenzied chase after his own wild thoughts, scratching down the first lyrics he'd written in months. Fingers dancing over invisible piano keys. Alone at last.

And that's when he saw it.

It scurried across the desk right in front of him, twitching and anxious and unlike anything he'd ever seen.

Instinctively, he smashed it with his fist.

Glancing about, he saw a second one near the corner of the rug. Then a third, a fourth, a fifth, sixth, seventh – zigging and zagging across its thick weave. And more still, crawling out from under it, one on top of the other. Tapping as they skittered away, like beach rocks under the waves. Yet soft, somehow – edges thin and quivering, fine blue outlines blurred together. Joining and disconnecting as their numbers grew.

Osha stood. Heart slamming, brain numb with terror, he rolled back the rug. And there they were: hundreds of glowing, fluorescent bugs, swimming up and out of the blood like a lake. Or an Oclian marsh. He could almost hear Waiter House moan as they dug in their claws.

For the first time in days, he felt he was going to be sick.

They were clumsy things, knocking each other over, fighting to right themselves from their backs. Twisting and writhing, as long as centipedes, tying and untying knots with one another. Pincers snapping and sparking as though they would ignite. And sure enough, along with the swarm, the tapping, the throbbing heat – there came the distinct smell of smoke.

Osha edged along the wall away from them, but they followed. Spreading evenly in all directions, folding neatly at the baseboards, they shot up the walls like a fresh coat of paint. He stomped them, kicked them, hit them off his clothing – but he couldn't stop them. They wriggled up his back, hot-cold on his skin, and he tore off his shirt with a cry.

Nadya bolted up in bed, eyes wide. "Are you alright?"

He groped for words, but found none. Nadya's eyes narrowed. The clock was ticking. His throat threw up a massive lump, leaving no room for his voice.

"Osha." Her gaze was steady. Like she saw nothing but him. No crackling hive of insects, thinning and dispersing, slinking under the door, into the loft, to the bathroom. A spare few still clung to his arm. He batted them off as casually as he could.

No, she couldn't see them.

He opened his mouth. "I, um. . . ."

"Good God, is that *blood?*" Nadya's eyes fell to the open floor, and Osha's followed. After resisting its fate for so long, the pool had finally dried to a flat, matte maroon.

"No," Osha said.

"What is it then?"

"A stain."

"I don't doubt that it is."

His tongue was a wad of cotton. "Wine," he managed.

"Wine," Nadya repeated. She rose, slip gently rustling against her legs as she moved toward him. Warm hand on his forehead, then his cheek. "You sure you're feeling alright?"

It took all he had to muster a smile, leaving nothing for speaking, nothing for moving.

"Come to bed," she said. "You need to sleep."

# FIFTY-EIGHT

Nothing had improved by morning. Day rang in to the tune of exoskeletons, crushed under Osha's bare feet. They were louder now, and bigger – easily as long as his hand. Hot to the touch, if not ablaze.

It was impossible to behave like nothing was amiss. If Nadya's moods posed a threat to his euphoria, these bugs were bona fide terrorists. When they skittered into Nadya's teacup, Osha slapped it out of her hand. When they shot across the table, smoking and flickering, he doused their fire with water from the kettle. There was no wonder and oneness with fear in the room; the last thing Osha wanted was unity with these bastards.

Nadya barely touched her breakfast – just one slice of bread, no butter. She watched the table warily, apricots overrun with elaborately patterned, fan-tailed centipedes – looking ill. And yet she couldn't see them. Couldn't hear the tapping of their claws, the clacking of their teeth.

It was Osha that bothered her.

Whatever trust they'd rebuilt the night before was stripped away – along with the finish on the cupboards and Osha's fragile sanity. He did what he could to calm her nerves, but it took all his strength just to maintain composure. And she could tell.

So he gave her space. While she gathered the last of the orchids, cradling them like babies on her way to the car, he retreated to the cellar to panic in private.

And good thing he did. The cellar was wholly *paved* in bugs – choked with smoke, walls singed, sooty beams folding in on themselves as the beasts bore deep into the pithy wood.

Osha knew his time at Waiter House was over. The power was off. The water was nearly dry. His bed, the desk, the soap in the bathroom – all gone before he was even fully dressed. If he left now, he'd probably never see the place again. Loosing a battalion of violent vermin was no way to say goodbye, but if this was how they had to part, so be it. Let the house swallow these monsters up, fold them like egg whites in the ether.

But not till after Nadya left.

Her footsteps sounded above, the ceiling shaking, dusting him with wood chips as she passed. It was going to collapse right from under her.

So he did the only thing he could. He attacked.

His assault was furious. He smashed them with fists and boot heels, beating them from the walls, knocking bottles to the floor, shattering glass. Splashing through spilled wine, he pried a shelf from the cupboards, screws and all, and wielded his weapon against their crisp little bodies in mass. Eruptions of glittering lava, syrupy volcanoes of blue guts. He pounded until the board cracked.

"Osha!" Nadya's voice broke through the clamor. "What are you doing down there?"

"Nothing!"

She moved rapidly down the stairs, and soon stood in the doorway. Flecks of anxiety, lightning bolts all around her. "What are you doing?"

Osha forced a grin. "Killing bugs?"

"You're tearing the place apart!" She gaped at the chewed-up posts, the broken glass, the rivers of wine.

"No, I'm not!"

"Why would you do this?" She approached one of the beams, but stopped just shy of touching it.

"Bugs, Nadya!" Osha's mouth had no reason to cover for him now – his actions had given him away. "There are bugs in this house!"

She looked at him now, not at the bottles or beams, and definitely not the glowing, pulsing hordes chattering and gnawing and sizzling all around her. They fell like fat raindrops as she shook her head, eyes gleaming. "This. . . ." She gestured broadly. "What's happening to you?"

He grabbed her by the shoulders, turning her toward the wall. "Open your eyes! Look at them!"

"You're mad!" She drew back roughly. "You're still sick, Osha – it's just gone to your brain!"

"Listen—" he tried to level with her "—we're not safe here. You have to leave now!"

"I will." She folded her arms, recoiling. "I'm going."

She turned for the stairs.

"Nadya, wait!" Osha dropped the shelf and hurried after her, but she was far ahead of him. Up the stairs and out the door – leaving him caught in the fracas. In the car and driving away as he shook bugs from his shirt.

He slumped down on the porch, burying his face in his arms. Maybe he had gone crazy. Maybe he was meant to be dead. Life made no sense anymore, and he'd already lost sight of death's lessons. The uniformity of things, the cohesion of life – gone with the polish of the floorboards. Why had he even come back to life? He was more broken now than ever.

A bug crept onto his shoulder and he slapped it to the ground. It wiggled, upside-down, a triple-looped ribbon with a thousand legs. Osha climbed to his feet, lifted his boot, and stomped down – slicing its middle with his heel. Two halves, silent.

But the silence was short-lived.

From the main room came an earsplitting screech. Twisting metal like untuned violins. Osha stumbled in just as the eclipse split apart – sun and moon separating, sliding down the wall, scraping the hearthstones, crashing to the floor. With a clang, the sun fell flat, its shining corona warped and dented. But the moon rolled forward, heavy and rhythmic, making a wide arc around the empty room before tipping, wobbling, and ultimately collapsing at Osha's feet. A three-foot-wide pancake.

And where it had hung: nothing but insects. They'd eaten clean through the wall.

"You—" Guttural voice – Osha hardly recognized it as his own. "You *ruined* me!" He charged at the fireplace, at that steaming, teeming hive. Ripped off a boot. Threw it at them. "You ruined my life!" Then he turned, stomping back toward the cellar stairs, tearing off the other boot. "Do you hear me?" He flung it down into the dark. "Come up here and face me, you cowards!"

Much to his horror, they did. They rose up the stairwell like a flood, shrieking and spitting and squealing.

Osha ran. They followed.

He paused at the back door, glancing over his shoulder. They braked as well, piling upon one another, spinning off the ceiling, pelting the ground. Waiting, chewing and churning – as though for direction.

Could he control them?

They were multiplying. Expanding before his very eyes. The walls were barely visible now, the whole building built with throbbing blue. Just as he'd been their home for so long, they now housed him – and then some. Out the window, he could see them trickling through the grass, flowing all the way to the bay.

*The bay.*

They *thrived* in bays.

But they couldn't survive the waves of open sea. Even in Oclia, restless waters were disease-free. Old things only lingered in stagnation. These ancient beasts couldn't handle change. Dynamism was death.

Osha squinted at the beach. The dock was still there. The rowboat tied to its side: still there. He took a deep breath. "Well, come on then!"

They charged.

He tumbled out of the house and into the yard – slipping on the muddy slope, sliding on his side down to the dock. Shoeless, half his clothes heavy and wet, he clambered into the boat. Water slapping the stern, he unwound the rope, loop after infuriating loop. And all the while, that sizzling, gritting buzz grew louder. Closer.

Good.

At last, he lifted an oar, jamming it into the rocky bank – a sloppy shove away from the shore. Letting the water carry him farther, he fixed his eyes on the beach. "Are you coming?" He hollered. "I'm leaving!"

And there they were again, in shimmering streams.

He rowed.

He rowed until his arms caught fire, sides stuck with spears, face drenched in sweat. His wound felt torn open anew. Pausing to rest, he checked it. It was sealed, cemented in its grisly scab. His body was a closed vessel. That was reassuring. This was no place for open sores.

The bugs caught up quickly: a single organism, a floating algae bloom, a mutant cloud on a strong wind. They surrounded him. He could hear their claws and teeth – digging into the frail wood of his raft.

"Stop!"

They did as instructed. No more noise but the lapping water. Somber foghorn. Distant ocean. Ragged breath.

The bugs could have been lily pads.

"Is this how you are? Up north? Just waiting like this? Hungry?"

They didn't answer.

Osha glanced around, past their metallic gleam. Over his shoulder – quite a ways away – was the jetty. Once he felt ready, he started toward it.

The bugs stayed put.

"Well?"

A liquid light rippled through them.

"Let's go, then."

The noise rose again, cacophonous. Osha clenched his teeth, ears searing from the onslaught. Oars in the water – but less effective now. They were shrinking. Softening as he paddled. Thinning – as was the boat.

Back on shore, only the dimmest outline of Waiter House remained. He had to do this fast.

It wasn't strength that brought him to the jetty – other forces took over. Fear. Panic. But he reached it: a tall stone wall, seaweed-strewn and seashell-encrusted. Barnacles crawled up the boxy blocks, a patchy white façade stretching nearly as high as the wall itself. The bugs swarmed past him and into it, spraying in a full, sparkling rainbow. Almost beautiful.

He was certain they'd flourish here. Certain they'd find their way into someone else's veins. He had to find a way over the wall. The jetty stretched serpentine in either direction, arching up in spots, sinking in others – at points all but vanishing below the tides. He studied the length of it, looking for a way out, a break, anything.

And he found one. A gap. A space where the ocean chewed at the bay like a foaming mouth. Again and again, the sea reared its frothing head, gaping and slobbering. A rabid beast.

Perfect.

"Let's move."

He paddled toward it, struggling as he drew near. The water knocked him back, slamming his flimsy boat into the rocks.

"Go without me!" he tried. "Through that hole! To the sea!"

The bugs didn't understand. He'd have to show the way. But each time he rowed forward, another surge pushed him back. Powerful and frightening. Nearly capsizing him.

He pulled away. Watched the waves. He'd have to time this well, but the ocean didn't keep a steady beat. He could work with it, though. He could drum drunk. Eyes locked on the gap, he tapped on the boat, wood like cardboard now: 1, 2, 3 . . . 1, 2, 3, 4 . . 1, 2 . . . . . 1, 2, 3, 4 . . . 1, 2, 3 –

In he went.

He didn't hear the thud, but he felt it. The scrape. The tripping and ripping. The teetering, precarious moment perched atop the stones, followed at last by a slurping plunge into the sea. It only took a moment – bobbing in the churning water, glittering curtains of bugs falling around him – for Osha to notice the water in the boat.

Coming up from below.

The jetty had been submerged alright, but he'd misjudged how deep.

He had to move. He had to get where the wall was higher. He had to do something to keep these things from getting back into the bay. But he was paddling in quicksand. Frigid, biting quicksand. Arms all but cracking from the effort, the water pulled him farther and farther down, until finally the boat gave out from under him.

Ice in his lungs. He pulled his head to the surface just long enough to wail, then fell under again. Down in the thick thundering waves. Up into piercing insect whine. Gasping. He could feel them on his face. Sticky, itchy little legs.

He flung himself at the jetty – hard. Too hard. Wrists and ribs coming alive with pain, he sank again, deeper this time. Flailing for direction, he hit stone once more. With his face. Hands rising defensively, his fingers finally grabbed a hold. Digging in his toes, he began to climb. Not thinking. Not seeing. Not even feeling. He made it to the air – to the very top of the jetty – mindlessly. Miraculously. He was straddling the wall, arms and legs splayed, before he had a single thought at all.

The bugs.

They were all but lost in the sea foam, feet upon feet below. Trapped.

"Damn you!" Osha laughed. "Damn you to hell!"

They said nothing, silenced by the ocean's roar.

"Who's dying *now*?"

Still nothing.

They were drowning. Glints of light in the white caps slowly fading. He stared for some time, thinking of all they'd been through. How long they'd been with him. They'd made him who he was. "Monsters."

Nothing.

Osha turned away, toward the calm of the bay, letting his cheek fall upon the wet rock. The sky was brightening, sun burning through the mist. Sparkling on the water. Warm on his back.

Valena was far, almost too far to see, but if he squinted he could make it out: the tiny sails of the marina, jutting up like white blades of grass. The spires of the temple rising above the skyline. The brown covered market, docks caught in storms of seagulls. The glowing orb lamps over the bridge. The blinking lights of the streetcar.

It was the most magnificent city he'd ever seen.

In his head he began the letter he'd write home – at last – describing every delicate detail. So his sister could know beauty. So his mother could know hope. So his family could know *life*.

People strolled the waterfront, arm in arm, dressed in their finest. In blooming yellow heat, they shed their hats and swirling scarves, exposing strings of pearls and glossy spectacles, smart mustaches and circles of rouge. They were talking and reading and kissing. Petting cats, painting pictures, playing music. Laughing and crying and standing alone, gazing out over the bay, right back at him.

Their colors blended like melted wax, a glowing rainbow cap over the city. A shield. A quilt. It faded but didn't end – bleeding into the sky, blurring with all that lay beyond—

the past, the present, the future

the great accordion of reality

lovers and fighters

saints and sinners

wild beasts

plant spirits

—the whole grand menagerie that Osha was inextricably a part of. Ancient and infinite. Pulsing and alive. Just like him.

He smiled. He sighed. He closed his eyes.

And that's all I know about my father.

# ACKNOWLEDGMENTS

Writing a book can be both trying and inspiring, requiring meticulous attention to detail alongside an almost mystical probing of the psyche. The need for both patience and support cannot be overstated – and I thank everyone who endured my ever-shifting moods throughout this process. I'd especially like to thank my mother, Nadya Perala, who shared my joys and bore my frustrations as I struggled to decode the many myths and legends surrounding my father, the fabled Comrade O. My mother's memory has kept him alive for me, her stories moving me enough to ultimately pen this text. These words would simply not exist without her.

Polon Larami (who I've always known as Dad) also deserves my deepest gratitude – for sharing recollections of his own, for founding the Interisland Refugee Fund in my father's honor, and for raising me with a love and devotion few are lucky enough to know.

The journals of my granduncle, Nico Dov, also served as a rich source of information. Before his disappearance in the Nameless Province, he filled upward of seventy books, detailing everything from political happenings to his daily beauty routine. I thank the Union Library of Culture and Science for allowing me access to this private collection of intimate and interesting material.

My uncle Loren, through my mother's channelings, has clarified much of my father's storied "lost days." His disembodied whisper has proved an invaluable resource – as well as a point of great interest to Sagoma's growing mystics movement. He provides readings and guidance via my mother at 230 East Panetro Street, along the garden blocks of Sagoma's Marz District, for a nominal fee.

Iza Barsamina, the Great Lady of Valena, made time in her busy schedule for one lunch interview and three cocktails. Her stint in jail during the war was short and unremarkable. In her own words: "I flirted my way to freedom." Holic Tiademis, to the contrary, was not so lucky. His infamous wall of secrecy has only recently been cracked in Corin Coromo's new book, *Rebel Radio: Rimolean Airways and the Theater of War*, which I used extensively in my research.

Since falling under Barsamina family rule, complaints of crime and corruption in the city of Valena have sullied its reputation, but all told my time there was quite pleasant – thanks in no small part to Rika Belcov, owner of the boarding house in which I lived over the summer of 2552. Ma Belcov's generosity and humor surpassed all expectations, and I drew much inspiration (and editing advice) from the endless procession of artists and writers that Belcov House is famous for. House cook and Oclian native Esra Lazlo, in particular, provided many relevant insights – as well as free piano lessons. In him and his partner, nomad historian Julis Balestro (who claimed the Singing Spy personally saved his life), I found unparalleled knowledge of Valena's street music scene and prewar nomad culture. But I thank Mr. Lazlo, most of all, simply for making me feel at home. At only eighteen, I'd never traveled abroad before, and Esra took me in like his own daughter.

Finally, I'd like to thank Sagoma's Museum of Broadcast Media for sharing with me the few recordings of my father's voice that still exist. The small selection of his songs surviving in the museum's archives are something I particularly cherish. The moody crooning of 'Farewell, Everything,' I'm not ashamed to admit, brought me to tears.

Piecing together this narrative was a revealing and often brutal tour of the traumas I've known my parents to grapple with. While my generation has never suffered the horrors of war, there have been times that I've felt the anguish of my forebearers as though it was my own. It is my hope that my writing deals with our collective inheritance sensitively and respectfully. That said, this chronicle can only represent the experiences of one man. First and foremost, I've aimed to do justice to what I understand of his perspective.

There will likely never be a comprehensive biography of Osha Oloreben, but I hope that my account will at least dispel some rumors – ideally without raising too many new questions.


Véva Perala
Republic of Sagoma
Spring, 2553

# ABOUT THE AUTHOR

Véva Perala graduated from Sagoma Academy of Art, with a focus on stage and film theory. Since completing *Farewell, Everything*, she divides her time between Sagoma – performing seasonally with the Circle City Dance Company – and Valena, Rimolee. With Professor Julis Balestro, she recently opened the Museum of Nomad Culture and Lore at Perala House, in Valena's West Hills. She is regularly featured in *Façade*, a political satire column published by *The Anatine Herald*, where she writes under a pseudonym.

# ABOUT THE TRANSLATOR

H.B. Cavalier was born and raised in the Pacific Northwest, though nomadic tendencies have repeatedly taken her far from home. Over the course of many years, she translated *Farewell, Everything* from a series of dreams, visions, and peculiarities. When she isn't decrypting esoteric phenomena, she enjoys a quiet life with her small family.